PRAISE FOR THE NOVELS OF

WHITNEY GASKELL

Testing Kate

"A very readable, enjoyable story, and readers will root for Kate all the way through and cheer her decisions at the end."

—RomanceReviewsToday.com

"Whitney Gaskell delivers a vibrant story and memorable characters that will appeal to chick-lit and women's-fiction readers.... This story line about the first year of law school remains fresh yet familiar in the capable hands of Gaskell....A testament to the remarkable skill of its author to turn a stressful situation like law school into a delightful novel."

—FreshFiction.com

"Gaskell...relieves the high school–like atmosphere with sharp dialogue and various forays into New Orleans culture."

—Publishers Weekly

She, Myself & MAIN

"Engagingly written."

—Boston Globe

"A warm, funny, charming, and engrossing story that will hook anyone who has a sister—and any lover of quality fiction who doesn't."

—Valerie Frankel, author of Hex and the Single Girl

True Love (And Other Lies)

"Funny, romantic...an entertaining read with all the right stuff."

—RomanceReviewsToday.com

"A hilarious story about love and friendships...A compelling, thought-provoking and nevertheless entertaining book...breezy, delightful, and well worth reading."

—TheBestReviews.com

"Witty, honest, and refreshingly fun."

—RoundTableReviews.com

Pushing 30

"Feisty, poignant, sexy, and packed with delicious comedy."

—Sue Margolis, author of *Gucci Gucci Coo*

"A breezy romp."

—*Miami Herald*

"A sprightly debut...breezy prose, sharp wit...a delightful romantic comedy heroine."

—*Publishers Weekly*

"Gaskell takes a familiar 'oh-no' chick lit theme and turns it sprightly on its ear.... What sets *Pushing 30* apart from others in the genre is Gaskell's sharp writing and skillful handling of many plot strands as it weaves into a cohesive, thoroughly satisfying read."

—*Pittsburgh Post-Gazette*

Also by Whitney Gaskell

PUSHING 30

TRUE LOVE (AND OTHER LIES)

SHE, MYSELF & I

TESTING KATE

Mommy Tracked

Whitney Gaskell

BANTAM BOOKS

MOMMY TRACKED
A Bantam Book / September 2007

Published by
Bantam Dell
A Division of Random House, Inc.
New York, New York

Book design by Steven Kennedy

Bantam Books and the rooster colophon are registered
trademarks of Random House, Inc.

Library of Congress Cataloging-in-Publication Data
Gaskell, Whitney.
Mommy tracked / Whitney Gaskell.
p.   cm.
ISBN 978-0-553-58969-6 (trade pbk.)
1. Married women——Fiction.   2. Single women—Fiction.   3. Female
friendship—Fiction.   4. Domestic fiction.   I. Title.

PS3607.A7854M66 2007
813'.6——dc22
2007020378

Printed in the United States of America
Published simultaneously in Canada

www.bantamdell.com

BVG   10 9 8 7 6 5 4 3 2 1

For Sam:
Keep that breathless charm.

author's note

Many thanks to all of the usual suspects—

My editor, Danielle Perez, and the whole crew at Bantam, with special thanks to Katie Rudkin, Patricia Ballantyne, and Lynn Andreozzi;

My agent, Ethan Ellenberg;

My fellow Literary Chicks, Michelle Cunnah, Alesia Holliday, Beth Kendrick, Eileen Rendahl, and Lani Diane Rich, for their support and encouragement;

My husband, George, for everything he does;

And, finally, a special thank-you to all of the mothers I've known over the years: You're the inspiration for this book.

The world is full of women blindsided by the unceasing demands of motherhood, still flabbergasted by how a job can be terrific and torturous, involving and utterly tedious, all at the same time. The world is full of women made to feel strange because what everyone assumes comes naturally is so difficult to do—never mind to do well.

—Anna Quindlen, *Thinking Out Loud*

one

Anna

Anna Swann had been running late her entire life. And things had only gotten worse since she'd become a mother. Mommy Time, she called it. Mommy Time meant that you automatically had to add an extra twenty minutes just to get out the door, while shoes were located, diapers changed, sippy cups filled.

Anna was now late for her Mothers Coming Together meeting. She weaved in and out of the traffic clogging up U.S. 1, swearing silently at every red light. The monthly get-together was a more organized version of what Anna's mother, Margo, had always called a Girls' Night Out. Thirty or so women would get together at a restaurant, drink wine, eat too much, and spend some precious adults-only time away from the demands of children, husbands, work, and life.

Anna's eyes flicked to the red numbers lit on the dashboard clock. If she got there right this minute, she'd be only five minutes late. Unfortunately, she was still two miles away from the restaurant, and traffic had slowed to a crawl.

Shit, she thought. *Mommy Time strikes again.*

Her cell phone started to sing—"Another One Bites the Dust" by Queen—and Anna fished around in her purse for the tiny silver phone, trying not to drive off the road as she did so. She finally grabbed hold of it, checked the caller ID, and groaned when she saw who it was—her ex-husband, Brad. Which could mean only one thing: bad news.

She clicked the phone on and said, "So where are you this time?"

"What, no hello?" He sounded like he always did—charming, upbeat, good-natured. Mr. Vegas, she used to teasingly call him, because of his effortless Rat Pack charm. He was the sort of guy everyone liked immediately—men, women, children, dogs, even cats.

The bastard.

"Where?" Anna asked again, her voice cold.

There was a pause. "I'm in Tampa."

Tampa. That would make it difficult to kill him. Difficult—but not impossible. Of course, the fact that she'd have to drive over an hour down to the West Palm airport, purchase a plane ticket, and then fly across the state in order to murder him might weaken her temporary-insanity plea.

"My boss sent me out to handle a meeting," Brad continued blithely. He worked in sales for a pharmaceuticals company, and he was, unsurprisingly, quite successful. Brad was a natural sales-man, which was another way of saying that he was full of shit. "I thought I told you I might have to cover it."

Ha! Anna thought. He knew damned well he hadn't told her. She considered taking her cell phone and beating it against the car window, hopefully rupturing one of his eardrums in the process, but then a Ford Explorer zipped in front of her, nearly hit-ting Anna's station wagon as it did so.

"Shit!" Anna said, hitting the brakes. "Asshole!"

"What did you say? You're cutting out. Why don't you call me back later when you get to a land line," Brad suggested.

Typical, Anna thought. He knew she was pissed off, and, just like a turtle, Brad always snapped into his shell at the first sign of trouble. He had a truly remarkable instinct for self-preservation.

"No!" Anna bellowed at her ex-husband. "Do not hang up on me! Brad, you're supposed to watch Charlie tonight. You *promised.* I already told him you were coming to see him."

Their son, Charlie, was two, and therefore too young to

understand that his father was ditching him. Yet again. *But how long would that blissful ignorance last?* Anna wondered. She had visions of Charlie in his pajamas, the blue ones with the glow-in-the-dark rockets on them, sitting up and waiting for his father to appear. Her heart pinched at the image.

"Yeah, about that. I'm not going to be back in time to take him."

"What a surprise," Anna said. She hated how bitter she sounded, hated that he'd turned her into this, but even more, she hated that Brad was letting Charlie down.

"Anna, don't start. It was a last-minute thing, and I didn't have a choice. Tell the little guy I'll see him this weekend," Brad said.

"Brad! Seriously, you can't do this! I have plans tonight," Anna said, her voice rising.

"Can't your mother watch Charlie?"

"That's not the point. The point is that you said *you* were going to take Charlie tonight, and you can't just back out of it at the last minute. It's irresponsible, and it's not fair to me or to my mom or to Charlie," Anna said evenly.

There was a weird cellular pause, then Anna thought she heard a female voice speaking in the background, and then there was the unmistakable rustling of a hand being placed over the phone to muffle the sound. Anna rolled her eyes. Obviously, Brad had not gone to Tampa alone.

Anna got pregnant after a condom malfunction when she and Brad had been dating for only six months. They were still in that early golden stage of the relationship, past the awkwardness of the first few dates and yet still oblivious to the other's less forgivable traits. Anna—who was thirty-one at the time and making peace with the likelihood that marriage and babies weren't going to be in her future after all—had been terrified and thrilled when she found herself perched on the toilet seat in her bathroom, staring down at the two blue lines that had appeared on the home pregnancy test.

I'm pregnant! I'm going to be a mother! she had thought, the knowledge cresting inside her, a soaring rainbow of happiness. And then, suddenly, a cold fear washed the rainbow away. *Oh, God...I'm* pregnant....*I'm going to be a* mother.

She was still vacillating between happy disbelief and terrified disbelief when Brad came over for dinner that night. Her original plan was to tell him over a dinner of pasta carbonara, and she'd even engaged in a brief fantasy of how it would go down: She'd be sitting at the table when she told him. She'd remain calm and serene and poised, Princess Diana posing for the cameras with her chin tucked in, a sly smile playing on her lips. Brad would be gallant and thrilled. Maybe he'd even get a little teary and insist on kissing her stomach, which would be cheesy but sweet. And then they'd agree that although their relationship was still relatively new, maybe this baby was a sign that what they had together was right. That it was Meant to Be.

Instead, Anna panicked and ended up blurting out the news while she was salting a boiling pot of water before adding the pasta.

"I have something to tell you," she'd said. Her back was turned to Brad, who was leaning against the kitchen counter, sipping a glass of chardonnay.

"Let me guess," he'd said. She could hear the smile in his voice as he continued, "Your ultimate sexual fantasy is to have a three way, and you're not sure how I would respond to the idea. Well, have no fear, I'm all for it. Provided, of course, that we're talking two women, and not two men."

It was just the sort of joke Brad would make, with a teasing growl that would normally make Anna laugh. But right now it was all wrong, and Anna didn't laugh.

Instead, she said, "I'm pregnant."

Brad was silent. When Anna finally worked up the nerve to turn around and face him, she saw that he'd responded to the news of their impending parenthood by blanching the greenish-white color of bad yogurt, while his mouth opened and closed soundlessly, making him look like a fish. It was this fishlike expression—combined with her taut nerves—that made Anna laugh. Nervously.

After absorbing the news—Brad actually had to sit down, and she noticed that his hands were trembling—he looked up at her and said, "Are you going to keep it?"

"Yes, I'm going to keep it!" Anna folded her arms over her chest and glared at Brad. He visibly wilted.

"Oh. So . . . what do we do? Should we get married?"

And Anna—who had never been one to fantasize about Vera Wang white silk dresses or headlining the sort of overstylized event profiled in *Martha Stewart Weddings*—had felt a keen sense of loss.

Still. Even though it wasn't the proposal of her dreams, Anna tried to focus on the positive: She was getting married. They were having a baby. She had her dream job as the food critic at the local newspaper. After ten years of bad dates, selfish boyfriends, and crappy jobs, life was finally falling into place.

Five months later, Anna—enormously pregnant and retaining so much water the only shoes she could wedge her swollen feet into were a pair of Old Navy flip-flops—had stopped by her new husband's office unexpectedly, planning to surprise him with the picnic lunch she'd packed. It had been one of those fabulous late-winter Florida afternoons. The sun was softly filtered through the cottony clouds, a salty breeze rippled up from the intracoastal river, and the idyllic weather seemed to have filled everyone in their small seaside town of Orange Cove with a feeling of communal goodwill. Anna had thought she and Brad could take the deli sandwiches she'd packed over to the beach, something they used to occasionally do while they were dating. To be honest, Anna was trying to recapture some of those stomach-fluttering feelings they'd had back in the beginning, which had been fading away over the months as they adjusted to married life and the prospect of a new baby on the way.

We'll just make it work, Anna thought. *You can make anything work, if you put enough effort into it.*

But then she walked in on her new husband sticking his tongue down the throat of one of his coworkers.

Debbie. That was her name: Debbie, spelled with an *ie*. Debbie, with her perky breasts, tiny waist, and freakishly large lips. Debbie, who didn't even have the grace to look embarrassed when caught making out with another woman's husband. Instead, while Anna stood there, mouth gaping open, Debbie raised her chin defiantly and smirked at her.

Anna had stared at the two of them, waiting for the shock and anger to writhe up inside her, waiting to feel the sharp pain when her heart shattered. Instead, there was only an oddly hollowed-out feeling, as though it wasn't really a surprise but something she'd been expecting all along. And then, distantly, a fluttering *thud* as the baby shifted and turned before settling directly on top of her bladder.

"I have to pee," Anna finally said, and then she turned and left.

She regretted that more than anything, wishing she'd had the poise and quickness of mind to think up a Dorothy Parkeresque quip. *I have to pee.* It had to be the worst exit line in the history of scorned women.

Afterward, Anna realized she had known, had even had a premonition when her hand curled around the doorknob to Brad's office, that she didn't want to see what was on the other side. There had been signs that later seemed obvious, and in an annoyingly clichéd way at that. Suspicious phone calls. Late nights at work. Odd excuses for where Brad had spent a Saturday afternoon or Wednesday evening. But it wasn't until she'd actually seen the kiss, seen Brad's hand resting on Debbie's perfectly aerobicized bottom, that she'd faced up to the truth: Her husband was a cheating rat-bastard piece of shit. And Anna wasn't about to give him a second chance.

Two hours later Anna had the locks on their modest bungalow changed. By the time Charlie was born, the divorce proceedings were under way. Anna took sole custody of their silver-fawn pug, Potato. Sharing a child had proved to be a little more difficult.

"Brad," Anna now said, struggling to stay calm. It wasn't as though she cared whom he slept with these days, but he was supposed to be coparenting Charlie with her. Ditching their son for work was annoying, but ditching him to jet off to Tampa with his girlfriend was unacceptable.

"Look, I've got to go. I'll call you when I get back in town. Give Charlie a kiss from me," Brad said.

"Brad!" Anna tried again, but he was gone. The words CALL ENDED blinked up at her from her phone.

The traffic came to a sudden stop at yet another red light. Anna slammed on her brakes again, narrowly avoiding plowing into the Explorer, and glanced at the clock to confirm that, yes, she was now very, *very* late.

"Gah! How is it that I'm always late? How? *How?*" she said out loud, thumping one hand on the steering wheel.

Most days, Anna didn't mind being a single mother. Sure, it was hard at first, when Charlie was a newborn and totally dependent on her for everything, but Anna had lots of help from her mother, Margo—or Gigi, as Charlie called her. His baby-babble name for her had stuck, despite Margo's attempts to brainwash Charlie into calling her *Grandmère*. And Anna couldn't get enough of Charlie. After she'd spent nearly twenty hours in labor and one solid hour pushing, Charlie entered the world with a birdlike shriek. The nurse laid him across Anna's chest, and she'd taken one look at her squalling, blood-covered infant and fallen helplessly in love. Now just breathing in the powdery scent of his head or feeling his solid little body relax against her while she read to him brought Anna an indescribable joy.

But then there were days like today, days when Anna felt the full weight of single motherhood, of having to do everything on her own. Her morning had begun when she took Potato out in the pouring rain for her morning tinkle. Potato flatly refused to lay one paw on the wet grass and mulishly resisted all of Anna's attempts to wheedle her into peeing. Anna, soaking wet and insanely late, finally gave up and dragged Potato back inside. Five minutes later, Potato deposited a puddle of urine and one large, stinky turd in the middle of the bathroom floor. Anna cleaned up the mess, took the fastest shower in modern history, and then raced around getting Charlie's breakfast ready. Charlie—who had recently thrown himself into the terrible twos with alarming enthusiasm and was having the mood swings of a premenstrual teenage girl—wept bitterly when Anna presented him with a toasted whole-grain waffle spread liberally with cream cheese.

"Bagel!" he'd cried piteously, pushing the waffle away as though it were poisonous. When Anna—running on only one cup of coffee and thus not awake enough to fight about it—had given up and toasted a cinnamon-raisin bagel for him, Charlie poked at the bagel unenthusiastically, looked up at her, and said in a hopeful voice, "Waffle?"

And then, when Anna dropped Charlie off at his Montessori day care, which he normally loved, Charlie had clung to her like a baby koala.

"Mama has to go to work," Anna said in a singsong voice, as she attempted to detach him from her legs. "But guess what? Gigi is picking you up today!"

"Noooo!" Charlie screamed, reattaching himself to Anna's legs.

In the end, the teacher had to hold back a sobbing Charlie while Anna rushed out the door, feeling like the worst mother in the world.

Now, after a long day at work, Anna was stuck going to the Mothers Coming Together meeting. Not that she didn't normally enjoy the get-togethers; she did. But work had been stressful as she'd rushed to meet a deadline, and she hadn't slept all that well the night before—Charlie had gotten up twice, once with a wet diaper, once wanting a drink. Now she was so tired, it felt like her eyes had been rubbed over with sandpaper. Sharing a grilled-cheese sandwich with Charlie and then curling up for a few rounds of *Brown Bear, Brown Bear* sounded infinitely more appealing than engaging in the sort of grown-up conversation that took effort. So appealing, she nearly turned her car around.

I promised Grace I'd be there, Anna reminded herself, and, swallowing back a yawn, she dialed her mother's phone number.

"Hello," Margo said brightly when she answered the phone.

"Hi, Mom, it's me," Anna said. "How's Charlie?"

"Hi, honey! Charlie, it's Mama," Margo said. "Do you want to say hello to Mama?"

There was suddenly the sound of heavy, stalker-like breathing on the line.

"Hi, baby," Anna cooed. "Are you having fun with Gigi?"

More heavy breathing. And then a high voice piped, "Mama?"

And just like that, Anna fell in love with her son all over again. It was always this way. One sight of his radiant smile or a whiff of his sweet little-boy aroma, and Anna was overcome with a wave of love and longing.

"Yes, baby, it's Mama! How are you? How's my baby?" Anna continued.

Margo returned to the phone. "You'll never believe what Charlie said to me today. He looked up at me with those big blue eyes and said, 'Gigi *beautiful.*' Can you believe that?" She giggled breathily. "At least we know he has good taste."

Breathe in, breathe out, Anna reminded herself, as she tried to squelch the irritation that always flamed when her mother went off on one of her narcissistic tangents.

Anna's editor, Teresa Picoult, had always been great about letting Anna work flexible hours, but Anna was still a single parent, and one with a flaky ex-partner at that. So on days like today, when Anna wasn't able to pick Charlie up at day care, she had to rely on her mother to fill in for her. And although Margo was great about it—she and Charlie adored each other—Anna felt guilty every time she had to lean on her mother. It didn't help that Margo could, at times, be the most infuriating woman in the world.

"I thought you had your moms' meeting this evening," Margo continued.

"I do, and I'm already late. You wouldn't believe how bad the traffic is."

"It's all the snowbirds down for the season," Margo said. "What time is Brad picking Charlie up? I thought he'd be here by now."

"That's why I called. Guess what?"

"He's not coming," Margo said.

"He's not coming," Anna confirmed.

"What was his excuse this time?"

"Apparently he went to Tampa and only just now bothered to call and tell me," Anna said.

Margo made a *pfft* sound. "What a surprise," she said tartly.

Anna knew that the only reason her mother didn't launch into an anti-Brad tirade—A Complete List of Brad Lewis's Faults, Annotated—was that Charlie was close enough to overhear her, and Anna had made her mother promise not to run Brad down in front of Charlie.

Besides, even though Anna shared Margo's low opinion of her ex, she knew from experience that this conversation would quickly turn into the familiar rant of how Margo had known from the first time she met him that Brad was all fizz, no substance, and how you can never trust a man who pushes out his lower jaw when he smiles, but oh, no, Anna wouldn't listen, and then she had to go and marry him, *blah blah blah blah blah*.

This was all true, but Anna wasn't in the mood for a session of *I told you so* just at the moment.

"Supposedly it was a last-minute work thing," Anna said.

"I just bet," Margo huffed.

"Mom, I hate to ask, but could you possibly keep Charlie a little later than usual? I promised Grace I'd be there tonight. It's her first meeting as president, and she says she needs the moral support."

"Of course. Don't worry about us at all," Margo said.

"Thanks, I really appreciate it," Anna said, feeling a rush of warmth toward her mother. Two-parts gratitude and one-part guilt for her earlier knee-jerk irritation.

"In fact, why don't you leave Charlie here for the night, and go out and do something fun afterward? Go out to dinner or get a few drinks," Margo urged her.

"No, that's okay. I'll just go to the meeting, and then I'll swing by to pick Charlie up. I don't think I'll be much later than eight or so."

"I mean it," Margo said, warming to the topic. It was one of her favorites. "There must be dozens of nice men who'd like to take you out to dinner. You're still a very attractive girl, Anna. You get that from me. Well. Except for your chin. That's your father's, unfortunately. It should have been my first clue as to what he'd be like. Men with weak chins are always unreliable."

"What's wrong with my chin?" Anna, horrified, peered at her reflection in the rearview mirror. Had she always had an ugly chin and never known it?

"All I'm saying is that if you just took the time to do something with your hair and makeup, you'd have loads of men interested in you."

If she hadn't been driving at the moment, Anna would have banged her head against something hard.

"Believe it or not, I don't know any nice men. And I doubt I'm going to meet one at Mothers Coming Together," Anna said wearily. Her phone beeped out a warning. "Look, Mom, I've got to go. My phone's running out of power. Give Charlie a kiss and a hug from me. Bye."

Anna tossed her cell phone onto the passenger seat. The traffic started to move slowly, reluctantly even. It was as though every driver in front of her dreaded reaching their destination and wanted to draw out the trip as long as possible. The light turned yellow, and although the LeBaron now in front of her could have easily sped up and allowed them both to make the light, it came to an abrupt stop, trapping Anna behind it.

"Oh, come on," Anna groaned.

She could feel her frustration swelling in her chest, pushing up and out until even her fingers were tense. She drew in a deep breath, then another, opening her throat the way the yoga teacher had instructed at the one class Anna had attended. She'd always envisioned herself as a calm, serene yogi, smugly turning down coffee and capable of wrapping her legs behind her neck.

Instead, she found the stretching and breathing…breathing…
breathing…for ninety straight minutes to be excruciatingly boring. Afterward, when Anna asked if they offered a shorter class—
"Like, maybe one for people on a tighter schedule?" she'd said
hopefully—the teacher gave her a pitying look.

Now stuck at the light, Anna glanced around. There was a
new strip mall to her right, wedged between a discount furniture
store and an auto-parts supplier, that seemed to have gone up
overnight. The signs lined up over each new store were uniform—
cream rectangles with the names set in a black Engravers font.

**Purrfect Pet Grooming. Map World.
Jenny Kay Interior Design. Bacchus Fine Wines.**

Bacchus. Anna remembered her editor, Teresa, mentioning
the store.

"It's amazing," Teresa had enthused. "Very sleek and hip, and
they have an incredible wine selection. They're even set up to host
wine-tasting parties. Maybe you should do a piece on it."

Anna suddenly felt an irresistible urge to go into the store and
check it out for herself. She glanced at her clock; she was still late.
So would it really matter if she was a little later than usual?

When Anna stepped into Bacchus, a bell on the door signaled
her entrance; the reporter in her began to mentally record the details. The dark-stained wide-plank wooden floors. The white walls
lined with minimalist shelving. The Spartan yet artful way each
bottle of wine was lined up on the shelf, three deep. The long, dis-
tressed trestle table sitting in the middle of the room, also display-
ing wine. The glass-fronted counter along the back wall that held
a selection of cheeses, jars of olives, and loaves of pâté. The store
was empty of customers, or employees for that matter.

But then a man stepped through the door behind the
counter, presumably from a back office or storage room.

"Hi," he said. "May I help you? Or are you just browsing?"

He was a compact man, neither short nor tall, with an athletic build that ran to thin. His skin was pale, as though he spent most of his time indoors, and his hair was dark and recently cut. His brown eyes were kind behind silver-framed glasses, and his mouth was gentle, which made Anna like him immediately. She'd always thought that the mouth offered the best insight into a man's character. People learned to shutter their eyes but rarely made the same effort with their lips. Tense and pinched up, or twitching nervously, or turned down in permanent displeasure: All of these were bad signs.

"I'm just looking around," Anna said.

"Okay. Let me know if you need anything," he said. He picked up a case of wine and brought it out to the front, where he unloaded it onto the trestle table.

"Thanks," Anna said, smiling briefly at him before turning to examine the bottles on the shelf. It was an interesting selection, not the standard chardonnays and merlots from the same megawineries you could find in every grocery store.

And then a silver label emblazoned with the black silhouette of an owl caught her eye. Was that...? Could it possibly be? Anna looked closer. It was! A 2003 Snowy Owl pinot noir!

"You have good taste," the man said, noticing what she was looking at.

"I just read an article about this wine in last month's *Wine Spectator*," Anna exclaimed. "The reviewer was raving about it. Said it was one of the top wines of the year."

"That's right," he said, looking impressed. "I was lucky to get a case of it. It's been in such high demand since the article came out."

"I'm so glad you opened up. Orange Cove's really needed a store like this," Anna said. "How long have you been open?"

"One month," he said proudly.

Anna had originally estimated that the man was in his forties; now she readjusted it. Between thirty-five and forty, she thought. He was wearing a blue shirt and khaki pants, both crisply pressed, although the shirt was open at the neck and the sleeves were rolled up. He looked like the sort of guy who'd be an architect or lawyer, and she found herself wondering how he'd come to work in a wine-shop.

But she'd been watching him too intently for too long, and she suddenly realized he was looking back at her, his expression puzzled.

Oh, no, she thought. *He probably thinks I'm coming on to him. Or, worse, that I have some sort of disorder where I stare at people for inappropriate lengths of time.* Like Phillip who used to write obits for the paper, and who never seemed to blink when he spoke to you.

Suddenly, with rising panic, she wasn't so sure that a staring disorder would be worse. After all, what was worse than being seen as a desperate, man-crazy, lonely divorcée? That was far more pathetic than having a medical disorder that you couldn't even help.

So Anna did what she always did when she was nervous: She began to interrogate the man. Which, she realized, was probably not the best way to convince him that she wasn't stalking him.

"Is this your store?" she asked, although she was fairly sure she already knew the answer from the proprietary way he was survey-ing the stock.

"Yes, it is." He smiled again. "I was an investment banker in my previous life."

Aha! I was right, Anna thought. *He's the sort of guy who looks naked without a tie on.*

"Why did you change careers?"

"Um . . . well, this was always my dream, I guess," he said, with a self-conscious shrug, as though he was embarrassed to be talk-ing about his dreams with a stranger.

"Really? That's interesting. Were you an investment banker here in Orange Cove?" Anna asked.

"No. Palm Beach," he said. His voice was still friendly, but his brow was crinkled quizzically.

Stop interrogating him, Anna told herself firmly.

"Oh," she said. And as she forced herself to squelch her next question—*Why did you open your shop here, instead of in Palm*

Beach?—an awkward silence spun between them. Anna waited a few beats, until she couldn't stand the silence any longer.

"So why'd you open your shop here? Instead of down in Palm Beach, I mean?" she asked. Then quickly she added, "I'm sorry, you don't have to answer that. You can just ignore me if you want."

"That's okay," he said, shaking his head. "I don't mind. I opened it up here because I thought there was a market for an upscale wine store in this town, and not a lot of competition, whereas the market in Palm Beach is already pretty tight. Glutted, even. Plus it costs a lot less to open a business up here…although that's probably way more detail than you wanted," he finished dryly. "I did warn you that I was in finance before this."

"That's okay. I asked," Anna said.

"Yes, you did. Actually, you ask a lot of questions," he said, and then he grinned at her.

"I'm sorry," Anna said, feeling her cheeks grow hot.

"No, don't apologize. It's just, most of the customers who come in here are more interested in the wine than they are in my business plan," he said.

"You mean all of your customers don't do this?" Anna asked in mock surprise. "And here I thought that was how everyone shopped."

He laughed. "I'm Noah, by the way. Noah Springer."

"I forgot to ask you your name." Anna thumped herself on the forehead. "Clearly I'm losing my touch. I usually start off with names and only then start asking about business plans."

"And what comes after business plans?" Noah asked, still grinning at her.

Wow, that's a great smile, Anna thought. It kept catching her off guard. He'd look like a normal, nice-enough-looking guy, and then he'd smile, and—*wow*.

"Oh, then I downshift into the really embarrassing and inappropriate personal questions. You know—how much money do you make, how's your love life. Stuff like that," Anna said.

"So basically you'll be channeling my mother," Noah deadpanned, and Anna laughed.

"I come by it honestly," Anna said.

"What? You mean...you are my mother?" Noah asked. "Wow, you look amazing for a seventy-year-old. All of those ballroom dance lessons have really paid off."

"I meant I'm a reporter. Or I was a reporter, anyway. Once upon a time," Anna said.

"And now you just go from store to store interrogating strangers?" Noah asked. This time when he smiled at her, she actually felt her stomach do a flip-flop.

It had been a very, very long time since Anna had experienced the flip-flop. Not even Brad had inspired a flip-flop.

"Now I'm a restaurant critic for the local paper. I write a weekly column," Anna corrected him, and she couldn't help feeling pleased at how impressed he looked.

"What's the name of your column?"

" 'Silver Spoons.' I know, Ricky Schroder flashback. But my editor thought it sounded punchy," Anna said.

"No, I think it's excellent. I've always been a Rick Schroder man myself," Noah said, patting himself over the heart. "I loved him in *NYPD Blue.*"

Anna laughed, and reluctantly glanced at her watch. "I better go. I'm late for a meeting."

"Are you off to review a restaurant?"

"No, not tonight. I have a Mothers Coming Together meeting," Anna said.

"Excuse me?"

"That's the name of my group. Mothers Coming Together. I know, it's a stupid name. My best friend, Grace, thinks it sounds like the title of a porn movie," Anna said.

"Then I'd be safe in assuming that it's not porn related?" Noah asked.

"No, not porn related. Just a bunch of moms getting together."

"You have kids, then?"

"Yes. Well, kid. Just one," Anna said. "A little boy."

"So where's he tonight? Home with your husband?" Noah asked.

"Oh, God, no," Anna said, remembering her earlier argument with Brad. "I mean…I'm not married. And my mom's watching my son. So…anyway. I really should get going."

"Wait…before you go…you haven't told me your name," Noah said.

"Oh! Sorry. I'm Anna," she said, and held out her hand.

Noah took it in his and shook it solemnly. "It was very nice to meet you, Anna," he said.

It wasn't until after Anna was back in her car, fighting her way up U.S. 1, that it occurred to her that Noah had made a point of asking if she was married. And that realization made the flip-flopping start up all over again.

two

Grace

Thinner than me, thinner than me. Oh, good, she's fatter than me. At least there's one, Grace Weaver thought, looking around her.

The Mothers Coming Together meeting was supposed to start in five minutes, and the private back room at Luna Pasta was filled with about thirty chattering women. Most were drinking wine and picking at the platters of calamari and antipasti. Their laughter swelled to fill the room.

Thinner than me, thinner than me, fatter—oops, no, she's pregnant. Technically fatter than me, but it doesn't really count.

Grace always played this game when she was around other women, tallying up how many were thinner than she was. She'd never won, not before she had kids. And now... well, now forget it. Natalie was three months old, and not only had Grace not yet lost her pregnancy weight, she was pretty sure she might have actually gained a few pounds since the baby was born.

She took a deep breath, willing away the nervous flutters. In a few minutes she was going to have to stand up in front of all of these women to introduce the evening's speaker.

And there's nothing more judgmental than a group of women, Grace thought, trying to swallow her surging terror.

She looked back out over the room, at the sea of pink and citrus green. Orange Cove was such a preppy town, you couldn't swing a dead cat without hitting a woman dressed in head-to-toe Lilly Pulitzer.

Thinner than me, thinner than me, thinner than me...Shit. Is every woman in town on a diet? Grace wondered, with a shock of panic. *And I'm going to have to stand up in front of them looking like this?*

Suddenly, she felt huge, like a big blob of fat molded into a woman shape. Worse, she was starting to sweat. She could feel the moisture beading up on her forehead and trickling down between her breasts.

That's just great. Fat and sweaty—it doesn't get any sexier than this.

"I'm here," Juliet announced. "You owe me big. I had to cut out of a meeting early."

Thinner than me, Grace thought, turning to meet her friend. *But then, that's nothing new.*

Juliet was tall—almost six feet in her high heels—and very, very thin, with the sort of long, skinny legs Grace had always coveted. Even when Juliet was pregnant with her twins, and her stomach was tight and round, the rest of her body stayed twiglike. It would be enough to make Grace hate Juliet, if she didn't love her so much. Well, that and knowing that Juliet was a neurotic, type-A mess. It was always easier to like your friends when they had really noticeable flaws.

Juliet and Grace's husband, Louis, were both associates at the law firm of Little & Frost. Grace had met Juliet when they were seated next to each other at the firm's Christmas party one year. They'd hit it off over cocktails, were friends by dessert, and had been close ever since.

Tonight, Juliet was wearing a tailored navy-blue pantsuit, and her dark hair fell to her shoulders in sleek waves. She reminded Grace of Snow White's evil stepmother in the cartoon version of the movie—striking, poised, and more than a little scary.

"I'm glad you're here. I need all the support I can get," Grace said. "And I think tonight's meeting will be fun. I'm going to use my presidency to spice things up around here."

"Yeah, well, I still hate these meetings. They're like torture by estrogen. Where's Anna?" Juliet asked.

"I don't know. She said she'd be here."

Juliet snorted. "Late, as usual. Whenever I'm supposed to meet her, I always figure in a thirty-minute delay."

"Here I am, stop talking about me," Anna said, breezing into the room. As usual, she was out of breath from hurrying, and her long, light-brown hair was pulled back in a messy ponytail.

Thinner than me, Grace thought ruefully. *And totally adorable.*

"So I think the guy at the wine store thinks I was hitting on him," Anna announced.

"What guy at what wine store?" Juliet asked.

"Bacchus. It just opened on U.S. One. I stopped in, and the owner was there, and he had this great mouth—"

"What is it with you and mouths?" Grace asked. "I'm an ass woman myself."

"—and he caught me staring at him," Anna continued, ignoring the interruption. "I was mortified, so I did that thing I do where I ask a zillion questions—"

"I hate it when you do that," Juliet said.

"—and it was bad. Very, very bad. Clearly I can never go into that store again, which really sucks, because they had a great selection," Anna finished.

"I'm sure it wasn't as bad as you think," Grace soothed.

"It was worse," Anna said darkly. "He probably thought I was completely ridiculous. And desperate. A ridiculous, desperate divorcée just shamelessly throwing herself at him."

"Is he single?" Grace asked.

Anna looked at her, exasperated. "How should I know?"

"I don't know. Did you ask him out? That would be one way to find out."

Anna rolled her eyes. "Be serious."

"I am serious."

"And how would that work, exactly? 'I know you don't know me, other than as the crazy question lady, but would you like to go out with me?' "

"I'd drop the crazy-question-lady part," Grace said. "But, yes, that's generally how it's done."

"First of all, since I don't even know the guy, I have no idea if he's single. And second, I'm not interested in dating anyone. As I've already told you time and time again. Like when you tried to set me up with your dentist. And Louis's friend from college. And that random guy you met in the produce section of the supermarket—"

"Oh, now, he was a good catch. You shouldn't have passed him up. He had really great hair," Grace said.

"You didn't even know his name. You gave my phone number to a total stranger," Anna said.

"I gave your phone number to a total stranger *and* signed you up for a self-defense course," Grace countered. "That way all the bases would be covered."

"Not even I can argue with logic like that," Juliet said.

Anna rolled her eyes. "I'm not interested in dating. I've already resigned myself to being an old maid. I'm going to have seventy-three cats and live in a house filled with crocheted doilies and Charlie's old school photos hanging on the wall," Anna said.

"Technically speaking, I don't think you can be an old maid if you've been married," Juliet said.

"I thought it was sex. Only virgins can become old maids, right?" Grace chimed in.

"Yes, maybe that's it," Juliet agreed.

"And then someday Charlie will get married and have kids, and I'll be the cool grandmother who spoils them rotten," Anna continued, ignoring her friends' commentary. "Unless Charlie ends up marrying some awful woman who will allow me to visit them only once a year for two days. The bitch. I hate her already."

Her friends looked at her.

"Charlie's *two*. It's a little early to start worrying about whom he's going to marry," Juliet said.

"I can't help it. It freaks me out when I think about it," Anna said.

"Then don't think about it. I've already made a deal with my girls that we're going to just skip right over the hellish teenage years," Grace said.

"How does that work?" Juliet asked.

"I'm not sure yet. But I don't think I can deal with three teenage girls all living under one roof. Between them and me, there are good odds that one of us will be premenstrual at any given time. Which is a very scary thought," Grace said. She picked up a cookie from a platter and bit into it. *Mmmm.* Molasses, her favorite.

"Hi, Anna." The pregnant woman Grace had been eyeing earlier approached them. She was young, maybe in her late twenties, and petite, with curly blonde bobbed hair, wide blue eyes, and a smattering of freckles across her snub nose. Upon closer examination, Grace realized with horror that she had been wrong earlier. *She's thinner than me. Oh, my God. She's pregnant, and she's still thinner than me. That's it, I have got to go on a diet. Immediately.* Self-revulsion curled through Grace, and she could practically feel the calories oozing out of the cookie and right onto her ass. This was such a disgusting image that, if it had been at all socially acceptable, Grace would have spit the cookie back out. Instead, she chewed and swallowed, then wrapped what was left of the cookie in a paper cocktail napkin and tossed it in the garbage can.

"Chloe, hi, I'm glad you could make it. These are my friends Juliet Cole and Grace Weaver," Anna said brightly. "This is Chloe Truman. She lives just down the street from me. I met her when Charlie and I were out walking Potato, and I told her all about how this group is a godsend for new mothers."

"It's true," Grace said. "Whenever someone in the group has a baby, we all take turns bringing dinner over for a few weeks. After I had my youngest, Natalie, the rest of my family probably would have starved if it hadn't been for MCT."

"I'm trying to talk Chloe into joining," Anna said.

"You don't have to talk me into it," Chloe said, looking both shy and pleased. "I want to join."

"Yeah!" Grace enthused. She grinned at Chloe. "You've picked the perfect time to join MCT, if I do say so myself."

"Grace is the new president of the group," Anna explained.

"Wow," Chloe said.

"You're looking at the power center of Orange Cove," Grace joked. "Did you ever see *The Godfather*? I'm basically the mom version of Don Corleone."

"You should get out while you still can," Juliet said to Chloe. "Run. Run as fast as you can."

"Why?" Chloe asked.

"Mothers' groups are always boring. I'm only here because Grace threatened me with physical violence if I didn't come."

"Don't listen to her. Juliet's a malcontent," Anna said.

"I am not. I'm a contrarian. It's different."

"How old is your baby?" Chloe asked Grace.

"Three months. That's why I still look pregnant," Grace said, feeling the need to explain away her still-swollen stomach, although she immediately regretted it when she noticed Chloe's eye flick down in that direction. "And I also have two other daughters. A five-year-old, Molly, and a three-year-old, Hannah."

"Wow. Three under the age of six?" Chloe looked shocked. "I can't imagine. I'm not even sure I'll be able to manage one." She rested a hand on her round belly.

"It's not so bad, especially once you've gotten over the loss of your sanity," Grace assured her.

Anna nudged Grace and nodded toward the front of the room. "Grace, who is that woman, and why does she have a bag full of dildos?"

Grace turned and saw a tall, shapely redhead, dressed chastely in a gray skirt suit and lilac silk blouse. She was pulling handfuls of dildos out of a preppy L. L. Bean tote bag and lining them up on the table like an army of plastic penises.

"Oh, good," Grace said, relieved. "Our speaker's here. I was starting to worry she wasn't going to show up."

"Who is she?" Juliet asked.

"Melinda Gibbons. She's a sexpert. She's here to teach us how to give better blow jobs," Grace explained.

"Did you say 'better *blow jobs*'?" Anna asked, frowning. Three lines appeared on her forehead, just between her eyes.

"You shouldn't frown like that. It'll give you wrinkles, and then you'll have to get Botox, and you'll end up with one of those scary, waxlike faces. And you don't want that," Grace said.

Anna rolled her eyes. "Grace? The dildos?"

"I told you, I want to spice the meetings up a little," Grace explained. "I thought a sex seminar might help boost our membership."

"Works for me," Juliet said.

The women watched as Melinda Gibbons set out a crystal punch bowl full of condoms on the table, next to the dildos.

"You know, Grace, you're right. Mothers Coming Together does sound like the name of a porn movie, especially when you throw in fifty flesh-colored dildos," Anna said dryly.

"See? This is going to be a whole new chapter for Mothers Coming Together," Grace said brightly.

"Oh, my God! Are those...*penises*?" one of the women milling around gasped, and suddenly everyone's attention was on the dildos.

Usually, someone had to flick the lights to get everyone's attention when an MCT meeting started. The first half hour of the meeting was reserved for socializing, and this precious adults-only time was the main reason many of the MCT members showed up. But tonight all of the moms hurried to sit down at the round tables without being prompted. A hush fell over the room, punctuated by a few excited whispers.

"I think she's selling sex toys," one woman said to a friend.

"Oh, my *God,* those dildos are *huge,*" another woman squealed.

"I guess it's time to start the meeting," Grace said. She smiled, but felt another wave of fear-laced nausea wash over her. What had she been thinking when she volunteered to be president? She was now going to have to stand up and speak in front of all of these women. *Gah.*

"Good luck," Anna whispered, and briefly squeezed Grace's hand.

"Come on, let's sit down. I want a good seat for this," Juliet said.

"Will you sit up at the front table? I want to see some friendly faces," Grace said nervously.

Anna nodded. "We'll save you a seat."

"Thanks." Grace sucked in a deep breath and walked slowly to the front of the room, where Melinda Gibbons was now setting out an assortment of sex toys—a black leather cock ring, an anal plug, and several different types of vibrators, including one that looked like a bullet and another that was shaped like a rabbit.

"Hi, Melinda?" As though she could be anyone else. "I'm Grace Weaver. We talked on the phone. Thank you for coming tonight."

"Yes, hi, Grace, it's nice to finally meet you in person," the red-head said pleasantly, reaching out a hand, which Grace took in hers. Melinda's hand felt small and cool, and her grip was surprisingly firm. "Thank you for inviting me."

"I thought I'd start off by introducing you to the group, and then I'll let you do your thing," Grace said. "Is that okay with you?"

"Sounds perfect." Melinda smiled serenely. Unlike Grace, Melinda didn't seem at all nervous about momentarily standing up in front of all of these women and talking. If anything, she looked loose and utterly relaxed.

Must be all of the orgasms she's having, Grace thought, and she made a mental note to buy a vibrator.

Grace turned to face the roomful of women and immediately became aware that all eyes were on her. She looked out at the crowd, swallowed hard, and hoped that she didn't look as fat as she felt in her black linen tunic and pants. She'd made a mad dash to Stein Mart yesterday and bought the set without trying it on. She hadn't even particularly liked the outfit, but she was desperate. The only thing in her closet she could get into were maternity pants with the hideous stretch-panel waist. And even though she'd bought the outfit two sizes larger than she'd worn before having Natalie, it still felt a little snug. The pants dug into her waist, and the tunic stretched uncomfortably over her breasts.

She drew in another deep breath, although her lungs felt too small and too tight to contain the air. Grace's heart started pounding, and for a scarily long moment she wondered if she was having her first full-blown panic attack.

Thinner than me, thinner than me, thinner than me. The entire freaking room is thinner than me, Grace thought as she stared out at the women. They looked back at her, and Grace's anxiety continued to swell. *They're probably all thinking about how fat I look. I can see it in their eyes, that awful, awful pitying expression people get when they feel sorry for you.*

Grace gulped in some air and wished desperately she'd brought along the index cards on which she'd written her introductory comments. Louis had talked her out of using them, insisting that she'd sound more natural if she winged it.

Why the hell did I listen to him? Gah. I have to say something. I can't just stand up here, staring blankly back at them....

"Um...hi, everyone. Thanks for coming to the meeting tonight," Grace said haltingly. "I know we have a few new members here, so for those of you who don't know, I'm, um, Grace Weaver, and I'm the president of the Orange Cove chapter of Mothers Coming Together. Please feel free to talk to me after the meeting if you have any, um, questions. And now I have a feeling you're just dying to find out who the woman standing behind me is." Grace grinned despite herself, and it had the happy effect of relaxing her. She drew in a deep, cleansing breath and continued. "So I'll go right ahead and introduce her. Her name is Melinda Gibbons, and she's a sexpert."

Murmurs spread through the room, and a few women giggled.

"Melinda gives seminars all over the country on how to be a better lover." More titters. "And tonight she's here to tell us all about..." Grace paused to enjoy the buildup of suspense and the cheerful energy her audience was giving off. This was almost fun. "... how to give sensational blow jobs. So without further ado— Melinda Gibbons," Grace said, waving her hand with a game-show-hostess flourish. Melinda stepped forward, and Grace sat down at the front table between Juliet and Anna. Her heart was still pounding, and she was enormously relieved to be done with her bit, but she thought it had actually gone pretty well. The group applauded politely, and Melinda smiled as she waited for everyone to quiet down.

"Hello, everyone. As Grace said in her kind introduction, my name is Melinda Gibbons, and I'm a sex educator. Many years ago, I started out my career as a sex therapist. Clients began to invite me to speak at various functions, and my seminars grew from there. I've spoken to groups as large as a thousand college students down to bachelorette parties of a half-dozen women, and I cover topics on everything from safe sex to lovemaking techniques to libido issues. One of the most popular topics I cover is what we'll be discussing tonight: how to give an amazing blow job."

Melinda had a soft Southern accent, stretching out her words with just the hint of a twang. From the faint web of lines by her eyes, Grace guessed Melinda was in her early forties. She was curvy with a tiny waist, like a 1940s movie star, and her auburn hair fell to her shoulders in thick waves. She looked and sounded like the sort of woman who would serve you old-fashioned lemonade on the porch of an antebellum Southern home.

Thinner than me, Grace thought. *And probably better in bed too.*

"The first thing I'm going to do is hand out these." Melinda picked up a dildo from the table setting off another round of snickering among the mothers. "I have every imaginable color and size, so you can pick whatever you're most comfortable with, or..." Melinda's eyes twinkled. "Maybe what you've fantasized about."

Melinda began passing out the dildos. Grace ended up with an enormous Barbie-pink one.

"The spitting image of Louis," she joked, holding it up to show Anna.

"Way too much information," Anna whispered.

Once everyone had their dildos and condoms—the laughter and conversation swelling to a fever pitch—Melinda raised her hand, signaling for the group to quiet down.

"I want to begin with a fun technique for putting on a condom," Melinda said. "I call this the Kiss and Roll method. Watch me do it, and then I'll give you step-by-step instructions."

Melinda unwrapped a red latex condom and unrolled it a bit, so that it looked like a little hat. She placed a dab of lubricant from a small silver bottle inside the tip of the prophylactic, and then, pursing her lips in an exaggerated kiss, she popped the condom in her mouth, tip facing in. Her lips encircled the rim. Melinda picked up a dildo and, holding it by the shaft, leaned forward and rolled the condom onto it with her mouth in one graceful move. The women sat watching her, mesmerized.

"Wow," Grace breathed. "That was amazing."

"No kidding. It almost makes me wish I were a man," Juliet replied.

Grace thought she knew how to give a serviceable blow job. But, as she learned over the next hour, it was an area where she was sorely lacking in skill. There were a multitude of techniques she hadn't even heard of, much less tried. Like the Eight Ball, which involved using your tongue to draw the number 8 on a man's testicles. Or the Big Dipper, a move where the man hovered over you and lowered his testicles into your mouth.

"That's also called tea-bagging, because it's like dunking a tea bag in a cup of hot water," Juliet said loudly. Juliet was incapable of whispering, and Grace elbowed her to be quiet.

And then there was the technique that Melinda assured the group was the *pièce de résistance* of any woman's oral repertoire—the Tongue.

"Trust me," Melinda said, after demonstrating the technique on her condom-encased dildo. "Do it and he'll weep with gratitude."

Grace fished a dry-cleaning flyer out of her Kate Spade diaper bag and jotted down some notes. Anna raised her eyebrows at this, but Grace just grinned and shrugged.

"I don't want to forget anything," she whispered.

"And now we'll end with a quiz on what you've learned tonight," Melinda said. She held up a bag of silver Hershey's Kisses. "Call out the answer, and I'll throw a Kiss to whomever gets it right. First, what foods make a man's semen taste sweeter?"

"Strawberries!" Jana Mallin yelled out.

"Melon," Kari Clem said.

"Pineapple!" Grace called out.

"Very good," Melinda said, tossing the foil-wrapped chocolates into the audience.

"How many calories are there in an average ejaculation?" Melinda asked.

"Six calories," Justine Silkey said, with a giggle.

"That's right," Melinda said, tossing her a Kiss. "So being on a diet is no excuse for not swallowing."

Laughter erupted. Over the last hour, almost everyone had lost their initial shock at the material, and the atmosphere was now more like a bachelorette party than a subdued MCT meeting.

"And last but certainly not least, what is our new motto?" Melinda asked.

"Tend to the Testicles," the group chorused back, and Melinda beamed out at them like a proud parent.

"Excellent. You'll be amazed by how far a little attention there goes. Your man will love it," Melinda said. "And I think we'll end on that note. Thank you for your time, ladies. It's been a pleasure."

Wild applause broke out, and Melinda smiled graciously.

After the meeting, Grace walked out to her car, accompanied by Juliet, Anna, and Chloe.

"Thanks for inviting me, Anna. This was fun," Chloe said. She yawned widely and then smiled sheepishly. "Sorry. I guess it's past my bedtime. Which is about eight o'clock these days."

"I remember that from when I was pregnant with Charlie. I was bone tired for nine months straight," Anna said.

Juliet also suppressed a yawn, and Grace looked at her, eyebrows raised. "Something you want to tell us, Jules?"

"What?"

"She's asking if you're knocked up," Anna said.

"Jesus, no. Bite your tongue," Juliet said with a shudder. "I was up late last night working on that damned dead-baby case."

"Oh, please. You never sleep, anyway," Grace scoffed. "You just plug yourself into a socket and recharge."

"Dead-baby case?" Chloe asked.

Grace heard the note of panic in her voice and turned to Juliet, willing her not to go into detail, but, as usual, Juliet was completely clueless.

"An otherwise perfectly healthy baby died during delivery. My firm is suing the doctor—well, suing his insurance company—for botching the C-section. And right now we're in the hellish bowels of discovery," Juliet explained.

Even in the dim lights shining over the dark parking lot, Grace could see that Chloe had paled.

"Juliet," Anna said warningly.

"What?" Juliet asked.

Grace sighed. Juliet was a brilliant and talented lawyer, but sometimes it seemed like she lacked even the most basic interpersonal skills.

"Ignore her," Grace said to Chloe. "She doesn't know any better."

"What? What did I say?" Juliet asked again.

Anna looked pointedly at Chloe's very pregnant abdomen.

"Oh," Juliet said, finally catching on. "Don't worry. Hardly anyone dies during childbirth anymore."

Grace and Anna exchanged an exasperated look. But Chloe seemed to rally.

"You're a working mom?" she said, looking at Juliet with interest. "I'm doing an article for *Mothering* magazine—I'm a freelance writer—and I'd love to interview you for my story. It's about women trying to balance work and family."

"Why not?" Juliet said. She pulled a business card from her pocket and handed it to Chloe. "Call my secretary, and she'll set up a lunch appointment."

"Which Juliet will cancel at the last minute, because she never eats lunch," Anna added. "But I think she would be a great addition for your story. Chloe's interviewing me too."

"How about you?" Chloe asked Grace, turning toward her with a keen interest. "Do you work?"

Grace hesitated, her lips pressed together as she swallowed back her annoyance.

Yes, I work, she wanted to say. *I run around after the children, and prepare three meals and two healthy snacks a day, and vacuum, and do the shopping and the dishes and the laundry, and run a zillion errands, and I even, for God's sake, produce milk from my breasts. In fact, I work so hard that at the end of the day I'm often too tired to brush my teeth before passing out in bed. I'm like a goddamned modern-day Cinderella.*

But that wasn't the sort of work Chloe meant, Grace knew. She meant office work. Paid work. *Important* work.

"No," she finally said, managing a rueful smile. "I'm just a stay-at-home mom."

"Just?" Anna protested. She shook her head. "Come on. I couldn't do what you do."

"Me neither. Grace is like the superhero of mothers," Juliet said.

"Supermom," Anna said with a grin.

"Yeah, that's me. I have the cape and suit with a big M on it and everything. Although I've sworn off my spandex superhero suit until I lose the baby roll." Grace laughed. She pressed the button on her remote-access key chain to unlock the doors, and her minivan flashed its lights in response. "And now I should probably get the Mom-mobile home. I left Louis in charge, and I'm afraid the girls are going to have staged a coup and taken over the house in my absence. I'll catch you guys later."

"Hey, hon," Louis said, when she walked in the back door.

He had changed into sweats and was standing at the kitchen sink, loading dishes into the dishwasher. Grace felt a stab of guilt. She had meant to do the lunch dishes before she left for the MCT meeting, but then she'd gotten busy with the girls, as well as monitoring an eBay auction for a pair of sixties-era Lucite lamps—which she ended up losing in the final seconds of the auction—so she never quite got around to the dishes. So much for being Supermom.

"Hi. Sorry, I didn't mean to leave you with the dishes." Grace put the plastic storage container full of brownies that she'd brought home from the meeting on the counter.

She walked around the island and gave him a perfunctory kiss hello.

"No biggie." Louis smiled at her. He had a little blob of dish soap foam on his cheek, which Grace wiped off.

Louis had a lightly freckled face, thinning copper-red hair, and the square, boxy build of the wrestler he'd once been. Like Grace, he'd put on some weight since their marriage a decade earlier, but unlike her, Grace thought, he carried it well. It was one of the great injustices in life: men aging better than their wives. Louis's laugh lines and gradual loss of hair just made him look more distinguished, more likely to be taken seriously by his colleagues.

"How are the kids?" she asked.

"Everyone's in bed and asleep." Louis gave her a mock salute.

"Wow. Miracles do happen."

"Nat took a while to go down, so I told her all of the gritty details about one of my tax cases, and that seemed to do the trick."

Grace laughed. "I bet."

"How was the meeting?" Louis asked. He began to scrub out a frying pan crusted with eggs from that morning.

"It was fun. The sexpert seemed to go over well. I don't know how I'm going to top it next time."

"I hope you took notes," Louis said, grinning at her. "It's been a while."

It had been months, actually. The last time had been before Nat's birth. Grace's libido always went into a freefall while she was nursing. Still, Louis looked so hopeful that she didn't shoot down the idea immediately.

"I might have picked up a tip or two," Grace said, smiling back at him.

The phone rang, echoing across the kitchen. Grace picked up the cordless phone and clicked it on.

"Hello," she said.

"Hey, it's me." It was Anna. From the slight delay on the line, Grace guessed that she was calling on her cell phone. "I just wanted to make sure everything was okay. You scooted off so quickly after the meeting."

Grace cupped her hand over the phone and turned to Louis. "It's Anna."

"Say hi from me. I'm going to take a shower," Louis said. He headed out of the kitchen.

Grace uncovered the phone. "Hey. Louis says hi. No, I'm fine."

"Oh, good. Chloe was worried she'd offended you when she asked if you worked," Anna said.

"Oh, no, not at all." Grace felt a warm trickle of guilt. She should have made more of an effort with Chloe; it was always hard being the new one in a group. "It's just..."

"What?"

Grace turned and stared out the back window overlooking the pool. The backyard was dark and still, lit only by the small lantern that hung over the back door. Grace reached over and turned on the pool lights, flooding the backyard with light, but then thought better of it and switched them back off. She didn't want Mrs. Christie—the crotchety old bat who lived next door—to complain, as she unfailingly did whenever they used the pool at night.

"Well, sometimes I do feel like I'm the odd man out around you and Juliet. You both work, have careers. I'm just a housewife."

"Will you stop with that 'just a housewife' crap? I wish I could have stayed home with Charlie, at least for a little while," Anna said wistfully.

Grace snorted.

"I'm serious," Anna insisted.

"Anna, you're a restaurant critic. Which means you have the most amazing job in the world. It's better than being a rock star. You don't have to deal with tours, or groupies, or your band ending up in rehab," Grace said.

"Yeah, well, I love my job, you know that. And I don't think I could have stayed home full time; I would have been climbing the walls. But still. It's hard sometimes leaving Charlie all day," Anna said, and she sighed heavily. "It was especially tough at first when he was a baby. In fact, he was fine with it; I was the one who was a mess at the day-care drop-off."

Grace thought of Natalie lying upstairs in her crib and tried to imagine leaving her every morning at a day-care center. Just the thought made her stomach roil.

"You're right, I don't think I could stand handing my baby over to a stranger like that," she said.

The silence went on for a full three beats before Grace realized what she'd just said. She slapped her hand against her forehead.

"Oh, shit, Anna, I'm so sorry. I didn't mean to sound like such a judgmental bitch."

"That's okay," Anna said, although Grace could hear how hurt her friend sounded, and it made her want to beat herself to death with the telephone.

"Anna, really and truly—I envy you. I wish I had something outside the house and kids that was just mine."

"Well, you know what I think."

"Yeah, I know." In her premom life, as distant as it seemed, Grace had worked as an interior designer. Well, she'd worked *for* an interior designer, anyway, although she had handled a few smaller projects on her own. As much as she loved design work, she'd mostly hated the job. Her boss had been such a demanding diva—she actually snapped her fingers at Grace when she wanted something handed to her—that Grace hadn't been at all sorry to quit when Molly was born. Occasionally, Grace wondered aloud if she'd done the right thing giving up her career, and Anna had told her time and time again that she could pick up some part-time clients if she wanted.

But the truth was, Grace didn't think it was as easy as all that. She hadn't exactly been a huge success in her chosen field. In fact, being a mom was the only thing she knew she was good at. She was the fun mom, the one who played Barbies and dress-up and who baked batches of chocolate chip cookies with her kids and was there to apply *Dora the Explorer* Band-Aids to their boo-boos. She kept the art-project cupboard stocked with glitter and feathers and washable paints, regularly took her kids on outings to the zoo and the children's museum, and custom-made all of their Halloween costumes (every year, Grace got desperate last-minute calls from other moms, begging to borrow the *Blue's Clues* costume she'd sewn with fake blue fur or the green tulle fairy-princess outfit complete with gossamer wings).

"So Chloe seemed nice," Grace said instead, changing the subject. "I think I'll invite her to our pool party."

"Yeah, she's great. Very shy, but sweet. She and her husband just moved into the neighborhood a few months ago. I think they came here from Texas."

"When is she due?"

"I think in about a month. She looks ready to pop."

"I thought she looked adorable," Grace said.

"Yeah. I never looked that cute when I was pregnant. I just swelled everywhere," Anna said.

"Tell me about it. Only in my case, the swelling never went away. I still look like one of those dancing hippos from *Fantasia*. You know, the ones with the tutus?" Grace laughed—*this is what the fat friend is supposed to do*, she rationalized, *make funny, self-deprecating jokes*—but Anna didn't join her.

"Don't do that," Anna protested. "Don't run yourself down."

"I was just kidding," Grace said quickly.

"Hey, I have to go. I just pulled up to my mom's house," Anna said.

"Okay. I'll talk to you tomorrow."

"Bye."

Grace clicked the phone off and continued to stare out the back window into the darkness for a few minutes, mentally going over the day's events. Her bit introducing Melinda had gone all right—at least, she hadn't spoken too fast or stumbled over her words. She just wished she'd had more time to get ready. She'd spent the afternoon helping Molly learn about traditional Japanese tea parties for the next Foreign Friends Day at school. Then Hannah had insisted on getting her finger paints out, which had been fun but messy. And Natalie needed to be fed, so Grace had to give up trying to wipe the remaining smears of paint off Hannah's hands and turn her attention to nursing the baby. By the time Louis got home from work, Grace hadn't had time to do much more than pull a brush through her hair and swipe a lipstick on before she had to run out the door. The previous president of MCT, Tara McFadden—a thin, elegant woman whose straight ash-blonde hair was always frizz-free—had always looked so polished at the monthly meetings.

Pretty much the opposite of me, Grace thought unhappily. When had she become so frumpy? It seemed like just yesterday that she was paging through fashion magazines, trying to imitate the styles she found there. Nowadays, she lived in sweats and sneakers.

She looked gloomily down at the now-rumpled linen pantsuit, which she'd already decided to burn, and saw a streak of powdered sugar smeared across the top. Gah. Had that been there earlier? Had she stood up in front of everyone covered in sugar?

Grace turned and popped the lid off the storage container and took out a brownie. Three bites later the brownie was gone, and she took out another one. And when that one was gone, she ate another. Twenty minutes later she looked down and saw that the storage container was empty. She blinked. Had she just eaten... How many brownies had been in there, anyway?

Revulsion surged up inside her, hot and fierce. The brownies felt heavy in her stomach, and suddenly Grace felt like she was going to be sick.

Thank God, she thought.

She ran to the bathroom. After taking care to turn on the water, so Louis wouldn't hear, she knelt down in front of the toilet and waited. But nothing happened. Grace panicked. She couldn't allow her body to digest five thousand calories of sugar, butter, and chocolate. Finally, she did something she hadn't done since she was in high school—she stuck three fingers down her throat until she began to gag, until her stomach cooperated and began to heave. She did it again, and again, and again, until there was nothing left to purge.

three

Juliet

Juliet was already awake when her alarm went off at five a.m., and she hit the buzzer before it woke Patrick. She always woke up a minute before the alarm went off and didn't know why she even bothered to turn it on every night. Habit, probably. Habit, and the fear that the one time she didn't set it would be the one morning she'd oversleep. And that would be a disaster. Juliet barely had enough time in the day as it was.

She slid out of bed, shucked off the oversize Tulane Law T-shirt she'd slept in, and pulled on her running clothes. Ten minutes later she was pounding down Ocean Street, the main avenue that ran from downtown Orange Cove to the public beaches on Pelican Island. Duran Duran played on her iPod, and Juliet matched her pace to the music.

It was still dark out, although the sky had the ethereal glow it got just before sunrise, changing so slowly from inky black to sorbet shades of pink and orange that it always took her by surprise when the morning suddenly dawned. She ran past the Dunkin' Donuts, which was already lit up inside, and the oil-change place, which wasn't. She sprinted by an assisted-living center for seniors, with its clusters of mod, seventies-built condos, and then past the fences of the few houses that backed against Ocean Street. And then she was running up the bridge that arched over the intracoastal river, connecting Orange Cove to the island. The wind was stronger at the top arch of the bridge and tasted sharply of salt. Juliet tucked her head down as she ran into it.

This was her favorite time of day, the one hour when there were no demands on her other than the physical ones she placed on herself. She didn't have to think, or be anything for anyone. No one was asking her for the status of a case, or pushing her to stay late at the office, or putting her on a guilt trip for staying late at the office, or begging her to turn on the television so they could watch *Kim Possible* over their morning bowl of cornflakes.

And it was the only time when she wasn't worrying. Worry had become Juliet's default state. She worried about *everything*— about the twins, about work, about money. How they were going to swing all of the extras that were constantly cropping up—new tires for Patrick's minivan, the roof repair they'd been putting off for months, the girls' dance lessons—on top of the fixed monthly costs. The mortgage. School tuition. Her law-school loans.

She'd turn the rest of the day over to her worries. But not now. Now she just focused on her lungs expanding with the humid salt air, the way her leg muscles strained up the incline of the bridge, and the rhythmic pound of her heartbeat. Juliet ran two and a half miles, which took her just over the bridge, and then turned around and ran back home.

A little less than an hour after she left, she walked in the back door of her house, sweating but not winded. She tossed the morning paper on the kitchen counter, poured herself a cup of coffee, and took it into the office, where she settled down behind her desk and switched the computer screen on.

This was her routine, every day, even when it rained. She knew her friends—Grace, in particular—thought she was crazy to get up so early just to work out, but it kept Juliet sane, made her feel like she actually had a grip on her life.

And her friends would never know just how important that grip was to her.

Juliet opened up her e-mail and sipped the bitter coffee as the messages downloaded from her office account. There wasn't much in her in-box; she'd checked it last night before going to bed. Mostly spam, and a note from a client asking for clarification on the documents Juliet needed from him to comply with a document request the plaintiffs in his case had made. At this, Juliet sighed. She'd already told the client, Peter Hamilton, what she needed—in explicit detail—three times. Hamilton was a nervous man, so distracted by the sexual-harassment lawsuit that had been filed against him that he needed constant hand-holding. He was her least favorite sort of client.

Juliet knew she wasn't any good at being emotionally supportive. She lacked whatever gene it was that made people want to reach out to one another, to share feelings, to listen empathetically. It was why she'd gone into the law; no one expected an attorney to be warm and cuddly. Although sometimes she thought that maybe she'd have been better off if she'd become a doctor instead—a surgeon, maybe, where the patients would be unconscious when she saw them.

And then, with an electronic chime to announce its arrival, another e-mail popped up in her in-box. One that made Juliet sit up a little straighter, that made her pulse buzz and her heart give an excited lurch. It was from her boss, Alex Frost. Juliet clicked on it.

TO: COLE, JULIET <jcole@littlefrost.com>
FROM: FROST, ALEX <afrost@littlefrost.com>
RE: lunch

Juliet—Are you free for lunch today? We need to go over the status of the D.B. case. I'll have Gail make a reservation for us at the Treehouse.
Alex

Lunch with Alex! And not just a sandwich in the conference room but an actual lunch out at one of the nicest restaurants in town.

Will it be just the two of us? she wondered, enjoying the way the thrill fluttered through her. *It must be. No one else has worked on the dead-baby case. Well, no one other than Richard, but he's only done a few motions here and there.*

Juliet's next thought was an uncharacteristically feminine one: *Oh, my God—what am I going to wear?*

She got up abruptly and, carrying her coffee with her, headed up to the master bedroom. The bed was rumpled and unmade but empty. There was the sound of a toilet flushing in the attached bathroom, and then Patrick appeared in the bedroom doorway, wearing a white V-neck T-shirt and striped pajama pants and looking sleepy. His black curly hair was standing up in peaks, and there was a red sheet mark on his left cheek.

"Is that coffee for me?" he asked hopefully, yawning widely.

Juliet shook her head. "Not a chance," she said, pulling her mug closer, as though he might try to fight her for it.

Patrick's face fell, and he scratched his side. "How was your run?"

"Fine. Shouldn't you get the girls up? They're going to be late for school."

Juliet stepped past Patrick and into their walk-in closet to appraise her wardrobe. She usually wore tailored pantsuits to work, but lunch with Alex Frost called for something…sexier. Juliet began pushing through her clothes, whipping one hanger over at a time. A tan Brooks Brothers pantsuit. A gray tropical-wool Brooks Brothers pantsuit. A navy-blue pinstriped Ann Taylor pantsuit. Another gray wool Brooks Brothers pantsuit.

Jesus, Juliet thought. *When was the last time I bought girl clothes?*

Masculine was usually her preferred look. Despite articles in the bar magazines about family-friendly law firms, flextime, and paternity leave, the law was still a male-dominated, old-school profession. The only chance a woman had to succeed was if she turned herself into a virtual man, at least during business hours.

She paused at the black strapless Nicole Miller dress she'd worn to a wedding two summers ago. It was sexy, in a tailored, minimalist sort of way. *Would it work if I wore it with a blazer? No, probably not*, she thought, and pushed the dress aside.

Just when she was about to give up and pull out her standard black pantsuit, she spotted the chocolate-brown skirt suit she'd bought at The Limited back when she was in law school, broke, needed something for interviews, and still thought that showing her legs off might benefit her professionally.

Perfect, she thought. The skirt was short without being slutty, and the jacket nipped in at the waist. Suitable for work but not too masculine. And maybe, just maybe, Alex *would* notice her legs.

Juliet pulled out the suit, neatly hung on a wooden hanger, and retrieved a white oxford shirt that had been crisply pressed at the dry cleaner. She laid the suit and shirt out on the bed, then stripped out of her sweaty jogging clothes. Just as she was tossing her shorts in the clothes hamper, Patrick returned with a steaming mug of coffee. He took in her naked body, looking her up and down, and raised one eyebrow. He suddenly looked much more awake, and his eyes glittered with interest.

"Can you be late for work?" he asked suggestively.

"No," Juliet said, walking into the bathroom. "Not today I can't. Did you get the girls up?"

She didn't wait for his answer. And fifteen minutes later, when she returned from her shower, wearing a fluffy white robe, her legs cleanly shaven and her hair freshly washed, Patrick was back in bed. Asleep.

Juliet closed her eyes briefly and tried to swallow back her irritation. How could he fall asleep? It was almost seven. She had to get ready for work and didn't have time to get the twins off to school too. Was it really too much to expect Patrick to handle this on his own, without her nagging him every step of the way?

"Patrick!" she said sharply.

"I'm awake. I am."

"Your eyes are closed."

He opened one eye and looked at her blearily.

"It's already seven," Juliet said.

"Oh, crap. Is it really?"

"Yes. Really. How late were you up last night, anyway?" she asked. Patrick had still been watching a basketball game on television when she'd gone to bed. She hadn't heard him come up.

"Midnight. Maybe a little later." He stretched and scratched his chin. His beard was heavy, giving him that scruffy, unkempt look she'd found so sexy when they first started dating. His eyes started to shut again, and Juliet had to clamp down her jaw and count to five to keep herself from doing something drastic, like throwing a glass of cold water at him.

But just as she opened her mouth, ready to calmly but firmly tell him that if he didn't get a move on they'd be late, *again*, there was knock at the door. Muffled giggles and whispers could be heard outside, and then in unison Emma and Izzy called out, "Little pigs, little pigs, let us come in!"

Patrick's eyes were still shut, but he grinned. "Not by the hairs on our chinny chin chins," he yelled back.

Juliet's irritation started to fade. It was hard to stay annoyed in the face of such silliness. And the twins excelled at being silly. It shimmered from them, infusing everyone they came in contact with. It was impossible to look at their identical faces, at the creamy skin, dancing blue eyes, snub little noses, and not grin.

"Then we'll huff, and we'll puff, and we'll blow your house in!" the twins shrieked.

The door swung open and the girls came running in, their arms waving and their long dark hair streaming behind them. They threw themselves on the bed, landing squarely on Patrick's chest and stomach, and began tickling him.

"Argh!" Patrick cried out, laughing and grunting at the same time. He curled up to protect his testicles from getting kicked. "Enough! You win!"

But the girls weren't inclined to grant their prisoner mercy. Giggling, they tussled with their father, elbows flying, bare little feet waving in the air.

"Help!" Patrick yelled to Juliet.

But she just shook her head and grinned at him. "You're on your own. It serves you right for going back to bed."

Patrick let out a yelp as Izzy tickled him under his armpit—his most ticklish spot, Juliet knew—and then the three of them rolled over onto Juliet's side of the bed, right onto her neatly laid-out suit.

"Stop!" Juliet cried, her amusement drying up. "You're going to wrinkle my clothes!"

She dashed forward to grab the suit, but it was too late. The great huddle of father and daughters was rolling around, oblivious to Juliet's protests. Arms and knees were akimbo, three pairs of feet, one large and two small, were trampling the suit and shirt. By the time Juliet pulled the garments off the bed, the shirt was crumpled and the skirt had an enormous crease over it. The jacket had mostly escaped, although it did look as though it could use a touch of ironing to freshen it up. Juliet glanced at the clock. *Shit.* She was already late and didn't have time to iron. Anger flared up inside her, pressing hotly in her chest.

Patrick and the girls were still rolling around, giggling like mad things.

"Hey," Juliet said tightly.

"No fair tickling Daddy!" Patrick yelped. The twins shrieked with glee and redoubled their efforts.

"Hey!" Juliet said again, louder than she meant to. Her voice was like a whip cracking across the room. All antics immediately ceased, and her husband and daughters looked at her, identical expressions of surprise on their faces.

"Why are you yelling?" Patrick asked her.

"I'm not yelling. I was speaking loudly to get your attention. Girls, get off Daddy and go get dressed. You're going to be late for school," Juliet said, fighting to keep her voice calm and upbeat. She hated playing the heavy, hated that the girls would inevitably see them as Fun Daddy and Mean Mommy.

"Okay, Mommy," the girls chorused. They tumbled out of the room, still giggling and whispering to each other.

Patrick was looking at her as though she were the Bitch Queen from Hell.

"What?" she asked defensively.

"You just seem a little pointy this morning."

"Look at my suit," Juliet said irritably. She held up the wrinkled garments. "And I don't have time to iron. I'm going to have to find something else to wear."

"I'll iron it for you," Patrick said. He swung his legs off the bed and stood up. "Here, give them to me."

Juliet felt a wash of guilt. Even if she had no intention of actually cheating on her husband, she was wearing the suit for Alex's benefit.

"No, I'll do it," Juliet said, clutching the suit to her chest when Patrick reached for it.

"Come on, give it to me," Patrick said, stretching his arms up over his head as he yawned again. He was a tall man, nearly six foot five, and broadly built. It was another trait that had attracted Juliet to him when they'd first met at a dinner party thrown by mutual friends. She'd been tired of always wearing flats for her date's benefit and loved being with a man who was taller than she, even when she wore her highest heels. Standing next to Patrick had made her feel petite and dainty for the first time in her life. She'd also loved that he was a firefighter. It had seemed like such a manly-man sort of job, so much sexier than the lawyers and tech executives she was used to dating.

Still, when she'd gotten pregnant a few months after they married—a surprise souvenir from their weekend scuba-diving jaunt down to the Keys—it had only made sense for Patrick to be the one to stay at home with the girls. Juliet earned nearly three times what he made, and they would never have been able to pay their mortgage on his salary alone.

Juliet had to talk Patrick into leaving his job. He hadn't wanted to at first.

"I don't want to be a kept man," he'd said every time she brought up the subject.

"Is that what you think of stay-at-home moms? That they're 'kept women'?" Juliet would counter.

"No, of course not. It's just . . . different," Patrick had said.

And Juliet, ever the litigator, would pounce. "It's only different if you're approaching it with a dated, misogynistic point of view," she argued.

"It just doesn't feel right having you bear all of the financial responsibility," Patrick would respond somewhat feebly.

Juliet knew it was only a matter of time before she'd wear him down. There were so many reasons it made sense for him to stay home with the twins. Day care was expensive for one child; for twins it would end up being nearly two grand a month. A nanny would cost even more. Patrick would have to pick up extra shifts at work to cover the additional costs, and then he'd hardly ever see the girls. And Juliet was already stuck working long hours until she made partner at her law firm.

Finally Patrick had agreed. Reluctantly. At first Juliet was thrilled with the arrangement, happy that she could leave the twins every day knowing they were being cared for by the one person in the world who loved them as much as she did. If that meant she'd miss out on all of the firsts—first smiles, first words, first steps—well, that couldn't be helped. And if one of the twins woke in the middle of the night, shaken to tears by the aftereffects of a nightmare, and called for Daddy, not her, Juliet tried not to take it too personally. The same applied when she got home in time to supervise the bath-and-bedtime routine, only to have one of the twins bossily inform her that Daddy poured lots more bubble bath into the tub and that the pajama tops covered with little red hearts could not, under pain of torture, be worn with the purple striped bottoms.

It's a small price to pay, knowing that the twins are safe and happy, Juliet had thought.

As Patrick took the crumpled suit from her and laid it back out on the bed, she hesitated for a minute, wanting to apologize for her irritable outburst, to explain that the stress of the dead-baby case had been getting to her, to fold her arms around Patrick and rest her head against the flat plane of his chest, absorbing his calmness.

But Patrick was in the closet for a long time, noisily trying to extract the ironing board from where it was stored behind the luggage, for some inexplicable reason. Juliet noticed the clock. *Shit.* Now she was really, really late. She hurried back to the bathroom to finish getting ready, instantly forgetting her intentions to apologize.

"I have to cancel our lunch," Alex Frost announced.

Juliet looked up from the deposition she was reading, startled at the interruption. She hadn't heard Alex approach, hadn't realized he was standing in the doorway to her office until he'd spoken. Excitement fluttered in her stomach at the sight of him.

Alex was in his late forties but looked young for his age. He was tall and muscular, with blond hair that he wore back off his face, vivid blue eyes, and a sharp jaw that rounded at the chin. He was, as usual, dressed impeccably in one of his custom-made suits, this one a gray sharkskin. Alex wasn't a traditionally handsome man—his eyes were too squinty and his nose too snub—but he had a sleekness about him and the sort of forceful alpha-male personality that Juliet had always found irresistible.

Juliet smiled coolly at him, pushing back the swell of intermingled excitement at seeing him and disappointment that their lunch was off. *Shit.* "Okay. Would you like to go over the dead-baby case later this afternoon?"

"I can't. I just got called into court for an emergency hearing on the Dunder case, and then I'm going to be in client meetings all afternoon," Alex said. He grinned sexily. "Life of the busy lawyer."

"Tell me about it," Juliet said, gesturing toward the stack of depositions on her desk.

"Let's get together tomorrow. I have a client meeting at four that will probably run late, though, so it'll have to be after that."

The twins had a tap-dance class tomorrow afternoon, and Juliet was planning to slip out of work early to watch, since she hadn't yet made it to one. But that wasn't exactly something she could admit to her boss. Not if she wanted to make partner. Most women lawyers who had children were shunted onto the mommy track, with no hope of making partner. It was the price they paid for taking advantage of maternity leaves, flextime, and weekends off. Juliet wasn't about to let that happen to her, even if it meant working twice as hard as every man in the office.

"Fine. I'll put it on my calendar," Juliet said.

After Alex left, Juliet returned to her deposition, quickly scanning each page before flipping to the next, and marking down notes of what she thought was important. She'd gotten through one deposition and started on another when her phone rang.

Juliet picked up the phone. "Juliet Cole," she said briskly.

"Hi, Juliet? This is Chloe Truman? We met at the Mothers Coming Together meeting?" The woman's voice was tentative, so that everything she said sounded like a question.

Juliet frowned and tried to place the name.

"You don't remember me," Chloe said, reading Juliet's hesitation accurately.

"No, I'm sorry, I don't," Juliet said.

"I'm the pregnant one. Anna Swann introduced us," Chloe reminded her.

"Oh, that's right."

"I called because I'm writing an article for *Mothering* magazine on mothers who are balancing work and family, and you said you might be interested in being interviewed for the article," Chloe continued.

"I did?"

"Yes. I understand if you don't have time, but it would be great if I could talk to you. I haven't interviewed any moms who work full-time in a traditionally male-dominated profession yet, so I think your insights would really round out my article. We can do the interview whenever you're free. I could come to you? Or we can do it over the phone, if you'd prefer?"

Juliet had no idea why she responded as she did. She should work right through lunch, on the off chance that she might finish the depos and get home in time to see Emma and Izzy before they went to bed. But the words popped out on their own, completely out of her control.

"How about lunch today?" Juliet said, and immediately wanted to kick herself. Lunch! She didn't have time for lunch, she thought, her eyes flicking back to the mountain of work piled up on her desk. "Although, maybe—"

But before she could yank the invitation back, Chloe pounced on it. "Lunch would be great! Where should I meet you?"

At twelve-thirty, Juliet walked into the Dolphin Street Café, a little sandwich shop in downtown Orange Cove. It was a pleasant restaurant that did a brisk breakfast and lunch business, specializing in paninis and homemade coleslaw. The windows were open, letting in a cool breeze, and ceiling fans rotated lazily above. The bistro tables were already filled, as were the tall stools that lined the counter. Enormous photographs of Orange Cove hung on the wall—scenes of the river, the bridge, a stop-action shot of a train chugging past downtown.

Chloe was already there, sitting at a table in the corner, her blonde head bent over a plastic-laminated menu. She looked up and waved when she saw Juliet approaching.

"Hello," Juliet said, sitting down.

"Hi! Thanks so much for meeting me," Chloe said, leaning back in her chair. Her voice was just as perky as it had sounded on the phone, but Juliet noticed that Chloe looked tired; there were black smudges under her eyes, and her face was pale and slightly bloated. Her pregnant stomach swelled in front of her, and her belly button had already popped out, like one of those plastic temperature gauges that come with turkeys.

Oh, Christ, Juliet thought with dismay. *I hope she isn't going to want to talk about her pregnancy. That's right up there with having to listen to someone blather on about their diet or whatever dream they had last night. Like anyone's ever interested.*

"The timing worked out well. The lunch engagement I had scheduled was canceled." Juliet made a point of checking her watch. "But I don't have a lot of time, so why don't we order and get right to your questions."

Chloe hesitated and blinked a few times, clearly startled by Juliet's brusqueness.

"Oh … okay," Chloe finally said.

The two women studied their menus in silence for a minute,

and then the waitress came by and took their order. A cheese-burger with extra cheese, extra mayo, and a side of fries for Chloe, and a raisin–walnut chicken salad for Juliet.

"I'm always hungry lately. I know I'm supposed to be eating for two, but most days it's like I'm eating for twelve," Chloe said, sounding apologetic, once the waitress had left. "Anna told me you had twins."

"Yes. Four-year-old girls," Juliet said, unable to keep a note of pride out of her voice.

"Wow. I've always thought that being pregnant with twins would make you twice as hungry—and have to pee twice as often," Chloe continued, with a conspiratorial laugh.

"To tell you the truth, I don't really remember. It's been a while since I was pregnant," Juliet said.

She'd found this was the best way to avoid the sort of intimate conversations most women loved jumping into. It started with shared pregnancy cravings, which sounded harmless enough, but—as Juliet knew from experience—that would just open the floodgates. All of a sudden she'd be listening to whines about husbands who didn't do their share of chores around the house, or bouts of postpartum weepiness, or episiotomies that went astray, leaving the new mom with a numb vagina. None of which Juliet wanted to know about.

As Juliet had hoped, her unwillingness to discuss the fre-quency of her urination while pregnant seemed to dampen Chloe's enthusiasm for the subject. The younger woman fell silent and busied herself by rummaging through her brown shoulder bag. She pulled out a small tape recorder and a yellow legal pad on which she'd neatly written a series of questions.

"I must admit I have an ulterior motive in writing this story," Chloe confessed. "I work at home—I'm a freelancer—and I haven't figured out how that's going to happen after the baby's here. I know I want to keep working, but I want to spend time with the baby too. I guess I'm trying to figure out a way to have it all." She laughed again, this time a little self-consciously, and pushed her short blonde curls back from her face. "In fact, this might sound a little...well, weird, but I was sort of hoping to find a mommy mentor."

"A what?" Juliet had no idea what Chloe was talking about. She thought again of the pile of depositions waiting for her back at the office and glanced at her watch.

"A mommy mentor," Chloe repeated. "Someone who's already been through it. You know, balancing work and family? Someone who could give me some advice and pointers along the way? I thought maybe, you know, you could..."

Juliet stared at Chloe for a moment. *Is this chick for real? A mommy mentor?*

Finally she cleared her throat and said, "My schedule is a bit full at the moment."

Chloe blinked at her, and her mouth formed a round pink O. "Oh...I didn't...I wouldn't bug you or anything. I didn't mean to make it sound like some huge, time-consuming thing."

A little voice in Juliet's head, one that sounded disturbingly like Grace, piped up. *Be nice, Juliet. You're terrorizing the poor pregnant woman.*

"Well...what exactly would you want me to do? I've never heard of a—what did you call it?—a mommy mentor before," Juliet said.

Chloe colored. "It's just something stupid I made up," she mumbled. "Forget it."

"Okay," Juliet said.

Juliet. It was Grace's voice again, and it sounded disapproving.

Crap, Juliet thought. *Go away, Grace.*

"If you really want some advice, I could probably give you some pointers," Juliet said, somewhat reluctantly.

Chloe perked up. "Really?"

"Sure, why not," Juliet said, with a resigned shrug. "Although today's not a great day for me—I'm under the gun at work."

Chloe looked relieved. "No, I totally understand. Some other day, okay?"

"You've got a deal," Juliet said.

Good girl, Grace's voice said.

Thanks, Juliet thought dryly. *Now get out of my head. You're creeping me out.*

"Shall we get started with the interview?" Chloe asked. She shuffled her papers. "First tell me a little about yourself."

"What do you want to know?"

"Well, what do you do for a living? I know you're an attorney, but what sort of law do you practice?"

"I'm a litigator. I'm an associate with a midsize firm that handles both plaintiff and defense work," Juliet said.

"How long have you worked there?"

"Seven years. After law school I clerked for a judge on the federal court in Miami for two years. Once I finished my clerkship, I accepted a position with my firm."

"Is your husband a lawyer too?"

"No, he was a firefighter—"

Chloe interrupted her. "Your husband's a firefighter? That's so exciting! Do you get nervous when he's called in to a big fire?" she exclaimed breathlessly.

Juliet smiled, bemused. Firemen always seemed to have this effect on women.

"He doesn't work anymore. He stays at home with our girls," Juliet said.

"Really?" Despite the microphone that was recording the interview, Chloe was furiously scribbling notes on her pad. "That's interesting. How does that work?"

"How does what work?"

"His staying home. Does he like it? Does he miss work? Is he planning on going back? Does he consider himself a Mr. Mom?" As she rattled off the questions, Chloe seemed to gain some composure and her voice lost its little-girl breathiness. "This is great; it will give a really unique slant to my story."

Juliet frowned and shook her head. "Honestly, I'm not sure why it's always such a big deal when the father is the one to stay at home. It just made more sense for us to do it that way. I earn more money than Patrick did, and since I'm hoping to make partner at my law firm, it would have been a setback if I took a long maternity break." She shrugged. "I'm sure Patrick will go back to work some-day. We haven't really talked about when that will be, though. Maybe once the girls are in school full-time. They go to preschool three mornings a week right now."

"But is he happy staying at home?"

This was just the sort of touchy-feely question Juliet hated. Was Patrick happy? Was anyone really happy?

"I think he enjoys the time he spends with the girls," Juliet said carefully.

"And what about you? Do you feel like you've missed out by working long hours?"

Juliet paused. Yes, she had missed out on some things, and the guilt over that often kept her company late at night. Then again, she got the fun side of things. Patrick was the one who had to deal with potty training, pediatrician visits, and carpools. She got to have the career, the nice clothes, and the lunches out, and when she came home, dinner was made, the laundry was done, and the girls were always excited to see her, greeting her at the door with screams of pleasure. Well, on the nights when she made it home before their bedtime, anyway. And on the nights when she didn't, she'd stand in the doorway of their shared bedroom and watch as they slept, each curled up around a favorite stuffed animal, their breath heavy and rhythmic. She knew that whatever it was she'd missed, at least she was giving the girls a positive role model. Her daughters would grow up knowing that there was more to life than getting married and changing diapers.

Her daughters would never watch their mother spend all of her time grooming herself because her bland prettiness was her only currency and she lived in terror that her husband would lose interest in her. Juliet's daughters would never be told to smile and flirt because "men don't like serious girls, they like fun girls," or to wear more eyeliner because "you have pretty eyes, but you just need to make them stand out more." Her daughters would never find her passed out in bed, fully dressed, after she'd "mistakenly" washed down six Valium with a bottle of California chardonnay as a way of coping with a temporary separation from her husband.

In other words, her daughters would never have to endure what Juliet went through with her mother. Growing up as Lillian Campbell's daughter hadn't been easy, but it did teach Juliet a valuable lesson in how not to parent.

So, yes, maybe she did occasionally miss a dance class, or the latest Disney movie, or taking her daughters to the park and pushing them on the swings. But she was giving them more than that. She was giving them a role model. And if they didn't appreciate it now, they certainly would when they were grown.

"It's worked out fine," Juliet said. She smiled coolly at Chloe. "Better than fine. Every working woman should have a housewife."

four

Chloe

*A*fterward, Chloe wasn't sure why she'd done it. It had been years since she'd felt the impulse, the compulsion lying dormant for so long that she'd actually been lulled into believing she'd overcome it.

She'd gone to Over the Moon, a posh baby boutique in picturesque downtown Orange Cove to look for a mobile for the baby's crib. Over the Moon was a beautiful shop, painted in shades of soft green and crammed with sterling-silver rattles, cashmere receiving blankets, Petunia Pickle Bottom diaper bags, and tiny outfits that cost more than what Chloe normally spent on her own clothes. Even so, she browsed through the racks of little blue sailor suits and pink linen dresses, wishing—not for the first time—that they'd found out what the baby's sex was. But James didn't want to know.

"Let's do it old school and not find out," James had coaxed, flashing his most charming, irresistible grin.

Chloe had finally acquiesced, not wanting to ruin the surprise for him. Not knowing the sex of the baby had seemed so important to James, more important than knowing had been to her. Except that she hadn't known whether to decorate the nursery with pink walls and the gorgeous floral crib set she'd seen in a baby catalog or blue walls and the dinosaur set from Pottery Barn Kids. And it had meant that she couldn't buy anything but the most gender-neutral clothes ahead of time.

She bent over to admire a fire-engine-red Bugaboo baby carriage—a steal at only $679—and suddenly felt another Braxton Hicks contraction. It pinched like a menstrual cramp, only stronger, and she closed her eyes tightly while she waited for it to pass. They'd been coming more and more frequently all day, each one taking away her breath and making her feel like she'd been punched in the stomach.

The first time she'd had what felt like a serious contraction, she called James at work and then rushed over to her doctor's office, sure that this was it, she was in labor. She wasn't. The nurse–midwife—a bossy woman with copper-red hair and Dolly Parton-size breasts—had checked Chloe's cervix and then sent her home.

"There's no point coming in every time you have a Braxton Hicks contraction. Most women have them for weeks before they actually go into labor," the nurse–midwife had said, so patronizingly that Chloe's cheeks flamed with embarrassment. She slunk out of the office, feeling like a complete failure.

Her due date had been yesterday. But when she went to see her obstetrician for her weekly appointment, he'd reported that her cervix was still closed as tight as a fist.

"First-time mothers are often late," Dr. Camp said soothingly. "It could be another week, or maybe even two."

Great, Chloe had thought. Just what she wanted to hear—another week with swollen elephant ankles, gut-wrenching contractions, and a belly stretched so large, her skin ached.

Although maybe it wasn't so bad. At least now they'd be able to attend the Weavers' cocktail party.

"I have to warn you up front, there are going to be a lot of lawyers in attendance," Grace had said when she called to invite Chloe and James. Grace had a warm voice that always sounded on the verge of fizzing with laughter. Chloe had instinctively liked her when they met and now felt a preteenish thrill of pleasure at being included.

The party was that night. Chloe glanced at her watch and saw that it was getting late. She should get home. She wanted to take a shower before the party, blow-dry her hair, and take time with her makeup. She was so nervous, it almost felt like she was single again and going on a first date with someone she had a crush on. Actually, making friends with a new group of women was worse than dating.

She looked around for a sales assistant who could hopefully point her toward the mobiles. And that's when Chloe saw them: a tiny pair of baby shoes. They were made of soft pink leather, and each had a red leather cherry sewn over the top. Chloe picked them up.

I have to have them, she thought, resting her hand on her swollen stomach as she suddenly pictured a little girl with blonde curls, wearing a starched white pinafore dress and these perfect little shoes.

Even before she'd decided to take the shoes, Chloe felt the familiar flare of exhilaration mixed with cold apprehension. What if she was caught? She had been once before, back when she was a teenager and had attempted to shoplift a fountain pen at an upscale stationery store. But Chloe had cried, and the manager who'd caught her tucking the pen into her LeSportsac had taken pity on her and shooed her out of the store. For a long while after that, Chloe had resisted the urge to slip lipsticks or silk scarves into her purse. But eventually she slid back into her old habits.

In college, she'd gone through a period where she filled her jacket pockets every time she went to the grocery store. It was never anything she needed; it wasn't like she was going to whip up a light gourmet meal in her dorm room. But even so, she couldn't seem to stop herself from pocketing jars of Grey Poupon, Swiss chocolate bars, boxes of soda crackers, and, once, a bloody steak that was turning gray at the edges. Each time, as soon as she left the store, Chloe had immediately driven to a homeless shelter and left the items by the front door, like a sacrifice to appease an angry god.

Chloe got control of the impulse again and went a long time without stealing anything. And then, a few years later, when she was in the throes of planning her wedding—an event far more stressful than she'd ever imagined, especially for Chloe, who always wanted to please everyone, which was pretty much impossible when you were gathering together three hundred of your touchiest friends and relatives—Chloe went on a binge. She took a purse from T. J. Maxx, a half dozen men's silk ties from Stein Mart, a pair of pink topaz earrings from Macy's, and a leaf-shaped air freshener from the car wash while she was waiting to pick up her recently detailed car.

She promised herself that she'd stop after the wedding, and, other than one tiny relapse on her honeymoon—she pocketed a Bermuda-themed snow globe in the hotel gift shop—Chloe had managed to kick the habit. It had been hard, but she'd finally done it. But now...now she could feel the urge creeping up and grabbing her, until she was overwhelmed with the need to take the cherry-adorned shoes.

Chloe looked around and saw that the salesclerk—who had been studiously ignoring Chloe—was now chatting away on the phone and had her back turned. Quickly, Chloe slid the shoes into her handbag, feeling a rush of excitement and her heart thumping wildly as she did so.

I did it! she thought, with such a fierce pleasure it took her by surprise. *I'm going to get away with it!*

She knew not to run out of the store immediately. A hasty departure might arouse the clerk's suspicion. Instead, she walked calmly over to the register and waited patiently—hands folded on her round stomach—for the young woman to finish what sounded like a personal call.

"Yeah, I know, he's, like, such an asshole. I totally don't know what she sees in him," the salesclerk was saying into the phone. She glanced back at Chloe and dropped her voice. "I gotta go. I have a customer. Yeah. Yeah. Okay. See ya later."

"Excuse me," Chloe said patiently, when the clerk finally hung up. "Could you please tell me where the mobiles are?"

Twenty minutes later, Chloe left the store with the mobile she'd purchased and the shoes she'd stolen. The mobile had stuffed bears, bunnies, and elephants hanging from a white hoop, and it played "Hush, Little Baby" when you wound a white knob on top. It was *perfect*, exactly what she'd wanted for the gender-neutral nursery. And the clerk had wrapped it beautifully, folding it in pink and blue tissue paper before slipping it into a cellophane bag with scalloped edges.

Chloe had waited until she got into her car—which took her a while these days—and locked the doors before she slid the shoes out of her handbag, cradling them in her hands.

But the pleasure at having taken them, that wild rush of victory, abruptly deserted her. It always did. Owning the things she took never brought her any pleasure. Instead, the shoes made her feel dirty and tainted and just a little nauseated, and she was overwhelmed with the urge to get rid of them.

Chloe started her car and quickly drove to the parking lot of a nearby Publix grocery store. She pulled up next to the Goodwill drop box, which was already overflowing with rusted bikes and faded curtains. She lumbered out of her tiny Jetta, pausing to catch her breath after she'd finally managed to push herself upright, and then—glancing around to make sure no one was watching her—she tossed the shoes into the donation box.

Chloe had just eased herself back behind the wheel when another Braxton Hicks contraction hit her. She held on to the steering wheel, squeezing it until the palms of her hands hurt, while the pain of the contraction washed over her.

Breathe, Chloe told herself, but her breath came in short, strangled gasps.

Even after the contraction ended and her breath stabilized, Chloe sat for a few minutes, feeling too shaky to drive. Finally, her hands still trembling, she turned her key in the ignition and backed her car out of the parking lot. She paused for a moment to push her curls back off her damp forehead, inhaled deeply, and pointed her car toward home.

The party was larger than Chloe had expected, and the laughter and chatter of the guests floated over the back patio. The night was cool—too cold to swim, really, Chloe thought—but even so, there were children bobbing in the heated pool, splashing and shouting at one another.

Grace was circulating, stopping to chat here and there while monitoring the platters of bruschetta, cold sliced tenderloin, pasta salad, steamed asparagus with sesame mayonnaise, and chocolate pound cake, making sure they were well stocked. Her husband, Louis, tended the bar, mixing up gin and tonics and handing out sweating bottles of Amstel beer. The backyard was lit with garlands of twinkle lights, and the scents of chlorine and mingled perfumes wafted toward Chloe.

"Chloe! I'm so glad you could make it," Grace said, hurrying over and kissing Chloe on the cheek.

"Hi, Grace! This is my husband, James," Chloe said.

"Hello, Grace. It's a pleasure to meet you," James said. He had a rich, deep voice softened by a Texas drawl that always became more pronounced when he was tired or had a few beers. James beamed at Grace, his teeth flashing white against his handsome tanned face, his deep-blue eyes sparkling, his dark-blond hair falling forward over his forehead. Chloe watched as Grace was hit by the full impact of James's charisma. He never failed to make a powerful first impression.

"Nice to meet you," Grace said, smiling back up at him and looking a bit like a starstruck teenager who'd just met her favorite boy-band singer. "Would you like a beer?"

"That would be great. Chloe's the designated driver tonight," James said, slinging an arm around his wife's shoulder.

"By necessity, not choice," Chloe said, smiling shyly, one hand resting on her stomach. She glanced down, suddenly feeling awkward and out of place.

Being with James in this sort of social situation always made Chloe feel even more inhibited than she normally was. It should have been the opposite—James had the sort of appealing, laid-back charm that smoothed the way through any social event. He was relaxed, witty, completely sure of himself. But instead of acting like a safety blanket for Chloe, his outgoing personality made her that much more timid, especially around people she didn't know very well.

And sometimes, especially when she was feeling insecure, Chloe wondered if maybe that's what James saw in her—a partner who would never outshine him. Just as her vain, fun-loving mother, who always insisted on being the center of attention, had chosen to marry a quiet man who preferred to spend his free time watching the History Channel, happy to let his wife be the one to spin around in the center of their shared life, twinkling and dazzling everyone around them.

Chloe had first met James at a much different sort of party. They'd both been undergrads at the University of Texas at Austin, and Chloe's friends had dragged her to an off-campus party. Chloe didn't know anyone there other than the friends she'd arrived with, and they quickly dispersed, leaving her on her own. The house where the party was being held was a pit. It smelled like stale beer and boy sweat and was filled with sickly-sweet clouds of marijuana smoke puffing out of an enormous plastic bong. Chloe had stood in a loose group of people, waiting patiently for the allure of cheap beer and too-loud music to wear off and for her friends to be ready to go to the movie they'd planned to see that night.

She noticed James before he saw her. He was hard to miss—he was so beautiful, even while lounging on one of the stained, ripped sofas and taking a hit off the bong. One of his friends said something to him—Chloe couldn't hear what over the din of music and raised voices—and James had burst out laughing, releasing the mouthful of smoke he'd been sucking in. A thin girl with long platinum-blonde hair and a prominent overbite was sitting next to James, looking at him hopefully. Every time James spoke to the blonde, she lit up with pleasure. It was obvious to Chloe that the girl was infatuated with him. And although he was going out of his way to be kind to her, it was equally clear that James had only the most casual interest in her. Chloe, watching from across the room, felt sorry for the girl.

Later, long after Chloe had given up any hope that she was going to find her friends much less make the movie, she decided to head back to her dorm. She made a quick stop at the bathroom, which was so grimy, she squatted over the toilet while she peed. Chloe used a piece of toilet paper to turn on the faucet to wash her hands and then another to turn the doorknob. She pulled open the door—and walked smack into James, who had been waiting his turn.

"I'm so sorry," Chloe said immediately.

"It was my fault," James said genially. His eyes were a little too bright, too unfocused, but he smiled warmly at her.

"No, I wasn't looking where I was going," Chloe insisted.

"In that case, why don't you apologize by buying me a beer?" James said with a grin that showed off his dimples and left Chloe feeling a little breathless.

Was he flirting with her? Because guys this good-looking didn't flirt with Chloe. Most days she rated as a solid *cute*, although if she took extra time with her makeup and had a good hair day, she could occasionally rise to *pretty*. But not nearly pretty enough to rate this attention.

"Um…I think the beer is free," Chloe stuttered, then gave herself a mental whack on the forehead for coming out with what might possibly be the dumbest response of all time. Handsome men always made her nervous.

"Even better," James said. He laughed, and even though she could feel her cheeks flushing, Chloe laughed with him.

"I don't think we've met. I'm James," he said, holding out his hand.

He was drunk, she knew. Drunk and stoned. That's why he was being so friendly.

But still, Chloe thought, *he's talking to me.*

"I'm Chloe," she said.

"Are you friends with Jay?"

"Who? Oh, is that who lives here?"

James laughed. "So I guess the answer would be no."

"Yes. I mean, yes, the answer is no," Chloe said. "I came with some friends, and now I can't find them, so I'm just going to head home."

James shook his head. "You can't go yet. Not when we haven't even had a chance to talk."

Chloe was flummoxed for a minute. Was he teasing her? Or did he really want to hang out with her?

"It's late," she said apologetically.

"It's not that late. Promise you'll wait here for me," he said.

"Well…"

"Promise."

"Okay," Chloe said, giving in.

"I'll be right out," James said, walking past her into the bathroom and gently shutting the door behind him.

And Chloe had waited for him. They'd spent the rest of the party together—the platinum blonde left in tears, and Chloe couldn't help feeling a thrill that she'd been the one chosen—and afterward James walked Chloe home to the tiny dorm suite she shared with two roommates. It was a clear, cloudless night, and a full pale-yellow moon hung low over the campus. James had casually taken her hand, lacing their fingers together, and they'd talked about a movie they'd both recently seen, and how they both regretted not spending a semester abroad, and how much they both hated cell phones.

James had kissed her good night—a soft, slow, gentle kiss that Chloe felt all the way down to her toes—and asked for her phone number. Elated, Chloe gave it to him, although she never thought he'd actually call her. Surely when he sobered up he'd go back to the thin blonde or some other flashy, sorority type.

But James surprised her: He did call. In fact, he called the very next day, wanting to see her again. And he called the day after that, and the day after that, until they were gradually and gently folded into the safe warmth of coupledom. But even then—even now, after all these years together—Chloe had never completely gotten over her surprise that he had chosen her.

On their wedding day, Chloe looked up at James while he repeated the wedding vows the minister had recited, and she had a moment of sudden clarity.

I love him more than he loves me, she thought as she gazed at him. James looked a little nervous and stiff in the unfamiliar tuxedo, and the hair curling against his stiff shirt collar was still damp from the shower. But then James glanced down at her, and when he saw that she was watching him, he smiled and winked at her. And she thought then that maybe it was okay if she was the one who loved more. Maybe it was the price she had to pay to be with him.

"The bar's right over there," Grace now said to James. "My husband's manning it. He'll set you up."

"Thanks," James said, and as he ambled off, Grace fanned herself with one hand.

"Wow. Your husband is seriously dishy," she said.

Chloe laughed. "Don't tell him that. His head is already swollen enough as it is."

"And that accent! So sexy!" Grace shook her head and sighed. "I've always loved men with accents. You're so lucky."

"Thanks," Chloe said. She tried to think of something witty to say, but, as usual in unfamiliar social situations, her brain froze. "You look nice. Your skirt is pretty."

Grace was wearing a filmy purple skirt and matching silk-knit short-sleeve sweater, and her dark hair was gathered back at her neck with a mother-of-pearl barrette.

"You're so sweet! I can't believe how much I've eaten tonight," Grace said, staring down at the plate of chocolate cake she'd been holding. "In fact, kill me if I eat one more bite of this cake." She looked at the dessert longingly. "Oh, fuck it," she said, and popped the last of the cake in her mouth.

"You look great," Chloe assured her.

"I was going to wear a sleeveless shirt, but look at my arms! They *jiggle*. Like Jell-O."

She held up her arm and shook it to demonstrate.

Anna appeared beside them. "Hey, Chloe, I'm so glad you could make it."

"Thanks," Chloe said, smiling at her shyly.

"Anna, look." Grace jiggled her arms again. "It's my new talent."

Anna rolled her eyes. "Will you please stop? You're gorgeous," she said.

"I'm huge," Grace insisted.

"You are not. You're curvy," Anna replied.

Grace snorted. "That's just a polite way of saying I'm huge."

"It is not. Men love curvy women. Ask anyone. They'd rather have a woman with real boobs and a real butt, rather than some silly girl with anorexia who's starved herself down to nothing," Anna continued.

"Yes! Starved down to nothing! That's exactly what I want to look like!" Grace enthused.

Chloe thought—although, of course, did not say out loud—that this was unlikely. Grace didn't have the build to be skinny, no matter how much she might diet. And Chloe wanted to tell Grace that she thought she was really very pretty, sexy even, as Anna had said. If Grace had been born a hundred years ago, Renoir would have painted her as a glorious nude sprawled across a French daybed, with the sun highlighting her shiny dark hair, her mischievous dark eyes gleaming, Chloe thought.

But she couldn't think of a way to say this without sounding sycophantic—and possibly gay—so Chloe just continued to smile at Anna and Grace and wait for a break in the conversation.

"Is your husband here, Chloe?" Anna asked.

"Yes, he's over there by the bar," Chloe said, nodding toward James, who was talking animatedly to Louis.

"He's the cute one in the blue button-down and khaki shorts. And you should hear him talk. He sounds just like Matthew McConaughey," Grace added, pointing in James's direction with her fork. "Louis is probably talking off his ear about golf."

"James will love that. He's practically obsessed with the game. He plays every weekend, without fail," Chloe said.

James was amused by something Louis had said. James laughed with his whole body—throwing his head back, his mouth grinning wide, his eyes crinkled at the edges.

"Well, those two seem to have hit it off," Anna commented.

"I'm glad. I was just telling Louis that he needed more guy friends," Grace said, and Chloe felt a small pang of jealousy. James made friends easily; Chloe had always envied him that. She felt like she always tried too hard with other women, was too eager to please, and they, in turn, sensed her desperation.

"Do you want to sit down?" Grace asked Chloe, suddenly concerned. "Get off your feet?"

Chloe hesitated. She was feeling tired, and the damned Braxton Hicks contractions kept washing over her, but she very much wanted to keep talking to Grace and Anna, sensing that they were exactly the sort of women she could be friends with.

Which reminded her of her interview with Juliet Cole. The memory caused Chloe's face to flush red. God, she'd made a fool of herself. She'd been so overeager, so hopeful that the elegant, poised Juliet would want to be her friend, that she'd made that stupid comment about wanting a mommy mentor. The term had sounded cute, and not at all pathetic, when she'd practiced it in her head while she waited at the restaurant for Juliet. But then Juliet had looked at her so oddly, as though Chloe was an extraterrestrial, not yet versed in normal human discourse.

Chloe looked around to see if Juliet was there. She was. Juliet was the only woman who'd dared wear a bathing suit in front of the crowd, and she was now paddling around in the pool with a pair of giggling, dark-haired twin girls. A man was with them, who Chloe presumed must be Juliet's husband from the way he was playing with the twins. He was good-looking and muscular and didn't look at all like the sort of man that any woman would even jokingly refer to as her "wife."

Chloe didn't realize Anna was watching her until Anna said, "I heard you interviewed Juliet. How'd that go?"

Chloe flushed and looked down at her protruding stomach, hoping that the others weren't watching her face. She'd always been too easy to read. "Your face shows everything," her mother had always told her. "It's like a window into your thoughts."

"It was fine," Chloe said brightly, hoping that the other two women would assume the stain on her cheeks was just a normal pregnancy flush.

"You interviewed Juliet? And lived to tell about it?" Grace asked, raising a disbelieving eyebrow.

"She's not *that* bad," Anna protested.

"Yes, she is. And I'm speaking as someone who loves her," Grace said. She turned to Chloe. "So how bad was she?"

"No, really, it was fine. Juliet was really nice," Chloe protested. She *had* been nice. Well, nice enough. Just not . . . overly warm.

"Uh-huh. She's pretty intimidating, huh?" Grace asked.

"Juliet intimidates everyone when they first meet her. Once you get to know her, you'll love her," Anna said.

Chloe smiled at Anna, but as her gaze drifted to Juliet— now playing Marco Polo with her family, all of them laughing as Juliet, eyes closed, made a lunge toward one of the twins—Chloe couldn't imagine being friends with the lawyer. Juliet scared the crap out of her.

A few hours later, the children had abandoned the pool in favor of watching *The Incredibles* in the playroom. The thrum of the party grew louder as people drank more. Laughter was bubbling forth, and inhibitions were lowered. Grace put on an ABBA CD, and "Dancing Queen" blared from the speakers.

Chloe's Braxton Hicks contractions had gotten worse, so she sat in a pool chair off to the side, feeling even more sober than usual. She sipped her glass of seltzer water and looked around for James.

She finally saw him standing with some of the other husbands, entertaining everyone with the story of how he and his friend Dan, a coworker at his old job in Austin, had gotten into a war of escalating practical jokes.

It had started when Dan stole James's parking space one morning, so to get back at him, James stacked a dozen bags of garbage in the back of Dan's truck. The next day Dan smeared toothpaste all over the receiver of the phone in James's office— which James didn't realize until after he answered the phone and got an earful of Colgate. James struck back by rearranging the pages on a report Dan had written just before Dan handed it in to the boss (which James ended up feeling rather bad about, especially after their boss—who had no sense of humor—called Dan into his office and reamed him out over the mix-up). But then Dan retaliated by breaking into Chloe and James's house while they were on a weekend trip to Corpus Christi and rearranging all of the furniture in their house. They came home to find their bed in the living room, the dining table and chairs set up in the bedroom, and the couch standing on one end, squeezed into the half bath. At that point, Chloe had begged James to give it up, but James went ahead and posted Dan's picture and home phone number at an online dating service, resulting in a flurry of interested phone calls. Dan's wife, Angela, was the one to answer the phone when several of the women called, and she wasn't amused. Later, when Dan and Angela divorced, Chloe couldn't help but wonder if the personals practical joke had been partly to blame for the split.

But everyone was roaring with laughter as James recounted the ongoing feud, embellishing the story where necessary to make it even funnier. He gestured wildly, beer bottle in hand, a wide grin on his handsome face, the center of attention. James had always had a way of working a crowd.

Still...maybe I'd better get him home, Chloe thought, worrying that if he was drunk, he'd end up doing something stupid, like throwing up in the pool.

And that's when it happened: Chloe wet her pants.

Chloe stopped breathing and went completely still, wondering if anyone had noticed. The warm water soaked through her panties and dripped down her legs onto the paved patio.

No, she thought wildly, so mortified she couldn't move. *Oh, please, no! Why didn't anyone ever tell me that pregnancy can cause incontinence?*

Chloe glanced around, terrified that she'd been seen. And just how was she going to clean up herself—not to mention the patio floor—without anyone noticing? Maybe James...but another glance in her husband's direction ruled that out.

He's definitely drunk, Chloe thought, with a fresh surge of horror as she realized he wouldn't be any help to her now. She was on her own. *At least intoxication is socially acceptable. Peeing in your pants? Not so much.*

"Hey, sweetie, is everything okay?" Grace asked brightly, touching Chloe's elbow. She was panting slightly from the exertion of dancing. "Do you need anything?"

Chloe turned to Grace, relieved at having help and yet mortified at what she would have to confess.

"I, um, I...oh, Grace, I'm so sorry. I think I just...I might have...wet my pants," Chloe said, her voice dropping to a faint, mortified whisper.

"You what?" Grace asked, leaning in to hear. Her face knit with concern.

And that's when the pain hit her. It started in her back, low and sharp, and was so intense she couldn't speak. The throbbing ache spread until it felt like it was tunneling through her, coring her from the inside out. Chloe heard someone groan and only belatedly realized that it was her.

"Oh, my God! Are you going into labor?" Grace asked loudly, her voice carrying across the pool over the strains of "Dancing Queen."

As the pain faded away, Chloe opened her eyes and was mortified to see that everyone had suddenly gone quiet and turned to stare at her. It was like those old E. F. Hutton commercials, only way, *way* more embarrassing. White-faced, Chloe turned to Grace, although she was too mortified to speak.

Grace reached out and patted Chloe's arm. "Everything's going to be fine," she said gently. "I'll go get James and find someone to drive you to the hospital. You just rest here."

"I'll take her," Juliet said, stepping forward.

"Great," Grace said.

"But…but…" Chloe said, thinking, *No, not Juliet! Couldn't someone less scary take me?*

Grace moved away through the now-quiet crowd, making her way across the patio to where James—apparently one of the only people who hadn't clued in to the fact that something was going on—was waving his beer bottle around, as he recounted another story to the group of men he was hanging out with. All of them hooted with laughter, James's the loudest of all. Grace whispered something in James's ear, and he turned sharply, the smile sliding from his face as his eyes searched for Chloe.

"Are you sure? Where is she?" James asked, his worried voice carrying loudly.

It was only then that it distantly occurred to Chloe that she hadn't actually peed in her pants. Her water had broken, which meant that Baby was on his—or her—way.

Chloe had thought this moment would be joyous and awe-inspiring. After all, her baby was coming! Finally! Instead, a cold terror gripped her, mushrooming in her chest.

I have to get away, she thought desperately. *I have to get away from all of this. Away from the party, away from James, away from Baby, away from the pain. Oh, God, I can't do this.*

And then another wave of nauseating agony hit her, and Chloe bent forward, closing her eyes against the pain.

"I'm preregistered," Chloe said, as James wheeled her into the hospital elevator. "Just take me right up to L and D. It's on the third floor."

James didn't move, so Chloe reached up from her wheelchair and hit the number three button.

"Are you okay?" she asked James.

Since James had been too drunk to drive, Juliet had driven them to the hospital. To Chloe's immense relief, Anna was coming too, although she'd driven separately in Chloe's little Jetta. Juliet was now out parking the car, and from the herky-jerky way James was pushing the wheelchair, Chloe was hoping she wouldn't take too long.

"What's L and D?" James asked hoarsely. He was swaying very slightly from side to side.

"Labor and Delivery," Chloe said through clenched teeth. She wanted to stay upbeat, wanted this to be the happy occasion she'd always dreamed it would be, despite the drunken husband . . . and the gut-wrenching pain . . . and her suspicion that even if women had been giving birth since the beginning of humanity, she, in fact, would not be able to do it. In fact, it was less of a suspicion than a strong, scary certainty.

"Oh, yeah. Right." James's voice sounded faint, and when Chloe glanced back up at him, she saw that his face had a sickly greenish cast to it.

"You're not going to throw up, are you?" she asked.

James pressed his lips together and shook his head. But then the elevator started to move, and he moaned. When the doors opened with a *ding* on the third floor, James sprinted off the elevator—leaving Chloe behind—and practically threw himself through the door of the men's room. Chloe stared after him, wondering, *Did he really just leave me here, by myself, on a freaking elevator, while I'm in labor?*

Chloe wheeled herself out—which took more effort than she would have thought, especially to get the chair to start rolling—and maneuvered herself over to the nurse's station. She could just see over the counter, where a nurse was standing, reading a file.

"Um, excuse me?" she said. The nurse didn't seem to notice her. "Hello?"

Another wave of pain flooded through her as another contraction started up. Chloe squeezed her eyes shut and gripped the arms of the wheelchair, waiting for it to pass. They were getting worse—more intense, more painful. She didn't know how much more of this she could take. Certainly not *hours*; she wasn't even sure she could last another five minutes.

The elevator doors opened with another *ding*, and Juliet came striding out, her long hair streaming behind her, looking like she was ready to take on the world. Chloe had never been so happy to see anyone in her life.

"What's going on? Where did James go?" Juliet asked, rattling off questions Chloe didn't have a chance to answer. "Why are you just sitting here? Hasn't anyone helped you? Excuse me, there's a woman in labor here. Could somebody please help us?"

Chloe was breathless as the contraction passed.

"I'll be with you in a minute," the nurse behind the counter said without looking up.

"I don't know if you heard me, but this woman is in labor," Juliet said, raising her voice.

"I did hear you. And I'll be with you in a minute," the nurse said in an artificially sweet voice.

"Oh, okay. We'll just wait," Juliet said. "And if my client ends up giving birth right here at the nurses' station, I guess *you* can be the one to explain all about how *you* were too busy with *your* file there to give her the medical attention she is so clearly in need of."

"Your client?" the nurse asked, frowning now.

"That's right. I'm her lawyer," Juliet said crisply.

Chloe looked up admiringly at Juliet. Usually, she despised conflict in any form, but now she was just grateful to have someone with her who was willing to take control of the situation. And

Juliet, standing with her hands on her hips and looking like she was ready to wrestle the nurse to the ground if necessary, was incredibly comforting.

The nurse sighed and, rolling her eyes, asked pointedly, "May I help you?"

"Hello? Woman. In labor," Juliet said, pointing to Chloe.

"I preregistered," Chloe offered.

"What's your name?" the nurse asked.

"Chloe Truman."

The nurse began to type, pausing every few moments to stare at the computer screen. Juliet tapped her foot impatiently, still bristling with irritation at the delay.

"Right, here you are. Have you started having contractions?"

"Yes. And my water broke, about forty minutes ago," Chloe said.

Oh, my God, I'm going to have a baby, she thought, with a fresh wave of terror. It was all so...surreal. That was the only word for it. When she left the hospital again, she was going to be a mother. A *mother*.

The elevator doors opened again, and Anna hurried out, her heels tap-tapping against the hard floor.

"Juliet! Chloe! I'm here," Anna said unnecessarily, as she hurried up to them. "Oh, good. The baby's still in there. I'm not late, then."

"That's a first," Juliet said dryly.

But Chloe hardly registered Anna's arrival. *I've changed my mind. I'm not ready for this.* Chloe looked around, hoping to find an escape route. A bright exit sign was lit up at the end of the corridor, and she wondered if she could make a break for it.

"I'm going to put you back in one of the exam rooms, where the on-call nurse will take your stats and get some information from you," the nurse said. She came out from behind the counter and began to push Chloe's chair firmly down the hall, in the opposite direction from the exit she'd considered dashing for. Not that she'd have gotten very far. Pregnant women aren't exactly built for speed.

I want my mother, Chloe suddenly thought, the need pinching at her so sharply, tears began to sting in her eyes.

"Can someone tell my husband where I've gone? He's in the restroom back there," Chloe said, nodding toward the men's room James had disappeared into. There was a loud retching sound from inside.

"Is he okay?" Anna asked, walking along next to the wheelchair.

"I think he had a lot to drink," Chloe said, glancing back worriedly. "That might have been him being sick."

"Thank God he didn't puke in my car," Juliet said.

The nurse rolled them into the examination room. "Here's a robe. Take everything off, and hop up on the table there," she said.

"Hop?" Chloe repeated. The idea that she, in her current state, was going to hop anywhere was ludicrous.

"Is there someone else you want me to call? Your parents?" Anna asked supportively.

Chloe shook her head. "They're in Austin," she said, swallowing hard so Juliet and Anna wouldn't see her cry. She wanted to impress them, wanted them to think she was the sort of woman they'd want to be friends with. "We don't know many people here yet."

The shame twisted like a knot in Chloe's throat. Even though they had only just moved here and hadn't met many people, she felt so pathetic to admit it. These two clearly had lots of friends, close friends, women who would drop everything to be with them in an emergency. Chloe didn't have anyone. Well, except James, of course—but that wasn't exactly a reassuring thought at the moment. He still hadn't made it out of the bathroom.

"I'll stay with you," Anna offered. "At least until James gets back, or longer, if you want me. Grace already said she'd keep Charlie for the night, so I don't have to hurry back."

"What the hell, I'll stay too," Juliet said.

Chloe looked at them wordlessly, her shame dissolving into gratitude.

Anna, mistaking the look, hurriedly added, "Although if you'd rather be alone, we'd completely understand. We don't want to intrude."

"No!" Chloe said urgently. "Please stay! Please!"

"We won't go anywhere," Anna promised, and she reached forward to squeeze Chloe's hand.

Two hours later, Chloe had had enough. She was sick of the contractions, sick of the waves of pain, sick of nurses waltzing in and sticking their hands up her crotch, sick of the steady beat of the fetal monitor, which she had initially found so reassuring. She was also fed up with the glaring fluorescent lights, the background noise of the *Friends* rerun playing on the television, and especially with James, who was sitting, relaxed and apparently recovered, in the orange vinyl upholstered visitors' chair, humming tunelessly, which was annoying Chloe to distraction. She gritted her teeth so she wouldn't snap at him.

Juliet and Anna had gone off in search of coffee—the nurse had promised it would be a late night—and Chloe hoped they'd be back soon. They'd been distracting her from the pain of the contractions. Juliet was telling a story about a deposition she'd attended where all of the lawyers, except for her, ended up in a fistfight, and Anna chimed in with a story about reviewing a restaurant where the chef was so drunk he'd mistakenly sent out a live lobster to one of her dining companions. Chloe was very, very glad for their company.

The door opened and her doctor came in. Dr. Camp had always reminded Chloe of a classic movie star. An older Jimmy Stewart, maybe, or Gregory Peck. He was in his late fifties and had a strong jaw, wide shoulders, and thick silver hair.

"Hey, Doc," James said. He stood and shook hands with Dr. Camp.

"How are you feeling, Mrs. Truman?" Dr. Camp asked.

"I'm fine," Chloe said, and then smiled at her knee-jerk politeness. "It's starting to really hurt," she admitted.

"Do you want an epidural?"

"Yes!" Chloe said, with such enthusiasm, the doctor smiled. "I asked for one earlier, but no one's come in yet."

"I'll see what I can do to hurry the anesthesiologist up," Dr. Camp assured her.

Dr. Camp was gentle and quick as he examined her. Chloe lay still, staring up at the drop-in tile ceiling.

"You're at seven centimeters," Dr. Camp said, snapping off his rubber gloves. "We've still got a ways to go."

Chloe nodded and swallowed, trying very hard not to let her terror show.

"Don't worry," the doctor said, patting Chloe's ankle. "You'll do great."

"I keep telling her that," James said, grinning proudly at Chloe. "It'll be a piece of cake."

"Easy for you to say," Chloe grumbled, and James laughed, as she knew he would.

The door swung open, and Anna and Juliet came in. Anna was carrying a big plastic cup and looking back at Juliet, who was saying, "Yes, really, I don't find Brad Pitt attractive. He's too pretty for me." But then Juliet saw Dr. Camp, and she grabbed Anna's sleeve to pull her back.

"Oh! Sorry," Anna said. "Should we wait outside?"

"No, come on in, I'm just finishing up," Dr. Camp said.

"Dr. Camp, these are my—" Chloe was about to say *friends*, but then worried that would be presumptuous. "Juliet and Anna," she said instead.

"It's nice to meet you both," Dr. Camp said genially.

"We were all at a party together when my water broke. Juliet was nice enough to drive us to the hospital," Chloe explained.

Dr. Camp laughed. "Sounds like you'll have a good story to tell your little one about the night he or she was born," he said.

"You know, you're right!" James said, clearly delighted with this idea. "It was a great party too."

"With a dramatic ending," Anna added with a laugh. "It was like something out of a movie."

"That's true! And I played the part of the idiot husband, who's so freaked out, he can't drive," James said. "So we had to hop into Anna's wagon—"

"Which didn't start," Anna interjected. "Piece-of-crap car."

But then another contraction hit Chloe, ripping her attention away from the story. It felt stronger than the ones she'd had before, and the force of it took her breath away. She curled her hands around the rough white bedsheet and squeezed hard. She had a vague memory that this was when she was supposed to start her breathing exercises, but she didn't know how she was supposed to breathe when it hurt so damned much. It felt like Baby was using a pickax to tunnel his or her way out of the womb.

"So then we had to move Chloe over to Juliet's SUV," James continued. "And then we hit every red light on the way here."

"Don't forget the train!" Juliet reminded him, laughing.

James cracked up. "That's right, the damned train."

The contraction started to ebb, leaving Chloe feeling weak and gasping for breath. Why wasn't anyone paying attention to her? Shouldn't James be sitting with her, holding her hand, helping her breathe through the contractions, and bullying the anesthesiologist into coming in and juicing her up with an epidural, rather than joking around with her friends and distracting the doctor?

"The crossing gate came down, and I was going to try to make it, but James screamed and scared the hell out of me, so I stopped," Juliet continued.

"I did not scream. I just…yelped a little," James said. He was laughing so hard, he had to lean against the wall to keep from falling over.

"It was a full, horror-movie scream," Juliet said, shaking her head in mock disgust.

Dr. Camp was laughing now too. Chloe wondered if she'd somehow turned invisible; she tried to swallow back her mounting frustration. Didn't they understand that all this chatter was holding up her epidural? She wanted to stop them, interrupt their story, demand they take notice of her and how much pain she was in.

"Excuse me?" Chloe said apologetically. "Dr. Camp? About that epidural?"

Which was about as demanding as Chloe was ever able to get. *Why,* she wondered miserably, *can't I just once be poised and self-assured and articulate? Because if there was a time for me to take charge, this would be it.* And yet she just couldn't do it.

Great. I'm the only woman in the world who can't do the bitchy-and-demanding thing while in labor, Chloe thought sadly.

"Oh, Chloe, I'm so sorry!" Anna looked mortified, and she covered her mouth with one hand. "We shouldn't have been monopolizing your doctor."

"No, no, it's okay," Chloe rushed to assure her. "It's just ... the pain isn't really getting any better. In fact, I think the contractions are getting more intense." She laughed self-consciously. "It feels like the baby is clawing his way out."

"Like that scene in *Alien,* where the alien bursts out of John Hurt's stomach?" Juliet asked interestedly.

"Juliet," Anna said, elbowing her in the side.

"What? Sorry. This is all new to me. I had a scheduled C-section with the twins," Juliet said.

"I'll send the anesthesiologist right in," Dr. Camp promised.

"He'd better hurry," Anna murmured after the doctor left. She was speaking in a low voice to Juliet and James, and Chloe could just barely hear her. "If the baby starts to drop, it might be too late for the epidural. That happened to me."

"Christ," Juliet said with a shudder. "Childbirth without meds? That's practically medieval."

"It wasn't fun," Anna said darkly.

"But that won't happen, right? They'll get Chloe the epidural in time, won't they?" James asked, his voice anxious and his face pale.

But Chloe didn't hear Anna's response. Another contraction gripped her, and she let out a soft cry, tensed up, and turned inward, as her body's violent attempt to evict the baby started again. In her fog of pain, she wondered briefly if God was punishing her for stealing the baby shoes. But then another contraction came, and then another, until she couldn't think of anything at all.

five

Grace

You have a date with the sexy wine-store guy?" Grace whispered excitedly.

"Don't rub it in," Anna sighed. "I don't know how it happened. I guess he tracked down my work number. And he has this great voice—don't you think he has a great voice?"

"I don't know him," Grace said, bemused.

"Oh, right. Well, trust me, he has the greatest voice. It's really, deep like...like..."

"Like James Earl Jones?"

"No. Not that deep. More like..."

"George Clooney?"

"No."

"Alan Rickman?"

"No! Grace, will you please let me finish my story," Anna whispered.

"Sorry. Go ahead."

"Anyway, I said yes. But I shouldn't have. If I could think of a way to get out of it, I would."

"Are you nuts? Why would you want to get out of it?" Grace exclaimed.

"*Head, shoulders, knees and toes, knees and toes,*" Miss Emily, the children's librarian, sang.

"*Eyes and ears and mouth and nose,*" the mothers chorused along, some more enthusiastically than others.

Grace and Anna were sitting with the rest of the mothers in a circle in the children's room on the second floor of the library. Some of the calmer kids camped out in their mothers' laps, while others were dancing in the center of the circle, bouncing around as though they'd been guzzling down espressos before heading to story hour.

"I'm just not ready to start dating again," Anna whispered.

"It's been over two years since you and the a-hole split up," Grace replied. This was Grace's way of making her language child-friendly: *a-hole* instead of asshole. She was also fond of spelling out curse words: F-U-C-K, S-H-I-T, etc.

"No, it's not *Brad*," Anna said, wrinkling her nose, as though even his name carried a bad odor. "It's Charlie. I decided when he was born that I wasn't going to date. At least, not until he's in college. I remember what it was like when I was a kid, and my mom had a stream of men coming in and out of the house. I don't want to do that to him."

"One date is hardly a stream of men. And there's nothing wrong with being happy," Grace whispered back.

"There is if it's at Charlie's expense," Anna replied.

"What shall we sing next? How about 'The Hokey Pokey'? Come on, Mommies, let's all get up and dance," Miss Emily said, leaping deftly to her feet.

Emily was in her early twenties and had a softly rounded face, ivory-white skin, wide green eyes, red ringlets falling down her shoulders. Grace could just picture her as a character in one of the historical romance novels she adored. The ones where the heroine's breasts were always on the verge of spilling out of her bodice, and penises were referred to as *throbbing members,* and there was a steamy sex scene every other chapter. The sort of book you sink into with a glass of red wine and a bowl of pistachio nuts. Or maybe a decadent slice of cheesecake... or melted brie spread on thick slices of crusty bread... *Mmmm,* Grace thought dreamily. All she'd had for breakfast was black coffee and half a grapefruit, and now her stomach was growling. This is what happened—she'd start the day with the best of intentions to stick to a strict diet, then she'd get so hungry she couldn't stand it, and it would all go to hell.

"Tell me again why you talked me into a personal day from work to come here?" Anna asked as they struggled to their feet.

"Wholesome family fun, remember?" Grace said.

The truth was, she didn't know why she insisted on dragging Hannah to story hour week after week. Hannah was not a fan of circle time or of sitting quietly, which meant Grace spent most of the half-hour session chasing around after her independent-minded daughter. But the group dancing was the worst part. Grace felt so self-conscious dancing in front of the other moms, awkwardly swaying her hips and swinging her arms along with "Hot Potato" by the Wiggles. She only liked to dance when she'd had a few drinks; at ten o'clock on a Tuesday morning, not so much. "When did they stop reading stories at story hour? All she's done since we've gotten here is sing one stupid song after another."

"Just hope she doesn't get out the parachute," Anna said darkly. The rainbow-hued parachute—which the moms would hold by the edges and billow up and down over the kids' heads—always got the kids overexcited. "I need Charlie to nap this afternoon so I can finish my column."

"*You put your right leg in, you put your right leg out,*" Miss Emily sang, shaking a shapely leg that ended in a gorgeous tan Stuart Weitzman high-heeled sandal. If Grace wasn't mistaken, they were the same sandals she'd ogled at Bloomingdale's last week, before deciding that they were both too expensive and impractical for a stay-at-home mom.

Charlie and Hannah were ignoring the song and instead cracking themselves up by turning around and around in circles, their heads tipped back until they got dizzy. Grace stopped dancing. She was all for spending quality time with her daughter, but if Hannah wasn't going to do the Hokey Pokey, Grace didn't see why she should. Anna stopped too.

"Four-inch heels on a Tuesday morning?" Grace said under

her breath, eyeing Miss Emily's slim figure critically. "Oh, I forgot, she doesn't have kids. I knew there was a reason I hated her."

"I don't hate her because she doesn't have kids. I hate her because she's gorgeous, weighs ninety pounds, and is disgustingly cheerful at all times. If there's one thing I can't deal with, it's relentless perkiness," Anna grumbled back.

"Do you think she ever eats?"

"She must eat something."

"I think some people can survive on coffee, cigarettes, and the odd salad," Grace said thoughtfully. "They're like thin freaks of nature."

"No talking, Mommies. Remember, we're supposed to be setting a good example for the children," Miss Emily chirped, looking directly at Grace and Anna. "Now, who wants to play with the parachute?"

The kids all cheered wildly. Grace and Anna exchanged a grim look.

"If she really weighs only ninety pounds, I think we can take her down," Grace whispered. "What do you say? Are you with me?"

Twenty minutes later Grace and Anna left the library, blinking as their eyes adjusted to the dazzling south Florida sunshine. Grace was lugging the baby in her car-seat carrier, staggering under its weight, and Anna was holding Charlie's and Hannah's hands.

"So tell me about Chloe's baby. You said she had a boy, right?"

"Yes. William Thomas," Anna said. "Seven pounds, eight ounces."

"How did the birth go?"

"Chloe did great. It was a long labor, but she was a real trooper. Her husband, on the other hand..." Anna's voice trailed off, as though it were so bad, it pained her to say it aloud.

"Oh, no! What happened?"

"At first he was great. Holding Chloe's hand, coaching her along, making her laugh between contractions. But then she started to push, and he suddenly turned green. Seriously: green. I've never actually seen someone turn that shade before. The next thing I know, he goes running into the bathroom. I checked on him after a while; he was lying on the floor in the fetal position. He didn't come out until after William was born."

Grace gasped. "Are you serious?"

Anna nodded grimly. "He said that he couldn't cope with seeing Chloe in that much pain. I thought Juliet was going to clobber him."

"*He* couldn't cope? What about *her*? God, I would have killed Louis if he'd left me alone like that."

"That's pretty much exactly what Juliet said. Only she was yelling at him, while he was still curled up on the floor."

"Grace! Wait up! I want to see your baby!" a high voice trilled out.

They turned to see Mandy Rider, the most competitive mother in Orange Cove, hurrying after them, with her twin three-year-old boys in tow. Jeremy and Duncan Rider were dressed alike in head-to-toe Ralph Lauren, and they each wore their blond hair parted on the left and slicked across their foreheads. They looked like a pair of miniature bankers.

"Save me," Grace said, looking around desperately for an escape, while Anna smothered a laugh.

Thinner than me, Grace thought, watching Mandy Rider lope up. *And a real pain in the ass to boot.*

"You know I hate to brag, but we had the twins tested, and they were off the charts. The pediatrician said that they have genius-level IQs," Mandy would say whenever she got the chance. She claimed Jeremy was already composing music and Duncan showed an early interest in Shakespeare. No matter what the milestone, the Wonder Twins—as Grace called them—got there first. According to Mandy—who Grace was pretty sure was a pathological liar—the Wonder Twins supposedly rolled over at two weeks, sat up at two months, and were crawling by four months.

"Not only is that a lie," Grace had said indignantly when she'd first heard this claim, "it's just plain weird. What kind of a creepy baby crawls at four months?"

"Oh, she's beautiful," Mandy now said as she peered down at Natalie, her long dark ponytail falling over her shoulder. Mandy was pretty in a bland, preppy way. She never wore makeup and favored pastel capri pants with grosgrain belts. Today the pants were pink and the belt was aqua blue with green alligators marching around it. "What's her name?"

"Natalie Marie," Grace said proudly.

"Oh, how . . . interesting. Is that a family name?" Mandy asked.

Interesting.

Grace saw Anna wince and glance nervously at her, as though she half-expected Grace to set down the car-seat carrier and slug Mandy. But Grace just took a deep breath and tried to center herself. Women like Mandy, the sort who viewed mothering as a competitive sport, were definitely not worth getting yourself worked up over.

"No," Grace said, smiling sweetly if insincerely. "Louis and I just liked it."

"You certainly favor girls, don't you?" Mandy said. "This is your fourth, right?"

"Third."

"Oh, right, sorry. It just seems like you've been pregnant forever," Mandy said, with a trill of laughter. She showed a lot of teeth when she laughed.

Grace rolled her eyes. "Tell me about it."

"Were you disappointed? I mean, you must have been," Mandy pressed.

What, Grace wondered, *does she mean by that?* Usually, Grace gave people the benefit of the doubt. But not Mandy, who had thrown one too many bitchy barbs in Grace's direction over the years.

"Why would I be disappointed?" Grace asked, tipping her head slightly to one side, as she took in another deep centering breath and tried to imagine what Mandy would look like with a bad perm and her face covered in pimples.

"Well, I just assumed that you were hoping for a boy. I mean, girls are wonderful, of course," Mandy said hastily. But then she smiled beatifically and rested her hands on the twins' shoulders. "But there's nothing like the bond between a mother and son."

That's it, Grace thought. *It's payback time.*

"Mandy, I don't think—" Anna began, clearly looking to defuse the situation, but Grace cut her off before she finished the thought.

"So, Mandy, did you hear the news about Winston Academy?" Grace asked.

"No—what?" Mandy asked.

"Well…," Grace said, pausing for effect. She leaned forward and lowered her voice. "They had so many legacies apply for next year's pre-K class, they've decided not to take on any new families."

The color drained from Mandy's stricken face, the way it might when a doctor told someone they had an inoperable tumor. In Mandy's world, the news was almost as bad.

Winston Academy wasn't just the best private school in Orange Cove, it was the Shangri-la of elementary schools. And it was the only one a woman like Mandy would ever consider sending her progeny to. The school was built on a nature preserve covering five acres, where the children could study local vegetation and observe a butterfly garden. It also offered private French and music lessons, had a hutch full of English lop rabbits, and on the second Friday of every month the school celebrated Foreign Friends Day, where the children learned about a different culture. There was always a buffet of native dishes for lunch and an assembly showcasing dancers or other traditional entertainers from the country being studied.

Mandy's boys were, Grace knew, scheduled to start attending classes at Winston in the fall. But since Jeremy and Duncan were Mandy's only children, news that the school had decided to take only legacies—the younger siblings of children already attending the school—meant the twins would be boxed out.

"Luckily Hannah's getting in, since Molly's already a student there," Grace continued blithely.

"But...but...that can't be," Mandy said. Her eyes were wide and a little manic-looking. "I would have heard; the school would have called me."

"They just made the decision a few days ago. They're keeping it hush-hush until they get a chance to notify all of the parents. In fact, I really wasn't supposed to tell anyone," Grace said regretfully, as if the thought had just occurred to her. "Don't say anything, okay?"

"Oh...um...right," Mandy said distractedly. She glanced down at her watch. "Oh, look at the time. I have to run."

Mandy grabbed each twin by a wrist and—to their loud protests—began dragging them off toward her gold Lexus SUV. Even her ponytail looked like it was drooping.

"Bye, Mandy!" Grace called after her.

"Is that true?" Anna asked.

"What?" she asked, the very image of innocence.

Anna rolled her eyes. "What do you think? What you just told Mandy about Winston only accepting legacies."

"Oh, that," Grace said. She smiled, pleased with herself. "As a matter of fact, it's not. Poor Mandy. She'll spend the next two days burning up the phone lines and pestering Mrs. Gregory for information." Mrs. Gregory was the no-nonsense headmistress of Winston Academy. All of the parents were a little terrified of her. "With any luck, Mrs. Gregory will be so annoyed she'll ban the Wonder Twins from attending next year."

"Grace!" Anna exclaimed. "I can't believe you lied to her like that!"

"Oh, please. She totally deserved it," Grace said, waving an airy hand. "After that 'boys are better than girls' crap. I'm surprised Mandy didn't ask me if we were going to try again for a boy. Do you know I've already had fourteen people ask me that? As though it's any of their business."

"What do you tell them?"

"I tell them the truth," Grace said, grinning wickedly. "I'm making Louis get the big V. He's going in next week. Snip-snip." Grace pantomimed a pair of scissors. "That usually shuts them up. Now, come on. Let's go get some lunch and figure out what you're going to wear on your big date."

"Mommy! I don't want pancakes. I want cereal," Molly whined.

"Me too! Cereal!" Hannah chimed in. She lifted up the top of her *Little Mermaid* pajamas, baring her round belly.

"We're having pancakes," Grace overruled, raising her voice over the cacophony of protests. She'd gotten up early to mix the healthy pancake batter—oatmeal, whole-grain flour, organic milk and eggs—and to toss together a salad of sliced strawberries, bananas, and blueberries. She served the round pancakes—and, okay, yes, they were a little tough—on scarlet Fiestaware plates, alongside the fruit salad and a scoop of organic yogurt, reaching around Natalie, who was strapped to Grace's chest in a BabyBjörn carrier, to plunk the plates down on the table. Molly and Hannah sat down, still grumbling at being forced to choke down a lovingly prepared, healthy breakfast rather than bowls of overprocessed, sugar-coated cereal.

Ring-ring! Ring-ring!

The ring of the telephone caused Grace to start. She glanced at the clock—it was quarter to seven. Grace suppressed a groan. There was only one person in the world who called this early: her stepmother, Alice. Grace hadn't consumed nearly enough coffee to deal with Alice, but she'd learned from past experience that ignoring her stepmother's calls just backfired on her. Alice would grow increasingly agitated and continue to call again and again until Grace finally picked up, and then Grace would be subjected to a lecture on how thoughtless it was not to return Alice's phone messages in a timely fashion.

"Hello," Grace said, once she'd clicked the phone on.

"Hello, Grace."

"Hello, Alice," Grace said, forcing her voice to sound upbeat, when what she really wanted to do was beat herself into unconsciousness with the phone. "Wow, you're up early. Were you out catching worms?"

"Excuse me?" Alice asked, a chill creeping into her tone.

"You know: The early bird catches the worm. Forget it, it was a bad joke. That's about all I'm capable of at half-past dawn."

"You weren't asleep at this hour, were you?" Alice asked, with a disbelieving snort of laughter.

As if it were inconceivable that anyone would still be lazing in bed at quarter to seven—although it sort of was inconceivable in Grace's house. Hannah routinely woke up at five-thirty and hurtled into her parents' room first thing, and Natalie woke up soon after. Grace couldn't remember the last time she'd had the luxury of sleeping in until seven.

"No, we're up. As up as one can be at not quite seven a.m.," Grace said. "But I'm just getting the girls their breakfast, so can I call you back?"

"This will just take a minute. Guess who I saw yesterday?"

"Who?"

"Guess," Alice insisted.

Gah. "I don't know. David Hasselhoff?"

"Who?"

"You know: the Hoff. Of *Knight Rider* and *Baywatch* fame?"

"I have no idea what you're talking about, Grace."

"I was just joking. Who did you see?"

"I want you to guess," Alice insisted.

"Alice, since I'm never going to be able to guess, this could take a really, *really* long time, and I have to get Molly ready for school. So why don't you just tell me?" Grace asked, struggling to keep her voice pleasant.

"Mary Beth Fisher."

"Who?"

"Mary Beth Fisher. You remember. You met the Fishers at our

Christmas party. He's a lawyer, retired now, and she's on the hospice committee with me."

Grace had no idea who Alice was talking about. There had been approximately two bazillion people at the Christmas party, and besides, Grace had spent most of the evening sequestered in the guest room with a newborn who insisted on nursing every half hour.

But this was all besides the point. Clearly, Alice wanted to tell her something, and Grace wasn't going to be able to get off the phone until she did.

"Right. How is Mary Ann?"

"Mary *Beth*. Mary Beth Fisher," Alice repeated.

"Okay. How is Mary Beth?"

"She's fine. Actually, she looked fabulous. She's been getting chemical peels, and, I swear, she looks ten years younger. You know, it wouldn't hurt you to get one, Grace. It would really brighten up your skin."

Breathe in, breathe out, Grace told herself.

Alice continued, undaunted by Grace's silence. "*Anyway,* Mary Beth's daughter, Lana—do you know Lana?"

Grace swallowed back her exasperation. Why on earth would Alice think that she knew these people? They lived in a different city, for God's sake.

"No. I don't know Lana."

"Lana just had a baby a few weeks ago. A little girl. Terrible pregnancy; she was on bed rest for months."

"That's too bad." Grace looked over at Hannah and Molly; they were sitting quietly at the table, spooning fruit salad and pancakes into their mouths. It always made her nervous when the girls were too quiet. It usually meant they were plotting something. Grace held her hand over the phone and whispered at them, "What are you two up to?"

"Just eating, Mommy," Molly said innocently. She ruined the effect by flashing her evil smile. Grace looked closer.

"Just eating, huh? Then why are you hiding your pancakes in

your napkins?" Grace asked. The girls squealed with laughter—getting caught made it that much more fun—and put the pancakes back on their plates.

"How'd she see that?" Hannah asked Molly.

"I'm the all-seeing, all-knowing Mommy. And don't ever forget it," Grace said.

"Grace? Are you there?" Alice was saying into the phone.

"Yup, I'm here. I've heard every word you said," Grace lied.

"Well, as I was *saying,* Mary Beth told me that Lana has already lost all of her baby weight," Alice said triumphantly.

And now we come to it, Grace thought. *The real reason for this early-morning phone call.*

"She's fitting into her old jeans already. Can you believe that?" Alice continued.

"It's truly a miracle. Right up there with those portraits of Jesus that cry real tears," Grace said flippantly. She rested a self-conscious hand on her stomach, which had, since Natalie's birth, deflated into not one but *three* noticeable folds. Natalie shifted in the baby carrier, one tiny sock-covered foot bumping against Grace's hand.

"So I told her how you've been struggling to get your baby weight off," Alice continued blithely. "And she told me that Lana drank this amazing diet tea she found at the health-food store, and the weight just fell off her."

Inside Grace, a war raged between annoyance and genuine interest. Finally, the interest won out.

"What kind of tea?" she asked grudgingly.

"It's called Miracle Diet Tea. Did you write that down? I know how bad your memory is. I was just talking to Mark yesterday, and he said you forgot to send him a birthday card last week."

Mark was Alice's son, and Grace's stepbrother. Grace hadn't forgotten his birthday—she'd deliberately not sent a card, having decided that it was hypocritical to go on pretending she had any affection for Mark, who was a world-class prick.

Natalie began to stir in her baby carrier and make fretful

mewling sounds. *Excellent timing,* Grace thought. A hungry baby was the world's best excuse for getting off the phone.

"Alice, I have to go. Nat's tuning up," Grace said.

"All right. Give the girls my love."

"Will do," Grace said, and then she clicked the phone off.

She closed her eyes and counted to ten, until she felt the Alice-induced stress begin to ooze away.

"Good morning, everyone," Louis said cheerfully, as he walked into the kitchen through the garage door. Grace opened her eyes and even managed a smile for her husband. Louis was wearing his royal-blue biking shorts, and his T-shirt was drenched with sweat.

"Daddy! Daddy!" the girls shrieked, nearly upsetting their plates in the excitement. Even baby Natalie cooed happily. She reached out fat little hands, opening and closing them like a crab.

Louis kissed his two older daughters on the top of their sleep-tousled heads, and then turned to look at his wife. "What's wrong?" he asked.

"Alice," Grace replied, waving the phone in explanation.

"Ah," he said, immediately understanding.

"My eye is twitching. She actually gave me an eye twitch."

"Look at it this way: She's turned driving you crazy into an art form."

"That's true. She's like the Mozart of annoying stepmothers," Grace said. "So. Did you have a nice ride?"

Every Wednesday and Saturday morning, Louis got up early and biked around Orange Cove with his cycling club. There was a whole group of them that did this—insanity, Grace thought privately—winding their way up along the intracoastal on Ocean View Drive.

"I did," Louis said. He bent over to kiss Grace, and she was suddenly all too aware of her morning breath and rumpled flannel pajamas. She lifted a hand to smooth back her hair, which was a snarled mess after yet another rough night with Natalie, who'd wanted to nurse every hour. Grace had finally just brought the baby into bed with them, so she could catch some sleep between nursing sessions.

Grace could suddenly hear her stepmother's voice in her head, so clearly that she actually started and looked around, half-expecting to see Alice standing there, perfectly coiffed, with a sour expression on her bony face.

You shouldn't let yourself go, Gracie. Louis is a good catch, and there are plenty of women out there who'd be happy to take him off your hands. If I were you, I'd get up and do my hair and makeup every morning before he leaves for work, so he remembers what he has at home before he gets around all of the cute young things in his office.

Grace gave a shudder. It was bad enough to have Alice annoying her over the phone; hearing her stepmother's voice talking inside her head was just sick and wrong.

Besides, how the hell was she supposed to find the time to doll herself up every morning? Louis left for the office at seven forty-five sharp. If she were going to curl her hair and slap on some makeup in time to kiss him good-bye, she'd have to start getting up at five a.m. And Grace couldn't afford to lose that precious half hour of sleep.

Anyway, since when was Louis the one who was considered the catch? Not that Grace didn't love Louis—she adored him—but when they'd started dating, *he'd* been the one to pursue *her.* Unbeknownst to Grace, Louis had nursed a crush on her all the way through high school, when he'd been a band geek and she'd recently lost twenty pounds and developed the largest breasts in the freshman class. Louis was a late bloomer, and it wasn't until the two ran into each other the summer after they'd graduated from college that Grace noticed how sexy he was now that his acne had cleared and how muscular he'd become since joining his college's wrestling club.

Wait. What was she doing? Grace gave her head a forceful shake. "Ugh," she said.

"What?" Louis asked, confused. Grace glanced over at her

husband, the Catch, and realized he'd been talking all along and she hadn't heard a word he'd said.

"Nothing. I'm just having an argument," Grace said.

"With whom?"

"Alice. Sort of. Only obviously I'm not actually arguing with her for real, just inside my head."

"Uh-oh," Louis said. "That doesn't sound good. Do you two need a minute alone to sort out your disagreement?"

"No, that's okay. I think I've shut her up for the time being. What were you saying?"

"I *said* we took Ocean View all the way up and back again," Louis said. "Nearly twenty miles. Not bad for an old man, huh?"

"That's great, hon. Did you eat breakfast?" Grace asked.

"Yeah, we stopped for bagels and coffee."

"Oh. I would have loved a bagel," Molly said sadly, poking at her pancakes.

"Me too. I would have loved a bagel too," Hannah mimicked.

Grace rolled her eyes. She held her own plate with the now-cold health pancakes—which, she had to admit, really did taste like cardboard—up over Natalie's head and attempted to spoon food into her mouth without dropping any on the baby.

"Do you want me to take Nat so you can eat in peace?" Louis asked.

Grace gratefully unbuckled the baby and handed her over to Louis. He leaned against the counter, snuggling the baby up against his chest.

"How's my baby girl? What a big girl you are, sleeping through the night," he cooed.

Grace shot him a filthy look. "She *didn't* sleep through the night. Did you seriously not hear her?"

Louis shook his head, looking surprised. "Not a peep. I saw that she was in bed with us this morning, but I figured the two of you fell asleep while she was nursing."

"We did. But that was after she'd already gotten up five times—every hour, on the hour. Sort of like a cuckoo clock, only with bloodcurdling screams in place of the cuckoos," Grace said pointedly.

"Oh, poor Mommy," Louis said, looking down reproachfully at his youngest daughter. She beamed up at him with a gummy grin. He smiled back at her, then looked up at his wife, his eyes crinkling with sympathy. "I'd love to stay and help out, but I can't be late for work today. I have an early client meeting."

"That's okay. I've already had two cups of coffee. Ten more, and I'll just coast right through the day," Grace said.

"Mom, can we be excused?" Molly called from the table.

"Yeah, can we be 'scused?" Hannah asked, as always, parroting her big sister.

"Go ahead. Molly, you'd better get dressed or you'll be late for school. And no television, Hannah," Grace called after the girls, as they clattered out of the room sounding like a herd of baby elephants.

"I heard some juicy gossip today," Louis said, as Grace poured them each a cup of coffee—black for him, cream and sugar for her—and set the mugs on the newly vacated table, which was now in need of a wipe-down. Soggy chunks of pancake stuck to the wood table and yogurt dripped off the rims of the plates, as though the girls had eaten their breakfasts facefirst. Grace sighed. Maybe they had, and she just hadn't noticed.

Louis settled Natalie down in her vibrating bouncer seat, and then sat across from Grace, who had perked up at the prospect of hearing some juicy news.

"Gossip? What kind of gossip?" she asked eagerly.

"You know the Meyers from down the street?"

"No. Oh, wait…are those the ones with the three teenage boys? The ones who had that big party last year when their parents were out of town, and the cops had to come and break it up?"

"That's right. Anyway…" Louis paused for dramatic effect. "I found out today that the parents are *swingers*."

"No! Really?" Grace asked, her mouth dropping open. The wife——Grace was pretty sure her name was Ellen—sort of looked the type: blonde, busty, and just a little trashy. She favored low-rider jeans, halter tops, and short-shorts, even though she was at least fifteen years past the age where she could pull off that sort of look. But the husband—Glen? Gary? Gene? What was his name?—was a troll. He was fifty pounds overweight and as hairy as a bear (which Grace knew because he insisted on mowing his lawn shirtless). Who would want to have sex with him? Except, presumably, Ellen. Or maybe that's why they were swingers— maybe she was just desperate for the opportunity to sleep with someone who had more hair on his head than on his back.

"That's what I heard. Skylar Banks was telling me this morning that Ellen invited her and Pete to a swingers party. Can you believe that?"

"Wait—Skylar's in your biking club?" Grace asked, thinking, *Ugh. Skylar Banks.* Skylar was tall and skinny, with a long swish of shiny black hair, and probably looked amazing in her cycling shorts. The bitch.

"Yeah. I thought you knew that."

"No, I didn't. Did Skylar and her husband go to the party?"

"No." Louis laughed, and took a sip of his coffee. "She said they talked about it—just to see what it was like—but chickened out."

Grace frowned. She didn't at all like Skylar Banks discussing her sex life with Louis. Then another thought occurred to her.

"So how does that work?" Grace asked.

"How does what work?"

"Swinging. I mean, I know you swap partners with another couple, but how? Do you all do it in the same bed, or do you go into separate bedrooms?" Grace continued.

"How would I know?" Louis said. He grimaced. "And I don't want to know. Although Skylar did say that those sort of parties are more common than you might think."

"*Really?* But, wait—why haven't we ever been invited to one?" Grace asked, suddenly feeling put out at the idea. "What's wrong with us?"

"I didn't think you were into that sort of thing," Louis said, looking at her oddly.

"Of course I'm not. It's just a fidelity loophole, a way to screw around on your spouse and not feel guilty about it. But still. It's nice to be asked. Like when Molly had her birthday party last year, we invited all of the kids in the neighborhood. Even those awful Tyler kids. You know, the ones with the mother who tells them to wipe their noses on their sleeves?"

"They're nothing at all alike. One is a sex party, the other is a children's birthday party."

"But it's only polite to ask everyone."

Louis shook his head and got up to pour himself another cup of coffee.

"I'm sure we just don't give off the right vibe. People don't look at us and think: *wild sex parties.* Which is, I think, a good thing," he said dryly. "More coffee?"

"No, thanks."

Grace stared down at her now-empty plate, which looked like it had been licked clean. She didn't even remember eating; she'd just mechanically lifted the fork to her mouth, over and over and over again. She could feel the pancakes forming a thick mass in her stomach.

And suddenly, sitting there with her slack stomach resting on her thighs, Grace began to blink back tears. She had a pretty good idea why they'd never been asked to swing. Louis had actually gotten better-looking with age, and women—women like the horrible Skylar, with her tacky overbleached teeth and nonexistent ass—were forever flirting with him, laughing girlishly up at him as they tossed their hair back.

So obviously it's me, Grace thought, miserable. *I'm so fat and unattractive, no one wants to swing with me.*

Grace had always thought that once you were married, you wouldn't have to ever face sexual rejection again. But now she felt like the girl who hasn't been asked to the prom and ends up having to take her geeky cousin as a date instead.

That afternoon, while Louis was at work, the baby was napping, and the girls were busy coloring at the kitchen table, Grace settled in at the computer. She clicked on Internet Explorer and typed in a new search: DIET PLANS. The results—all 38,200,000 of them—popped up. Grace began to browse through the list but quickly lost interest when she saw it was the same-old-same-old. Just calorie-counting plans, or the ones where you have to buy ready-made meals that taste like congealed chemicals. She wanted something different. Something that would work fast.

Miracle Diet Tea, Grace thought, remembering what Alice had told her that morning. She typed the words DIET TEA into the search engine. This time there were only 19,800,000 results. And about halfway down on the first page, a blurb caught Grace's eye:

> Having trouble losing that spare tire or excess baby weight? Miracle Diet Tea can help! Adding Miracle Diet Tea is a healthy way to speed up your metabolism so you burn off those unwanted pounds! And now, with our special 30-day money-back guarantee, there's no reason not to give Miracle Diet Tea a try!

Grace clicked onto the Web site. And ten minutes later, after reading about the Chinese herbal ingredients that had been proven effective and gushing testimonials from dozens of happy Miracle Diet Tea customers, she was convinced. Grace went to fetch her credit card from her wallet.

six

Anna

"I was thinking of something like this," Anna said, showing her hairstylist, Jean Luc, a picture of Julia Roberts she'd clipped from *InStyle* magazine. Julia was walking her twins in a double stroller, and her hair fell in shiny waves around her lovely, glowing face. "I'm going on a date Saturday," she confessed. "The first date I've had in years."

"We cut," Jean Luc announced in a thick French accent. He was almost frighteningly good-looking, with his broad shoulders, piercing green eyes, and thick, glossy blond hair.

"Not too much," Anna said worriedly.

"We cut," Jean Luc said again firmly. "I make you *très* chic, *très* glamorous."

Chic and glamorous. Perfect, Anna thought with a twinge of excitement.

It wasn't until he started shampooing her hair that Anna noticed how sad Jean Luc looked. He kept sighing heavily, and at one point Anna thought she saw tears glistening in his eyes.

"Is something wrong?" she asked.

"Yes," he said simply. "My lover is left. Bastard. My life, she is *finie*."

"Oh, Jean Luc, I'm so sorry," Anna said. Her heart squeezed with sympathy.

"Marcus was—how you say?—sleeping around," Jean Luc said. He pursed his thick lips together in a pout and began to scrub roughly at Anna's scalp.

"I know exactly you how you feel. The same thing happened to me, only in my case it was another woman," Anna said, flinching. It felt like Jean Luc was ripping her hair out by the roots. "Ouch!"

Jean Luc rinsed the shampoo from her hair, lifted the seat back to the upright position, and wrapped a towel around her dripping locks.

"Men," he pronounced, "they are pigs. Swine. How you say? *Asshole*." The last word left his mouth in an angry hiss, and he turned and kicked the wall so hard, his Dr. Martens left a black mark on the light-blue paint.

Later, Anna knew that's when she should have stood up and walked right out of the salon, wet hair or no. Because while Jean Luc was a brilliant stylist, easily the best in town, the quality of his cuts depended greatly on his mood. When he was happy—in love and high on life—he was phenomenal. He'd lean back and scrutinize the hair to be cut, picking up a lock here and there. And suddenly he'd leap into motion, his hands moving nonstop, like a French Edward Scissorhands. Hair would fly through the air, and all you would hear would be the metallic *snip-snip-snip* of the scissors. Then, just as suddenly as he started, he'd stop. He'd set down his scissors, clap his hands, and say, "Is finish! *Très belle!*" And the client would turn her head from side to side, marveling at how gorgeous she looked.

But when Jean Luc was in a dark mood, it was entirely possible that you'd leave the salon looking like a poodle who'd met up with the wrong end of a weed-whacker. Now, hearing Jean Luc mutter Gallic curses under his breath, Anna felt a twinge of concern. In fact, it wasn't so much of a twinge as a big blaring siren, warning her to get away before it was too late.

"Um," she said. "Maybe..."

But before she could finish this thought, Jean Luc sprang forward and began to cut. The scissors were moving so fast, they were almost blurred. He crouched down, hopped from side to side; all the while his hands were in constant motion. Hair flew everywhere, fluttering down around Anna like brown confetti.

Ten minutes later, Anna was staring at the mirror in horror. Hot tears burned in her eyes, and all she could do was shake her head from side to side.

"*Très belle*," Jean Luc said sullenly.

"You…you…you balded me," Anna croaked.

Her formerly long locks were gone, lying limply on the floor around the chair. Jean Luc had shorn her hair so that it was about an inch long all around, except for in the back, where there was some sort of weird Mrs. Brady flip. And the bangs—that was the worst part. He'd cut her bangs into a freakish asymmetrical eighties-style slant. One half was sticking straight up, the other bent back at a ludicrous forty-five-degree angle.

"*C'est très chic! Très Parisienne,*" Jean Luc said, fluffing at the crown, teasing the hair up with his comb so that it was practically standing on end. It wasn't making anything better. Now she looked like a human Q-tip. "You no like?"

"No! I no like! I *hate*! I look hideous!" Anna said through clenched teeth.

Jean Luc threw up his hands and started muttering in French. He opened a silver cigarette case, tapped a cigarette out, and lit it, seemingly unaware of the Florida health code.

"But it's *très belle,*" he tried again, although he really couldn't muster up much enthusiasm for it. He blew two long streams of smoke out of his nose.

"No," Anna hissed, waving away the cloud of smoke. "It. Is. Not. *Très. Belle.* You *balded* me."

Jean Luc sighed resignedly, stubbed out his cigarette on a vintage art-deco ashtray, and gave a dramatic shrug.

"So I fix," he said, picking up his scissors again.

With tears still hot in her eyes, Anna just shook her head and slid off the seat. She snapped the black cape off and tossed it onto her vacated chair.

"Forget it," she said, thinking that if she let Jean Luc anywhere near her with those scissors again, she'd probably end up leaving with a buzz cut.

"Hat," Charlie said happily, looking up at Anna.

"That's right," Anna said. "Mama's wearing a baseball hat."

"Sba hat," Charlie repeated.

"Close enough," Anna said with a sigh and wondered if she could get away with wearing a hat on her date with Noah.

Anna and Charlie walked down the long boardwalk to the beach. Anna held on to Charlie with one hand, helping him navigate the sand-covered walkway, and in the other she carried a kite shaped like an enormous red and gold butterfly. As the boardwalk crested, the ocean came into view. The water was midnight blue and shimmering in the sunlight. The gentle roar of the waves instantly relaxed Anna. The tension in her shoulders disappeared, her lungs opened up, and she rallied for the first time since Jean Luc had butchered her hair that morning. The sea always had this effect on her. It was part of the reason Anna had never left Florida—she couldn't bear to live away from the beach.

A strong breeze blew off the water, causing the kite to ripple and jump, and Anna had to let go of Charlie's hand to keep the kite from getting away from her. The wind had kept sunbathers away from the beach, for the most part. Only a few people were spread out on the sand, hunkered down in beach chairs with striped towels spread across their laps. No one was braving the water—the late-February afternoon was cool, and the waves were churning—but a few intrepid souls were out parasurfing, skimming effortlessly along the water, pulled by the brightly colored parachutes.

"Look!" Charlie called out. "Bird!"

He pointed a chubby finger at a pelican that was skimming the water, dipping the tips of its wings in the sea as it fished for its dinner. Overcome with excitement, Charlie began to run down toward the ocean.

"Charlie, don't go too close to the water," Anna called after him. He turned to look at her, a mischievous smile lighting up his face. *Uh-oh.* She knew that smile well. It meant: *I'm going to do something so breathtakingly dangerous, it might actually cause the remaining hair on your head to instantly turn gray.* "Let's see if we can make your kite fly," she said.

But the temptation of the sea was too much. Charlie turned back toward the water, his face alight with interest. He'd always been fascinated with the ocean, and Anna knew that if she didn't stop him, he'd end up marching right into the surf, fully dressed, and keep marching until he was quite literally in over his head and swept out to sea.

Anna retrieved Charlie and, keeping one hand firmly on the back loop of his pants, began to unwrap the kite string with the other hand. Between the wind and Charlie's struggles to get free of her grasp, it was slow going, but finally the kite was ready to fly. The wind rattled against the plastic, making the butterfly look like it was eager to jump up and test its wings.

"Okay, sweetheart, are you ready?" Anna asked.

Charlie's eyes were round with wonder as Anna tossed the kite up into the brisk wind rolling off the ocean, and the butterfly took off, somersaulting through the sky. Charlie shrieked happily as he watched the kite's flight.

A heavy gust of wind blew toward the shore. The kite dipped dangerously and looked like it might make a crash landing. Anna tightened up on the string, trying to regain control. Once the kite had righted itself and begun soaring again, she glanced down at where Charlie was standing just a moment ago. He was gone.

"Charlie?" she said, looking around.

And there he was, again inching toward the water. In fact, much too close to the water.

"Charlie," Anna said again, her voice rising nervously.

But Charlie didn't even turn around. Instead, he continued to stride right into the surf, wobbling a bit as a wave rocked into him, the water sweeping up over his feet. The waves were treacherously high, white-capped and powerful as they rolled toward shore. Anna immediately had a nightmarish vision of Charlie being sucked into the undertow.

"Charlie!" Anna shrieked. She let go of the kite string and ran after her son. The butterfly took a sharp turn up, spun a few times, and then dived into the grass-covered dunes at the back of the beach.

Anna sprinted across the sand and snatched Charlie up just a moment before an enormous wave crashed into the shore, soaking her canvas sneakers. Charlie wrapped his plump arms around her neck and giggled happily.

"You can't run away from Mama like that," she scolded him, as she carried him away from the water. "You scared Mama!"

Charlie relaxed against his mother, clearly unfazed by the danger his adventure had put him in. In fact, Anna was pretty sure that if she put him down, he'd head right back toward the water.

"Now, where did our kite go?" Anna mused aloud.

"It's up there." An older woman in a pink warm-up suit, sitting nearby in a beach chair, pointed in the direction of the dunes.

"Thank you," Anna called back, and still holding Charlie, she began trudging up the soft sand.

Technically, you weren't supposed to go onto the dunes. They were fenced off, and there were signs warning of all the hideous things that would happen—exorbitant fines, draconian jail sentences—if you were caught frolicking in the protected areas. But Anna could see the butterfly kite fluttering just over the first dune, where it had caught on a low green bush. The string was tangled in the thorny branches.

I'll just run in and grab it before anyone sees us, Anna decided, and stepped awkwardly over the fence. Charlie was heavy and bulky in her arms, but Anna didn't dare put him down. He'd head right for the water again.

When Anna reached down for the kite, though, Charlie began struggling in her arms so much that she had to set him down.

"Oof," she said. "When did you get so big? Here, hold Mama's hand."

But Charlie didn't answer her. Instead, he immediately threw himself down on the sand and, giggling maniacally, began log-rolling down the side of the dune. Sand stuck to his bare feet and wet pants legs. Anna glanced around nervously. She was pretty sure this was exactly the sort of activity the authorities had meant to prohibit.

"Come on, let's take the kite back to the beach," Anna said. She waded into the green vegetation after her son. When she caught up to him, Charlie was holding a plant he'd plucked from the ground.

"Pretty," he said.

"Oh, no." Anna groaned. "Honey, you're not supposed to pick the plants here."

"Green," Charlie said, thrusting it at his mother.

"Yes, it is green," Anna agreed. She picked him up.

"Three," Charlie said next. He proudly held out the plant and counted, pointing to each shiny leaf as he did. "One, two, three!"

Anna felt a flush of pride. Just two years old, and Charlie was already counting!

I wonder if it's too early to look into gifted-and-talented programs for him, she wondered. *Wait...three leaves? Three shiny green leaves...?* Anna felt a prick of discomfort. She looked closer at the plant Charlie was clutching in his small round hand and immediately recognized what it was.

Oh, shit, Anna thought.

Poison ivy.

Two days later, Anna was doing what she always did when she was stressed out: cooking. She peered at the recipe for exotic mushroom pâté—a complicated process that required three types of mushrooms to be chopped in tiny, uniform squares—while talking to Grace on the phone.

"I can't go on this date," Anna insisted. She tucked the phone under her chin and scratched her arms. The itch was maddening, like a million fleas crawling over her skin. "Noah's supposed to pick me up in eight hours, and I look like hell."

"I can't believe you got poison ivy," Grace said. Anna could tell that her friend was trying not to laugh.

"Grace! It's not funny! It's on my arms and my legs—it's even on my face! I smeared calamine lotion all over, like the doctor said to do, but I'm still itching. I'm itching *everywhere*. And to add insult to serious injury, the police caught us walking off the dunes and gave me a ticket. The fine is five hundred dollars!"

Anna rummaged through the utensil drawer until she found a plastic pasta fork. She used it to scratch her arms and legs, closing her eyes in bliss at the momentary relief. But as soon as she stopped scratching—and her doctor had sternly told her not to scratch—the itch returned, even worse than before.

"Oh, poor you," Grace said, sounding more sympathetic. "How's Charlie?"

Anna glanced down at her son. He was sitting in the middle of the kitchen floor, pushing his trains around a wooden oval train track and occasionally announcing, "I love trains! *Toot, toot!*" Their pug, Potato, was sitting next to him, staring at Charlie's bowl of Goldfish crackers with a hawkish interest.

Anna smiled at the familiar messy sight. She loved the chaos Charlie brought into their house. She loved the Duplo blocks strewn about the living room, the pajama top smelling of baby lotion and boy sleep discarded on the overstuffed chair, the turned-over sippy cup slowly leaking a puddle of milk onto the tile floor.

Charlie looked up and smiled at Anna, his face alight, and she could almost feel her love for him pouring out of her.

"He's fine, thank God. The poison ivy didn't affect him at all. He's apparently immune."

"That's good. What are you going to do?"

"I don't know. But I can't go out. Not tonight, not looking like this."

"So call him and cancel."

"Don't you think I've thought of that? I can't!"

"You're starting to sound a little hysterical."

"Well, I have an insane person's haircut, and I'm covered with pink calamine lotion. There's no way I can sit across the table from a man I'm that attracted to, while I scratch at myself. I can't do it. It's too mortifying to contemplate."

"Aha! So you *are* attracted to him!"

"That's so not the point. I wouldn't want anyone to see me like this."

Anna checked the saucepan—the stock was reducing, and the kitchen was filled with the earthy smell of the mushrooms.

"Why can't you call him?" Grace asked patiently.

"I tried. I don't have his home phone number, so I called his store and left a message with some dippy salesclerk he has working there. But he didn't call back, not that I'm surprised. I gave the clerk my name and number, and she just said, 'Okay, dude,' and hung up. I don't trust anyone who calls me *dude* to be capable of delivering a phone message," Anna ranted.

"She's probably in love with him herself and trying to sabotage your romance so she can have a crack at him," Grace said darkly.

"Do you think it would be rude to just not open the door when he gets here? To pretend that I'm not home?"

"Yes. That would pretty much define rude."

"But I can't let him see me like this. It'll scare him off."

"I thought you weren't interested in him. I thought you said you didn't even want to go on this date."

"You are not helping!"

"I'm sorry. Look. When he gets there, just open the door a crack and tell him you're really sick and don't want to infect him with your germs, and ask if you can reschedule the date."

"Like when my hair grows out?"

"I told you not to let Jean Luc touch your hair when he's upset. Once, when he was sulking over this teeny-tiny little pimple on his chin, he gave me a horrible hippie, center-part haircut. It was a nightmare. I looked like Mama Cass. I can't imagine how bad he'd be in the middle of a breakup," Grace said.

"Come over and look at my head."

"Do you want me to? Maybe I can fix it."

"No, that's okay. I put some hair gel in it and pushed it back with a headband." Anna sighed heavily. "I know it's only hair, and it's not the end of the world. It's just . . . my head looks like it's covered in pubic hair."

Grace let out a shriek of laughter. "Pubic hair?"

"Yes! It's short and frizzy. Pubic hair," Anna repeated darkly. "I can't let Noah see me like this. I just can't. I'd better go. I have to call my mom and tell her I don't need her to babysit tonight after all."

The doorbell rang promptly at eight o'clock. Potato began to shriek as though Nazi storm troopers were invading the house. The small fawn pug skidded across the tile floor and threw herself against the door with a thud, barking wildly the whole time.

"Potato! Stop that!" Anna hissed, trying to ignore the nervous fluttering in her stomach.

For as much as she'd protested to Grace that she didn't want to start dating anyone, there had been a definite spark between her and Noah. And a part of Anna—a larger part than she'd been aware of until just this moment—wanted to see what that meant.

Anna glanced in the direction of Charlie's room, listening carefully. He was already tucked into his crib, fast asleep, and the doorbell and Potato's yapping hadn't seemed to wake him.

Right, Anna thought, steeling herself as she walked to the door. *Time to get this over with.*

She'd considered wearing her trusty baseball cap, but then thought it would be harder to pull off her flu excuse if Noah caught a glimpse of her. Sick people don't walk around the house with a baseball cap on. Still, she'd carefully pinned back her crazy bangs and put on the one robe she owned that wasn't covered in coffee stains. Just in case.

Her heart was pounding when she reached the door. She pulled it open just a crack, only as far as the safety chain would allow, and peeked outside, trying to keep as much of her rash-covered face and insane hair out of view as possible. Potato, still huffing with outrage, stood on her hind legs and danced like a circus bear.

"Anna?" Noah leaned over to one side to peer through the crack at her. Anna jumped back before he could see her. "Is everything okay?"

"Hi! Yes, everything's fine," Anna said, too brightly, before remembering she was supposed to be sick. "Well...actually, no. It's not fine. I'm sick."

"What's wrong?" Noah sounded concerned.

"Nothing too serious. I'm just running a fever, and I have a sore throat, and...um, the chills, and the sniffles," Anna said, wondering if that was enough symptoms to sound contagious—or was it too many?

Oh, God, she thought. *I sound like I'm making it up. Probably because I am making it up.* "It came on suddenly. I woke up feeling fine this morning. And then after lunch it just hit me. Wham!"

"Well, do you need anything?" Noah asked. "I could go get you some medicine."

How sweet is he, Anna thought, her resolve going mushy for a moment.

"Or maybe I could come in and fix you something to eat?" he continued.

"No!" Anna bellowed, before she got ahold of herself and remembered her fictitious sore throat. People with sore throats

don't shriek. She lowered her voice to a husky whisper. "I mean...
no. Thanks. I'll be fine. I have some cough medicine; that should
do the trick." Then, not remembering if she'd listed a cough as one
of her phantom symptoms, began to fake-cough into her hand for
effect.

"Oh...well. Okay," Noah said.

"I'm so sorry," she said. "So, *so* sorry. I tried calling your store
this morning to tell you. I left a message with your clerk. Didn't
she give it to you?"

"I thought you said you just started feeling bad this afternoon."

"What?" Anna asked, feeling a stab of panic. What had she
said?

"You said that you just started feeling sick this afternoon. So
how would you have known this morning that you would need to
cancel our date?"

Now Anna thought he sounded a little angry. She wanted to
peek back out at him, but she was afraid that her calamine-
covered face would repulse him, maybe even cause him to stum-
ble over backward off the porch and then race off so fast, he'd
leave a dust cloud behind him, like the cartoon Road Runner.

"Um," she said. "I, um, wasn't...really...feeling all that great
yesterday, um, either...." Her voice trailed off guiltily.

Crap, Anna thought. *This is why I don't lie. I've always sucked
at it, and I always end up getting caught.*

"I brought you these flowers."

A flash of an enormous bouquet of tropical blooms appeared
in the door crack.

"That's so nice," Anna said, feeling even worse for her lies.
She wanted to open the door, wanted to thank him properly,
but she couldn't. She just couldn't. "Would you mind leaving
them there by the door? I really don't want to expose you to my
germs."

"Right." Anna could hear a rustling as he propped the bouquet by the door. "Well, I guess I'll just be going, then," Noah said
coldly.

"Oh. Okay. Bye," Anna said. She peeked out the door and saw that Noah had descended the two front steps and was starting down the walk. But suddenly he turned.

"You know, if you didn't want to go out with me, you should have just said so. You could have saved me the trouble of coming out here," Noah said. Now he sounded hurt.

Anna cringed. She couldn't let him leave thinking that she'd blown him off.

Anna fumbled with the chain, opened the door, and rushed onto the porch. Noah was already striding angrily down the walk, practically bristling with righteous indignation. Potato streaked down the front steps, chasing after him like a shameless hussy.

"Oh, no! Potato, get back here! Noah! Please wait," she said.

Potato threw herself against Noah's legs with a soft, furry thump, and Noah grunted and stopped. He peered down at the sausage-shaped dog, who was wiggling ecstatically by his feet, as though not sure what it was.

"It's okay. Potato won't bite. Well, unless you're a jelly donut," Anna said.

Noah looked back at Anna. "You named your dog Potato?"

"Long story," Anna said. "Look, Noah...I can explain about tonight. I wasn't blowing you off. At least not the way you think," she said haltingly.

Noah paused, but then shrugged and started back up the walk. Potato pranced along at his feet and looked adoringly up at him. Feeling self-conscious, Anna wrapped her robe tighter around her and then crossed her arms, gripping her waist. When Noah reached her and looked at her for the first time, the anger suddenly disappeared from his face.

"Oh, good God!" he exclaimed, visibly starting. "What happened to your face?"

Great. Just great. Just what every girl wants to hear on a first date, Anna thought. This was why she'd sworn off blind dates back in her pre-Brad days. She'd always dreaded the possibility of being met with a fleeting look of disappointment. Actually, this was worse than disappointment. Noah was peering up at her as though she'd sprouted a second head.

"Poison ivy," Anna said shortly, immediately regretting her decision to not let Noah leave mad. Anger was vastly preferable to out-and-out repulsion. "It's on my face and my arms and—well, everywhere."

Noah seemed to be working to regain control of his emotions. "Oh…that's…wow, that really sucks."

Anna sighed and lifted her hands to hide the rash from his view. "Please don't look at me. I know it's awful."

"No, it's not that bad," Noah said. He was a bad liar too. "Really, it's not. So is that the reason why you canceled dinner?"

Anna nodded. "I'm sorry I lied," she said, her voice muffled by her hands. "But I couldn't go out in public looking like this."

"That's okay." Noah laughed ruefully. "At least you weren't just blowing me off. And it's really not that bad."

"Yes, it is. It's awful." But Anna looked up reluctantly and lowered her hands from her face. She scratched absentmindedly at a particularly itchy patch on her right arm.

"No, it's really not."

Is that the third or fourth time he's said that? Anna wondered, and she remembered reading an article about how when people lie, they tend to repeat themselves. Which meant…disaster. *Well, try to look on the bright side. At least now I won't have to tell him about my whole nondating policy. It's not like I'm ever going to hear from him again after this.*

But then Noah surprised the hell out of her when he said, "Look, have you had dinner yet?"

"No. I was just going to scramble some eggs or something."

"Why don't I go pick up a pizza and we'll eat here?"

Huh? Isn't this the part where he's supposed to make his excuses and hightail it out of here, never to be seen again? Anna looked at him doubtfully. "That's sweet, but…honestly, I really don't want you to see me looking like this either."

"Hey, I can handle a little rash."

"I don't know..."

"I'll tell you what. We can eat outside, if you like." Noah looked at the postage-stamp-size front yard. "We'll have a picnic out here in the dark."

"Well. Okay. But let's eat in the backyard. I have a little table and chairs out there," Anna said. She knew this wasn't a great idea, that this was no way to have their first date. But at the same time—and this was the kicker—she didn't *want* him to go. Especially since he was sticking around even after being confronted by a rash-covered date. It must mean that her gut instinct was right: he really *was* a nice guy.

"Great. I think I saw a pizzeria back around the corner."

"That's right. Angelo's. It's excellent," Anna said.

"High praise from a restaurant critic. I'll be back as soon as it's ready," Noah said, turning to go. But then he stopped and glanced back at her, his eyes narrowing as he studied her. "Did you do something to your hair? It looks...different."

The pizza was delicious, especially when accompanied by Anna's mushroom pâté, which, Noah pronounced, was the most delicious thing he'd ever tasted. They ate out on the back deck, which was lit only by the citronella candles Anna kept out to ward off mosquitoes. She was hoping that the flattering effect of candle-light would extend to rash-covered skin.

Anna had found a dusty bottle of red wine in her pantry and mounded the pâté on a plate with an accompaniment of rosemary crackers while she was waiting for Noah to return with the pizza. She'd also hurriedly changed out of her robe and into her favorite jeans and a coral cotton sweater and made sure that her bangs were still secured by the barrettes. Unfortunately, the gel she'd put in her hair to slick it back had also made it crunchy and just a tad sticky, but still. It was better than the crazy bangs.

And by the time Anna and Noah downed a few slices of pizza and made a respectable dent in the bottle of wine, Anna had stopped thinking about her hair. Hell, they'd been so busy talking and laughing, she'd even forgotten to scratch herself. In fact, Noah was so charming, smart, and funny that Anna—who firmly did *not* believe in the Prince Charming myth—was trying to figure out what was wrong with him. All men had something wrong with them. It was a law of nature.

He'd never been married. *(Commitmentphobe?* she wondered.) He was close with his parents. *(His mother probably hates all of his girlfriends.)* He didn't have any siblings. *(Only children can be self-centered.)* He jogged and played tennis. *(Athletes were always assholes.)*

They talked about their favorite music (Anna liked eighties' new-wave pop, Noah loved seventies' Southern rock), books (Anna's favorite writer was Maeve Binchy; Noah had read everything Tom Clancy had ever written), and movies.

"*Dirty Harry,*" Noah said immediately. He sneered suddenly. "Do you feel lucky, punk? Do you?"

"What's wrong with your eyes? Why are you squinting like that?" Anna asked, amused.

"Don't you know a master Clint Eastwood impression when you hear it?"

"Oh, is *that* what that was?" Anna teased him.

He grinned at her and popped a cracker in his mouth. "So, what's your favorite movie? Let me guess—you're the arty sort. French movies without proper endings, right?"

"Ummm..." Anna considered lying and saying *Howard's End,* or something similarly highbrow. But, again, she was a horrible liar. "*Pretty Woman,*" she admitted.

Noah groaned. "What is it with women and that movie? I mean, it's about a hooker falling in love with her john. That's not romantic—it's gross."

"It is romantic! Richard Gere rescues Julia Roberts at the end! After she's given up hooking."

"For about five minutes. And presumably before he finds out that she gave him chlamydia."

"How can you say that? It's a classic redemption story!" When Noah just rolled his eyes, Anna exclaimed, "I can't believe you! It's like you haven't even seen the movie."

"I haven't seen the movie," Noah admitted.

"You haven't seen *Pretty Woman*? How is that possible?" Anna exclaimed.

"It's a chick flick. And it's not exactly a classic. Like, say, *Dirty Harry*."

"Actually, I have to admit: I've never seen *Dirty Harry*."

"What? And you're criticizing me?" Noah asked with mock outrage. "Okay, that's it. On our next date we'll have to rent *Dirty Harry*."

Our next date. Anna felt a thrill of excitement at the words. So her hair and rash really hadn't scared him off.

"Only if we also rent *Pretty Woman*," Anna countered.

"Okay. Deal. It'll be a double feature."

They smiled at each other. Potato, who had been snuffling around at their feet, hunting for dropped pizza, suddenly reared up and placed her feet on Noah's leg. She grinned at him, her pink tongue lolling out one side of her mouth and her wide eyes blinking coquettishly.

"I think your dog likes me," Noah said, reaching down to rub Potato's belly.

"She likes everyone. Especially people who slip her pieces of pizza under the table."

"When did you get her?"

"Three years ago. Right after I got married. I got custody of her during the divorce."

Noah whistled. "Divorce. That's tough. I'm glad I've never gone through that."

"Have you ever come close to getting married?" Anna asked. She leaned back in her chair, feeling a little tipsy, in a comfortable, loose-limbed way. Enough so that she felt bold enough to wander onto the minefield of asking a date about old loves. But the candle was glowing, casting small circles of warm yellow light onto the table, and one of her neighbors had put on an old jazz album. Strains of the music drifted toward them. It all lent itself to an atmosphere of intimacy.

"Yeah. I've come close," Noah said.

"So you've been engaged?"

Noah hesitated, just long enough to pique Anna's interest. Could that be the fatal flaw she'd been waiting for? Was there a woman in his past who he'd never gotten over? Maybe someone who had broken his heart? Anna leaned forward a little, and her breath caught in her throat while she waited.

"Yes, I've been engaged. In fact...more than once," Noah said.

More than once?

Anna furrowed her brow. "You've been engaged twice?" she asked.

"Um..."

His obvious discomfort was even more worrying. What had he done—left his brides at the altar? Anna had a sudden vision of two women, one blonde and one brunette, dressed in Vera Wang bridal gowns, standing side by side, sobbing quietly into their bouquets moments after being told that their groom was a no-show.

"Actually...more than twice," Noah finally said, sounding a little sheepish.

Three jilted fiancées? Three empty reception halls, three lists of gifts that had to be returned, three sets of nonrefundable honeymoon packages to Bermuda? One fiancée might not have been his fault. Two could have been a run of bad luck. But three? The only way a guy this attractive, smart, and funny could have discarded three different fiancées was if he'd been the dumper.

Aha! Anna thought grimly. *That's it. He's a serial monogamist, like Hugh Grant's character in* Four Weddings and a Funeral. *I knew he was too good to be true. I knew it.*

"More than twice?" Anna repeated.

Noah looked down at his wineglass, twirling the stem in his hands, while Anna waited for the explanation. Surely he'd have an explanation, however lame it might be. But she wasn't prepared for what he said next.

Noah cleared his throat. "Actually ... four times."

"What?" Anna thought she hadn't heard correctly. Because she could have sworn he'd just said "four times." Which was insane. No one got engaged four times. Well, no one other than Elizabeth Taylor. It was ridiculous.

"I said, I've been engaged four times," Noah said again. And as flabbergasted as Anna was by this news, she noticed that Noah didn't look her in the eye as he said it.

seven

Juliet

Obviously, you have to dump him," Juliet said, a few nights later. Juliet, Grace, and Anna were having dinner at The Tortoise and the Hare, which Anna was reviewing for her column.

The restaurant was housed in a converted cottage. The walls had been painted a deep lacquered red and were covered with ornate gold-framed mirrors. Each of the four small dining rooms was lit by a crystal chandelier, candles gleamed in silver candelabra, and the round tables were dressed in starched white linens. The three women sipped glasses of chilled white wine.

"No, she shouldn't!" Grace argued. "You don't dump someone over a little misunderstanding."

"Technically, it's not dumping when you've gone out on only one date. It's not returning a phone call. And I don't think that four fiancées counts as a misunderstanding," Anna said. She consulted her menu again. "Now, remember, you can order whatever you like, but everyone has to get something different."

"I'm having the pan-fried conch and the rainbow trout," Juliet said, closing her menu and pushing it off to the side.

"I was going to have the conch," Grace complained.

"Too late. I called dibs."

"Okay, fine, as long as you'll give me a bite."

"Everyone has to give everyone a bite. I need to taste everything," Anna interjected.

"Well...maybe I'll just have a dinner salad," Grace said, frowning as she looked over her menu.

Anna and Juliet both stared at her.

"What?" she said. "I told you, I'm on a diet."

"Order a real meal," Anna said.

"But I'm not that hungry."

"You don't have to eat it all, but I need to try as many dishes as possible," Anna said.

"Okay, fine. I'll get the crab cakes and the wood-grilled venison," Grace said. "But I'm not going to eat it."

They placed their order with the waitress—Anna ordered the roasted beet salad and miso-glazed tuna—and then, their wine-glasses refreshed, turned their attention back to Noah and his bevy of ex-fiancées.

"At least, I hope they're all exes," Anna said gloomily. "It would be just my luck if he was still engaged to one of them. I knew he was too good to be true."

"I think you're being too hard on him," Grace said.

"Oh, please. Like you wouldn't freak if you found out Louis was engaged four times before you met him," Juliet snorted.

"Well. Yes. But, then, Louis and I started dating when we were only twenty-one, and I'd known him since we were ten, so it would have been freakishly weird if he'd already been engaged four times. How old is Noah?"

"I'm not sure. Thirty-seven, thirty-eight. Somewhere around there," Anna said.

"So he's probably been dating for twenty-plus years. Four serious relationships over that long a period of time isn't abnormal," Grace said sensibly. She picked up a piece of bread from the basket, dipped it in olive oil, and started to take a bite. But then she suddenly jumped as though she'd been shocked and quickly dropped the bread back on her plate.

"What's wrong?" Anna asked.

"Yeah, why are you being so twitchy?" Juliet asked.

"I'm not," Grace said. "I just forgot for a minute that I gave up bread."

"Well, I haven't." Juliet picked through the basket and helped herself to a slice. Grace watched her hungrily. Juliet noticed and frowned. "Stop staring at me."

"I'm not staring at you," Grace said huffily. She pushed her bread plate away and turned back to Anna. "Did he tell you what happened with his exes?"

"No. Right after he dropped the bombshell, Charlie woke up crying. I was worried that seeing a strange man in the house would scare him, so I asked Noah to leave," Anna said.

"Are you going to see him again?" Grace asked. "I think you should. Give him a chance to explain."

"Well, we already made plans for a second date. We're going to have dinner."

"Good! Over dinner, ask him in a roundabout way what happened with his ex-fiancées. Just be subtle about it."

"Like: 'Did you dump them all at the altar?'" Anna asked teasingly.

"Or, 'Do you have a sexually transmitted disease they found out about?'" Juliet suggested.

"Oh, my God, I hadn't even thought of that," Anna exclaimed. "Do you think that's it?"

"No," Grace said.

"Yes," Juliet said at the same time. "But it could be something minor, like crabs."

"You are so gross," Grace said.

Anna looked a little pale. "I don't have a good feeling about this," she said.

"Look on the bright side. At least he wasn't scared off by your rash and that awful haircut," Juliet said.

"Juliet!" Grace exclaimed, and kicked her under the table.

"Ouch! What?"

"Your rash looks much better," Grace assured Anna. "You can hardly notice it at all."

"Thanks." Anna sighed. "But my hair is a different story."

"No, it looks cute all slicked back like that. You look like one of the Robert Palmer girls," Grace said brightly. "All you need is a guitar and a little black dress."

"I don't know why you didn't stop Jean Luc before he did that to your head," Juliet said.

"Obviously I didn't know it was going to be this bad," Anna said.

"That's why I don't go to him anymore. I switched salons after the time that Jean Luc was in a snit because he'd found out *Sex and the City* was going off the air. Remember? He tried to give me Farrah Fawcett hair, circa *Charlie's Angels*. You know: wings." Juliet shuddered. "You should go see Marta at the Seashell Salon. She might be able to do something with those weird bangs he gave you."

"Juliet!" Grace said again, her voice exasperated. "Are you completely incapable of tact?"

"Would you rather I lied?" Juliet asked.

"Yes!" Grace said. "It's called being nice."

"I don't do nice," Juliet said, with a philosophical shrug.

"No kidding!"

"Speaking of being nice, I need a favor," Anna said. "It's for Chloe. She didn't have a baby shower—she doesn't know many people in town—so I thought we could throw her a postpartum shower. We could just stop by with some gifts and a little cake and maybe a bottle of champagne. Nothing big, just the three of us. I stopped by her house the other day when I was out walking Potato, and I thought she seemed really down. I think she could use some cheering up."

"Absolutely!" Grace said.

"Absolutely *not*," Juliet said. "I also don't do baby showers."

"Oh, come on. It'll be fun. And I promise we won't play any of those annoying shower games or anything silly like that," Anna said.

"I think it's a fabulous idea," Grace said.

"I don't. Count me out," Juliet said.

"Don't worry, I'll make sure she shows up," Grace said to Anna.

"No you won't," Juliet said. "I was present at the birth. I saw the baby crown, for Christ's sake, and I've been having post-traumatic stress flashbacks ever since. I think I've discharged my duty on this one."

Grace just fixed her with her best stern-mother look. It was the look she saved for when her kids were really acting up, the one that caused her daughters to instantly cease and desist all naughty behavior. It was a look so powerful, even Juliet was no match for it.

"Okay, fine," Juliet acquiesced with a sigh. "But you owe me big."

"Hey," Patrick said, yawning as he entered the kitchen.

"Good morning," Juliet said.

Patrick planted a sleepy kiss on her cheek and then went to pour himself a mug of coffee.

"Where are you going?" he asked.

It was Saturday morning, so early the girls weren't awake yet, but Juliet was already dressed. She was standing by the kitchen door, keys in hand, while flipping through yesterday's mail.

"The office," Juliet said briefly. She opened the American Express bill and scanned the charges. "Why did we spend ninety dollars at Omaha Steaks? Oh, right, your father's birthday."

"It's Saturday," Patrick said. The obvious irritation in his voice caused Juliet to look up from the bill in surprise.

"I know. That's why I'm wearing jeans instead of a suit," she said.

"The twins have a soccer game this morning. You promised them you'd be there," Patrick said. His face looked stiff and angry, and he folded his arms over his chest.

"And I will be. The game isn't until eleven, right? I'm just going to pop into the office, work on my time sheets, and then I'll meet you over at the field," Juliet said.

Patrick's face softened a bit. "Oh. Okay, then. I just don't want them to be disappointed."

He didn't say *again*. He didn't need to. It hung between them, like a stiff-fingered accusation.

Juliet had a sudden flashback to the weekend when she and Patrick got married. They'd eloped to Vegas. It had been hot and crowded and tacky as hell, and they'd loved every minute they spent there. They got married by an Elvis impersonator at the Graceland Wedding Chapel and then spent one decadent night in a suite at the Bellagio. Instead of a reception, they'd eaten at Le Cirque, played blackjack, and finally fell into bed and made love for hours.

It hadn't been all that long ago. Only five years, Juliet realized. And yet now they couldn't be further away from the impulsive, sex-crazed couple they'd once been.

"You know what my job is like. It's not forty hours a week, Monday through Friday," Juliet reminded him.

"Tell me about it. I think the last time you worked only forty hours was our vacation," Patrick said, only half joking. It didn't help that the vacation was still a sore subject between them.

They'd driven up to Orlando to take the twins to Disney World in early January, on the tail end of the girls' school break. On the second day they were there, just moments before they were about to head off to Epcot, Juliet's office had called with a work crisis. Joanna, one of the other associates, had lost track of a case she was responsible for and the court was going to dismiss it for lack of prosecution, which would have opened the firm up to a potentially devastating malpractice lawsuit from the clients. Joanna was fired, and Juliet had to rush back to the office to handle the case. Patrick hadn't forgotten it, even though, Juliet remembered, he didn't exactly mind when the bonus she'd earned purchased the flat-panel television set he'd been salivating over at Best Buy.

"I don't have time for a guilt trip right now," Juliet said crisply. She picked up her travel coffee mug and a file of papers to bring in with her and turned to leave.

"I didn't know you were capable of feeling guilt," Patrick said to her back.

Juliet paused for a minute, her shoulders stiffening. And then she walked out the door and closed it behind her without looking back at him.

"Working on a Saturday? Are you trying to impress the boss?"

Juliet looked up. She'd been kneeling in front of the filing cabinet in her office, trying to track down the notes she'd made on her billable hours worked that month, when she heard his voice. It was Alex. She felt a frisson of excitement as she met her boss's cool gaze. He was also dressed casually, in chinos and a navy polo shirt that turned his eyes a vivid aquamarine.

"Always," she said, trying to keep her voice cool. She stood up to greet Alex, suddenly—and foolishly, she knew—glad that she'd worn a body-hugging V-neck T-shirt and her new flattering dark-rinse jeans, rather than the sweats she normally favored on the weekends.

"What are you working on?"

"Time sheets. I was in a deposition all day yesterday, and I didn't have a chance to get to them. How about you?"

"I just stopped in to clear my desk off. But, as long as I've got you here, let's go over the Richardson case. I have a meeting with the client on Monday," Alex said.

Juliet glanced at the clock. It was already quarter past ten. In order to make the twins' game, she would have to leave in twenty minutes. And, if past history were any guide, a meeting with Alex would take longer than that. Much longer. He was a detail man, the sort of lawyer that wanted to have every last issue spelled out for him before he went into a client meeting. Alex liked to say that the secret to his success was that he knew when and how to delegate, but this was bullshit. He micromanaged everything, and nothing got by him.

Juliet couldn't very well refuse. She was going to be up for partner in the next six months; she needed to take advantage of every opportunity she could find to impress Alex. He was the seniormost partner, and having his approval would make all the difference when it came time for the partnership to consider her.

Besides, it meant spending the morning with Alex.

"Okay," Juliet said, her decision made. "I'll get my notes together and come down to your office."

I'll still be able to get to the game by halftime, she thought. *And as long as they see me there at some point, the girls won't know the difference.*

"So I think that's everything," Alex said some time later, after Juliet had fully briefed him on the status of the Richardson case. "You want to grab some lunch?"

"Lunch? Why, what time is it?" Juliet asked, checking her watch for the first time since the meeting had begun. She gaped down at it. *Shit.* It was already noon. She'd completely lost track of time. The girls' game had started an hour ago.

How long do preschool soccer games last, anyway? she wondered. *Will I still be able to catch the end?*

"I can't. In fact, I have to get going. I'm running late as it is. Rain check?" Juliet asked.

"Sure," Alex said. He leaned back in his chair and smiled at her in a way that made Juliet suddenly aware of how close they were sitting. Just an arm's reach away. Close enough that she could smell his clean, fresh scent.

Juliet was suddenly overcome with the desire to touch Alex, to brush her fingers along the smooth skin on the inside of his wrist. She glanced at his hand; Alex was married, but he wasn't wearing a wedding band.

God, get a grip, Juliet told herself. *You're married. He's married. And to him, you're just one of the guys.*

But there was a flicker in Alex's blue eyes that made her not quite believe that.

"Do you have plans with your family today?" Alex asked.

Juliet made it a policy to never talk about the girls or Patrick at the office. First, she didn't think her family was anyone's business. And second, she didn't want her coworkers to think of her as a wife or a mother, which was—in Juliet's mind—synonymous with feminine weakness. She wanted them to think of her as a shark, someone who was ruthless, ambitious, and even slightly dangerous. Someone they didn't want to cross.

"Yes," she said vaguely. "You know, this and that."

Suddenly Alex leaned forward, reaching toward Juliet. She froze, and—for the first time in as long as she could remember—she had no idea what to do. She could feel the tips of Alex's fingers brush against her clavicle.

What is he doing? she wondered, nervous and excited at the same time. She inhaled sharply, then held the breath.

Alex fingered the emerald cross hanging on a delicate gold chain that she always wore. His touch was innocent enough and yet somehow managed to be incredibly sexy. Juliet could feel her body flood with warmth, as every last inch of her skin went on high alert.

"You never struck me as the religious type," Alex murmured.

"I'm not," Juliet said. She surprised herself with how self-possessed she sounded. "It was my mother's."

"Was?"

"She died when I was in law school," Juliet said briefly.

"I'm sorry." Alex's fingers withdrew abruptly. "You must miss her. You wear that necklace every day."

I don't wear it because I miss her, Juliet thought, feeling almost rebellious at the idea that her mother was someone she'd want to enshrine around her neck. *I wear it to remind myself of what happens to a woman who loses her power.*

Alex leaned back and glanced at his watch.

"All right, Cole, you'd better get out of here. You don't want to spend your whole Saturday stuck at the office," he said. He straightened the stack of papers in front of him on the table and slipped them into his leather binder.

It felt like a dismissal. Hell, it was a dismissal. Feeling stung, Juliet stood.

"Right, then. Good-bye, Alex. Have a nice rest of your weekend," she said. And then she turned and walked out of the room, hoping that she didn't look as disappointed as she felt.

Patrick was wrong: Juliet did feel guilt. As she walked into her house, the guilt clung to her, sticking thickly in her throat. She'd missed the girls' soccer game; by the time she'd raced across town and pulled into the park, the field was empty.

Still. She was at the office, she tried to convince herself. Not that it was working. She was well aware that Alex wouldn't have minded if she'd left earlier, in time to make the last part of the game. So why had she stayed?

But she knew why. She'd wanted to spend the morning with Alex, to watch his square, sure hands as he jotted down a note on a legal pad and to listen to the raspy bark of his laughter.

And knowing this made Juliet feel like five shades of shit.

Will Patrick know? she wondered, the thought causing her heart to skitter inside her chest. Juliet's mother had always sworn that she knew when her father was being unfaithful, insisted that he was incapable of hiding his guilt. Not that she'd been unfaithful to Patrick—at least not physically. And fantasizing about another man didn't count as cheating...did it? No. No way.

The house was buzzing with familiar sounds—the intake of the air conditioner, the hum of the dishwasher, "Hakuna Matata" from the *Lion King* soundtrack playing in the twins' playroom.

"I'm home! Where is everyone?" Juliet called out, setting her leather bag—large enough that it could double as a briefcase—on the front hall table.

"Mom's home! Mom's home!"

The girls came stampeding down the stairs, shrieking with happiness, and threw themselves against her legs. It was not the welcome she deserved after missing their soccer game, Juliet knew, and it made her feel even worse than she would have if they'd pouted.

What am I doing? she wondered, as she rested a light hand on each girl's head. *I'm missing everything.* Sometimes, their childhood seemed to be passing with terrifying speed. In the blink of an eye, they'd gone from roly-poly babies to these long-limbed big girls. What would they become in another blink? Surly, secretive teenagers? College students never at home?

"I scored a goal!" Emma piped up, beaming up at her mother with a toothy grin.

"You did? That's fantastic, sweetheart," Juliet said. Emma was still in her soccer clothes—a white T-shirt with *The Bumblebees* emblazoned on the front, red nylon shorts, and high white tube socks ringed at the top with red stripes. Izzy had already changed, swapping her soccer clothes for a purple *Dora the Explorer* T-shirt and a pink tutu.

"I didn't," Izzy said carelessly. Izzy wasn't a soccer aficionado like her sister and played only because she hated to be left out of anything.

"You came close," Emma reminded her.

"That's true," Izzy said.

"I think this calls for a celebration. Who wants to go to the beach? I think it's warm enough that we can brave it. And out for cheeseburgers afterward?"

"I do! I do!" the twins began to scream, hopping up and down with excitement.

"Go change into your swimsuits," Juliet said, and the girls streaked upstairs, chattering with excitement.

Juliet followed them, at a somewhat slower pace. Patrick was in their bedroom, lying on the four-poster bed and reading a novel. He looked up when she came in.

"Hi," she said, bracing herself for what was almost certainly going to be an argument.

"Hi," Patrick said curtly.

"Did you get my message? I tried calling, but your cell phone wasn't turned on," she said, as she peeled off her shirt and jeans. She opened a dresser drawer and rummaged around for her orange tankini.

"I did," Patrick said.

"My boss showed up at the office. He pinned me down," Juliet said. A brief but vivid image flashed through her thoughts: Alex holding her wrists on either side of her head against the conference table while he made love to her.

Christ, what is wrong with me? she wondered, forcing the unwanted fantasy out of her thoughts.

"You missed Emma's first soccer goal." He kept his voice conversational, but Juliet wasn't fooled. He was clearly pissed and intent on letting her know it in his typical passive–aggressive way. It annoyed her. Why couldn't he just come out and tell her he was angry? Why did he have to always play these games?

"She told me," Juliet said shortly. She peeled off her panties, tossed them in the hamper, and stepped into her bathing suit. "I'm going to take the girls to the beach and then to the Orange Cove Grill for dinner. Do you want to come?"

"Juliet."

"What?"

"This can't continue," Patrick said.

Juliet froze. *Oh, shit.* Had he already figured out that she'd been fantasizing about another man? How?

"The girls are only going to be young once. And you're missing out on their childhood," Patrick continued.

Juliet closed her eyes, feeling the cool rush of relief. She pulled on the top of her bathing suit and turned to face her husband, who was looking sternly at her.

"Don't be so dramatic. I'm not missing their childhood. But I have a very demanding job. And until I make partner, it's going to be like this." Juliet shrugged. She suddenly felt tired. "Do we really have to go over this again?"

"I know that you work hard. But shouldn't the twins be just as important as your job?"

"Jesus, Patrick. Who do you think I'm working for?"

"Do you really want me to answer that?"

Juliet and Patrick stared at each other, facing off like a pair of boxers. Juliet crossed her arms, and Patrick raised his eyebrows.

"She'll never have a first goal again. Just like she'll never take a first step again or say her first word. And you've missed all of it."

"It's not like I'm out partying," Juliet said. "I'm *working*. For the girls. For our family. Jesus. It's not like they'll remember that I wasn't there."

It was just the wrong thing to say. Patrick looked thunderous, his brow furrowing angrily. "Do you even hear yourself? They're your children."

"I know who they are," Juliet said coolly. "But I don't have the luxury of staying home all day to record every minute of their childhood. Someone has to pay for their school tuition, and the mortgage, and the car payments. Someone in this family has to be the provider."

"Right," Patrick said coldly. He got up off the bed and stormed across the bedroom.

Shit, Juliet thought. Why had she used that word? *Provider*. It was the same word Patrick had used back when she was still pregnant and they were arguing about whether or not he'd stay home. She'd known it was a hot button for him.

"So do you want to come to the beach with us?" Juliet called after him, by way of apology.

Patrick didn't answer.

eight

Chloe

Chloe wheeled William, sleeping in his navy-blue Peg Perego carriage, down the winding path into Manatee Park. It was a lovely space, located on the bank of the Intracoastal Waterway, where manatees could sometimes be seen lolling about in the shallow warm water. The weather was sunny and mild, and the sky was a wide-open blue.

A perfect day, Chloe thought, her spirits rising.

And there were certainly quite a few people who'd had the same idea. Older couples walked dogs along the boardwalk, and joggers and bikers huffed by. A group of teenagers with shaggy hair and too-long shorts were playing basketball. Past the basketball court, down by the water, Chloe saw a group of mothers congregating at the playground, and she resolutely pushed the carriage down toward them.

It was Chloe's first outing since William was born. Actually, it was the first day she'd even bothered to get dressed. Most days she just slumped around the house wearing a nursing bra and a pair of James's pajama bottoms, too exhausted to bother with anything else. But she was so sick of sitting at home and watching daytime television—there was only so much Judge Judy a girl could take before her brain actually crumbled into dust—and sick of seeing her puffy-faced reflection. She hadn't even brushed her hair, much less put on makeup, in weeks, and her short blonde curls were clumping up into snarls. She was starting to scare herself and did her best to avoid mirrors.

And so even though it had been yet another long night—William had woken up every two hours, squawking to be fed—and even though Chloe was so tired it felt like she was moving in a fog, she'd made the bold decision to shower, condition her hair, get dressed in real clothes, slick on some lip gloss, and head down to the park. She'd walked there occasionally during her pregnancy and stood just outside the playground, her hands folded on her belly, as she watched the children swinging, pumping their legs to go higher and higher, or climbing the wrong way up the slide and then shrieking with laughter as they inevitably slid back down. And she'd shyly watched the moms, who stood together, chatting companionably, as they watched their children play.

And now, Chloe thought triumphantly, *I finally have an in. Now I have William.*

The toddler park was enclosed by a chain-link fence, which probably should have been depressing, but the view of the river was so pretty it managed not to be. Chloe hesitated at the gate. The playground was covered with fine white sand, like a beach, so she couldn't wheel the carriage inside the fence. Instead, she leaned down and picked up William, still heavy with sleep, and a blanket, and awkwardly pushed his carriage next to the two other strollers lined up at the gate.

Three moms were grouped together near the huge jungle gym, which was shaped like a pirate's ship, half-watching their kids tumbling around but mostly focused on one another.

"Hi," Chloe said, approaching the group.

They didn't acknowledge her, didn't even look up.

Chloe went hot and cold at the same time. Were they really ignoring her? No, that was ridiculous; they were adults, *mothers.*

"Um, hi," she tried again, raising her voice. "I'm Chloe, and this is my son, William."

The three women glanced over at her, their eyes flickering as they looked her up and down. One of the moms gave her a half smile and nodded—*So I'm not invisible!* Chloe thought—but the other two just looked at her blankly for a few seconds and then turned back to their conversation.

"So, I was, like, if you're going to basically invite yourself to my kid's birthday party, you should at least bring a decent present," a thin woman with heavily highlighted hair and sharp features was saying. She was overdressed for the park, in a pink sweater and floral Lilly Pulitzer skirt. She'd dressed her kids to color-coordinate with her outfit: Her daughter had on the identical skirt and shirt, and her little boy was wearing a pink polo shirt and green canvas shorts. Chloe didn't like to be judgmental, but this seemed a bit...well, *much* for an afternoon park outing.

"So what did she end up giving Tatum?" another mom asked. This one was a fair, top-heavy redhead, whose skin was turning pink in the afternoon sun.

"A Barbie doll. And not even a nice Barbie but one of the cheap ten-dollar ones," the mom with highlights announced, and the other moms groaned in disbelief.

"That is *so* tacky," a petite Asian woman wearing green capris and a black halter top announced. She had a tattoo of a butterfly on her lower back, and she was doing an admirable job of ignoring her daughter, a tiny girl wearing rhinestone-embellished hip-hugger jeans and a cut-off tank top, who was pulling at her hand, saying, "Swings, Mommy, swings! Come push me!"

"Tell me about it," Highlights said, rolling her eyes and shaking her head.

Chloe turned away and pretended to busy herself with William, while she tried to figure out the best way to retreat before she burst into tears in front of the awful women. Suddenly it felt like she was back in high school, being ignored by the clique of mean, popular girls. The sort you knew wouldn't make very good friends and yet still wanted them to accept you anyway.

"Did you get Ava into Temple Beth El's preschool?" Highlights asked the redhead.

"Yes, *finally*. They took forever to let us know. I was really starting to sweat it. How about you?"

"Tatum's going to Winston." This was said with not a little bit of smug self-satisfaction.

The women set off on a loud and animated debate on local

preschools and the benefits of Montessori versus traditional schools. Chloe settled down on the warm sand, William cradled in her arms, and wondered why she thought she might fit in here.

Stupid, she thought fiercely. *Who brings a newborn to the park? It's not like William's going to be able to swing or climb up on the pirate ship. What was I thinking?*

But still. She couldn't leave, not now. The clique would think that they'd run her off. And she did have some pride. Shifting William to one arm, Chloe spread out his blanket and then gently set her sleeping son on it. He didn't wake up, and she gazed down at him, admiring the curve of his tiny shell-like ears and the Clark Kent dimple in his chin.

"Sure, sleep now. I know you're going to make me pay for it at three in the morning," Chloe told him.

"My shovel! Mine!" A little girl with a mop of orange curls began to scream, as the pink-and-green-dressed boy, so pale he almost looked albino, fled with the shovel at issue.

"Connor!" Highlights called after him. "Give Ava her shovel back!"

Connor ignored his mother and ran pell-mell toward where Chloe was sitting, his bare feet churning up sand as he approached.

"Be careful," Chloe warned him quietly—too quietly, really, since she didn't want his mother to hear her correcting him—but even if she'd screamed, it still would have been too late. The boy flew by her, and as he passed, he kicked a pile of sand right onto William's face. William woke with a start, throwing his arms back in a panicked reflex, and then started to scream. It was a high, thin cry, not at all like his hungry and tired cries, and for a sickening moment Chloe thought that he might really be hurt.

Could sand in a newborn's eye or ear be a serious problem? she wondered, as her stomach gave a lurch. *Could he end up blind or deaf?*

"Shhh," Chloe said, lifting his flailing body up to her shoulder. She rubbed his back soothingly. "It's okay, sweetie. It's okay."

William started to calm down, comforted by his mother's

embrace. His cries continued, but they were softer and less agitated.

Chloe looked over at Highlights, expecting her to apologize or, at the very least, to correct her son, who was now standing up on the swing, the shovel still clutched in his hand, and yelling, "Mine! Mine! Mine! Shut up! Mine!" The little redheaded girl dissolved into hysterical tears and rushed to her mother's arms.

Highlights looked at Chloe coolly and then said to her gaggle of friends, "Don't you think that baby is awfully young to be here?"

She didn't bother to lower her voice.

"I was thinking the same thing," the petite Asian woman agreed.

"You can't really expect the bigger kids to watch out for babies," the redhead added.

"Exactly," Highlights said.

Chloe stared down at the sand, her hand still rubbing circles on William's back, as he continued to mewl pitifully, pausing now and then to inhale raggedly. And as soon as the other mothers turned away, their attention distracted by another clash between two toddlers grappling over a plastic pail, Chloe got up and left.

When Chloe got home, she called William's pediatrician. The receptionist put her right through to the nurse, who soothed Chloe and assured her that William—who had fallen back asleep and was now dozing happily in his Moses basket—was in all likelihood fine, although Chloe was supposed to watch him for the next twenty-four hours and call back if his eyes or ears appeared to be bothering him.

After Chloe clicked off the phone, she burst into tears. She sat huddled on one end of the couch, her feet tucked under her, and sobbed until her eyes stung. She felt stupid, even pathetic, to be breaking down like this. So what if a few nasty women didn't want to include her in their awful clique? But she couldn't seem to stop.

She just felt so overwhelmed, so strung out, so *tired*. That was the worst part of it, the exhaustion. She'd never been so tired in her life, so tired her bones felt too heavy for her body.

She loved having William, adored every delicious inch of him, but the work—it never stopped. The nursing, and the diaper changes, and the crying fits. And then when he napped, she ran around the house, trying to take care of the laundry and the dishes and the vacuuming. The baby books instructed new mothers to sleep when the baby sleeps, but how could she? That was the only time she had to get anything done.

And James was never around to help. He was always at work, or out golfing, or at the gym. Had he been gone this much before Wills was born? Chloe tried to remember. It hadn't seemed like it...but maybe she just hadn't noticed. Now that she was being held hostage by a very small, very demanding person all day, every day, her husband's prolonged absences were starting to really bother her. Just this afternoon, when she'd gotten home from the disastrous park outing, there was a message from James on voice mail.

"Hey, hon. It's me. I'm going to be late tonight. The boss is taking a few of us out for drinks after work. Love you. Bye."

Chloe had been too frantic calling the pediatrician and worrying about Wills to pay much attention to the message. But now resentment began to burn in her chest. She knew what the message meant. James wouldn't be home in time to help her get William to bed. Again.

The doorbell rang, and Chloe started violently at the sound. Wiping her eyes with a Kleenex, she stood and picked up William, who was just starting to wake, and padded over to the door, expecting it to be the UPS man.

But it wasn't a UPS delivery. It was a group of women congregating on her front step. And, unlike the last trio of mothers she'd faced, these women were all smiling at her. Or, at least, two of the three were smiling. The third looked like she'd been dragged there against her will. Chloe blinked at them for a minute, while her sleep-deprived mind processed what was going on.

"Hi, Anna," Chloe said tentatively. "Oh, hi, Grace. Hey, Juliet."

"Surprise!" Anna said, holding up a large gift box wrapped in baby-blue tissue paper. Grace beamed too, hoisting a huge white gift bag with an enormous bow stuck to the front. Juliet was holding two bottles of champagne.

"We're here to throw you a baby shower!" Grace announced. She looked down at William, cradled in his mother's arms. "Oh, he's just gorgeous," she cooed.

"He really is," Anna chimed in. She looked at Chloe again and suddenly seemed concerned. "Hey, are you okay?"

Chloe lifted a self-conscious hand to her tear-stained face. "Oh. Yes. I was just...well. Hormones," she said weakly.

Anna nodded knowingly. "I cried every day for weeks after I had Charlie," she said.

"I cried for months after Hannah was born. Hell, I still cry every day, and she's three," Grace added. "He really is gorgeous, Chloe. He looks just like you."

"You think so?"

"He has your chin," Grace said. "Don't you think so, Juliet?"

"No, not really. Although, you know, he does look a little like Winston Churchill," Juliet said thoughtfully. Grace elbowed her. "Ouch!" Juliet exclaimed. "Will you please stop elbowing me!"

"Come on in," Chloe said, stepping back. She hesitated. "I have to warn you, though. My house is a mess."

"It's supposed to be a mess. You just had a baby. It would be freakishly weird if your house looked perfect...," Grace said, her voice trailing off as she looked around. "Um...your house looks perfect. Okay. Just ignore that whole freakishly weird part."

"It's not perfect," Chloe said, hurrying to move a pile of books—*Secrets of the Baby Whisperer; The Happiest Baby on the Block; What to Expect the First Year*—stacked on the front hall table. "I would have picked up if I knew I was having company."

"First of all, your house is immaculate. And second, we came here to spoil you, not make you clean for us," Anna said.

"Exactly," Grace said. "If you want to see what a real mess looks like, come over to my house. I swear, the kids just fling

Cheerios all over the place. Wherever I step, it's crunch, crunch, crunch."

"Go ahead and sit down. I'll bring out some drinks," Chloe said.

"Don't be ridiculous," Anna said. "We're waiting on you, not the other way around." She held up the plastic grocery store bag she'd been carrying. "We have cake."

"And more important, champagne," Juliet added.

"That's just so nice. I don't know what to say," Chloe said. She held a hand to her chest, feeling so overwhelmed that the tears welled up in her eyes again. Chloe wiped at them. "Oh, no. I'm sorry. This is embarrassing."

Crying seemed to be her immediate reaction to everything these days. She'd expected it while she was pregnant but had assumed the tears would dry up once William arrived. But, if anything, it had only gotten worse. Her emotions were always so close to the edge, ready to bubble over at the slightest provocation. She cried when she was tired, overwhelmed, emotional—which was pretty much all the time.

"Hey, don't worry," Grace said, touching Chloe's arm. "It's totally normal. It just feels like you're losing your mind."

"You mean I'm not?" Chloe asked, with a soggy smile.

"Oh, no, you probably are. But just give it a little time, and you won't even miss it," Grace said.

Chloe laughed. It was the first time she could remember really laughing in...how long? Since William was born? Before then?

"Go ahead and sit down. We're here to wait on you hand and foot," Anna said. "Juliet, you keep Chloe company. Grace and I will get everything ready and bring it out."

Chloe thought that she saw a flicker of panic in Juliet's eyes. Despite her embarrassment, she found a glimmer of humor in Juliet's obvious discomfort at being trapped with a weeping, hormonal new mom.

"Come sit down," Chloe said, leading Juliet to the living room at the back of the town house. William had begun to make mewling sounds in her arms. "Do you mind if I nurse while we talk?"

"You know, I did witness you giving birth. In vivid detail. It's probably a little late to worry about your modesty around me," Juliet said, sitting on the edge of the gray armchair. From the kitchen, there came the popping sound of a champagne bottle being opened.

Chloe laughed again. "Thank you again for staying with me that night. You and Anna were amazing. It was really above and beyond."

Juliet shrugged and looked a little embarrassed. "Don't worry about it. We couldn't exactly take off and leave you. Not when your husband was curled up in the fetal position, weeping softly."

"He wasn't that bad," Chloe protested, although she had no idea why she was defending James. He had been pretty useless at William's birth.

"I think at one point he actually fainted," Juliet said.

"Yeah, well, James has never been great with blood," Chloe said. She grinned suddenly. "Can you believe he was premed when I met him in college?"

"No, I can't," Juliet said, with a snort. But she smiled back at Chloe, and it felt like a barrier had suddenly fallen away.

Chloe fumbled with her nursing bra and then winced as William latched on, her entire body tensing with the momentary pain. For someone who didn't have any teeth, William had a fierce bite.

"I've been meaning to call you. *Mothering* magazine contacted me. They want to come and take your picture to run with the article I wrote," Chloe said.

"They do? Oh. Okay, I guess," Juliet said.

"They'd like your husband and daughters to be in it too, if that's okay," Chloe said apologetically. "I gave them your office number, so they'll contact you there to set up a time."

Before Juliet could reply, Anna and Grace appeared with the champagne, glasses, the cake, and a stack of plates.

"We just went through your cupboards and helped ourselves. I hope you don't mind," Grace said.

"That's fine," Chloe said.

"Your kitchen is so neat," Anna said. "Even your pots and pans are perfectly lined up."

"I know, I'm sort of anal about it," Chloe said.

"You'd probably have a heart attack if you saw what my house looks like right now," Grace said cheerfully.

Grace poured out four glasses of champagne, while Anna sliced the cake. It was chocolate with white buttercream frosting and topped with a baby rattle outlined in blue icing.

"No champagne for me," Chloe said apologetically. "I'm nursing; I can't drink."

"So? I am too. A single glass won't hurt," Grace said.

"Well...okay," Chloe said, feeling like a naughty schoolgirl as she accepted the champagne flute.

"It was so nice of you all to do this," Chloe said. She balanced her plate on the armrest of her chair and took a bite of the cake. It was delicious, and so sweet, it sent shivers down her back. William had his fill of milk, and he popped off her nipple, looking contentedly milk-drunk. Chloe pulled her shirt down.

"Of course we had to celebrate. It's not every day you have a baby," Anna said warmly. "It's a really big deal."

"Which is why we got presents for you, not for the baby. I'm sure he has three of everything he needs already," Grace said. She handed the white gift bag to Chloe. "So these are just for you."

"Oh, my gosh," Chloe exclaimed, as she pulled out a Philosophy Amazing Grace gift set. "This is too much! Shampoo, shower gel, bubble bath...Oh, it smells so good!" she said, sniffing at the bottles.

"Don't forget the firming cream," Grace said. "Because every new mom needs firming. And if you don't, I don't even want to talk to you."

"No, I definitely do," Chloe said, with a rueful laugh. Everything that had once pointed up on her body had fallen down since having William. She hoped it was a temporary state of affairs.

"And along with that theme, here's my gift," Anna said, handing over the box.

"It's too pretty to unwrap," Chloe exclaimed.

"I've never understood women who say that," Juliet said. "It's just wrapping paper. Whatever's underneath is pretty much guaranteed to be better, unless the person giving it to you is complete crap at picking out gifts."

Chloe tore off the tissue paper, opened the box, and pulled out a pair of pink toile pajamas from Victoria's Secret.

"When you first have a baby, you spend all of your time in your pjs, so I thought you should at least look pretty while you're doing it," Anna explained.

"Yes! That's so true! This is the first day I put real clothes on!" Chloe exclaimed, causing everyone else to giggle. "Thank you so much, Anna."

Juliet opened her handbag and pulled out a white envelope. "And this is from me," she said gruffly, handing the envelope over.

Chloe opened the envelope. "A gift certificate for a manicure and pedicure at the Gloss Salon and Spa," she read aloud. Chloe gaped down at the gift certificate for a moment before turning her gaze to Juliet, who looked sheepish and yet proud of herself. "Juliet! This is...oh...it's so nice! Thank you!"

"You're welcome. Just please don't start crying again," Juliet said.

"You did such a good job picking out a present!" Grace exclaimed.

"Don't talk to me like I'm five. I am a grown woman. And an attorney. And a mother. I'm capable of picking out a shower gift," Juliet said irritably.

"Did you help her?" Grace asked Anna, ignoring Juliet.

Anna grinned, while Juliet rolled her eyes. "Nope. She did this all on her own."

"Hello, family!" James said, bursting through the front door.

Chloe looked up from what had become her favorite chair to nurse in, yet again feeding the seemingly insatiable William.

"Hey, you," she said, brightening as her husband bounded into the living room. He was grinning and jingling his keys in one hand. His other was behind his back. "How was your day?"

"Excellent. And these"—James produced an enormous bouquet of coral tulips, the stems wrapped in cellophane—"are for you!"

"For me?" Chloe asked excitedly. She turned her face up toward James, and he kissed her warmly. "Thank you," she said.

"For the kiss or for the flowers?" James teased, resting his forehead against hers so that their eyes were only an inch apart.

"Both. Would you mind putting these in a vase for me?"

"Consider it done," James said, turning and heading back to the kitchen.

Chloe smiled after him and snuggled William toward her. She couldn't remember the last time James had bought her flowers. Oh, wait, yes, she could. It was back when they were still living in Austin, and James had gone out carousing with some of his college friends. He'd lost his cell phone at the bar and so didn't get any of Chloe's increasingly frantic calls. When he finally rolled home at four a.m., he was so drunk, his friends had to carry him in and put him to bed. He'd stayed there for nearly thirty-six hours, groaning and asking Chloe to bring him Diet Coke and aspirin. When James finally got over his hangover and climbed back out of bed, he'd bought her a dozen red roses as an apology.

The time before that was when he'd forgotten their two-year anniversary and hastily sent a huge basket of Gerber daisies the next day. And the time before that, a vase of simple white lilies, when he'd neglected to meet her at a restaurant where they'd had dinner reservations. James had gone to happy hour with his coworkers, forgotten all about his plans with Chloe, and she'd sat alone at the table, sipping her white-wine spritzer and feeling incredibly stupid and self-conscious, imagining that the other diners were whispering about how pathetic she looked.

Remembering this, she felt a prick of apprehension about the tulips.

"What's the occasion?" she called out to James, who was clattering around in the kitchen.

"Where are the vases?"

"In the cupboard to the left of the sink," Chloe replied, as she shifted William to the other breast. She waited, feeling the sharp pain as William's mouth pulled at her nipple and the responding tingle as milk flooded into her breast.

James came back into the room, carrying the tulips, which had been rather artlessly arranged in a vase. It wasn't the vase Chloe had wanted him to use—a gorgeous crystal Mikasa one they'd gotten as a wedding gift. Instead, he'd stuck the flowers in a cheap glass urn, the sort that comes free with flower arrangements.

It was, Chloe suddenly realized, the very vase the apology lilies had arrived in.

"So what did I do to deserve flowers?" she asked again.

"It's not every day my wife gives birth to our first son," James said proudly.

"No. But it wasn't today either."

James smiled sheepishly. "I meant to bring you flowers in the hospital, but then … Well, I sort of lost track of the idea," he said apologetically.

Chloe relaxed. The tulips were apology flowers after all, but at least not harbingers of bad news.

"That's so sweet," Chloe said, her face relaxing into a warm grin. "I love them. The perfect end to a perfect day."

She was about to tell James about her lovely surprise shower, but he was too impatient to tell her his own news.

"I had a great day too. Joe Mackie"—Joe was James's boss, the department head at the securities firm he worked at as a broker—

"invited me to his house on Key West this weekend. It's right on the golf course, and I've been dying to play there. He actually invited both of us, but he understands you just had the baby."

"Understands?" Chloe repeated.

"That you can't come. No one would expect you to travel with a newborn."

"You mean—wait, you aren't going, are you?"

"Of course I'm going. I have to. I can't turn down an invitation from the Big Guy."

"But...but...," Chloe began. What she wanted to say was: *How could you even think of going? We just had a baby! I need you here to help me. I can't do this on my own. You're already gone all day, every day during the week. Don't leave me alone for the weekend too.*

"What's wrong, hon?"

Chloe opened and closed her mouth, then opened it to speak, and then changed her mind and closed it again.

"Nothing. I'm just...tired. I'm just really tired," Chloe said slowly.

James yawned. "I know. The no-sleep thing is tougher than I thought it would be."

Chloe stared at him. James hadn't gotten up once with William. Not once. She'd been the one startled awake by the sudden high, fretful cries, the one to drag her bone-weary body out of bed every time, while James slept right through it all. But she hated the feeling of anger, hated the way it tightened in her stomach and caused her cheeks to feel too hot. She pushed it back down, struggling to gain control against it.

"This is great news. You know how this business works. It's all about who you know. And my boss taking me under his wing like this could be a really big step for us." James leaned over and kissed Chloe on the head. "I'll get you stocked up on food and diapers and everything you could possibly need before I go, so you don't have to worry about anything. I'll take care of everything."

And even though James had been taking a hands-off approach with William, leaving all of the diaper changes and nighttime

wake-ups to Chloe, the idea of being home on her own with the
baby for three full days frightened her. She was still getting used to
being a mom, still trying to figure out why William's poop was
sometimes neon green, or whether it was normal for him to start
so violently when he was waking up, or whether the red spot on
his bum was just standard diaper rash or something more serious.
It was all so overwhelming.

"Wait, James," Chloe said.

But he didn't hear her. Or he didn't stop if he did. Whistling
jauntily, James bounded upstairs to change out of his work
clothes. And, tied to the chair by her nursing baby, Chloe couldn't
chase after him.

nine

Grace

The turnout for the March meeting of Mothers Coming Together was the best ever. Grace stood in the back of Tapas and looked out over the crowd of women, which included at least a half dozen faces she hadn't seen before. Membership had picked up briskly after the blow-job seminar. Apparently, all it took to drum up interest in MCT was one woman with a bag full of dildos. And tonight was going to be even better. Or, at least, it would be if she could shake her headache. Grace pressed her fingers against her temples and willed the dull ache away.

"Excuse me, are you Grace Weaver?"

Grace looked up blearily at a woman standing in front of her. *Thinner than me. Thinner* and *younger.*

In fact, the woman was quite young, with light-blonde hair pulled back in a low ponytail, glossy pink lips, and funky black plastic glasses. She was wearing a white lab coat over a slip dress and was pulling a metal suitcase on wheels behind her.

"Yes, I'm Grace. Are you Ivy?"

The woman nodded and chewed on a wad of gum. She looked like she was about fifteen years old. Grace stared at her doubtfully.

"Do you have a lot of, um, experience with this sort of thing?"

"Waxing parties? Uh-huh. I've done, like, tons."

"Oh, good. I should warn you: This is a surprise," Grace said, leaning forward and whispering so that she wouldn't be heard. "It may take the group a little time to get used to the idea of getting a bikini wax in front of everyone."

"Oh, yeah. It always does. It helps when people have a chance to down a few drinks before I start waxing them."

"Where are you going to set up?" Grace asked, with a sudden not-so-pleasant vision of having to stand up in front of an audience of half-naked women with wax dripping off their genitals. Or, even worse, having everyone see *her* without her skirt on.

No way. No one is going to see my thighs, she thought, with no small amount of panic. She was starting to realize that she hadn't thought this idea through.

Ivy glanced around the restaurant's banquet room. "Hmmm. Well, I usually set up in a separate room, for privacy and stuff, but you don't have one here. So I guess I'll just hang a sheet in the back corner of the room. Once I'm set up, you guys can just, like, take turns coming back. I'm booked for two hours, so I'll wax as many of you as I can during that time," she said, tossing her ponytail back.

"Great. Let me know if you need anything," Grace said.

Ivy wheeled her suitcase off to the back corner of the room and busied herself setting up the white privacy drape she'd brought with her—a portable version of the ones hospitals use—and getting out her waxing paraphernalia. The moms, noticing that something was up, abandoned the platters of tapas and hurried to their chairs, wineglasses in hand. Everyone was seated and looking up at Grace expectantly by the time she reached the front of the room and set her notes down on the lectern. She wasn't as nervous about speaking in front of everyone this time, although a jolt of adrenaline did shoot through her when she felt everyone's brightly interested eyes focusing on her.

"Hi, everyone, thank you all for coming. At tonight's meeting, we need to brainstorm ideas for our new fund-raising project. We're going to hopefully raise enough money for the Starfish House—which, as you all know, is a shelter for abused women and children—to redecorate the common rooms. Right now the living areas are depressing, to put it mildly. So we want to help them create a more pleasant, soothing environment to live in. And while you're all thinking up fund-raising ideas, I have a little surprise for you. In the past, we've gotten some feedback that many of you would like to see your membership dues go toward doing something fun. So at tonight's meeting…we're having a waxing party!" Grace paused while the women reacted to this news. There were exclamations of surprise and a tittering of nervous laughter. Grace waited a few beats and then continued, raising her voice to be heard above the excited buzz. "I'd like to introduce you to Ivy."

Grace gestured toward the back corner of the room, where Ivy had finished setting up and was now standing with her hands clasped behind her back. When everyone turned to stare at her, Ivy waggled her fingers in a wave and smiled.

"Ivy's an aesthetician. She'll be waxing anyone who's up for it back there behind the white curtain while we hold our meeting. So if any of you are interested in getting waxed, Ivy's your go-to girl," Grace continued.

"What kind of waxing do you do?" Jessica Swanson called out.

"You know. Pretty much everything. Standard bikini, Brazilian—I can even do shapes, if you want," Ivy said. "Like hearts and letters and stuff."

"You mean shapes in your…pubic hair?" Rachel Baum ventured.

"Uh-huh. Whatever you want. Well, almost anything. I used to do monograms, but it takes too long to get all of the initials to overlap," she said.

"So how do you want to handle it, Ivy? Should we do a sign-up sheet or have those who are interested line up?" Grace asked brightly.

"Whatever." Ivy shrugged. Clearly, she was not going to take it upon herself to impose an order to the project. "But whoever's going first, come on back. The wax should be, like, hot enough by now."

Ivy disappeared behind her white privacy curtain, and there was another wave of nervous laughter. For a minute it looked like no one was going to take Ivy up on her offer. But then Nadia Cohen stood up.

"I'm not going to pass up a free wax job," Nadia said with spunk. "I'll go first."

Some of the mothers cheered for her as she marched to the back of the room. A few others stood and followed her back, forming a short line.

Who knew there were so many women interested in getting their pubic hair shaped into four-leaf clovers? Grace thought. She smiled. Maybe this would go over even better than the sexpert. And she'd be remembered as Grace Weaver, the hippest president in the history of MCT. Maybe she'd even be invited to speak at the national meeting on how to liven up meetings and increase membership.

"Okay, so let's get started with our brainstorming ideas for the fund-raiser. We'll have only three months to plan and execute the fund-raiser, so we can't get too elaborate. But I think we can come up with something a bit more creative than a bake sale or jumble. One of my ideas was—" Grace began.

She was interrupted by a sudden loud ripping sound from the back of the room. Everyone turned in their seats, necks craning as they looked back at the curtained corner.

"Ouch!" Nadia yipped.

Grace cleared her throat and raised her voice. "Um … to have a charity luncheon. Maybe one of the local department stores would even host it for us and put on a fashion show. I know that Saks sometimes does events like that."

"That's a great idea," Anna said supportively, and Grace smiled at her. "We could have door prizes."

"It sounds expensive," Kari Clem said.

There was another loud rip. This time, Nadia let loose with an expletive.

"Um …" Grace was momentarily distracted. *What's happening back there?* "Ah … well, we'd sell tickets. If we sold enough, we should be able to cover the costs plus clear a nice profit."

Ivy's curtain suddenly snapped open, and Nadia shuffled out, walking with her legs spread unnaturally far apart. She looked like a crab scuttling down the beach.

"That woman is a sadist," Nadia said, not bothering to lower her voice.

"Next," Ivy barked.

Kelsey Jennings, who was at the front of the line, flinched visibly and then went reluctantly behind the curtain.

"Take your pants off," Ivy said loudly, her voice carrying clear across the room. "How much do you, like, want to have taken off?"

Kelsey murmured her reply.

"Yeah, that's what we call the landing strip. Basically everything comes off but, you know, a thin line right here at the top."

Everyone in the room winced, and three of the women who were standing in line returned to their seats.

"Um, so back to the luncheon. I'll need volunteers, of course, especially if there are any marketing or advertising whizzes out there," Grace said gamely, trying to focus on the business at hand. But no one was paying any attention to her, especially when there was another set of loud ripping sounds, accompanied by Kelsey's sharp exclamations of pain.

"Ow!" she squeaked. *Rip.* "Oh, dear God...Eep!"

"What is she doing to Kelsey?" Liza Green asked.

"I don't know, but I'm not about to find out," Sarah Dunn replied with a grimace.

"I've never had a waxing hurt that much," Nadia announced. "I think she took off a few layers of skin along with the hair. Seriously. I may have to go to the ER after this."

Grace rolled her eyes. Nadia Cohen had always been a drama queen. But even so, maybe this hadn't been such a good idea after all.

"So, uh...back to the fund-raiser?" Grace suggested hopefully.

"It was a total nightmare," Grace said the next day. Louis was driving her minivan, and Grace sat in the passenger seat, her bare feet propped up on the dashboard.

"I'm sure it wasn't that bad," Louis said.

"It was that bad. It was humiliating. Britt Howard—do you

know her? She's sort of mousy with really short man hair?—got a second-degree burn on her thighs. God, I hope she doesn't sue."

"Is she a lesbian?"

"Who? Britt? No. Actually, I'm not sure. She's never mentioned it. Why?"

"The man hair."

"Mom, what's a lesbian?" Molly asked. Molly and Hannah were strapped into their car seats in the backseat of the minivan, listening to a Hilary Duff CD on headphones, but they always seemed to develop bionic hearing at the least opportune times.

"Um...a lesbian is a woman who likes other women," Grace said. Louis snorted, and Grace shot him a look. "You want to explain it to her?" she hissed at him.

"No, you're doing just fine," he said, his mouth twitching with amusement.

"You mean, like I like Sasha?" Molly persisted. Sasha was Molly's best friend.

"No, not quite. It's more like...like how Mommy likes Daddy. How married people like each other," Grace explained.

Molly went silent, and Grace hoped that she'd lost interest in the discussion.

"So, you mean, I could marry Sasha?" Molly asked.

"Well...," Grace began, not sure exactly how she was going to explain the politics of same-sex marriages to a five-year-old.

"I want to marry Izzy and Emma," Hannah piped in. She worshipped the Cole twins, who were a whole year older than her and already knew how to swim without water wings.

"Good job clearing that up, honey," Louis said, snickering.

"But then who would get to be the bride and wear the fancy white dress?" Molly said, frowning. She had a way of putting her finger on an issue.

"We all would," Hannah said dreamily. "Me, and Emma, and Izzy. We'd all wear princess dresses, like Cinderella wears."

"You can't," Molly said, with the certainty of one who's halfway through kindergarten. "There can only be one bride in a wedding."

"There can too be more than one! Mommy just said!" Hannah said.

"There can *not.*"

"Can too!"

"Can not!"

"I probably could have handled that better," Grace said.

"Live and learn," Louis said.

Grace looked out the window. They were driving through the front gates of the subdivision. A big sign that read

WHISPERING OAKS

hung over a decorative fountain. *Just what the hell is a whispering oak anyway?* Grace wondered. Louis stopped and gave their name to the guard, who—after taking an unnecessarily long time to check that, yes, they were on the approved list of visitors—raised the security bar and allowed them to enter.

"Tell me again why we're doing this?" Grace asked softly, so that only Louis could hear.

"Because they're your parents, and if we don't show up with their grandkids every few months they start threatening to visit us," Louis reminded her, as he drove into the subdivision and turned onto her father and Alice's street.

"Not my parents," Grace reminded him. "My father and step-mother."

Alice and Victor Fowler lived just outside Orlando, in a gated golf-course community. They'd moved there three years earlier, after Victor retired from his medical practice in Orange Cove. The reason for the move: Mark, Alice's son. He lived in Orlando with his bitchy wife and their two sociopathic children.

"Now we'll be able to see the grandchildren every day!" Alice had told Grace, after announcing they were moving.

Grace had bit back the obvious observation—that the move would actually take Victor away from *his* biological grandchildren—but what was the point? Alice always got her way.

The grounds at Whispering Oaks were impeccably kept by a crew of vigilant landscapers. Hibiscus trees stood in precise rows, each covered with enormous red flowers. Ornamental grasses were planted in neat clusters, surrounded by bunches of purple queen. The grass was lush and even. Retirees dressed in pastel golfing clothes were zipping around in golf carts, stopping to chat or wave their hats at one another.

"It's like a whole other world here," Grace mused. "Everything's so … perfect. So neat. So unspoiled."

"Unspoiled?" Louis looked amused. "Every last inch of this place has been landscaped into submission."

"You know what I mean. People here don't have to worry about anything," Grace said wistfully.

Louis snorted. "Except for cirrhosis and heart disease."

As soon as Louis pulled into the driveway, Hannah and Molly started to shriek with excitement.

"Nana! Papa!" they yelled out. Molly unhooked the straps of her booster seat and hopped up before the car came to a complete stop.

"Molly," Grace said in warning voice. "What have I told you about getting out of your seat before we park?"

"You said it's a crime, and if the police see me, they'll put me in jail," Molly said in a small voice.

"That's right," Grace said approvingly.

"Nice," Louis said, giving his wife a sidewise grin. "Did you get that one out of the parenting manual?"

"I tried telling her that they'd put me in jail, but she didn't take that threat very seriously. In fact, I think she liked the idea. You know how Molly's always fantasizing about being an orphan, like Sara in *A Little Princess*," Grace explained.

Alice and Victor Fowler walked out the front door, smiling and waving. The sight of their grandparents caused the girls to start shrieking again. Grace smiled wanly at her father and stepmother and raised one hand in greeting.

"Hi, Louis," Alice cried out, throwing her arms around her

son-in-law as soon as he was out of the car. Grace couldn't help rolling her eyes. Alice would probably prefer it if Louis and the girls came to visit without her.

"Remember me?" she said, climbing out.

"Gracie," her dad said, folding her into his arms.

Victor Fowler was a tall, thin man, with a full head of hair, now gray, and a trimmed mustache. He was meticulously neat, with knife pleats ironed into his shorts. Grace inhaled deeply, smelling his bay-rum aftershave, a scent that had always made her feel safe and protected.

"Hi, Daddy," Grace said. "Hi, Alice."

Alice kissed Grace's cheek and then stood back to look at her stepdaughter. "You've lost a little weight, Grace," Alice said approvingly. "Your stomach is finally going down."

"Um, yeah, a little," Grace said, stiffening at the observation. But before she could say something healthy, like, *I'd rather we didn't discuss my weight,* Louis was letting the inmates out of the van. Chaos ensued as grandparents and children were united, and the moment passed.

I'm not going to let her get away with another crack like that, Grace promised herself, as she turned to pluck Natalie out of her infant car seat. At the same time, she couldn't help feeling a tickle of pleasure that her stepmother had noticed her weight loss. Grace rested a hand on her stomach, which was indeed finally starting to go down—thanks to the Miracle Diet Tea—and felt a wave of pride.

"How does she do it?" Grace whispered to Louis later that night, when they were lying in the double bed in the cramped guest room. The room doubled as a home gym, and Grace was constantly stubbing her toe on Alice's treadmill. "How does she always manage to make me feel like I'm this big?"

Grace held her thumb and index finger an inch apart.

"Mmm," Louis said, nuzzling her shoulder. "Want to feel how big I am?"

"Oh, please." Grace batted him away. "We are so *not* going to have sex here."

"We used to have sex in your parents' house all the time when we first started dating," Louis reminded her.

"Not my parents. My father and my stepmother. And, besides, look where it got us," Grace said, with a nod toward the travel crib where Natalie had finally—mercifully—fallen asleep, after exhausting herself with an hour-long screaming fit. Hannah and Molly were sleeping in the den on the uncomfortable pullout couch, which they seemed to think was a treat.

"Yeah, but now I'm shooting blanks," Louis reminded her.

"Thank *God*," Grace said fervently. "But still. No. I'm too annoyed at Alice to have sex right now."

Louis sighed and rolled back over. "And that pretty much takes care of that," he said.

"What?"

"I'm good, but it would take a stronger man than me to stay in the mood while you're talking about Alice," Louis said.

Grace snorted with laughter.

"Shhh," Louis warned her. "You'll wake the baby."

"I just don't know why Alice has to be so awful to me. And if I have to hear one more story about how successful and wonderful Mark is, I'm going to hurl. Right there at the dinner table."

"That would be subtle," Louis said.

Louis grew up in a bizarrely normal family, where everyone actually liked one another and wanted to get together; they didn't just show up at holiday dinners because they'd been guilt-tripped into attending. He was the second of three sons, all still close even now that they were grown and married, and his parents—Sissy, a middle-school French teacher, and Malcolm, a retired dentist—were still happily married. So while he'd known Grace's family long enough to be familiar with its myriad problems, he'd never really experienced such dysfunction firsthand.

It was, Grace suspected, the reason Louis was so irritatingly vice-free. He didn't drink too much, or do drugs, or gamble, and he wasn't addicted to Internet porn. All good qualities in a spouse—but sometimes it just made her feel even more imperfect.

"Don't you think it's weird how close Alice and Mark are?" Grace asked. "Did you know he discusses his sex life with her?"

"He does? You never told me that."

Grace turned on her side to face him, bunching the pillow up for support. She curled her legs under the cool weight of the cotton sheets.

"Yeah. She said he was worried he had prostate cancer, because he couldn't—you know, get it up," Grace said. She wrinkled her nose.

"Mmm, yes, I do know," Louis said. His eyes glittered, the way they always did when he was feeling horny. He reached over and put an exploratory hand on Grace's bum.

"Louis," Grace said, exasperated, removing his hand. "Absolutely not."

Louis sighed. "So does he have cancer?"

"Of course not. He's fine, he's just a hypochondriac. But Alice was all up in the air about it. Seriously, what man talks about his erections with his mother? It's freakishly weird."

"I'd actually prefer not to talk about Mark's erections," Louis said. "I thought Alice was on her best behavior tonight."

Grace rolled her eyes. "Well, of course *you* would think that. 'Louis, would you like another slice of cake? I baked it just for you. I know carrot cake is your favorite,' " she said, mimicking her stepmother's voice perfectly. " 'Gracie, you probably don't want to eat that. The frosting has two sticks of butter in it.' Which was just gratuitously controlling, since I'd already told her I didn't want a piece of her stupid cake."

"Maybe she just likes me better," Louis conceded. He grinned wickedly. "But can you blame her?"

Grace picked up her pillow and whacked Louis in the side of the head with it.

"Ouch!" he said.

"Shhh! Don't wake the baby!" Grace said, and then she bopped him in the head with the pillow again.

The next morning, Louis and Victor had plans to take Hannah and Molly to Disney World. Grace didn't want to drag Natalie around the amusement park, so she elected to stay home. Alice also abstained from the trip.

"As far as I know, hell hasn't yet frozen over," Alice said. "And that's what it would take for me to go to Disney World."

"It's supposed to be the happiest place on earth," Grace said, as she blew on her Miracle Diet Tea to cool it. It tasted disgusting, like a mixture of brewed grass and dirt, but the results were worth it.

"Please," Alice said, waving a dismissive hand. "Bloomingdale's is a far happier place. Besides, I need your help. I've decided to redo the living room, and I wanted to get your opinion on the fabric samples I picked up."

"Really? That sounds like fun," Grace said, pleased. Alice had never asked her for decorating help. "Let me just help Louis pack up the girls, and then I'll take a look."

It took nearly an hour to get Hannah, Molly, Louis, and Victor fed, dressed, and equipped for a day at Disney World. The girls were already so excited, neither one of them could sit still before rushing off to make sure that all of the essentials—autograph books, mouse ears, Fairytopia Barbies—had made it into the knapsack, along with granola bars, juice boxes, bottles of water, hats, and an extralarge tube of sunscreen.

"I'm already exhausted, and we haven't even left yet," Louis said wearily, as he tried to contain a squirming Hannah long enough to tie her sneakers.

"Welcome to my life," Grace said. She knelt down to help Louis with Hannah's shoes, and as she did, she whispered excitedly, "Did you hear her? Alice actually wants my advice on decorating! I can't believe it. She's never asked me for help before. I wish I'd have known; I would have brought that notebook I keep all of my clippings in."

"Just be careful," Louis said evenly.

"What do you mean?"

"Just don't get too excited, okay? You know Alice. She always has a way of yanking the carpet out from under you."

"I know. It's not a big deal," Grace said unconvincingly. "I just thought it sounded like fun."

As screwed up as their relationship was, Alice was the only mother figure Grace had known. Grace's real mother, Jocelyn, died in a car accident when Grace was three. Her father had married Alice five years later, and at the time Grace was happy about it, thinking she'd lucked into a new family. Besides, she and her new stepbrother, Mark—a surly, acne-pocked fourteen-year-old— were the wedding attendants, and Grace had worn a heavenly cream puff of a white satin dress with a crinoline petticoat and matching white Mary Janes. She'd walked down the aisle just before Alice, strewing rose petals along the white satin carpet while the congregation oohed and ahhed over her.

But then Alice and Mark moved in. Up until then, Grace's entire concept of blended families was based on reruns of *The Brady Bunch*. She quickly learned that, at least in her family, life did not imitate art. On *The Brady Bunch*, Mrs. Brady didn't openly prefer Marcia to Greg. Mrs. Brady didn't ask Peter to help her bake cookies for the PTA bake sale and then chide him for eating one, insisting that no one would ever like him if he was fat. Mrs. Brady didn't promise to take Bobby shopping for a prom tuxedo, then claim to have a migraine and drop him off at the mall with a credit card and strict instructions not to spend more than seventy-five dollars. And when Jan hit puberty, Greg never teased her about how large her breasts were getting or "accidentally" walked into the bathroom while she was taking a shower, nor had he ever stolen panties out of Cindy's dresser drawer and masturbated into them. At least, not that they showed on the air. And Mr. Brady didn't spend all of his time at the hospital where he was an orthopedic surgeon, ignoring the dysfunction raging out of control at home.

Grace's memories of her real mother were all shadows. The lemony-floral scent of Jean Naté, auburn hair gleaming in the sun, a deep, rich belly laugh. Just wisps of smoke, flashes of light that made Grace's eyes flood with tears, while a wave of longing crested inside her. Longing that would turn to sadness, even anger, when she realized that she didn't even know if these were actual memories of her mom or if she was only remembering the mother she'd later daydreamed about having, until the fiction had blurred with reality.

But despite Louis's warning, despite her lengthy experience with her stepmother, despite the two years she'd spent in therapy after her high-school guidance counselor caught her throwing up her lunch in the girls' bathroom, Grace's enthusiasm for the decorating project wasn't dampened. On the contrary, as soon as the minivan had pulled out of the driveway, she plunked Natalie into the BabyBjörn carrier, strapped her to her chest, and turned her full attention to her stepmother's living room.

First and foremost, the room needs color, Grace thought.

The Travertine tile floors were taupe, and the walls were the same industrial white paint that the builders had slapped on. The furniture wasn't much more daring: shades of cream and ivory, from the striped fabric on the Queen Anne couch to the ecru wing chairs. The carpet alone infused some color into the room, but it was so muted—sage greens and soft roses and gentle golds—that it didn't provide much zip.

The room was elegant and appropriate and completely lacking in personality, which, Grace thought, practically rubbing her hands together with relish, made it the perfect setting for a makeover. The only question now was, where to start? Some designers began with the carpet, others with a wallpaper or fabric scrap. But Grace liked to think of the room in a more integrated way, to understand how all the elements would work together before committing to any one piece. She needed a cohesive vision.

"Oh, here you are. I wanted to show you the fabric samples I picked up," Alice said, breezing into the room. Her stepmother looked flawless, as usual—her short dark hair was neatly brushed, her white sweater was spotless, her navy linen slacks ironed perfectly to a knife-edged pleat. And she was so thin that her sharp clavicle bones stood out prominently. Grace felt her stepmother's eyes flick over her, the judgment unspoken but clear.

Grace glanced down at herself. She was wearing baggy gray sweatpants and, under Natalie and the BabyBjörn, a milk-smeared gray Florida Seminoles T-shirt. She lifted a self-conscious hand to her hair. There was a glob of jelly in it, probably deposited there by one of the girls when she was wiping them down after breakfast.

Well. So what? Grace thought, with a surge of rebellion. It wasn't like they were going out anywhere. Why shouldn't she be comfortable when they were just going to be sitting around the house all day? Besides, Grace wasn't in the mood to argue with Alice about her appearance. Today was going to be about spending time together, not just rehashing the same tired, toxic fights they'd been mired in for the past twenty-five years.

No. Today will be different, Grace thought with a burst of optimism.

"So I was thinking," Grace said, trying to sound bright and upbeat. "I saw a gorgeous house featured in a magazine last month, and I think it's a look that would work really well in your house. It had the same type of traditional furniture you have, but they'd updated the pieces with new fabric. Linen on the wing chairs, and an amazing hot-pink chevron stripe on the Queen Anne sofa. And then they had lots of gorgeous accents—coral sconces, a gilded mirror, a modern glass coffee table. We'd have to do a little shopping, but I think the end result would be fabulous."

"Hot-pink chevron stripes?" Alice repeated, looking at her blankly. "That sounds … bright."

"It was. But the rest of the furniture was muted, so it worked. The sofa provided a nice focus point for the room."

"I *don't* want pink," Alice said. She sounded definite. Almost defiant.

"Oh. Okay. Well. What were you thinking of?" Grace asked.

Alice handed Grace the fabric samples she'd been clutching. "I was thinking of this for the sofa, and this for the chairs," she said.

One swatch was striped with light and dark creams; the other was an ivory with cream crewel.

"But...it's almost exactly like the fabrics that are on there now," Grace said.

Alice nodded. "I know. I like it, and I already know it works well in here."

But it doesn't work well! It's washed out and boring and bland!

Grace could feel the words bubbling up inside her, propelled by frustration, not just over the living room—it wasn't her living room, after all—but all of those years of Alice never once taking her word for something. She swallowed hard, forcing them back down.

"Okay. If that's what you want," Grace said, handing the samples back over.

Alice looked pleased. "Yes, I think it is. I'm glad you agree."

Just let it go, Grace told herself. *It's not worth it.*

And yet...she couldn't.

"I don't agree. In my professional opinion, I think you need to bring some more color in here. Some oomph. The room's too bland, too monochrome. But if that's what makes you happy..." Grace let her voice trail off and shrugged one shoulder. *If being boring is what makes you happy, what can I do about it?* the shrug said.

Alice flushed and held the fabric up to her chest, as though Grace might rip it out of her hands at any moment.

"This fabric is very expensive," Alice informed her. "This striped one costs a hundred ten dollars a yard." She gave a little shrug of her own, only she lifted both of her bony shoulders. "I'm not surprised you don't like it. You've never been one to go for quality fabrics."

"What's that supposed to mean?" Grace asked, so sharply that Natalie—who had just been drifting off—started and looked up at her mother with wide, surprised eyes.

"I did tell you when you bought your sofa that the microfiber wouldn't wear well. But you wouldn't listen," Alice said.

Un-fucking-believable, Grace thought. Her anger tasted hot and coppery in her mouth.

"The sofa *is* wearing well," Grace said. Her sofa looked gorgeous, like new, like the day they got it. Well, okay, except for the tiny splash of chocolate milk one of the girls had spilled on it, but that had happened recently, and Alice hadn't even seen it yet.

"If you say so," Alice said diffidently.

"Fine. Whatever." Grace lifted her hands and shrugged, as though she were giving in. Although, as Anna was fond of pointing out, when a woman said *whatever,* it was really just a passive–aggressive way of saying *fuck off.* The sentiment was not lost on Alice.

"Fine," Alice said coolly. "But, you know, dear, I wouldn't go around telling people that you're a professional decorator."

"What?" Grace stared at her stepmother, at the face that was more familiar to her than her own. It was a face she had loved and hated in turn. The overplucked eyebrows. The hazel eyes. The narrow nose with the flared nostrils. The thin lips that were rarely, if ever, seen without lipstick. The crepey skin of her neck.

"It's just that you never really were a decorator. And if you tell people that you were, and they find out that you only worked for one, they're going to think you've just made it up to sound important," Alice said. She smiled then, as though she were just offering some well-meaning motherly advice.

Grace's heart began to pound, and she could feel her skin warm as it flushed. But she couldn't find the words she needed, the words that would make her stepmother understand how much these insults, these gibes, these never-ending digs meant to undermine her self-esteem hurt her. How they instantly turned the clock back and made Grace feel like the chubby, insecure young girl she'd once been, desperate for the approval that was never forthcoming.

Then again, Grace suddenly realized, the heat of anger suddenly turning cold, *maybe she already knows that.*

Natalie started to fuss, making fretful birdlike sounds and opening and closing her small round hands.

"I think Nat's hungry. I'd better go feed her," Grace said.

She turned and padded out of the white living room, away from its awful blandness, away from her over-tweezed stepmother, without saying another word.

ten

Anna

When Noah called to ask Anna out for a second date, she hesitated.

Four fiancées, she reminded herself. *That's bad. Really bad. Like, forty-and-still-living-with-your-mother bad.*

So what if he was smart, and handsome, and funny, and had a steady job, and seemed like a genuinely nice person, and, yes, did not actually live with his mother? Finding out that he had four former fiancées was the romantic equivalent of seeing a huge blinking sign by the side of the road that read:

DANGER! ROAD FLOODED AHEAD! TURN BACK!

Which was why Anna was shocked when she heard herself accepting his invitation to dinner when he called a few days after their first date. It was as though the sex-deprived side of her brain had locked up the logical side in a trunk and was now making decisions all on its own.

"Great," Noah said. She wondered if she imagined the note of relief in his voice.

They met the following Saturday evening at Swordfish. Anna had eaten at the restaurant many times in the past, and although the food was wonderful if a bit idiosyncratic—the restaurant had both a sushi menu and a separate menu with more-traditional fare, like Caesar salads and filet mignon—it took second place to the extraordinary view. The restaurant overlooked the water, and now, as the sky darkened into a smear of hazy purples and smudgy pinks, it occurred to Anna that it was actually quite romantic.

Which was not something she'd planned on. Well, it wasn't something the rational side of her brain had planned on. God only knew what the sex-deprived side that had gotten her into this in the first place was planning. Noah looked over the wine menu with interest before finally ordering a bottle of Oregon pinot noir.

"Are you reviewing this restaurant for your column?" Noah asked, once the waitress left. He knit his brow, concerned. "I probably should have let you pick the wine."

"No, I'm not, and besides, you're the wine expert," Anna assured him.

"Expert." Noah gave a self-deprecating snort. "I don't know about that. I'm sure you know a whole hell of a lot more about wine than I do."

"I doubt that," Anna said.

"I didn't think this date through," Noah said. "Taking a restaurant critic out to dinner is a tricky proposition. What if I order shrimp cocktail, and it turns out that shrimp cocktail is now considered gauche and horribly out of style?"

"Actually, shrimp cocktail is definitely back in right now, although I've never cared for it myself. Too bland," Anna pointed out.

Noah grinned. He really did have a great smile. One corner of his mouth curled up just a little higher than the other, and his brown eyes smiled with his lips, squinting so that faint lines fanned out from the corners.

"And there's the benefit of dating a restaurant critic," he said. "I'm guaranteed to always eat well."

Anna knew he was joking, and yet his words—and what they implied—caused a jolt of excitement to shoot through her. She pressed her lips together into a smile and tried not to think of the trail of fiancées he'd left in his wake. Although the more

she tried not to think of them, the more she did. She was starting to imagine what each one was like—the smart one, the
funny one, the demure one, the pretty one. No, they'd all be
pretty, of course. But one would be movie-star gorgeous.

The waitress—a zaftig woman with hair dyed the color of
black shoe polish—arrived with the wine and a bread basket.

"Do you have any questions about the menu?" she asked
pleasantly, after pouring the pinot noir.

"No, I think we're all set," Anna said.

Noah had apparently decided against the shrimp cocktail: He
ordered a house salad and the crab cakes.

"Good choice," Anna said approvingly. She also ordered a
salad, and the filet mignon.

Once the waitress had left, Noah turned back to Anna, wineglass in hand. She thought he was going to make a toast.

Please don't let it be too cheesy, she thought. She didn't think
she could bear it if he was one of those nice-in-theory, cheesy-in-
reality guys. It would be such a disappointment.

But instead he said, "I think I owe you an explanation."

"What do you mean?"

"I got the feeling that you were a little surprised when I told
you about my past," he said.

He's certainly not beating around the bush, Anna thought.
Although I guess that's better than cheese.

"Well. Actually . . . yes, I was, a little," she admitted.

"I thought so. And I want to explain."

"You don't have to. It really isn't any of my business," Anna
hastened to add.

"Isn't it?" Noah looked at her, his eyes dark and inscrutable,
and Anna felt another thrill rush through her. There was definitely possibility here—although she still wasn't sure how she felt
about that.

There was something different about Noah tonight, she
thought. And then she realized: He wasn't wearing his glasses. His
face looked bare and vulnerable without them.

"I have to admit, I am curious," Anna said.

The waitress arrived with their house salads. She ground pepper over the beds of lightly dressed baby greens studded with blue cheese and pecans, topped off their wineglasses, and then left again. Anna took a bite. *Delicious,* she thought, and sighed happily. She felt Noah's eyes on her and looked up.

"Good?" he asked, a smile twitching at his mouth.

"I love this dressing," Anna enthused. "It has just a hint of citrus in it. I've attempted re-creating it at home, but I can never get the flavor right. I've tried lemon juice, and lime, of course. But now I'm thinking it's a bit sweeter than that. Tangerine, maybe."

Noah laughed, and Anna suddenly felt defensive.

"What?"

"Nothing. I'm not laughing at you. I just like how your face lights up when you talk about food."

"Oh," Anna said. She looked down at the beautifully arranged plate, pleased yet self-conscious. "So...you were about to tell me all of your dark, sordid secrets."

"I don't have any dark, sordid secrets," Noah protested. "At least, none that I'm going to tell you."

"Damn. I was hoping for some good dirt."

"Alas, my life isn't that exciting."

"Four fiancées? That's not exactly dull."

"Right, them. Well, where should I start?" Noah asked, carefully spearing some lettuce and blue cheese together on his fork.

"The beginning is always good," Anna suggested. "How about fiancée number one?"

"Number one. That was Caitlyn," Noah said fondly. "We met our sophomore year at Brown."

"Young love."

"That's right. We were together all through college, and I proposed to her the weekend we graduated. I was going off to business school, she was going to law school in a different state. I was probably worried that we were going to grow apart."

"So what happened?"

"We grew apart." Anna and Noah both smiled. "We broke up during Christmas break. Last I heard from her, she and her husband had just had their third kid," Noah continued.

"You stay in touch?"

"A bit, although life tends to get in the way. The break was as amicable as they get."

"So you weren't heartbroken?"

"No. I already knew by then that the engagement was a mistake. Mostly, I was relieved that she agreed with me."

"So you'd met someone else," Anna surmised.

Noah looked startled. "How'd you know that?"

Anna shrugged. "In my experience, people are relieved to get out of a relationship only when they're either, one, with someone really annoying, or, two, when there's someone else," she said.

"Well, okay, you're right. There was someone else. Nothing had happened yet—"

"But you wanted it to."

"But I wanted it to," Noah agreed. "And it did, when school started back up again after the holiday break. Her name was Olivia, and she was in one of my classes. We'd only been dating a few months when she got pregnant. When she told me, I proposed—or I did right after I recovered from the shock."

This sounded so similar to the beginning of her own ill-fated marriage that Anna nearly dropped her fork. And, wait: he had a kid?

But Noah saw what she was thinking and shook his head before Anna could ask. "Olivia lost the baby early on in the pregnancy. Later, after the miscarriage, Olivia told me she'd reconsidered and had already decided she was going to have an abortion, since she didn't want to have a baby while she was still in school. And I was angry that she was making decisions like that without me," Noah said. "It was a lot of stress for a new relationship. We didn't last long after that."

"I'm sorry. That's really hard," Anna said.

"Then I took a break and managed to get through the rest of business school without proposing to anyone," Noah said. He smiled sheepishly.

"Which brings us to number three."

"Maria." Noah's smile became a bit dreamy. "She was a professional dancer. She had really long legs."

"Really," Anna said, more tartly than she meant to, and decided that so far Maria was her least favorite of the group. Clearly, she was the gorgeous one.

"Yeah. But, unfortunately, she was also really screwed up. We had a brief, very intense affair. I was so convinced she was the great love of my life that I proposed to her after knowing her for only a month," Noah said. He shook his head and took a sip of wine. "Looking back, I have to wonder if I sustained some kind of a head injury."

"Why? What happened?"

"I found out she was stealing from me," Noah said sheepishly. He blushed.

Anna laughed, delighted that Maria—whom she could just imagine, with a long, lithe dancer's build, flowing dark hair, liquid eyes—was a criminal. "What did she steal?"

"Money, mostly. I couldn't figure out where all of my cash was going. I'd go to the ATM, take out a hundred bucks, and the next day it would be gone. I thought I was just being really careless. But then I got up one night to go the bathroom and I caught her in the act."

"What did she say?"

"She cried and said she was sorry. Said she'd lost her job, her rent was due, and she was desperate. So I gave her the money."

"Sucker. Let me guess—she kept stealing from you?"

Noah nodded. "A week later I caught her sneaking a bottle of vodka out of my apartment. And after we broke up, I realized that a bunch of other stuff was missing. The watch that my parents gave me when I graduated from college. My grandfather's cuff links. Even small stuff, like groceries and toiletries. She cleaned me out of shaving cream and deodorant. I'm lucky I ended it when I did. Another week and she might have managed to strip my apartment bare."

"No kidding. And after Maria?"

"And after Maria...there was Jessie. Jessie broke my heart," Noah said flatly. He stopped eating and rested his fork on the edge of his salad plate.

Anna felt a stab of jealousy. Even if Maria had been sex on legs, she obviously didn't hold any power over Noah. But Jessie— just the way he said her name made Anna's mouth taste bitter, as though she'd bitten into a rancid nut.

"When I met her, I thought, *This is it, this is the real thing.* Finally. We dated for two years. I proposed to her in Venice, by the Bridge of Sighs as the sun set. It was a beautiful day, like something out of a movie. We—well, I should say, *she*—planned a huge, formal wedding to be held at her parents' country club." Noah's laugh was a short, humorless bark. He was looking back into his memory now, and his eyes were far away. "She spent months driving me crazy by obsessing over what entrée we should serve. Salmon or chicken? Beef Wellington or beef bourguignonne? Or maybe we should have a buffet, she'd say. Only it wouldn't be a real buffet—not what I think of as a buffet, with a long table and lots of dishes—but instead stations all over the place. A crepe station, and a sushi station, and a seafood station. And the cake. God, she was obsessed with the cake. We visited four different bakeries, and I had to remember if the lemon chiffon at this bakery was better or worse than the white chocolate at that one. I couldn't wait for it to just be over, to get the wedding behind us, so that we could start our life together. Buy a house, have a few kids, you know. The usual."

Anna was starting to regret her curiosity. She didn't like the hurt flickering in Noah's eyes, didn't like the note of bitterness creeping into his voice. If he was still angry with this Jessie, it meant he still felt something for her. And men who had feelings for the women who'd come before were certainly not safe to get involved with.

The waitress came by to pick up their salad plates. Anna hadn't even noticed she'd finished hers, only now realizing that her fork had been rising and falling mechanically as Noah spoke.

"And then one day I came home to the apartment we were sharing, and my bags were packed and waiting for me by the door. She said it was over. And that was it. It was over. She wouldn't even talk to me about it."

"Did you ever find out why?"

"She eventually told me that she knew I'd been cheating on her," Noah said.

Anna had been lifting her wineglass to her mouth, but at those words she abruptly plunked it back down. *He's a cheater? I knew he was too good to be true!*

"I told her I hadn't cheated on her—and I *hadn't*—but she said she didn't believe me. And just like that, everything was off. The wedding was canceled, the presents were sent back. I had to somehow explain it to everyone. And, of course, no one believed me when I told them I hadn't been unfaithful to her. I don't think my parents even believed me, although they said they did," Noah continued. "I didn't even know who I had supposedly cheated on her *with*. When I asked her, she just said, 'I know.' *I know.* But I sure as hell didn't."

"Well. It does sound…odd," Anna said, trying to ignore the siren in her head that was blaring *cheat-er, cheat-er, cheat-er.* "Were you ever able to sort it out?"

"Oh, I sorted it out." Noah's voice was bitter again. "I found out that Jessie had been seeing her ex-boyfriend. They got married six months after we broke up. On the same day, and in the same place where we were supposed to get married. I guess after all of her hard work planning the wedding of her dreams, she figured it was pointless to start over from scratch. She just substituted a new groom." Another humorless chuckle. Anna had liked it better when Noah was smiling with his eyes, although the *cheat-er* siren had faded away. "I heard they served salmon and beef Wellington."

"That's awful," Anna said. She reached out and touched his hand. "You must have been devastated."

"It wasn't a fun time," Noah admitted. "I was angry for a long time, and then I was bitter for a while. I worked a lot. And then, after a while, I just got over it."

"I think that would be a hard thing to get over. It would be hard to trust anyone again," Anna said, doubting very much that Noah *had* gotten over Jessie or the way that she'd gone about leaving him. He still seemed stuck on bitter. Then again, it was a phase she knew only too well, so who was she to judge?

"It took a while. But eventually, I did. And I haven't been engaged since." He flashed her a wry smile. This time, it reached his eyes.

The waitress appeared again, carrying their entrées on a round tray. She put the plates down with a flourish, again attended to their wineglasses, and said, *"Bon appétit!"* before flitting away. Anna picked up her fork and knife and cut into her steak. It was perfectly cooked, and there was a pat of herbed butter melting on top.

And yet, for once, the conversation was holding Anna's interest more than the food.

"Anyway. There you go, that's my—what did you call it?—dark, sordid past. Crazy, huh? Four engagements, no marriages, no kids, no pets. Although I have been thinking of getting a dog," Noah said.

"I'll let you take Potato out for a day, if you want to work up to it," Anna joked.

"I just may take you up on that. So, did I succeed in scaring you off?"

"Is that what you were trying to do?" Anna asked lightly, flashing him a smile.

"No," he said, and his voice was serious. "Just the opposite, actually."

Anna looked at Noah, who gazed steadily back at her. In the movies, a moment like this would be accompanied by a swell of music and some meaningful dialogue about how they completed each other.

But all Anna could think was, *Oh, my God, do I have lettuce in my teeth? Is he segueing into a meaningful conversation while I have bits of green gunk wedged into my gums?*

She tried to subtly run her tongue over her front teeth to check for the lettuce but stopped when she realized how odd this would look.

"How are your dinners?" their waitress asked, pausing by their table and smiling down at them expectantly.

"They're fine, thank you," Noah said, and Anna used the distraction to lift her napkin to her mouth as a shield. She performed a quick finger-check on her teeth—and discovered that, yes, indeed, there had been a bit of lettuce trapped there.

Great, Anna thought darkly. *First poison ivy, now lettuce teeth. What next? Will I come out of the ladies' room with toilet paper stuck to my shoe?*

"Can I get you anything else?" the waitress continued.

"No. I think we're all set," Noah said.

Anna tried to set aside the lettuce trauma and think back to what Noah had just said and how he'd looked at her as he said it.

Did I succeed in scaring you off?

Anna hadn't given him her answer. The truth was, she wasn't yet sure.

Anna and Noah had driven separately to the restaurant. As they waited out front for the valet to bring their cars around, they didn't speak at first. But Noah took Anna's hand in his, and as their fingers curled together, she shivered.

"Are you cold?" Noah asked. His lips were so close to her ear, his warm breath tickled her skin.

"No," Anna said truthfully.

Noah drew her to him, so that the length of her body molded

against the hard planes of his. His hand tightened over hers, and Anna swallowed. She suddenly felt like she was sixteen again, overdosing on teenage hormones and the close proximity of a cute guy. It was like every nerve ending in her body was poised, waiting for his touch.

A party of four, two couples in their mid-to-late fifties, came out behind them, laughing and talking, and another valet approached to take their ticket. Anna nodded at the approaching station wagon the first valet was pulling up in.

"That's my car," she said.

"Right," Noah said.

She stepped forward, away from him, although he didn't let go of her hand. The valet opened the door and hopped out. Noah slipped him a tip.

"Thank you, sir. Have a good night," the valet said, touching a finger to his forehead.

Anna turned to look at Noah. "Thank you for dinner," she said. "I had a great time."

"You're welcome," Noah said. He leaned forward.

He's going to kiss me, Anna thought. She inhaled sharply, and her pulse felt like it was skittering out of control.

Another valet pulled up in Noah's Lexus sedan, and, at the same time, the door of the restaurant opened again. Another group of diners, this one rowdier and louder than the last, spilled out onto the carport. They'd obviously had a few too many cocktails, and they roared with drunken laughter.

Noah stepped back and smiled ruefully.

"It's a bit crowded here," he said. The valet flashed the lights and looked around to see where the driver was. Noah raised his hand and said, "That's mine. I'll be right there."

He turned back to Anna.

"I don't suppose ..." Noah began.

The third valet arrived with a giant Lincoln Navigator. The SUV was so big, he couldn't wedge it up under the carport. The valet waited patiently for Anna and Noah to move their cars.

"I think we're blocking the way," Anna said.

"Are you going to stand there all night?" one of the men—presumably the driver of the Lincoln—asked irritably. His face was a ruddy red, although Anna couldn't tell if that was due to sun or liquor. Probably both, she thought.

"Shhh," his wife shushed him. "Can't you see he's trying to kiss her good night?" She turned back to watch Anna and Noah, not bothering to hide her interest.

Anna and Noah looked at each other, and they both laughed.

"I should go," Anna said apologetically.

"Home?" Noah asked. "Because I rented *Dirty Harry*. Just in case you really wanted to see it."

It sounded innocent enough, but Anna knew what he was really asking: *Come home and sleep with me. Come on. You know you want to. You practically had a spontaneous orgasm when I almost just kissed you.*

Her answer, also unspoken, echoed back: *Four fiancées. Four! Not a normal number, like one. Or maybe two, tops. But four! That's a freakishly large number of ex-fiancées for one person to have, no matter how you look at it.*

"No, I can't. Not tonight," Anna said, and tried not to feel too flattered when she saw the obvious disappointment on his face. She stretched up and kissed Noah chastely on the cheek. Then she leaned back and looked at him, her brow furrowed. "Did any of them give you the engagement ring back?"

"Not a one," Noah said, smiling wryly. He let go of her hand, and Anna's fingers, freed from his, felt suddenly cold.

"I'm home," Anna called out, as she walked in her front door.

Her mother was in the small, cozy family room, just off the front hall, curled up on the couch and watching *Breakfast at Tiffany's* on television. "How was your date?" she asked.

"It was fine," Anna said. She kicked off her heels and sank down on the couch next to her mother with a sigh. "How's Charlie?"

"Sweet as a bug. He had a grilled cheese sandwich and an

orange for dinner, and then I took him out for an ice cream cone, which he immediately dropped on the ground."

"Oh, no! Was he upset?"

"No, I gave him mine. I didn't need the calories, anyway," Margo said, patting her flat stomach. "And after that, we came back home, and I gave Charlie a bath and tucked him into bed. He went down without a peep."

"Good." Anna leaned back against the couch. "Thank you again for watching him."

"I'm always happy to babysit my sweet boy, you know that. Now. Tell me about your date. I want all the juicy details."

"There aren't any juicy details. But it was"—she searched for the right adjective—"nice."

"Good! So you like him?" Margo asked eagerly.

Anna could tell her mother was already mentally writing the wedding invitations: *Mrs. Margaret Swann requests the honor of your presence at the marriage of her daughter, Anna Elise, to Noah Springer.* She'd probably even tack an *MBA* on after his name.

"Yes, I do like him. He's sweet. And smart, and funny." She nodded, and smiled a bit wistfully. "Actually, I really like him."

"So what's the problem?"

"I didn't say there was a problem."

"I know you better than that. I can always tell when you're fretting about something. Your forehead furrows up, and you look just like your father."

Anna knew her mother well enough to know that this was not a compliment.

"Well, we both have a lot of baggage."

"You don't have any baggage," Margo said.

"I'm a single mother, Mom. I pretty much define the word *baggage*."

Margo shook her head impatiently. "You kids make this more difficult than it has to be, what with your online dating and your AIDS tests."

"My what?"

"Dating is supposed to be fun. You have a few drinks, eat a couple of steaks, play a few records. Have a good time. Your generation makes it more difficult than it has to be," Margo said.

"We're not making it anything. It just is what it is. The world is a difficult place these days," Anna said.

"When I was your age, I was a single mother, and I went out all the time. I had a date lined up every weekend."

"I remember," Anna said, raising her eyebrows.

"And don't give me any more of that nonsense about how your dating will somehow hurt Charlie. You turned out just fine."

"When I was fifteen, one of your dates grabbed my ass when I was leaning over to get a can of soda out of the fridge. Another one was driving drunk when the two of you picked me up from a friend's house and kept swerving out of his lane the entire way home," Anna said flatly.

"Oh, that," Margo said, waving her hand dismissively. "He wasn't drunk. Just a tiny bit...tipply."

"That's not even a word, Mom."

Anna knew Margo would never have purposely exposed her to jerks. And, to give her mother credit, she had reamed out both men for their bad behavior, then refused to see either one again (two of the few times she didn't give her dates second, third, and fourth chances). Yet her mother had never exactly had a surplus of common sense, especially when it came to men.

"Then there was the guy who used to pee with the door open," Anna continued.

"Well, yes, that was odd. But he was ex-military."

"What does that have to do with it?"

"Oh, you know. When soldiers are living in the barracks, they lose a lot of their inhibitions," Margo said vaguely.

Anna rolled her eyes. The man—his name was Ed Armstrong, Anna remembered—had been discharged from the army some twenty years before he even met her mom. He was just a weirdo. Who goes into someone else's home as a guest and fails to close the door while peeing? It was appallingly gross. Even worse, her mother had continued to date him even after the first time he'd left the bathroom door open.

"Oh! And do you remember that one guy who told me all about how he didn't believe in wearing deodorant, that he preferred his own natural fragrance?" Anna asked, grinning at this memory.

Margo shuddered. "Yes, I remember him. But give me some credit—I went out with him only once, *and* it was a blind date. I couldn't possibly have known that he was going to show up smelling like a pair of dirty sweat socks."

Anna laughed and bent her knees up in front of her, propping the heels of her feet on the edge of the sofa cushion. This reminded her of being little, when her mom had been the one to go out and she'd lie in bed, pretending to be asleep while she waited for Margo to come home. As soon as the babysitter left, Anna would scamper out of bed to see her mother, and the two would curl up on the couch together, talking and giggling late into the night.

"Mom, why don't you ever go out anymore?"

"I do go out."

"You know what I mean: go out with men, out on dates."

"Oh, I'm too old for that."

"You're only sixty."

Margo shrugged and sighed. "Well, I guess it used to make me feel young to date. Now it makes me feel old. Besides, the only available men my age are all widowers, and they're just looking for someone to take care of them."

"That's men of any age," Anna said.

"You sound so bitter." Margo's forehead crinkled into a concerned frown.

"I know. But I've earned my right to be bitter."

"I just hope you're not punishing Noah for Brad's crimes," Margo said reprovingly.

Anna didn't reply, because she didn't know what to say. She

liked Noah, and she was certainly attracted to him. But she didn't trust him. It wasn't personal—although the four fiancées didn't exactly help his case. It was just that she doubted she'd trust any man automatically at this point, at least not before she got to know him. And even then? She had no idea.

"Didn't it make you bitter when Daddy left?" Anna asked.

Her parents had divorced before Anna's fourth birthday. Her father relocated to Miami, remarried within a year, and had three more children. For a while, Margo had driven Anna down to her father's house every few months to visit, but as she got older—and as his new family expanded—the visits had grown infrequent and then stopped altogether. Anna still saw him on occasion—her father had a passing, sentimental interest in Charlie—but it had been a long time since he'd had any sort of presence in her life.

"No, honey, it didn't make me bitter. Angry as hell for a while, but I got over it." Margo leaned back, and tucked her feet up under her. "But I do wish I'd been able to find someone else, the way your father did. Someone to settle down with. I would have liked to have had another baby," she said wistfully.

"Really? I never knew that."

"Well, it's not worth dwelling on. Those days are far behind me," Margo said, waving a dismissive hand. Then she grinned suddenly. "Do you remember that one man I went out with a few times, the one you always called the Hummer?"

"Oh, how could I forget the Hummer?" Anna said, chortling. He hummed constantly, wherever he went. He even hummed while he was eating. On the one occasion when her mother had invited him for dinner, Anna spent the entire meal smothering her laughter, while Margo glared at her across the table. "Do you think he ever realized that he was doing it?"

"No, I don't, the poor dear. You know, he asked me to marry him."

"You never told me that!"

"Well, I said no, obviously. The humming was too large an obstacle to overcome. But don't think I didn't consider it for a while."

"Why? Were you in love with him?"

"God, no. But he was a plastic surgeon, and quite a successful one at that. Just think of it—free face-lifts for life," Margo said dreamily.

And at this, the two women dissolved into another fit of giggles.

eleven

Juliet

Richard Healy stuck his balding head into Juliet's office.

"Come on. We're having a team meeting," he said.

"Now?" Juliet asked, looking up from the discovery motion she'd been drafting.

"Yup. Alex wants to meet down in the conference room," Richard said.

Crap. Juliet threw her pen down on the desk. She didn't have time for a meeting, not today. She had to leave work early to go to the photo shoot for *Mothering* magazine, and she absolutely had to finish this motion before she could go. She had told Alex last week about the photo shoot and sent him a follow-up e-mail this morning to remind him. But that was the thing about Alex: He was a good attorney—no, he was a *great* attorney—but work always came first, before family, or vacations, or free time. And he expected the same commitment from his associates, as Juliet knew all too well.

She picked up the phone to call Patrick and warn him she might be running late but then thought better of it. She didn't want to hear Patrick's irritated sighs and the inevitable lecture about how she was yet again putting work first. So instead, she texted him from her BlackBerry:

IN MTG, MAY B LT.

And then she picked up her yellow legal pad and dutifully trooped down the hall to the conference room.

"Richard, what's the status on your motion for summary judgment?" Alex asked.

Alex was sitting at the head of the big mahogany conference table as he met with his associates. Juliet sat to his left, Richard to his right, and the third associate, Neil Upson, sat next to Richard.

"The MSJ is done and ready for your John Hancock, Alex," Richard said. A smug smile stretched across his doughy face.

Juliet had long suspected that Richard was a graduate of one of those make-friends-and-influence-people courses. He always made a point of making eye contact and using your name when he spoke to you. This didn't make him more likable. If anything, it was creepy to be stared down while having your name repeated over and over. In fact, whenever Juliet ended up in a conversation with Richard—something she tried to avoid—she always felt like he was trying to convert her. To what, she didn't know. Maybe he belonged to some sort of bizarre ass-kissing cult.

"What are you working on now?" Alex asked Richard.

"I've been working hard on the Patterson case, Alex. I stayed up late last night reviewing the file, so I could start drafting the complaint this morning," Richard boomed.

That was another thing about Richard: He always talked far too loudly.

A flicker of irritation passed over Alex's face. Juliet had to suppress a smile. For all of Richard's ass-kissing, she knew how much he annoyed their boss. Alex liked his associates to do their work quickly and competently and did not want to listen to them brag about how late they'd stayed at the office. Richard had yet to figure this out.

"You haven't finished drafting that complaint yet? I gave that to you weeks ago," Alex said, his voice flinty.

Richard's face fell. He looked down at the papers he'd brought into the meeting with him and began shuffling through them, as

though the answer was somewhere within. "Yes…Alex…umm…
it's just…" Then he got himself together. "Well, Alex, I've been taking depositions in the Steele Insurance case. You told me to make
those depos a priority." A petulant tone had crept into his voice;
Alex noticed it.

"It's *all* a priority," Alex said sharply. He turned to Neil Upson.

Neil was thin in a gawky, awkward way—all bones and sharp
angles. His thinning hair was red, and the eyelashes that framed
his watery blue eyes were so pale, they appeared nonexistent.
Juliet had long suspected that Neil was a depressive—there was always a drawn, sad air about him—but he was a hard worker. In
fact, Neil was a machine. He was single, didn't have kids, and
spent all of his time at the office. He consistently outbilled everyone else in the firm, which made Juliet uneasy. Neil had started at
Little & Frost right after her, and they were more or less on the
same rung of the partnership ladder. Juliet knew that she was the
favorite to make partner next—she'd won a couple of modest
cases recently—but compared to Neil's extraordinary billables…

Please let it be me, Juliet thought. The Winston Academy had
sent home a note last week announcing, in a vaguely regretful
tone, that there would be a tuition hike next year. She could
barely afford the double tuition at the current rate and the girls
were only going part-time now. Next year, they started kindergarten. And moving them to the poorly rated public school nearby
was out of the question. Their education was too important—
in fact, *the* most important thing. Knots of anxiety tightened in
Juliet's shoulders.

*What if Neil gets the partnership instead of me? Is it possible that
they'll make both of us partners? No, not likely. The firm's too conser-
vative to do that. Well, it will just have to be me. If I have to work late
every night and weekend until they make the decision, that's just
what I'll do—*

"Juliet?"

Juliet flinched involuntarily. She hadn't been paying attention, and apparently Alex was satisfied with Neil's update and
ready to move on to her.

Juliet cleared her throat. "This morning I wrote a status memo for the Hamilton file—it's in your in-box, Alex—and I was just drafting a discovery motion for the dead-baby case," she said smoothly.

"How about the Motor King hearing? Are we ready for that?" Alex asked.

Juliet nodded. "I wrote up a memo on the issue regarding past judgments that you asked me to research. That's in your in-box as well."

"Excellent," Alex said, making a note on his pad.

Juliet smiled to herself. She'd known that would impress him. Across the table, Richard was sulking, and Neil was staring down sadly at the papers in front of him. Juliet looked back at Alex. He was still writing, his gold pen dancing impatiently across the pad, and she took the opportunity to watch him, unseen. She loved the way his eyes tilted down at the outer edges and how they were fanned with laugh lines.

Alex suddenly looked up, before Juliet could avert her stare. As their eyes met, excitement twisted in Juliet's stomach. Her mouth went suddenly dry, and her pulse quickened, and she had a vivid image of what it would be like to kiss Alex, wondering what those firm, thin lips would feel like against hers ... or trailing down her neck ... or ...

The corners of Alex's mouth quirked upward, and Juliet was suddenly aware that she was holding her breath. She let it out in a *whoosh* and then quickly looked back down at her notes, pretending to review them, all the while thinking, *I cannot have a crush on my boss. It (a) is ridiculous, and (b) could seriously damage my career. I must stop fantasizing about him.*

"All right. We have a new case that just came in this morning. It's an investor-fraud case," Alex began.

As Alex detailed the background of the new case, Juliet's heart rate gradually slowed back down. She tried to clear her thoughts and focus on what her boss was saying.

But Alex shifted in his chair and straightened his legs, brushing against hers under the table. Another jolt of excitement shot through her—a thrill that was heightened when Alex didn't immediately move his leg away. Instead, his calf was pressing against hers, warm even through the wool of his pants.

Juliet dared herself to look up at Alex and saw that he was looking right at her. Then, unmistakably, his eyebrows crooked up.

Was it a question? Juliet wondered, her heart skittering. *A challenge?*

A moment later his leg moved away, and Alex turned to answer a question Neil had posed about one of the parties to the new lawsuit...and Juliet was left wondering what had just happened. Or if anything *had* just happened. Had she imagined the whole thing?

But as she could feel the rhythmic thrum of her heightened pulse, she knew she hadn't imagined it. Not at all.

By the time Juliet got out of her meeting, put the final touches on the discovery motion, had a quick conference with her secretary, Janine, and got out of the office, she was already late for the photo session. It was being held at a local photography studio *Mothering* had rented out for the afternoon. Patrick and the twins were already there, waiting for Juliet. The girls were wearing matching slightly rumpled pink dresses, and their ponytails were starting to droop. They raced around the waiting room, playing a loud, giggling game of tag. When they saw Juliet pushing open the glass front door, the game came to an abrupt stop.

"Hi, Mommy!" Emma called. She ran over and threw herself at Juliet, wrapping her arms around her mother's legs.

Isabel, who had always been more loyal to Patrick, held on to his hand and frowned up at her mother. Juliet touched her daughter's head in greeting.

"Hi, Izz," she said.

"You're late," Izzy said. She fixed Juliet with a disapproving stare.

"Where have you been?" Patrick asked her irritably. His hair was standing up on end, the way it always did when he was anxious and compulsively running his fingers through it. "The girls are reaching their limit. I tried calling your cell, and I couldn't get through."

"It ran out of power," Juliet lied glibly. She'd actually turned her cell phone off. She knew that Patrick would be calling her to find out why she was late, and she hadn't wanted to hear the re-criminations. It wasn't like his nagging would get her there any faster.

"Juliet Cole? Thank *God,* you're finally here." An officious man in his mid-twenties sporting a goatee and long sideburns appeared. "She's here," he called back over his shoulder, before looking Juliet over critically. "Is *that* what you're wearing?"

"Who are you?" Juliet asked.

"Simon Walker. I'm in charge," he said importantly. "The blue suit isn't doing it for me. Here, try taking off your jacket and undoing a few buttons on your shirt."

Simon reached out to unbutton Juliet's shirt for her, but she held up a hand, blocking him.

"Don't even think about it," she said. "I'm not unbuttoning my shirt."

"Fine. But it's not going to look right," Simon said huffily. "Come on to the back, we're running late."

Juliet and Patrick, each taking a daughter by the hand, followed Simon into the larger of two studios, which was filled with camera equipment, a few people—the photographer, his assistant, and a random woman with a bored expression who was yammering into her cell phone—and, oddly enough, an empty shopping cart set up in front of a blue screen.

"What's the shopping cart for?" Izzy asked.

"That's where we're going to take your picture," Simon said, affecting the slow, condescending tone of voice childless people often used with young children. He mimed pointing and shooting a camera.

Izzy rolled her eyes. "I know what taking a picture means," she said scathingly.

That's my girl, Juliet thought proudly.

"We're going to pretend that we're all at the grocery store. Won't that be fun? You and your sister are going to sit in the cart, and your mommy is going to push it," Simon continued.

"But we're not allowed to sit in the back of the cart," Emma protested. "It's not safe."

"And Mommy never goes to the grocery store with us," Izzy added.

"That's not true," Juliet said. "I go to the store. On occasion."

"But not with us," Izzy corrected her. "Only Daddy takes us. You're always too busy working."

Simon looked at Juliet. She could see the judgment on his face. "Have *you* ever tried grocery shopping with two young children?" she asked him, crossing her arms defensively.

"Hey, Juliet."

Juliet turned and saw Chloe standing there, baby William strapped to her chest in a sling. Chloe's face was so pasty and pale that the dark circles under her eyes stood out like bruises, and a pimple was erupting on her chin. She was still just as puffy and bloated as she'd been pregnant, and although her stomach had deflated a bit, it still protruded out, Buddha-like.

"Jesus, what happened to you? You look awful," Juliet said.

Chloe flinched as though she'd been struck. She blinked a few times and looked stunned—but then suddenly she shook her head and let out a short, startled laugh.

"I had a baby, remember?" Chloe said, pointing to William. "And you're the first person who's told me the truth. Everyone keeps lying and telling me how much motherhood agrees with me and how I'm just *glowing*. Please. I know I look awful. I *feel* awful. And I'm not glowing—my skin's just oily."

"It's hard in the beginning," Juliet agreed.

Chloe looked at her doubtfully.

"What?" Juliet asked. "I had two kids. Speaking of whom, these are my daughters, Emma and Izzy. And this is my husband, Patrick. Patrick, this is Chloe."

"Hi, Chloe," Patrick said. "I remember you from Grace and Louis's party."

"That's right. Although I don't think we officially met," Chloe said.

"No, but you're the chick who went into labor. That makes you pretty easy to remember," Patrick said, grinning.

"I'm never going to live that down, am I?" Chloe said with a laugh. She smiled down at the twins. "Hi."

"What's your baby's name?" Emma asked.

"This is William," Chloe said, smiling softly down at the sleeping baby in the sling, and for just a moment, as her eyes lit upon her son's sleep-slackened face, she really did look lovely.

I'll be damned. She is *glowing*, Juliet thought.

"Let's get going, people," Simon called out, clapping his hands together. "Mom, Dad, kids, come over here."

"I guess that's us. It was nice to meet you, Chloe," Patrick said pleasantly. Holding the girls' hands, he started over to the makeshift set.

"Are you coming over?" Juliet asked.

"No, go ahead," Chloe said. "William and I just stopped by to watch. I don't want to be in the way."

"That guy, Simon, wants me to unbutton my shirt," Juliet said. "But isn't the whole point of the article supposed to be that I'm a working mom? Lawyers don't go around with their shirts unbuttoned down to their navels. It's not exactly professional."

Chloe looked her over, furrowing her brow as she thought. "True. Although it might photograph better. And you might want to take your jacket off too. It'll give you better contrast."

Juliet hesitated, but then nodded. "Okay," she said, shrugging off her jacket and popping open the top two buttons on her shirt. "How's that?"

"Much better. Now you still look like a lawyer—but a hot lawyer. The one all the guys in the office are lusting after," Chloe said with a mischievous grin.

Juliet knew Chloe was joking, but she had a sudden flashback to Alex's ankle resting up against hers, warm and questioning. She shivered at the memory.

"Are you cold?" Chloe asked sympathetically. "It's freezing in here, isn't it? I had to put a sweater on William."

For just a moment Juliet felt an odd impulse to confess to Chloe what she'd really been thinking about. Why, she had no idea. It would be totally unlike her. But then she saw Patrick standing just across the room, looking back at her, his eyebrows raised in question: *What's the holdup? We're running late as it is!* Apparently they'd reached the point in their marriage where words were no longer necessary, and they could communicate everything that needed to be said by giving each other exasperated looks. She swallowed back the impulse to tell Chloe about Alex.

"No, I'm fine," she said.

"Mommy!" Simon called out importantly. He'd found a clip-board and a headset—why he needed a headset in a tiny studio, Juliet wasn't sure—and was happily bossing Patrick and the girls on where to stand and how to pose.

"See you later," Juliet said to Chloe.

"Good luck!" Chloe called after her.

"We have to talk," Patrick said later that night.

Juliet was sitting on the couch, a file propped open on her lap. She was skimming through a motion that opposing counsel in the dead-baby case had sent over earlier that day—apparently, the defense was not going to offer a quickie settlement—while she half-watched the late news. Juliet had once read a news article about how researchers had discovered that when a woman gives birth, her brain chemistry changes, most notably expanding the woman's ability to multitask.

I could have told them that, Juliet thought. She was probably the only one among her office of male colleagues who had actually managed to bill even as she changed diapers.

She glanced up at Patrick, who was glowering down at her. *Big surprise,* she thought wearily. *That's all he seems to do these days. He practically radiates disapproval every time he sees me.*

She ran a critical eye over her husband. Patrick was wearing a pair of stretched-out blue sweatpants, the ones with bleach spots on one knee that he'd owned when she met him, and a white V-neck undershirt. His beard was heavy, even more so than usual.

"Did you shave today?" she asked curiously.

"What?" He stared at her as though she'd spit at him instead of asking a benign question.

"I was just wondering if you'd shaved. Forget it." Juliet shrugged, already losing interest. "What did you want to talk about?"

He sat down heavily at the end of the couch and sighed. *Drama queen*, Juliet thought, freshly irritated. She had too much to do tonight and didn't have the time to indulge his moodiness.

"This isn't working. Our arrangement. Me staying home full time. You always at the office," he said. He looked straight ahead of him as he spoke, staring at the perky brunette newswoman on television, the one with the retro Dorothy Hamill haircut.

Juliet's head immediately began to hurt. She closed her eyes against the throbbing ache. She didn't have time for this. Not now, not when she still had a pile of work to get through before she could go to bed. It was her punishment for leaving work early.

"I want to go back to work, at least part time. And I want you to cut your hours back," Patrick continued.

"That's not what we agreed to," Juliet countered. "We can discuss your starting back to work eventually, but I'm not going to be able to cut my hours until I make partner. And maybe not even then."

Patrick's eyes darkened, and he shook his head. He finally looked at her. "This isn't open for discussion. I'm telling you what I decided."

"*You* decided that *I'm* going to work less?" Juliet asked. She laughed humorlessly and shook her head. "You don't get to decide that, Patrick."

Sometimes Patrick reminded Juliet of her mother, Lillian. Not that Juliet would ever share this with her husband, since he knew damned well how she felt about her mother, who had lived in a near constant state of agitation, flitting around the house nervously, never able to sit still. Her parents even used to have the same fight that she and Patrick were now having, only it was her father, Evan, who had worked the long hours, and her mother who railed against his absence from the house. When they were little, Juliet and her younger sister, Angie, would hide in Angie's closet, letting the darkness cocoon them, while they listened to the muffled screams of their parents.

"You're never here! I'm always alone!" Lillian would scream.

"Stop acting like a child," Evan would reply, his voice softer but scornful.

And the two sisters, who had never been close, would sit together and wait for it to pass. As they got older and the fights continued with a dreary repetition, Juliet and Angie eventually learned to tune their parents out and stopped hiding when the shouting began. Juliet would turn on her radio as she did her homework, and Angie would yak on the phone to one of her friends, and the shouts would subside into background noise.

Juliet had always assumed that her parents didn't love each other. Or, more accurately, that her father didn't love her mother. How could he? Lillian was such a weak, hysterical woman.

But then Lillian died when Juliet was in her second year of law school. Aggressive uterine cancer. It killed her three months after the initial diagnosis, when she'd gone to the doctor complaining of cramps, expecting to hear that she'd need a D&C. And, after Lillian's death, Evan withered like a neglected plant. He abruptly stopped practicing law, gained weight, and spent all of his time zoned-out in front of the television. A year later, he was dead too. Heart attack, the doctor said.

But Angie had other ideas. "He died of a broken heart," she'd said sadly on the phone one night, a few weeks after their father's funeral. Juliet normally avoided her sister's phone calls—her sister had inherited their mother's chronic anxiety—but there was paperwork to discuss.

"That's not even possible," Juliet had scoffed.

"Of course it is. Dad wasn't like you, Jules. I know you always thought you two were so alike, but you really weren't. He was a romantic at heart."

He was? Juliet wondered. *Since when?*

"God damn it! Will you listen to me? I'm not happy!" Patrick now shouted suddenly, startling Juliet away from her memories. She stared at his angry face, at his hardened eyes, furrowed brow, and flushed skin, and was shocked at the sudden transformation in her husband. Where was the gentle, soft-spoken Patrick who never yelled, who never lost his patience?

"Why are you yelling? You're going to wake up the twins."

"Because it's the only way I can get your attention!"

"Okay. You have my attention," Juliet said calmly. "But I don't know how you're proposing this would work. What do you suggest we do with the twins while you're at work? Or are you going to take them with you? Enlist them as mini-firefighters and let them ride around on the fire engine?"

"I thought we could work out a time-share arrangement. I'd go back part time, maybe take the evening shift. You could get home from work early," Patrick said.

"I told you, that's not going to happen."

"We could get a nanny."

"We could. But we looked into that before. It doesn't make financial sense to get a nanny. The extra income you'd bring in would hardly cover the cost," Juliet pointed out.

At this, Patrick flinched visibly. He stared down at his hands, which he balled into fists. Juliet knew that she'd probably damaged his fragile male ego, but Christ, he wasn't being reasonable.

"Besides," Juliet continued, "what about the girls? You'd rather a stranger came in and took care of them?"

Patrick stared at her as though he'd never seen her before. His eyes were so blank, so devoid of any of the warmth and love she was used to seeing there, that Juliet suddenly felt a little frightened.

"No. You don't get to do that. You don't get to put me on a guilt trip," he said quietly.

"What's that supposed to mean?"

"I've been raising those girls for four years, basically as a single parent."

"Bullshit," Juliet said, raising her voice for the first time.

"It's true. Tonight was the first night in a week you were home before they went to bed," Patrick said.

"When you were growing up and your father worked late, did you consider your mother to be a single parent? No, of course not. She was just doing what moms did back then, and your dad was just being a dad. So why is it different when the wife is the bread-winner in the family?" Juliet asked.

"Don't do that. Don't lawyer-argue me," Patrick said.

"I'm not lawyer-arguing you. I'm pointing out the fundamental sexism of your argument."

"So now I'm a sexist?"

"You're the one who's troubled by taking a nontraditional role," Juliet said.

"I'm not troubled by my quote-*nontraditional*-unquote role. I'm troubled that my wife is never home. I'm troubled that my daughters never see their mother. I'm troubled that you think your obligation to this family begins and ends with a fucking pay-check," Patrick said, his voice rising again.

Juliet opened her mouth, ready to argue back, as she always was. Patrick was right about that: Being a litigator was an inherent part of her now. But before she could speak, Patrick stood up abruptly. The anger had disappeared from his face as quickly as it appeared. Instead, he just looked tired, as though all the spark had drained out of him.

"Don't. Just . . . don't, Juliet. I don't want to hear it. Fine, I won't go back to work just yet." Patrick shook his head and turned to leave. "You win. Big surprise."

He stalked out of the room. Juliet pressed her fingers to her temples and waited for the wave of rage swelling inside her to pass.

Should I go after him? she wondered. *That's what he wants, for me to chase after him and apologize and then talk all of this out with him.*

But this angered her even more. It was already late, and Patrick knew she had work to do tonight; that was the trade-off she had to make to leave the office early. Why did he have to get into this whole debate now, tonight? And he didn't just confront her—he dropped an ultimatum on her, started a fight, and then sullenly withdrew before they'd resolved anything. It was manipulative. Worse, he'd done it to her before—he'd pick a fight, then run off, and she'd be stuck chasing after him, trying to coax him into making up with her.

I'm not going to do it, Juliet thought resentfully. *If he wants to make unreasonable demands and then walk off in a huff, that's his problem.*

Patrick hadn't always been like this. He used to be so much fun, and so *funny.* He'd always been able to make her laugh, get her out of her own head, and stop taking herself too seriously. They'd balanced each other out back then—Juliet crackling with energy and purpose, Patrick laid-back and gentle.

He'd even been old-fashioned, in a way; Patrick had been the first man Juliet had been with who had actually set out to court her. He'd cooked her lasagna on their third date, would stop by her office with a latte just because he was thinking of her, and told her that her hair smelled like the lilac tree that had grown outside his childhood bedroom window.

Above all, he'd always made her feel loved and treasured.

Now...now he was turning into her mother. When had that happened? And how? Wasn't she supposed to be the one to gradually morph into the weak and brittle woman Lillian had been? Juliet shuddered at this thought; it was the worst fate she could imagine. Or was it? What was worse; to become Lillian—or to be *married* to Lillian?

Now, that was a truly chilling choice.

Juliet gave herself a mental shake. *Work. I have to get back to work.* The dead-baby case could clinch her bid for a partner-ship.

She breathed in deeply and exhaled slowly. And once her temper had cooled and her mind had cleared, she switched off the television and turned her attention back to the file she'd brought home.

twelve

Chloe

Chloe! I'm so glad I got you! I know you just had a baby, like, five minutes ago and all…"

Chloe immediately recognized the rapid-fire voice on the other end of the phone. It was Maia Bleu, an editor at *Pop Art*, the entertainment magazine she'd done a few pieces for over the years.

"Hi, Maia," she said warmly. "Thank you so much for the rattle you sent William."

"I'm glad you liked it. Although I can't believe you already sent me a thank-you note. You must have written it, like, the day you got it. Aren't you crazy busy doing baby stuff?"

"Well, yes, but William takes long naps," Chloe said modestly. She didn't mention that she had a hard time falling asleep when she had unwritten thank-you notes hanging over her head. Her mother, ever the Southern lady, had long ago drilled the rules of etiquette into Chloe. But she knew just how hopelessly suburban and uncool that would sound to someone as hip as Maia. "What's up?"

"We have a bit of a situation here. Is there any chance you'd be interested in doing a piece for us?"

"Well—"

"And before you say anything, I have two words for you: Fiona Watson."

"Fiona Watson?" Chloe repeated, impressed. Fiona Watson was the current Hollywood It Girl and had been considered a front-runner for an Oscar after her recent turn as Fanny Price in a remake of *Mansfield Park*. She was too old for the part by at least ten years, but—thanks to her Crème de la Mer and a soft-focus lens—she had managed to pull it off to critical acclaim.

"She's agreed to do an interview with us, which is a huge scoop, but only on the condition that the interview take place in person, not over the phone. Said she doesn't trust a reporter she can't see. You know, typical actress bullshit. She's staying at the Breakers on Palm Beach, but only until tomorrow morning, so you'd have to do the interview today. This afternoon. It's so last-minute, we don't have time to fly anyone down. You're our only hope."

"Today?" Chloe hesitated. It was impossible. It was already ten a.m. There was no way she'd be able to do the background re-search in time. And who would she get to watch William? She couldn't exactly leave him at home alone, with instructions to make a peanut butter sandwich if he got hungry. Besides, she was exhausted—William had his days and nights mixed up and had been up every night, all night, for the past week. Chloe seriously doubted she'd be able to drive all the way down to West Palm without falling asleep at the wheel.

But *Fiona Watson*. It was easily the biggest story Chloe had ever been asked to cover. And even though she was tired, the idea of spending a few hours as a professional in the company of other adults was hugely appealing. A whole afternoon where she could function as something other than a human milk dispenser, where she could wear her dry-clean-only clothes without fear of getting them covered in hunks of cottage-cheeselike baby spit-up; where she could recapture her premom self, if only for a few hours.

"It has to be today," Maia repeated. "I know, it's short notice, so if you can't do it, I totally understand—"

"I'd love to!" Chloe blurted out, even as she wondered, *What am I doing? There's no way I'll be able to pull this off! I haven't even showered today, and I haven't shaved my legs in a week, and I still can't fit into any of my prepregnancy clothes....*

"Great! I knew I could count on you. You're always so depend-able," Maia said brightly. "I'll have my assistant fax over all the background we have."

"Right," Chloe said, trying to sound professional and worthy of Maia's praise. "I'll get right on it."

Twenty minutes later, Chloe was sinking fast into a panic spi-ral. She couldn't find anyone to watch William.

"Normally it'd be no problem, but we're dealing with the flu here," Grace said apologetically. "Hannah and Molly are both sick, and I know it's just a matter of time until Nat gets it too. The whole house is crawling with germs. I've never seen so much vomit in my life. I keep expecting their heads to start spinning around, *Exorcist*-style. Did you try Anna?"

"She's at the office today. Anna gave me her mom's phone number, but Margo isn't answering," Chloe said.

"Oh, *shit*. Molly just threw up all over the couch. I'm so sorry, Chloe, but I have to go."

"No, that's fine, I understand. I hope the girls feel better soon," Chloe said.

She hung up and dialed James.

"Hello," he said. His voice was clipped and businesslike when he answered. He always sounded so different when she called him at work.

"Hey, it's me."

"Hey, babe." James's tone immediately softened. "What's up?"

"Well...what are you doing today?" Chloe asked him. She tucked the phone under her chin and began to pace nervously around the living room, William cradled in her arms.

"Working," James said. "Why, is everything okay?"

"Fine. Only...is there any possible way you could take the rest of the day off? I just got an assignment to interview—you're not going to believe this—*Fiona Watson*! But it has to be today. This afternoon."

"No way," James said immediately. "Not today. I have a meeting with my boss right after lunch. I can't miss it."

Chloe could feel the thud of disappointment hit her. James had been her last hope.

"I thought you were taking some time off work, anyway," James continued.

"I was, but I don't want to pass this up. Are you sure there isn't any way you can do it? Can't you tell your boss you're sick and need to go home early?"

James laughed his easy, warm chuckle. "Nah, that dog won't hunt. I already saw the big guy, so he knows I'm not sick. Sorry, babe."

"No, I understand," Chloe said. She looked down helplessly at William. He cooed and blew a spit bubble at her. "It's just...getting to interview Fiona Watson is a really big deal."

But James wasn't listening to her. Instead, he'd moved the phone away from his mouth and was talking to someone in his office.

"Yeah, I got that memo.... I know it's total bullshit.... Yeah, I know exactly what you mean. Hey, Todd and I are heading over to Nemo's for lunch. Want to come with us?" he said.

"James?"

"I'm here," he said, as he returned to the phone. "Look, I've got to run. I have a ton of work to get through today."

Chloe suddenly had an idea. "Hey—what if I dropped William off at your office?"

"Chloe—"

"He won't be any trouble! He'll just sit there quietly the whole time," Chloe said. She looked down at her son, who was lying placidly in her arms, blinking sleepily. "You won't bother Daddy while he's working, will you, sweetie?"

Unfortunately, William's face suddenly purpled and crumpled up, and his tiny body went rigid with fury.

"AHHHHHHH!" William screeched. It was a surprisingly loud sound for one so little. Chloe could feel her breasts tingling in response as her milk rushed in to soothe. She tucked the phone under her ear and lifted William to her shoulder, patting his back softly.

James said something, but she couldn't make it out over William's screams.

"What did you say?"

"I said, it sounds like you've got your hands full. Hey, I've really got to go. I'll talk to you later, okay?"

"So can I drop William off at your office?" Chloe asked, raising her voice to be heard over William's screams.

"Sorry, babe, but there's no way that's going to work. Give the little man a kiss for me."

"No, wait!" But James was gone.

"What am I going to do now?" Chloe wondered aloud. "It's not like I can show up to an interview with a baby in tow—"

But then she stopped. Why couldn't she? It wasn't *that* crazy of an idea—was it?

"What do you think, buddy? Do you want to go down to Palm Beach with Mommy and hang out with a movie star?" Chloe cooed.

William began snuffling around at her neck, crying piteously.

"Okay, okay," Chloe said, sitting down to feed him. She positioned her horseshoe-shaped nursing pillow on her lap and rested William against it, while she fumbled with her nursing bra. He latched on with the enthusiasm of a drunk on a dry spell, his eyes wide open with relief as he gulped down the milk, his fingers splayed against the side of her breast.

It was only then that she remembered hearing the fax machine spitting out the background on Fiona Watson that Maia had sent her. Chloe should be reading while he was nursing.

Well, too late now. Good thing I've seen all of Fiona's movies, Chloe thought, running a finger over the curve of her son's cheek.

Chloe had never been to the Breakers before, although she'd seen it from a distance on the few occasions when she'd ventured down to Palm Beach. As she turned onto Breakers Drive, she realized the hotel was even more gorgeous than she'd imagined, like something out of a movie.

A long, palm-tree-lined drive, surrounded by extensive manicured grounds, led up to the hotel. The whole place radiated the smug confidence of money, and Chloe immediately felt underdressed. She glanced down at her straining blue oxford shirt and too-tight black trousers, purchased before she'd gotten pregnant, which meant Chloe practically had to shoehorn herself into them. And even then she couldn't fasten the top button. She'd had to loop a rubber band around the button and thread it through the hole, and leave her shirt untucked to cover it. Chloe glanced into her rearview mirror, which was lined up with the mirror hanging over William's rear-facing car seat. She could see William's reflection—he'd finally drifted off, his head lolled over to one side. His sweet round face was slack with sleep.

Maybe he'll sleep right through this, she thought hopefully. He'd been awake for most of the hour-long car trip, looking solemnly out the window, and so was due for a nice long nap.

She drove under the arched entrance to the portico, parking her car between the round pillars. A small army of valets milled about to the left of the front doors, which were manned by two extremely good-looking uniformed doormen. One of the valets sprinted up, eager to take control of her car.

"Just one minute," Chloe said, as he opened her car door. "I have to get my baby out."

She slid out of the car, popped open the trunk, and heaved the baby stroller out. One of the doormen hurried over to help her.

"I've got it," Chloe said, struggling with the unwieldy stroller. "I just have to push out this lever..."

"I think you're supposed to press one of those buttons first," the doorman said, looking down at it doubtfully.

They both fidgeted with the stroller, each getting in the other's way, while the valet stood patiently to one side, watching them. Chloe felt ridiculous, especially once they'd finally gotten

the stroller open and she lugged out her enormous black nylon
diaper bag. Small as William was, he required an extraordinary
amount of paraphernalia to get out of the house: hats, diapers,
wipes, two kinds of diaper balm, a changing mat, blankets, burp
cloths, a change of clothes, another change of clothes, three paci-
fiers, and a brightly colored Manhattan Whoozit, which all of the
baby magazines had insisted was *the* toy of the moment and
which Wills mostly ignored. She shoved the bulging bag into the
bottom of the stroller, pushing it down to fit, and then grabbed
the leather binder containing the background notes on Fiona
Watson.

"Okay," she finally said. "I think I've got everything." She
smiled at the valet.

"Your baby," he said, pointing at the car, where William was
still sleeping in his car seat.

"What? Oh! William!"

Blushing furiously, Chloe yanked open the car door and
fumbled with the lever that released William's infant car seat.
She was so embarrassed at having nearly forgotten her son—was
it her imagination or were the doormen smirking at each
other?—that she jostled the seat in her haste to pull it out.
William woke up with a start and looked at her with wide, un-
blinking eyes for a minute. Chloe recognized the expression
darkening his small face.

"Oh, no," Chloe said. "Oh, no, no, no, no, no. Please don't,
honey. *Please—*"

But it was too late. William stretched his mouth open wide
and began to howl in fury at the rude awakening.

"Shhh! It's okay, sweetie, it's okay, Mama's sorry," Chloe gab-
bled at him, desperate not to make a scene in this elegant place.
But William wasn't having any of it. Warmed up now, he began
to scream even louder, gripping his hands into round fists,
which he held up by his head, looking like a very tiny, very irate
old man.

"Maybe you shouldn't have woken him up," the doorman

said unhelpfully, as he peered down at William over Chloe's shoulder.

Like I did it on purpose, Chloe thought, gritting her teeth.

"Excuse us. I'm so sorry. So, *so* sorry," she said, as she struggled to latch his car seat on to the stroller. Finally, she pushed a still-wailing William and the stroller packed full to bursting with his assorted gear through the front doors of the hotel into the opulent lobby.

It was a long space, and elegant in a hushed way that made you feel like any noise would be a trespass. Couches and tables lined one wall opposite a row of square columns. Overhead, crystal chandeliers hung from the decorative plaster ceiling. It was the sort of place to walk through when you were wearing crisply ironed linen and high heels and meeting someone special for lunch.

It was not at all the sort of place you wanted to hurry through in too-tight clothes, wheeling a screaming baby, especially one who seemed to be taking a fiendish delight in the echoing quality of the high ceilings.

There were at least a hundred people milling about in the lobby, some sitting on the posh couches, others passing through the front doors into the sunlight. Chloe felt marginally better when she saw that she was actually more dressed up than most of the patrons, many of whom were wearing sweat suits or tank tops over shorts.

Chloe glanced at her watch. She was already running late, but she couldn't bring William upstairs while he was in the middle of a fit—and why had he been crying so much lately? she wondered with a twinge of anxiety. William had never been colicky before, but now he seemed to be fussing most of the time he was awake. She looked down at him, undecided whether she should pick him up and cuddle him or just wheel him around outside until he fell asleep, when thankfully—amazingly—he blinked, yawned, and then his eyelids snapped shut, so that his feathery eyelashes spread against the soft pillows of his cheeks. It always amazed her that he could do that, just fall asleep in mid-scream, as though an off switch had been pressed.

Thank you for that small miracle, Chloe thought. *Maybe I'll make it through this interview after all.*

The living room in Fiona Watson's suite had a stunning view of Palm Beach's white beaches and the blue-gray ocean beyond. It was exactly the sort of place Chloe would have imagined a movie star of Fiona's stature would stay. The furnishings were tastefully expensive—a low cream sofa, two pale-blue wing chairs mono-grammed with white Bs, a carved armoire, a sleek mahogany desk—and the living area alone was bigger than the entire first floor of Chloe's town house. Clearly, Fiona needed the space; the room was full of people, including two personal assistants buzzing around importantly, a stylist who had brought a selection of gowns for the actress's appearance that night at a charity ball at Donald Trump's Mar-A-Lago, and a hairdresser, a manicurist, and a cosmetician, who were chatting among themselves while they waited for their turn with Fiona. Just after Chloe arrived, a young woman with a caramel-colored tan also came in, shepherding Fiona Watson's two young sons, who looked as though they'd just come inside after having a swim, considering their damp hair and Hawaiian patterned trunks.

Chloe sat in the chair one of the assistants had pointed her to, parking William's stroller next to her. William was, thankfully, still asleep.

The assistant—who introduced herself as Nanette—was a tall, pretty girl with a shock of short pale-blonde hair. She looked at the stroller doubtfully.

"She's not going to like that," Nanette said.

Chloe didn't have to ask who She was.

"Right—sorry. I didn't have a choice." Chloe smiled apologeti-cally. "My sitter fell through. I hope Miss Watson likes children."

Nanette looked horrified. "You're not going to bring it into the interview with you, are you?"

"It?" Chloe asked, confused.

"The baby."

"Oh…my son? Well, um, yes. I can't leave him alone," Chloe said.

But Nanette was vigorously shaking her head from side to side before Chloe had even finished speaking. "Absolutely not. It's out of the question. She doesn't like having babies around her."

"But she has two little boys," Chloe pointed out.

"Chloe Truman? She's ready to see you," a second assistant—this one an impossibly good-looking young man with a square jaw and heavily highlighted hair—said importantly, as he swept into the room.

"Thank God you're here. You have to help me get rid of this baby," Nanette hissed nervously at the second assistant.

Chloe stared at her and took a step closer to William. She didn't know what this woman meant by "get rid of," but she wasn't taking any chances.

"I don't think—" Chloe began to say, but Nanette wasn't listening to her.

"Baby? What baby?" the second assistant asked.

"She brought a *baby* with her!" Nanette said, nodding in Chloe's direction.

"Well, she certainly can't bring it in there," said Assistant Number Two, looking scandalized. "Get Katie to watch it."

Again with the it, Chloe thought, her irritation and frustration mounting.

"His name is William," Chloe began.

"Katie," Nanette called out. The nanny had been trying to talk the two little boys into sitting still long enough for her to towel-dry their damp hair. The larger of the two boys—he looked to be about six—kept hitting the nanny's hand away, while the younger one, around four, was poking her in the bottom with the plastic shovel from a pail set.

"Quincy, stop it. Satchel, please sit still. You know how cross She gets when your hair doesn't dry right," Katie was saying, in a thick Australian accent.

"Katie! Quick!" the assistant hissed again.

Katie looked up, her expression wary. "What?"

"You're going to have to take this baby," Nanette said.

"A baby?" Katie asked, looking exasperated. "Nanette, I can't possibly take care of a baby on top of these two."

"Look, he's probably going to just sleep the entire time. I promise he won't bother anyone," Chloe said, standing up. She put a possessive hand on the handle of the stroller.

"No," Nanette snapped.

"Absolutely not," Assistant Number Two echoed.

"Fine, give him here," Katie said wearily. She left behind the two boys—who promptly ran over to the pristine white couch and began jumping up and down on it—and pulled William's carriage roughly away from Chloe.

"Um," Chloe said. Watching the nanny wheel her son away, toward the rowdy boys, made her incredibly uncomfortable. All of her mommy instincts were on high alert, whistling an alarm.

"Come on. We're running behind schedule," the male assistant snapped.

I'm only going to be one room away, and Katie is a professional child-care provider, Chloe tried to reason with herself. Finally, reluctantly, she turned and followed the bossy male assistant out of the living room, although she couldn't help casting one final worried look back at her sleeping baby before she left.

Fiona Watson was smaller than Chloe had expected her to be. Chloe knew the actress was thin—Fiona was known for her sticklike figure, which she claimed to maintain through a macrobiotic diet and four hours of yoga a day—but she hadn't known how short she was. The movie star looked like a little pixie curled up on the white chaise longue on one side of the master bedroom, an open script on her lap, her long blonde hair piled up on top of her head. Fiona had on a thick white terry-cloth robe, and her feet were tucked up underneath her. She looked delicately, ethereally beautiful.

"Fuck me," the actress muttered, not looking up when Chloe and Assistant Number Two entered the room. "This fucking script sucks. There's no way in fucking hell I'm going to play the cute little ingenue anymore." She mispronounced the word *ingenue* as *in-genuine*. "I'm fucking sick of it. I'm sick of wrinkling my nose and smiling, and sick of everyone thinking I'm the fucking prom queen. I want to be taken seriously!"

"Fiona," Assistant Number Two said, shooting Chloe a worried look. Suddenly, he seemed to realize that she was the Press and therefore someone they should tread lightly around. Chloe wondered why he hadn't thought of that before he and Nanette had referred to William as *it*. "This is the reporter from *Pop Art*, here to interview you."

"I'm Chloe Truman," Chloe said. She smiled uncertainly at Fiona Watson. It was surreal coming face-to-face with such a huge star.

For just a scant moment, Fiona Watson looked dismayed. But then suddenly her face transformed, lit up by her world-famous smile.

She's so beautiful, Chloe thought wistfully, as she took in the finely boned face, the perfectly straight white teeth, the clear pale skin.

"Thank you so much for coming. I'm a huge fan of *Pop Art*," Fiona said sweetly, tilting her head to one side fetchingly. "Please, sit down. Faber, get our guest a drink. What would you like, Chloe? Iced tea? Freshly squeezed juice?"

Chloe gratefully sank down on the white linen wing chair. She'd once read a gossip piece that claimed Fiona Watson always insisted that her hotel and dressing rooms be all white—white furniture, white flowers, white everything. And, actually, the bedroom was decorated in a white palette—a white upholstered headboard, white duvet, whitewashed armoire—although the walls were a pale blue and the patterned carpet was tan and gray.

"No thank you, I'm fine," Chloe said, smiling at Assistant Number Two. What had Fiona Watson said his name was? Faber? It didn't sound like a real name, and Chloe wondered if he'd made it up.

"Just let me know if you need anything," Faber said sycophantically, and closed the door behind him as he left the bedroom.

"So, I thought we could start off talking about your new film," Chloe began, nervously rifling through her briefcase for her tape recorder and pad. She checked to make sure she'd put a tape in and then turned the tape recorder on. "The name of the movie is *Lamp Light*, correct?" Fiona Watson nodded, still smiling beatifically. Chloe noticed that the actress's eyes looked a bit empty. "Would you tell me a bit about your character in the film?"

"I play Della Fox, a brilliant forensic psychiatrist working with the FBI to track a serial killer. I become concerned that one of the agents—played by Brad Ford, who's just *amazing* in the movie—might be the killer. And, of course, I'm falling in love with Brad's character, which further compli—what the hell is *that*?" Fiona suddenly snapped, her voice turning hard and shrill.

"That" was the sound of a baby crying. And not just any baby. *William*. Chloe would know his cry anywhere. She jumped to her feet and hurried out of the room, calling back over her shoulder to Fiona, "Um, sorry, excuse me, just give me one second!"

Chloe rushed toward the living room, which was down the hall from Fiona's bedroom, just past the kitchenette with its marble counters and skinny stainless-steel refrigerator. The stroller was still where Chloe had left it, but William wasn't in it. Chloe looked around anxiously. The stylists and beauticians were still lounging about the room, as was Faber, but the nanny, the boys, and—most importantly—*William* were nowhere to be seen. Where was he? Where had Katie taken him? Anxiety roiled up in Chloe, burning at her throat and mouth. She could still hear William's sobs, but as she turned around and around, she couldn't figure out where they were coming from.

"Faber, do you know where my baby is?" Chloe asked. She was trying to stay calm and not freak out, but her voice was high and strained.

"Back in the boys' bedroom," Faber said, nodding in the direction of the second hall. Chloe dashed off in the direction he'd indicated.

"Are you done with the interview already?" Faber called after her.

"No," she replied, trying to sound upbeat and professional. "Just give me one minute."

Chloe burst into the bedroom without knocking. Inside, a harassed-looking Katie was rocking a screaming William in her arms, while Quincy and Satchel were grappling over an enormous Super Soaker water gun. It wasn't until Chloe had reached for her crying baby, folding him into her arms, that she noticed his T-shirt was damp.

"What happened?" Chloe asked, cradling William against her.

"The boys were playing with their water gun," Katie said.

"It was an accident," Quincy protested.

"No, it wasn't," Satchel said.

"Was too!"

"Was not!"

Quincy lunged at Satchel, who nimbly sidestepped the attack and, as he did so, knocked over a glass of juice that had been resting on the side table. The juice splashed onto the snow-white duvet, staining it orange, and dripped down on the carpet. Satchel dove, aiming the Super Soaker at his brother, but Quincy batted the plastic gun barrel away from him—and right at Chloe.

"Ack!" Chloe yelped as a heavy stream of cold water doused her and William. William howled with fresh fury, and Chloe looked down at her now-dripping-wet baby—not to mention her own soaked cotton blouse and wool pants. William suddenly made a hacking noise and deposited a large glob of milky spit-up on Chloe's shoulder, before returning to his wailing with fresh enthusiasm.

Chloe patted William's back, made shushing noises, and kissed the downy hair on his head, but William, unmoved by these gestures of maternal soothing, continued to shriek.

"Boys!" Katie was shouting to be heard. "No!"

The boys, still tussling and still grappling over the water gun, both dove onto the floor. Chloe quickly backed up before they could hit her with a stream of water again, then turned and walked out, closing the door behind her. She heard Katie shriek and guessed that the nanny had also gotten Super Soaked.

I wonder how much Fiona pays her to watch those terrors, Chloe thought. Whatever it was, Katie earned every penny.

"Are you okay, sweetie?" she asked William, as she carried him back out to the living room of the suite. His cries grew more pitiful as he inhaled raggedly. Ignoring the annoyed looks of Faber and company, Chloe rustled around in the diaper bag, still stuffed at the bottom of the stroller, for a dry outfit. She set William down on the couch, unsnapped the wet one-piece romper he'd had on, and replaced it with a soft pair of green pants and a matching green-and-blue-striped T-shirt with a frog appliqué on the front. William stopped crying and looked up at his mother with solemn, blinking eyes, as if to say, "Please don't leave me alone with these people again."

"Ms. Watson's time is really much too valuable—" Faber began reprovingly.

"I know. I'm sorry," Chloe said. She glanced down at herself. The Super Soaker had hit her square in the stomach and her trousers. It looked as though she'd peed herself. Well. *Nothing I can do about that now,* she thought grimly, although she did clean the spit-up off her shoulder as best she could with a wet wipe.

Still cradling William in one arm, she unlatched his car seat from where it was docked to the stroller and carried both baby and seat back into Fiona Watson's room, moving quickly before

Faber could figure out what she was doing and stop her. Fiona was just where Chloe had left her, lounging prettily on the chaise. She smiled vacantly at Chloe—until her wide blue eyes fixed on the baby. And then the smile slipped from her face, and her lovely features rearranged into a scowl.

"Was that *your* baby crying?" Fiona asked, looking aggrieved.

"I'm so sorry," Chloe apologized. "So, so sorry. My son got wet from—" Then, thinking that it might be better not to implicate the star's sons, Chloe veered off in another direction. "Um, well, anyway, he seems to have calmed down now, so I'll just put him in his seat and we can continue the interview."

"I don't like hearing babies cry," Fiona said sulkily. "I find it very stressful."

Me too, Chloe thought dully. Her ears were still buzzing from William's screams. Although she would have expected a little more sympathy from Fiona, who was a fellow mom. Chloe wondered how Fiona had coped with her own sons when they were babies. Surely even the progeny of Hollywood film stars cried now and again. Then, remembering Katie, Chloe realized that Fiona had likely rarely, if ever, had to deal with her children when they were upset. There had probably always been someone standing nearby to whom she could pass off the baby.

Chloe gently settled William in his car seat and then returned to her chair. She switched on the tape recorder.

"So. Where were we? Oh, yes, we were talking about Brad Ford. So, um, I've read that there was quite a bit of chemistry between the two of you. Would you care to comment on that?" Chloe asked.

She was being delicate in how she broached this particular topic; the actual story that had been floated to the press by a disgruntled member of the crew was that Fiona and Brad had locked themselves up in Fiona's trailer for hours on end, during which time the sound of ecstatic moaning and squealing could be heard from within. Since Fiona and Brad were both famously married to other people—Fiona to Scott Wilder, a sitcom star, Brad to Jilly

Andrews, a former teen pop idol—the stories had been splashed around on the covers of the gossip magazines.

Fiona just smiled serenely. "Yes, Brad and I do have amazing chemistry, which I think really comes across in the film. Of course, there wasn't a bit of truth to those silly rumors, but that always happens. I guess it's more exciting to believe that two costars are sleeping together than the truth, which is that they're just very close, platonic friends, like Brad and me." She followed an eye roll with her trademark America's Sweetheart grin. It was an effective combination.

"What's your next project?" Chloe pressed on.

"I'm about to start work on—" But before Fiona could finish, William, already tired of his car seat, began to mewl unhappily. He wasn't particularly loud about it—especially considering that for such a small baby, he had an extraordinary capacity for volume— but even so, the smile on Fiona's face vanished and was replaced by a thunderous scowl. Chloe cringed and lunged toward her baby.

"Sorry, I'm so sorry," she muttered to Fiona. Chloe moved William's seat closer to her chair and rocked it back and forth, which lulled William into a dazed stupor. As soon as Chloe stopped rocking, William's eyes snapped open. Before he could start crying again, Chloe quickly began rocking him again. Fiona stared at her, expressions of distaste and disbelief mingled on her lovely face. Chloe colored. This was not going well.

"Um. So. You were saying? About your next project?" Chloe said.

"What's that on your shirt?" Fiona asked, pointing at Chloe.

Chloe looked down and saw that her milk—which apparently began flowing in response to William's cries—had begun leaking. Two large wet circles were bleeding onto the only dry part of her already soggy blue oxford shirt. How could she have forgotten to stick in her breast pads? *How?* When she glanced back up at Fiona Watson, she saw that the actress had turned paper white.

"Is that … is that … *breast milk?*" Fiona whispered.

"Yes, I'm sorry. It happens sometimes when he cries."

"Eww! That's disgusting!" Fiona said, with her famous nose wrinkle.

"Well, it's just breast milk," Chloe said apologetically, wishing desperately that the conversation could get off the topic of her lactation.

"You have to leave." Fiona pointed a thin finger at the door.

"What?"

"I can't have *that*"—Fiona made a vague gesture in the general direction of Chloe's breasts—"near me." She looked revolted, as though she might start vomiting at any minute.

"Can we just get through a few more questions?" Chloe asked. She couldn't leave now. She hadn't gotten nearly enough material for her story. Maia would never again entrust her with a big story. "I'll change my shirt if it makes you more comfortable."

"I can not have someone doing…doing…*that* near me!" Fiona was now so upset, her voice cracked.

"But…but…," Chloe stuttered. She felt like she'd been struck dumb with mortification. And then, even worse, she let out a small gulp of nervous laughter. It was just so ridiculous—freaking out about *breast milk*. It wasn't like she had plutonium leaking out of her breasts.

Fiona gasped, and two bright spots of red appeared on her cheeks. "How dare you laugh at me," she hissed.

"I wasn't laughing at you," Chloe said immediately. "I'm sorry, it was just a reflex, and—"

But Fiona didn't let her finish. "Get out!" the actress shrieked. She smacked her hand against the wall with a loud thud. William started at the noise and began to cry, and Chloe could feel her milk-swollen breasts respond again with a warm prickle.

"What's going on in here?" Faber and Nanette had appeared instantly, standing side by side at the door, wearing identical expressions of concern.

"Get her out of here! Now!" Fiona screeched. Her blue eyes bugged out and her lips were stretched back, toadlike. Suddenly,

she didn't look beautiful at all—in fact, she looked slightly de-
ranged.

"Nanette, call security," Faber said authoritatively. He
stepped forward to take Chloe's arm. William began to cry even
louder.

"No, it's okay. I'll go," Chloe said. Faber's grip on her arm was
so tight, it was starting to hurt.

"Make her take that horrible baby with her too!" Fiona
screeched, trying to make herself heard over William's screams,
which was no small feat.

"Like I'd leave him here," Chloe muttered. Hot, angry tears
burned in her eyes as she leaned down and picked up William in
his car seat. Then, with as much dignity as she could muster, she
marched out of the room.

Later that afternoon, after Chloe got William bathed, fed, and
tucked into his crib, she poured herself a glass of wine and collapsed on the sofa. She'd never been so tired in her life. Of course,
William had slept like an angel the entire way back home, which
Chloe supposed was a good thing, but she couldn't help feeling a
tad resentful.

Sure, now he sleeps, she thought.

Chloe had assumed that after she had William, going back to
work wouldn't be that hard. She already worked from home and
had a career that allowed her to keep flexible hours. Chloe had
figured that it would just be a matter of being disciplined about
sitting down at her computer every afternoon when William
drifted off to sleep. Instead, on her first postpartum work assignment, she'd manage to humiliate herself in front of one of
Hollywood's biggest stars and entourage before being escorted
out of the Breakers by hotel security. And while Chloe had tried
to explain that she hadn't done anything wrong, that the actress
had a bizarre phobia of breast milk, security hadn't been won over
by this argument. If anything, they'd hustled her out that much
faster.

And, typical me, I let them, rather than standing up for myself, Chloe thought bitterly.

Chloe now rested her bare feet on the edge of the coffee table. As she did so, she noticed that the glass top of the table was smudged. In her former, premommy days, Chloe would have leapt up for the Windex, but right now she was just too freaking tired to move. The smudge would have to stay for the time being.

Chloe reached into her pocket and withdrew a tube of lipstick. Her stomach pitched guiltily as she stared down at it. On her way home from the interview, Chloe had stopped at Publix to purchase the wine. While she was in the grocery store, she had—on impulse—pocketed the lipstick. It was a vampy red, a shade she'd never have the nerve to wear, not that she planned to. She would have tossed it in the Goodwill collection box on her way home, but William got fussy at the store and Chloe thought she'd better not stop.

But why had she done it? Why was she stealing again? She'd been doing so well—she hadn't even had the impulse to shoplift anything since the day she had taken the cherry shoes. And then, out of the blue, the urge had hit her. *Is it stress-related?* she wondered.

Or maybe, she thought with a dull wave of self-loathing, *I'm just a really terrible person. Other women are able to keep it together, and juggle babies and marriages and husbands, without screwing up their jobs or going on a crime spree. How do they do it? And why can't I?*

Then Chloe remembered Juliet's offer to give her some pointers on balancing work with motherhood. Chloe had never brought up the subject to Juliet again, but now, she knew, it was time. She needed help.

She finished her glass of wine and picked up the phone and dialed information. A moment later, she was being connected to the law firm of Little & Frost.

"May I speak to Juliet Cole, please? This is Chloe Truman."

"Hello, Juliet Cole." Juliet's voice was clipped. Chloe, realizing too late that she was catching Juliet at a busy time, suddenly wished she hadn't called.

"Hi, Juliet, it's Chloe."

"Hey, Chloe, what's up?" Juliet asked. She sounded distracted, her voice edged with tension, and Chloe almost lost her nerve. But then she looked at the lipstick, standing on end on the coffee table, and pushed ahead.

"I need some help," Chloe admitted.

Juliet was quiet while Chloe recounted the aborted interview with Fiona Watson.

"Jesus Christ. She freaked out over a little breast milk?" Juliet said.

"She acted like it was toxic. Like it was poison, instead of milk."

"So what do you need my help with? I don't think you have a cause of action against the hotel, unless the guards hurt you when they escorted you out. And even then—"

"Oh, no, I don't want to sue anyone. That's not why I called." Chloe hesitated, but then, feeling emboldened by the wine, she continued. "I need to learn how to handle situations like that. Working and being a mom and being bullied by people. I know you're busy, and I know this sort of thing probably comes easy to you, and I know it's a huge imposition, and I'm so sorry for that, but please—I just need a few pointers."

"Well, first of all, you don't put up with shit like that. I don't care if the woman is a big star, you shouldn't let anyone treat you like that," Juliet said.

"But how?"

"You have to be more assertive. Stop saying everything as though it's a question. Stop apologizing for taking up space."

"Do I do that?"

"Constantly."

"Oh, sorry—oops! I did it again, didn't I? Sorry," Chloe said. She shook her head and clapped a hand against her forehead. "I can't seem to stop."

"And that's just the beginning. Look, I'll tell you what—are you free for lunch tomorrow?"

"Yes," Chloe said.

"Let's meet at the Dolphin Street Café. I'll give you some tips, and we'll figure out how to get back at that Fiona chick."

"Really?" Chloe asked. She felt such a rush of relief that her voice cracked.

"Yes, really. I'll see you tomorrow," Juliet said.

And despite everything that had happened that day, when Chloe hung up the phone, she felt better than she had in a long time. Or at least she did right up until her gaze fell on the lipstick again, and a fresh wave of shame rolled over her.

thirteen

Grace

*S*he'd lost eleven pounds!

Grace hugged her arms around herself and did a little jig of happiness right there on the scale. Thank God for her Miracle Diet Tea! It really worked! Which made it all worthwhile: the headaches, the dizziness and, yes, okay, the occasional feeling that her heart was racing so fast it was going to explode. Really. She could handle a headache and the occasional discomfort if it meant that she might finally be thin.

"Mom." Molly was standing at the bathroom door. She looked at her mother curiously. "What are you doing?"

"I'm just weighing myself."

"Oh, let me," Molly said.

Grace stepped off the scale, and Molly stepped on.

"Fifty-two pounds," Grace announced.

Molly frowned. "That seems like an awful lot."

"Don't be silly. You're the perfect weight."

But Molly smoothed her hands down over her bottom—a gesture, Grace recognized with a twinge of discomfort, that she herself often made, when checking to see if her ass fat was disappearing—and announced, "I'm fat."

Grace stared at her oldest daughter. "You are *not* fat."

"I have a big butt," Molly insisted. "And my stomach sticks out."

"It does not!" Grace protested. Molly was only five. Surely, she was too young to be worrying about this.

"Mm-hmm. Hannah is too. She's even fatter than me. I was just telling her that. That's why you and Dad always call her Chugs."

Grace gaped at her daughter.

"Hannah is not fat! And Daddy and I call her Chugs as a *nickname*, as an *endearment*. The same way we call you Monkey. We don't think you really look like a monkey; it's just because you were always getting into everything when you were a baby and first starting to crawl," Grace explained. She sat down on the edge of the tub and took her daughter by the shoulders. "Molly. Sweetheart. You are not fat. You're perfect just as you are. So is Hannah."

"But Hannah's stomach sticks out even more than mine."

"That's because she's a little girl. All little girls have tummies that stick out."

"Not Emma and Izzy. They're skinny."

Just like their mother, Grace thought. Juliet was an ectomorph, and her twin daughters clearly took after her.

Molly seemed to be reading her thoughts. "When I grow up, will I have a big butt like you? I hope not. But I wouldn't mind having big boobs, although maybe not as big as yours."

"You think my butt looks big?" Grace asked anxiously. She stood up and faced away from the bathroom mirror, craning her neck around to get a look at her bottom. "You think I look fat?"

"A little," Molly said with the cruel honesty of a five-year-old. "But don't worry. Mommies should be fat. It makes them better at cuddling. I bet Emma and Izzy's mom isn't any good at cuddling."

And then Molly skipped out of the bathroom, while Grace continued to peer at her reflection, shifting from side to side to see just how enormous her ass really was.

"Have you slept with him yet?" Juliet asked Anna.

Anna shook her head. "No."

"Why not?" Grace asked.

"For one thing, I don't remember *how* to have sex," Anna said.

"Me neither," Chloe said gloomily.

Juliet, Anna, Chloe, and Grace were at the fountain park on Ocean View Drive, sitting at a picnic table shaded by a hardwood arbor. They sipped the iced coffee Anna had picked up for everyone at Dunkin' Donuts and watched their children streak around through the large jets of water shooting out of the ground. Molly—who, as eldest, considered herself in charge of the others—was trying to boss around Charlie and Hannah, who mostly just ignored her. The twins were setting beach balls on the water jets when they got low and then screeching with laughter when the water suddenly shot back up, rocketing the balls into the air. The two babies, William and Natalie, napped in their infant car seats on the shaded ground by the table.

"You're not supposed to have sex," Grace told Chloe. "In fact, it's our obligation as your sisters-in-arms to tell you the truth about postpartum sex: Don't do it."

Chloe laughed.

"I'm serious," Grace continued. She began ticking off the reasons on her fingers. "One, you're exhausted; two, you're sore; and three, you're leaking milk. You shouldn't even think about it until William is three months old. And even then I don't advise it. Better to put it off indefinitely."

"My doctor said six weeks," Chloe said.

"Well, he lied. Trust me. No one but another mother is going to tell you the truth about these things. Forget sex, and, oh, you're probably going to hate your husband for a while," Grace continued.

"What?" Chloe looked startled. "I don't hate James."

"Sure, you do," Grace said cheerfully.

"No, I don't."

"All new mothers hate their partners in the short term. How can you not? You're lucky to get in a shower, and they're off every morning, wearing real clothes and going out to nice lunches. The bastards," Grace added.

"I didn't hate Patrick," Juliet said.

"Yes, well, you were the one with the nice clothes and lunches out. He was the one stuck home with a screaming baby—make that two screaming babies. He probably hated you."

"I hated Brad." Anna shrugged. "Hell, who could blame me? And as for sex, I had five stitches with Charlie." At this, they all shuddered. "Even if Brad and I hadn't split up, I wouldn't have wanted him anywhere near that."

They all looked at Juliet.

"Jesus Christ. You know I hate talking about personal crap. And I'm certainly not going to tell you about my sex life," she said, exasperated.

"Come on, don't be like that," Grace said, nudging Juliet under the table with one sandaled foot. "You don't have to share your feelings, heaven forbid. Just tell us if your sex drive went down."

Juliet rolled her eyes. "Well, no," she conceded. "It really didn't. But I didn't breast-feed. And I did have a C-section, after all, so there weren't any stitches to worry about. At least, not at any access points."

The other women laughed at this.

"Three months? Really?" Chloe said, her brow puckering. "I don't know if James can make it that long. I was on pelvic rest for the last three months of my pregnancy. It's been a long time."

"Tell him to suck it up and be a man," Grace advised her. "Besides, that's what the shower's there for."

"Nice," Juliet commented.

"But you have no excuse," Grace said, turning on Anna. "So why haven't you slept with Noah yet?"

"We haven't really had the opportunity. We've gone out to dinner a few times, but I've always had to go home to Charlie afterward." Anna shrugged again. "Noah came over to our house to watch movies one night, but I felt weird doing anything there, with Charlie in the next room. I swear, it's like being in high school again, what with the out-of-control hormones and zero privacy," Anna continued.

"You could leave Charlie with your mom overnight and stay at a hotel," Grace suggested.

"Actually, tonight—" Anna began, but then she blushed and stopped.

"What?" Grace asked. "Oh! You mean...tonight is the big night?"

Anna nodded, and flushed an even darker red. "I wasn't going to say anything."

"Excellent," Grace said with relish. "Take notes. I'm living vicariously through you, and I want all of the details."

Anna looked at Grace, her eyebrows arched.

"My no-personal-details rule is looking better and better, isn't it?" Juliet said.

"Yes, it is," Anna said.

"Give us something. Are you going to a hotel?" Grace asked.

"No. I'm staying over at Noah's house," Anna said. "And to be honest, I'm nervous. I wasn't even sure I'd remember how to use my diaphragm, so I practiced putting it in and taking it out last night."

"Why don't you just use a condom? You can practice the Kiss and Roll technique we learned at the MCT meeting," Juliet suggested.

"That might be a little much for the first time, don't you think?" Anna said. "I always thought it was better to save the inventive stuff for when things were getting routine."

"That's true. You don't want to set the bar too high," Juliet said.

Suddenly there was a loud shriek, different from the background noise of shouts and squeals as the children darted in and out of the fountains. It was a cry of unhappiness, of pain, the sort of cry that caused every parent in the park to immediately look up sharply, eyes searching to account for their own child.

"Mom! Mom! Hannah fell!" It was Molly, running toward her mother. Grace looked for Hannah—who had fallen on the water-slicked ground and was now sobbing and clutching at her elbow—and quickly stood up. Too quickly. Suddenly, a horrifying dizziness washed over Grace, and her vision blurred and dissolved into tiny specks of light. She grabbed the edge of the picnic table to steady herself, and even then, she wasn't sure that she'd keep her balance. Her legs felt wobbly, and she wondered distantly if she was about to fall.

"Grace?" Anna's voice—sharp, nervous—echoed near her.

"Are you okay?" This time it was Chloe, sounding anxious.

Grace blinked, and her vision came back, although it was blurred at the edges.

"I'll get Hannah," Juliet said, swinging her long legs over the built-in bench and striding off toward the fountains, where the little girl was still sitting and crying.

"Sit down, right here." It was Anna again, now standing next to Grace—*How had she moved so quickly?* Grace wondered—taking her hand and guiding her down onto the bench. "Lean over and put your head between your knees."

"What does that do?" Chloe asked.

"Isn't that what you're supposed to do with someone who's about to pass out? Actually, now I'm not so sure. Grace, honey, maybe you should sit back up," Anna said.

"Do you feel sick?" Chloe asked.

"No. Well, a little, I guess. Just give me a minute. Hannah?" Grace's voice sounded weak and far away to her own ears. And for a minute she thought she might be sick; her mouth tasted unpleasantly metallic.

"She's fine. Juliet has her, and she's smiling now. In fact, there she goes; she's running off to play with the other girls. The crisis has passed," Anna said.

Grace opened her eyes. Even with her sunglasses on, the sun seemed unbearably bright. She squinted until her eyes focused and she could ascertain that her two older daughters were indeed fine. Hannah and Molly had gone back to running around the jets of water, laughing and shrieking as they played. She looked for Nat, who was still dozing contentedly in her car seat.

Juliet joined the others and fixed Grace with a penetrating look. "What was that all about?"

"I'm fine. I just felt light-headed for a minute," Grace said blearily.

"You don't look fine," Juliet said.

"You said you've been having a lot of headaches lately too," Anna said, frowning.

"Just a few," Grace said.

"I think you should see a doctor about this. You shouldn't let it go," Anna said.

"I bet it's that diet you're on," Juliet said. "You've hardly been eating anything lately."

"I know! Have you noticed how much weight I've lost?" Grace asked proudly. "Eleven pounds in a month! I can almost get into my skinny jeans, and I haven't worn those since 1994, right after I had mono."

"That doesn't sound healthy," Chloe said, frowning. "I thought you were only supposed to lose one pound a week."

"It's *not* healthy," Juliet said.

"Grace, why don't I drive you and the girls home?" Anna suggested. "You can pick up your minivan later when you're feeling better."

"They won't all fit in your wagon. Some of you will have to go with me," Juliet said.

"It's okay. Really, I'm fine. And I can drive," Grace protested.

"I know. Do it for my sake, so I don't worry," Anna suggested.

"It's not a bad idea," Chloe chimed in. "What if you get dizzy again while you're driving?"

"Well...I really think you guys are making too big a deal out of this," Grace said, hesitating. The truth was, she had been feeling dizzy a lot lately. More than she'd told anyone, even Louis. *Especially* Louis.

"Forget it, Grace. There's not a chance in hell we're letting you drive yourself home," Juliet said.

"Bossy pants," Grace said, borrowing her daughters' favorite insult.

"Bossy I can live with. You plowing your minivan into

oncoming traffic with your three children strapped in the back, I can't," Juliet said with a shrug.

The image caused Grace's mouth to go dry with fear. "You really don't mind dropping us off?"

"Not at all," Anna assured her. "Here, give me your keys. I'll go move the girls' car seats over. Who's going with me, and who's going with Juliet?"

Later that afternoon, while Hannah and Natalie were napping, and Molly was in her room playing, and Louis was outside mowing the grass, Grace made herself a cup of Miracle Diet Tea and sat down at the kitchen table to work on the upcoming fundraiser MCT was holding for the Starfish House.

Plans for the charity luncheon were coming along. Saks had agreed to host the group and was even putting on a fashion show and offering free makeovers. They'd put Grace in touch with a caterer who had worked events for Saks before, and she'd picked a menu of seared beef tenderloin on a bed of greens for the main course and gourmet chocolate cupcakes for dessert. Jana Mallin and Val Metcalf were working on getting local businesses to make contributions in return for ad space in the program. If they sold fifty tickets, at one hundred dollars apiece, they'd make a profit of—Grace punched numbers into her calculator—at least $3,750 to go toward the new furniture for the common room at the Starfish House.

Excellent, she thought with satisfaction. *And we'll make even more than that if we can drum up interest with the local businesses. I'll have to send an e-mail to Jana to see if she's had any luck.*

Grace took a sip of her tea and made a face. She'd been so absorbed in her paperwork, it had gone cold.

I'll just nuke it for a minute, Grace decided. With the mug in hand, she stood up, turning toward the microwave.

But before she could take a single step, the awful dizziness returned. It came on so quickly and forcefully, and overtook her so suddenly, that all Grace could do was wait helplessly for it to pass. She watched, as though from a distance, as the mug dropped from her hands.

It's going to break, she thought fuzzily, watching the ceramic mug fall in what seemed like slow motion. It was her favorite mug. Molly had painted it at a pottery store and given it to Grace for Mother's Day last year. It was pink and purple—Molly's signature colors—and there was a kitten with a bubbly head and big triangular ears painted on one side.

Black spots speckled Grace's vision, and a low thrum filled her ears.

I'd better get Louis, she thought. *Or maybe I should just sit down for a minute, until the dizziness passes....*

And then everything went black and still and quiet. Grace didn't even hear the mug when it finally hit the floor and shattered into pieces.

fourteen

Juliet

"We're home," Juliet called out, as she came in through the back door into the kitchen. It smelled like vinegar and lemon; apparently Patrick had been cleaning in their absence.

"We're home! We're home!" the twins echoed, as they kicked off their shoes.

"Hey! How was the fountain park?" Patrick asked, coming out from the office. The twins streaked by him, running upstairs to change out of their wet bathing suits, sending him careening into the counter. "Whoa! What's the hurry, shorties?"

"Mom said we could watch *The Little Mermaid*," Emma yelled back over her shoulder.

"If…?" Juliet called out.

"If-we're-good-and-promise-not-to-whine-when-it's-time-to-go-to-bed," Izzy parroted back.

Juliet and Patrick exchanged a smile—a rare occurrence, these days—both charmed by their silly, sweet girls.

"Just remember that when it's lights-out time," Juliet said.

The twins scampered up the stairs, giggling as they went.

"I have to go in to the office for a little while," Juliet said, and braced herself for the inevitable fight this announcement would cause.

But Patrick surprised her.

"Fine. What time will you be home?" he asked. His voice was polite, almost cool, but not argumentative. Which was a definite improvement.

"Not late. I'll be home for dinner," Juliet said. And then, to strike a conciliatory note, she added, "Do you want to go out? We could go to Cosmo's."

The twins adored Cosmo's, an Italian restaurant that served thick wedges of buttery garlic bread and mountains of meatball-topped spaghetti.

Patrick hesitated, then nodded. His face was inscrutable, his feelings shuttered away from Juliet's view.

"All right," he said.

And with this détente reached, Juliet left.

Juliet was surprised to find the office deserted. Even Neil was gone, which had to be a first. He was always there, bent studiously over his desk, working away in an office lit only by the dim light of a fluorescent lamp. It was refreshing to actually be completely and totally alone for once, free of the distractions of voices, coughs, and ringing phones.

Juliet sat down behind her desk, switched on her computer, and got to work. Richard had written a memo on the Patterson case that Alex—to Richard's barely concealed fury—had asked Juliet to review and change where necessary. And then she had to write a status memo on the dead-baby case. A settlement offer had come in from the defense. It was low—too low, Juliet thought—but still, it had to be considered.

Absorbed in these projects, Juliet quickly lost track of how long she'd been there. Between the airless quality of the office and the tinted windows that effectively masked the color of the sky—it always looked dark and gray out, no matter the weather or time of day—she often felt suspended in purgatory while she worked.

"Juliet."

Juliet started, dropping her pen, and looked up to see Alex standing at the door of her office. He was dressed casually, a white sweater draping over the muscular curve of his shoulders and jeans skimming his hips in a way that made Juliet very aware of his physicality. A jolt of excitement shot through her, warming as it rushed outward from her stomach.

Alex crooked his eyebrows in a question, and for a brief, awful moment, Juliet wondered if he knew what she'd been thinking.

Oh, God. Please don't let him have seen me looking him up and down, she thought, averting her eyes quickly.

But then Alex said, "What are you doing here so late on a Saturday?"

"Is it late?" Juliet checked her watch. Five o'clock. How had she been there for four hours and not noticed the time passing?

"Let's go grab a drink," Alex said. He tilted his head to one side casually.

Juliet hesitated. They'd gone out for drinks before, but always with the whole team, usually to celebrate a big win. Never alone. And never on a Saturday night.

"Come on," Alex said. "You've worked enough for one day."

Maybe it was the fact that Alex wasn't asking. Or maybe it was simple curiosity. Or maybe it had something to do with the excitement that skittered through her stomach whenever Alex's eyes rested on her.

"Okay," Juliet said. She stood, remembering only then, as she leaned down to pick up her briefcase, about her dinner plans with her family. *Shit.* She glanced up at Alex, who was leaning against the doorway, his pale eyes alert. "Just give me one minute. I'll meet you down by the elevators."

Alex nodded and left. Juliet picked up her desk phone—and then put it right back down again. Instead, she pulled out her cell phone and typed in a text message to Patrick:

WRK CRISIS. RUNNING LT.

And then, on legs shaking with nerves, Juliet walked out of her office, switching off the overhead light as she left.

———

The Sands was a newish hotel on the beach. It had been built in a modern style—all glass and chrome on the exterior, and slate-gray floors, Lucite chandeliers, and dark wenge wood accents on the interior. The hotel bar was quiet and spare, with sleek black leather chairs set around round metal tables and dimmed lights. Soft jazz music played in the background.

Alex and Juliet sat at a corner table, away from the other patrons, and ordered vodka tonics from the waiter. He placed the drinks and a white dish heaped with shelled pistachios in front of them before discreetly withdrawing.

Juliet held her glass with both hands and waited for Alex to say something. But he'd been unnervingly quiet since they'd arrived. She finally broke the silence.

"Are you still covering those depositions in the Patterson case on Monday?" she asked. She stirred her drink with a plastic swizzle stick, mostly to give her hands something to do.

Alex took a sip of his drink and then shook it gently, so that the ice cubes tinkled softly, before he finally spoke. "If I've learned one thing over the years, it's this: It never pays to tiptoe around an issue. If you want something from someone, you should just ask for it, straight out. Some people find that a bit"—he waved his hand—"strident, I suppose. But in my experience, being straightforward saves a lot of time and avoids misunderstanding."

What the hell is he talking about? Juliet wondered. But out loud she said, "I agree."

"Do you? That's good," Alex said. And then suddenly he leaned forward and lightly grasped Juliet's hand. "Because there's something I want from you."

Juliet looked down at the table, watching as Alex turned her hand over in his and trailed his fingers over the inside of her wrist. Goose bumps sprang up on her arm, and she shivered.

"I very much want you to go upstairs with me," Alex continued, his voice low. "But I don't want you to feel obligated. Whether you say yes or no, this won't affect our working relationship or your future at the firm."

For a moment, Juliet couldn't move. Or breathe. Or think. All she could focus on was the gentle pressure of his hand against hers, as the meaning of his words sank in.

He's asking me to sleep with him, she thought. *Alex is asking me to sleep with him. Is this really happening?*

When she looked up at Alex, she saw that he was gazing at her intently. For a moment she felt pinioned by his pale eyes.

"What do you say?" Alex asked.

Juliet hadn't been aware that she was holding her breath until she spoke.

"Yes," she said.

Juliet finished her drink, trying to steady her shaking hands, while Alex went to get a room. As she sat, the cold warmth of the vodka sliding down her throat, she felt oddly disembodied, as though she were on the outside of herself, watching the evening unfold with a detached interest.

What am I doing? she suddenly thought, as a sharp jolt of fear hit her, grounding her back in reality. But then Alex was suddenly there, reaching out for her hand, guiding her up and out of her seat, and the moment of indecision was lost.

He kissed her for the first time in the elevator, as soon as the doors slid shut. Alex reached for her, cupping one hand behind her neck and pulling her toward him, pressing his mouth onto hers. There was nothing remotely soft or romantic about the kiss; it was all heat and need.

When the elevator stopped and the doors slid open, they broke apart. Juliet felt almost dizzy and unsteady on her legs. But Alex's hand was firm on hers as he half-led, half-pulled her down the hall.

The hotel room was expensively spare—the furniture was all dark wood and low to the ground, and an enormous round paper lantern hung from the ceiling, suffusing the space with a soft light. The platform bed was dressed in a stark white duvet, and a gray cashmere blanket was thrown casually over one end.

Things happened quickly. Alex pulled Juliet's striped boatneck shirt up and off and reached down to cup her breasts. Her nipples hardened at his touch and jutted out through the thin white nylon of her bra. Alex leaned forward and kissed them through the fabric, then reached behind Juliet to unhook her bra. Juliet, still standing, heard herself gasp as heat flooded down and out through her limbs. His excitement fueled her own, and she tugged at his sweater, wanting it off, wanting to feel the warmth of his skin pressing against hers. Alex helped her pull off his sweater, and then pulled her down toward the bed, rearing up over her as he slid his hand down over her bare stomach, toward the zipper of her jeans. Juliet sucked in her breath and closed her eyes.

An electronic rendition of Beethoven's *Fifth Symphony* rang out. Juliet's eyes popped open.

"My phone," she said.

"Ignore it," Alex murmured. He lowered his head again, trailing kisses down over her breasts and stomach, his hand reaching down to unbutton and unzip her jeans.

Juliet gasped as his hand slid down under the waistband of her panties, and she tried to ignore the still-ringing phone. Finally, it stopped. And then, almost immediately, it began to ring again.

"Wait," she said to Alex, her breath coming in quick little puffs. "I have to check that. It might be important."

Alex rolled onto his back, lacing his hands behind his head, and watched Juliet as she scrambled off the bed, trying to get her briefcase open. She grabbed the cell phone and flipped it open, just as it stopped ringing. The screen read: CALL MISSED, 5:45 P.M. PATRICK.

Juliet stared down at the phone. It let out a beep, and then the message icon began to blink.

Patrick.

Patrick—who was home with the twins.

Oh, God, the twins. Home.

What the hell am I doing? Juliet wondered. *I'm in a hotel, about to fuck my boss, while my family is home, waiting for me to go out to dinner with them. How did this happen? How did I let this happen?*

She shivered, this time from fear. No, it was more than fear: It was revulsion. Juliet wrapped her arms around herself, all too aware of her nakedness.

"I have to go," she said, her voice wooden.

"Now?"

Juliet turned to look at Alex, who was now sitting up on the bed, staring at her incredulously. He looked incredibly sexy, his muscular bare chest covered with a swirling pattern of reddish-blond hair. Shirtless was a good look for him, Juliet thought, and she felt such a wave of wanting that she hesitated.

Alex, sensing her equivocation, got up and moved toward her, ready to pull her back onto the bed with him.

But Juliet took a deep, steadying breath and stepped back out of his reach.

"I'm sorry," she said, turning to retrieve her shirt from the floor. "I have to go."

Juliet sat in her car in the driveway for a few minutes, examining her face in the rearview mirror. The skin on her neck was red, rubbed raw by Alex's stubble.

Maybe Patrick won't notice it, she thought. *And if he does, I'll just tell him I must have gotten some sun today at the fountain park.*

Juliet closed her eyes briefly, hating that she had to sit here thinking up cover lies, hating herself for sinking so low. It took several long moments for her to work up the nerve to go inside. It was only when she was halfway down the front walk that she realized the minivan wasn't in the driveway.

Did Patrick park in the garage? she wondered. Odd. He didn't usually.

"Who's ready for spaghetti and meatballs?" Juliet called when she walked in the door. Her voice sounded oddly shaky to her, and she took a minute to draw in a deep breath and steady herself.

Just keep it together, she thought.

But then it occurred to her that the house was unnaturally quiet. She couldn't hear the girls laughing, or the blare of the television, or Patrick's heavy footsteps upstairs. "Patrick? Emma, Izzy?"

Juliet kicked off her shoes and walked from room to room, but her family wasn't there. The girls weren't in their bedroom or playing in the den; Patrick wasn't at the computer, browsing through the online news. She frowned. Did they go to the restaurant without her? If so, why wouldn't Patrick have mentioned that in his voice-mail message? All he'd said was to call him back. But when she'd tried to reach him on his cell phone, it had gone straight to voice mail.

Juliet padded into the kitchen. There, on the counter, next to a neatly stacked pile of mail, was the latest issue of *Mothering* magazine. And next to it was a note written on one of her yellow, lined legal pads, in Patrick's cramped scrawl:

I took the girls to my parents' house. I'll call you later. Patrick.

Juliet stared at the note. What the hell was going on? Patrick's parents lived all the way down in Boca. Patrick did occasionally take the twins down there for weekends—Juliet was usually too busy with work to go with them, not that she minded missing out on quality time with her in-laws—but it was always something he made plans to do in advance. He'd never just upped and driven down there without even telling her.

Something's wrong, Juliet knew immediately. Patrick's mother, Trish, had breast cancer a few years back. Was she sick again? Or was it his father, Sean, who knocked back three martinis every night and then insisted he was sober enough to drive everyone to dinner?

Juliet immediately reached for the phone and dialed her in-laws' house.

Trish answered. "Hello."

"Hi, Trish, it's Juliet."

There was a weird pause. "Oh . . . hello, Juliet," Trish said. Her voice sounded strange.

Juliet pressed her lips together in annoyance. She and Trish had never gotten along. Trish disapproved of Juliet working while Patrick stayed home and never let the opportunity pass to comment on it. In fact, Trish never missed the opportunity to talk, period. The woman was verbally incontinent.

"I got a note from Patrick saying he and the twins were headed down there. Is everything okay?"

Another pause. "Yes, they just got here. I'll, uh, let you talk to Patrick."

Juliet frowned. What the hell was going on? Surely, if Trish or Sean were sick, Trish would have told her.

"Hey," Patrick said, taking the phone. He sounded odd, like he was upset but trying to contain it.

"Patrick, what's going on? Is everything okay?" Juliet asked. Her concern made her sound more irritated than she felt.

"No. Everything is not okay," Patrick said flatly.

"What's happening? Why did you take the girls down there? When are you coming home?"

Patrick sighed deeply. "I'm not coming back," he said. "At least not right away."

Juliet felt an almost electrical shock of fear.

"What do you mean you're not coming back? What are you talking about?"

"We need to take a break, Juliet. We've needed that for a long time. And I need to...well, to decide. Where I want to go from here."

Oh, God, Juliet thought, with a great, nauseating lurch. *He knows about Alex. He must have found out somehow.*

But how? How had he found out? It was a two-hour drive down to Boca. If Patrick and the twins were already there, they had to have left home while Juliet was still at the office, before she'd left to go to the Sands with Alex, long before she'd almost—

Almost. That was the key word, Juliet thought. She'd *almost* cheated. But she'd stopped it in time. Well. Almost in time.

"Patrick, I don't know what's going on, but you can't just leave like this," Juliet said, trying to keep her voice steady.

"Yes," he said. "I can."

Juliet blinked. He sounded so angry. What was going on? She understood what Patrick was saying, but it didn't seem real. Surely at any minute the twins would come tumbling through the door, shrieking with delight to see her, and Patrick would be there, his lips curled up in a familiar grin, and everything would go back to normal. A dinner out, bath time, a DVD rental. Just another normal Saturday night.

Juliet suddenly wanted that normalcy with such a fierce longing, she had to grip the edge of the counter for support.

But the door didn't open. Instead, the house stood silently around her, until it seemed that the quiet would swallow Juliet whole. She noticed that her hands were shaking.

"But...what about the twins? What did you tell them?" Juliet asked.

"Nothing. At least, nothing yet. Just that we were going to surprise Gran and Pops."

"Look, I'm coming down there. We obviously have to talk," Juliet said decisively. She grabbed her keys off the counter.

"Please, don't. I know we'll need to talk—eventually. And that you'll of course want to see the twins. I wouldn't keep them from you, or you from them. But I'd appreciate it if you could give me a few days before I see you. I need to think things through," Patrick said.

"Think things through?" Juliet whispered. What was he thinking through? Had he somehow sensed her infidelity? Should she tell him that she didn't cheat? That although she'd walked right up to the edge, she'd stopped and turned back before it was too late? "Look, there's something I think you should know—" Juliet began.

"You're not going to tell me that you didn't say those things," Patrick said, his voice suddenly cold.

Juliet frowned, confused. "What things? What are you talking about?"

"The article?"

"What article?"

"The magazine is right there on the counter. The one we were photographed for," Patrick said.

Juliet's eyes fell on the copy of *Mothering* magazine. The

headlines of the articles stood out in white print against the aqua-blue cover, which featured the picture of a beaming pregnant actress, sitting with her legs crossed in a yogalike position: ARE PTAS A THING OF THE PAST? GO FROM MATRONLY TO HOT MAMA! CAN ANY WOMAN REALLY HAVE IT ALL?

She stared at the magazine for a few minutes, wondering why it had been sent to her—she wasn't a subscriber. Then it clicked. Oh, right! Chloe's article. Is that what Patrick was talking about? But wait. It still didn't make any sense, it didn't make any sense at all.

"You left because of an article?" Juliet asked.

"You haven't seen it yet?"

"No," Juliet said. She flipped through the magazine, until she found Chloe's byline under an article entitled MOMMY TRACKED. At first, all Juliet saw was the photo accompanying the article. It was one of the pictures from the photo shoot. In it, the twins were in the basket of the shopping cart, Izzy sitting and Emma standing at the end, on the verge of jumping out. Patrick was behind the cart, pushing it, grinning and looking adorably rumpled. Juliet was in front of the cart, one hand behind her, as though she were pulling it after her. In the photo, she was looking fixedly ahead of her, unsmiling and cold. She looked—well, God, she looked horrible. And so distant from the rest of her family. Juliet dropped the magazine back on the counter, recoiling from it.

But still. Patrick wouldn't have walked out because she looked lousy in a picture. Juliet leaned forward and skimmed the first few sentences of the article. There didn't seem to be anything particularly damning about it.

"Patrick. Look. I have no idea what's going on. And if you want to visit your parents for a few days, that is, of course, your choice. But I don't understand why you're making this all sound so . . . dire. You act like you're leaving this marriage." Juliet let out a frustrated noise, somewhere between a laugh and a sigh.

There was a pregnant pause. "Yes. That's exactly what I'm considering."

"But that's insane! Nobody leaves their marriage over a magazine article!"

"It isn't just the article. I've been unhappy for a really long time. I've tried talking to you about it, but you haven't been receptive. And then when I read that article, when I saw what you really think of me, it just clarified the situation for me." Patrick sighed heavily. "Look. Just give me a few days to think about things. I'll drive back up later on this week, or early next, and we'll talk then."

It wasn't the words that worried Juliet, it was the way he was saying them, with such a cool detachment. It was as though he'd already made up his mind.

"May I speak to the girls?" Juliet asked.

"They're swimming in the pool right now. I'll have them call you when they get out, okay?"

"Fine," Juliet said.

There was a long pause.

"Are you going to be okay?" Patrick asked. For the first time, she could hear an echo of the old tenderness in his voice.

Am I? Juliet wondered. She thought of her mother, remembering the messy, dramatic exhibit Lillian had made of herself during one of her many temporary separations from Juliet's father—he'd bang out of the house cursing under his breath with an overnight bag slung over his shoulder, and Lillian would dissolve into a wine-fueled sob fest, refusing to leave her bed for days on end, leaving Juliet to take care of her little sister, Angie. And Juliet remembered the promise she'd made to herself at the time: No matter what happened to her, she'd never, ever behave like her mother. Especially not over a man.

She drew in a deep breath and let it out slowly, so that by the time she spoke, her voice was calm and measured. "I'll be fine," she said.

There was a pause. "Right. Bye, then," Patrick said.

And then he hung up the phone, while Juliet stood there, still staring down at the awful picture.

It was only then that she began to read the article:

Can any woman really have it all? CHLOE TRUMAN takes a closer look at the culture clash between working and stay-at-home mothers.

As I write this, I'm pregnant with my first child, and I'm struggling with an important question. It has nothing to do with picking out a name for my new baby or the color I should paint the nursery walls. It's the far more weighty decision of whether I'll go back to work after having my baby. Do I trade in quality time with my child to continue building a career I enjoy? Or do I give up the perks of extra income and time among adults to stay at home?

The question divides American women.

"I didn't have children just to hand them off to someone else to raise," says Jenn Kreger, a Chicago mom who used to work as a financial analyst but now stays at home with her two children, Regan, 4, and Nathaniel, 3. "I went back to work after Regan was born, and most nights I was lucky if I got home in time to see her before she went to bed. After a while, I started to wonder what I was working so hard for."

But other mothers relish their time away from home.

"I'm a single mom, so not working isn't an option. But even before my ex-husband and I separated, I never considered giving up my job. I love what I do," says Anna Swann, a restaurant critic and mother to Charlie, 2. "My work fulfills me, which in turn makes me a happier mom."

Juliet Cole, an attorney and mom to four-year-old twin daughters, is more blunt about her decision to return to work after the birth of her twin daughters.

"I think I'd go crazy if I had to sit at home all day watching *Sesame Street* and coloring," Cole says. Her family's solution is one that's becoming increasingly popular in this modern era of women executives: Her husband has taken time off from his career as a firefighter to stay at home with their children. The arrangement has worked well for Cole. "Every working woman should have a housewife," she says.

Juliet didn't bother to read on. She just stared down at the article. It was a hit job. Chloe, the woman Juliet had come to think of as a friend, had backstabbed her in print.

Every working woman should have a housewife.

Did I actually say that? she wondered. *No. There's no way I said that. Jesus! It's libel! It's libel, and I'm going to sue Chloe and fucking* Mothering *magazine.*

Except... Juliet suddenly felt horribly sure that she *had* said it. As a joke. Obviously she hadn't *meant* it and certainly had never intended for Patrick to hear about it, much less read about it in a national magazine.

Patrick. At least Juliet no longer had to wonder why he'd left. He'd already been overly sensitive about his domestic role. To find out that his wife had snidely referred to him as her "housewife," and in a magazine article no less—he'd be devastated, his pride wounded. She knew him well enough to know that.

What she didn't know was if he'd ever be able to forgive her.

fifteen

Anna

"Hey, tiger," Brad said when he opened the door. He leaned over to plant a kiss on top of Charlie's head. Anna, standing behind Charlie on the doorstep, was pleased to note that her ex was starting to go bald.

Serves him right, she thought, unable to suppress a gleeful stab of pleasure. *Maybe next he'll become impotent.*

"Daddy!" Charlie exclaimed, beaming at his father. He held up a blue wooden Thomas the Train. "Look! Train!"

"Sweet," Brad said appreciatively.

"Hi," Anna said coolly. Brad stepped aside so that she and Charlie could enter his apartment.

Brad had offered to pick Charlie up, but Anna wanted to do her routine once-over to make sure the house had been child-proofed tonight. It wasn't that she didn't trust Brad—he was actually quite good with Charlie, or at least he was when he remembered he had a son—but her ex-husband's parenting style could be a bit lax at times. Sure, he didn't leave out open bottles of pesticide or shards of broken glass, but he didn't always think of less obvious dangers. Like remembering not to leave his razor on the edge of the bathroom sink. Or putting the soft protective bumper up around the perimeter of his glass-topped coffee table. Or installing child gates on the terrifyingly steep staircase that led up to the second-floor master suite.

Why Brad insisted on renting this house, I will never know, she thought, looking skeptically around the ultramasculine bachelor pad decorated in chrome and glass and black leather. He'd rented it after their separation, moving in just before Charlie was born, but it wasn't exactly child-friendly. She supposed he was trying to create his own Rat Pack bachelor pad.

The Rat Hole is more like it, Anna thought darkly.

She was still holding on to Charlie's hand, not yet ready to let go. Anna suddenly felt nauseated at the thought of leaving Charlie here overnight. It was the first time he'd slept over at his father's. And, as she looked out Brad's sliding-glass back doors at the spectacular ocean view beyond, she was flooded with the terrifying possibilities of what could go wrong. What if Brad took Charlie swimming and he got sucked down by the undertow? What if Brad forgot to use the special nonallergenic shampoo when he washed Charlie's hair and instead used the regular shampoo that caused Charlie's eyes to swell shut? Or what if Charlie fell and lacerated his hands and face on one of the decorative modern glass vases on the coffee table?

"Maybe this isn't such a good idea," Anna said, taking a step back.

Brad frowned at her as he reached for Charlie's bag. "He'll be fine, Anna. Stop worrying. And it's about time Charlie started spending the night over here once in a while. I didn't want to push it at first, especially when he was a baby, but now that he's a little older, I want to do this more often."

Anna looked around bleakly at the hard-edged house. "Well. Maybe if you made this place more kid-friendly," she said.

"It is kid-friendly! I even put up the gates. See?" Brad gestured toward the staircase.

Anna turned and saw a safety gate spanning the bottom of the stairs. She felt slightly better, although she couldn't resist giving the gate a small shake to make sure it was secure.

"He's my son too. Do you think I'd let anything happen to him?" Brad asked softly, and looked down at Anna with one of the melting stares that had instantly won her over when they first met. It had been, ironically, at a wedding. Anna worked with the bride and Brad had gone to college with the groom, and they'd both turned up dateless. Anna had been hit by the full force of one of Brad's irresistible grins, two parts charm, one part smoldering sex appeal, and was instantly smitten when she found herself seated next to him at dinner. She'd even, for a while, fancied that it had been love at first sight.

Which just goes to show what an idiot I was, she thought.

Now, as their adorably blond little boy let go of her hand and ran to his father, clinging to Brad's leg and beaming up at him, she felt the familiar conflicting emotions. Brad had been a mistake. Hell, her relationship with him pretty much defined the word. Yet without Brad, she wouldn't have had Charlie. And that was unthinkable.

Brad watched her watching Charlie, his dark eyes inscrutable.

"We'll be fine," Brad said again.

For a moment, Anna softened. She was overreacting, of course, letting her anxiety zoom out of control. But then Brad uttered the two words Anna knew she couldn't trust coming from him: "I promise."

Right. I know all about your promises, Anna thought. She felt her face stiffen as she turned away.

"Before I go, show me where Charlie will be sleeping," Anna said.

"This was obviously a better idea in theory than it was in practice," Noah said.

"What?" Anna asked.

"THIS WAS OBVIOUSLY A BETTER IDEA IN THEORY!" he bellowed.

"NO! THIS IS NICE!" Anna lied.

"YOU'RE A LIAR," Noah said, still shouting to be heard.

"Well, it is a little windy. But I'm still having fun," Anna said. And this time she wasn't lying.

"What?"

"I'M. HAVING. FUN," she shouted.

For their big night out—The Night, Anna remembered with

a thrill—Noah had surprised Anna with what was supposed to be a romantic picnic by the sea. He'd even tracked down an old-fashioned wicker picnic basket and filled it with grilled chicken and goat-cheese paninis, wild-rice salad, sliced melon, chocolate chip cookies, and a bottle of cold pinot grigio.

"Yum," Anna said, peeking in the basket. "This looks great. I didn't know you could cook."

"I can't," Noah admitted. "But I have a lot of experience at ordering takeout."

"Good to know," Anna said.

But no sooner had Noah spread out the plaid blanket on the sand for them to sit on than the wind had picked up, gusting off the water and spraying sand in their faces. Even though they were sitting only a foot apart, Noah and Anna had to shout at each other in order to be heard over the squalling of the wind, and the edges of the blanket blew up and flapped in the breeze. Gamely, Noah got out the food, but the napkins were instantly blown away and Anna's plastic wineglass toppled over.

"I don't think this is going to work," Anna said.

"What?" Noah asked.

"I DON'T THINK THIS IS GOING TO WORK!" Anna shouted. "IT'S TOO WINDY!"

She suddenly hoped that Noah hadn't been planning on seducing her here. Having sex on the beach sounded romantic in theory but wasn't actually all that fun in practice. Sand tended to get up into uncomfortable places. And Anna had never been turned on by the idea of having sex outside, or in public places, for that matter. She was really more of a plain-vanilla, sex-in-bed-with-the-lights-out sort of a girl.

"Do you want to go?"

"What?"

"DO. YOU. WANT. TO. GO?" Noah shouted.

Anna nodded and pointed toward the car. She packed up the as-yet-uneaten food, and Noah managed to somehow fold up the blanket, although it was a struggle. They jogged awkwardly back up the boardwalk to his car.

"Phew," Noah said, once they'd climbed inside the car.

Anna lifted a self-conscious hand to her hair. It was finally starting to grow out a bit and didn't look quite as insane-asylumish, but all the gel in the world wouldn't have helped against the wet monsoonlike winds. She patted at it, tucking the ends behind her ears.

"Sorry about that," Noah said, turning to look at her. "That wasn't quite what I had in mind."

"Oh, really? You weren't planning on eating a sandwich full of sand?" Anna asked lightly.

"Believe it or not, I thought this would be romantic. I had a vision of us sipping wine while the sun set over the ocean. Just like you always see in the movies."

The laughter fizzed out of Anna before she could stop it.

"What?" he asked, smiling along with her, even though he clearly had no idea why she was laughing.

"Wrong direction," Anna explained. "We're on the east coast. The sun rises over the ocean here. It sets over the beach on the west coast." She giggled again. "That's why you always see it in the movies. You know—Hollywood? California? All on the west coast."

The tip of Noah's nose turned red, which just made Anna laugh even more.

"Smart-ass," Noah said, reaching over to pinch her lightly on the waist.

"You think so?" Anna asked, her head resting on the back of the car seat.

Noah nodded. "Definitely," he said. And although he was still smiling, there was a gleam in his eye that caused the laughter to die in Anna's throat.

Noah leaned forward and brushed his lips—which tasted of salt from the sea wind—against hers. He gently rested his hand on the side of her neck, his thumb at her jawline, and pulled her into the kiss. Anna felt the rest of the world recede as she lost herself in the sensations of him. She touched the exposed triangle of skin just under his throat, her fingers grazing the coarse dark hair growing there. Her fingers dropped, and she unbuttoned the top button of his blue broadcloth shirt. Then she unbuttoned another one. And another.

When she'd finally gotten his shirt off and splayed her hands across his chest, Noah murmured, "Now it's my turn."

He pulled her short-sleeve cotton sweater up over her head before deftly slipping off her skirt. His pants followed, and then their underwear. It was all a bit tricky in the confined space, although they managed just fine (except when Anna banged her knee against the gear shift and let out an involuntary "Oh, shit!"). And then Noah was pulling her onto his lap so that she was facing him, her legs straddling his.

Anna hesitated then, looking at Noah, their faces only inches apart.

"I haven't done this in a long time," she said softly. It felt like a confession.

Noah looked back at her, a smile playing on his lips.

"And if I said it was just like riding a bicycle?" he asked.

Anna laughed in response. She leaned forward and caught his lips against hers.

And then they made love—in a very non-plain-vanilla way—right there in the front driver's seat of Noah's car in the deserted beach parking lot.

It wasn't until sometime later—after they'd gotten back to Noah's house and made love yet again in his big walnut four-poster bed—that Anna suddenly had the premonition: Something was wrong. They were lying quietly together, Anna's head tucked against Noah's shoulder, when the creeping dread suddenly spread through her.

Charlie, she thought, and her body stiffened with fear.

"What's wrong?" Noah asked sleepily, as he felt her body shift away from his.

"I don't know..." Anna hesitated, not wanting him to think she was crazy. And then suddenly she yelped, causing Noah to start. "My cell phone! I forgot to turn it on!"

She hopped out of bed and rummaged through her purse, until her fingers closed around the small silver phone. She powered it up and waited a minute to see if the message icon was blinking. It wasn't. Anna let out a relieved breath and closed her eyes for a minute. "I can't believe I was so stupid. What if something had happened to Charlie? Brad wouldn't have been able to get hold of me."

"You didn't tell him where you are?"

"No. I felt sort of weird about it. It felt too much like I was announcing to my ex-husband that I was off for a wild night of sex," Anna admitted, sliding back into bed.

"Mmmm. I like the sound of that," Noah said, pulling her to him.

"Really? Already?" Anna asked.

"Maybe in a few minutes," Noah conceded. "Are you hungry? We never did eat."

"Famished. Did you bring the picnic basket in?"

"No. But I'll go get it." Noah got up slowly, reluctantly, and pulled on his jeans. "I'll be right back."

"Okay," Anna said. Once he'd gone, she leaned back against the pillows, pulled up the navy-and-white-striped comforter to her chin, and stretched her hands over her head, trying to relax. Everything was fine—no, it was better than fine. It had been a perfect, perfect night.

That was when her cell phone rang. She looked at the caller ID. Brad. Anna frowned as she hit the answer button.

Don't worry, she told herself. *He probably just forgot what time Charlie goes to bed or something like that.* An irritating interruption, yes, but nothing to get worked up about.

"Hey, what's up," she said.

"Anna..." And just from the way Brad said her name, Anna knew something was very, very wrong indeed.

Charlie was missing.

After something bad happens, people always claim that it was all a blur. But not for Anna. Everything that happened that night was frighteningly clear, every moment precisely defined: Grabbing her clothes off the floor. Dressing faster than she ever had before in her life. Running out of the room, holding her shoes in one hand. Meeting Noah as he was just coming back in with the picnic basket. The color draining from Noah's face when she told him. Running outside, out into the darkness, to Noah's car. The seemingly endless drive to Brad's beachside house.

Oh, God, the beach, Anna thought. What if Charlie was out on the beach? He always ran straight to the water, always, with a fearless joy that never failed to make her heart lurch. What if he'd gone out intent on a midnight swim? It was nightmarish, but horrifyingly possible. A scream rose in Anna's throat, and she had to cover her mouth with one hand to stifle it. If she started screaming, she knew she wouldn't be able to stop.

"I put him to sleep in the guest room at seven-thirty," Brad had told her over the phone. "I went in to check on him at nine, and he wasn't there. Oh, Christ, he wasn't there. We've looked everywhere. He's not in the house." Then Brad had broken down in tears.

"We?" Anna asked dumbly, the news not immediately sinking in.

"We" turned out to be Brad and his new girlfriend, Bridget.

And where were "we" from seven-thirty to nine?

In the upstairs bedroom, of course. Charlie was downstairs, alone, sleeping in a big-boy bed for the first time (Brad had neglected to set up the portable crib, despite his promise to Anna that he'd do so). Apparently, Brad had been too busy fucking his girlfriend to remember to lock the front door.

"If anything's happened to Charlie, I'm going to kill Brad," Anna said, her voice sharp with fear, as Noah raced toward Harbor Ridge, the neighborhood where Brad lived. "And I don't mean that the way people usually say they're going to kill someone. I mean it literally. I will literally end his life."

"I'm sure Charlie's fine," Noah said.

But Noah didn't know that; he couldn't. He was just saying it, the way people always said that things will turn out fine when faced with a terrible reality. *But things don't always turn out fine,* Anna thought, going cold. *Some children really are kidnapped, or really do wander out of the house and drown. Bad things really can happen.*

"I have to call my mother," Anna said suddenly. "She'll want to know. Shit, my phone—I didn't bring it."

In her frantic hurry to leave, Anna had left her purse and all of her other belongings back at Noah's house. Noah didn't have his with him either.

"I'll call her for you as soon as we get there," Noah promised, and Anna nodded distractedly. She turned away and watched the darkened suburban landscape pass by. Oddly, she wasn't crying. It was as though the fear had dried her up on the inside.

When they got to Brad's house, her ex-husband was walking around outside, a flashlight pooling a weak circle of light ahead of him into the blackness. He was bellowing Charlie's name at regular intervals. Anna's heart sank, and the breath left her body when she saw him. If he was still looking...

Oh, God. OhGodohGodohGodohGodohGod.

Charlie.

She was opening the car door before Noah had come to a full stop, leaping out and running across the lawn.

"Have you found him?" she called out shrilly, although she knew the answer. But she had to hear him say it.

"No." Brad's reply was terse, and Anna could see that he was distraught. "Anna, I'm so sorry. So, so sorry."

"Not now." Anna held up a hand to silence him. "I can't listen to that now. Right now all I want to do is find my son."

"Have the police been called?" Noah asked, coming up behind Anna.

Brad looked at Noah blankly. "Who are you?"

"Noah Springer. I'm a friend of Anna's. Have you called the police?"

"Yes, I already did. Bridget's inside waiting for them."

"Give me your flashlight," Anna said, reaching for the large Maglite Brad was holding.

"I've already looked all around the house," Brad said.

"I'm going to look again," Anna said, clenching her teeth so hard, the muscles in her jaw ached. She'd keep looking for as long as she had to, until Charlie was safe in her arms.

And then she would never let him out of her sight again.

Brad found two extra flashlights, and he, Noah, and Anna prowled around Brad's house and the neighbors' houses, shouting Charlie's name. Lights came on at a few houses, and people stepped out onto their front porches, wearing robes and peevish expressions, looking to see what all the commotion was. But as soon as they heard a child was missing, most of them joined in the search, until a small army was combing up and down the street, looking for the small boy. The police arrived, first in one patrol car, and then—when it became apparent that this was more than just another case of a child hiding in a closet and a panicked parent calling the police too quickly—more uniformed officers showed up.

Margo came too, but she was hysterical, screaming all of the terror and panic and fear that Anna hadn't dared let out. She turned away as a neighbor led her mother off—to where, Anna had no idea, and at that moment she didn't care. She couldn't deal with her mother's emotional breakdown right now. Not when it was taking everything Anna had to keep it together herself.

Charlie.

Bridget had stayed inside Brad's house, which had been turned into headquarters for the search. She was a tall woman, big-boned, with a lovely face now pale and streaked with tears as she moved woodenly around the small kitchenette, brewing pots of strong coffee for the volunteers. She seemed nice, Anna thought, the sort of woman she might have been friends with in a different situation. If . . .

If this weren't happening.

But it was. *OhGodohGodohGodohGodohGod—*

No! I have to keep it together, Anna thought fiercely, another burst of adrenaline pushing her up from the swampy despair that kept threatening to drag her back down.

It was just after one in the morning, when expressions were growing grim, and the searchers kept looking worriedly toward the beach, and the first detectives had shown up on the scene, that a victorious shout rang out.

"I found him! I found him!"

Anna turned back from the beach—which she'd been going to search yet again—and began running toward the direction of the shout. She ran as hard as she could, her arms pumping, her feet flying beneath her, while her heart beat with hope. *Please oh please ohpleaseohpleaseohplease* . . .

And there he was! Charlie was in Brad's arms, looking groggy with sleep, and—oh, God, yes! He was okay!

Anna raced to them and threw her arms around her son, practically ripping him away from Brad. She pulled Charlie's solid, heavy body against hers, felt his arms slip around her neck and his head loll heavily against her shoulder.

"Mama," Charlie said, his voice muffled. And then he let out a throaty chuckle and pulled back to grin up at her. "Hi, Mama!"

Anna's legs suddenly gave out. She sank to her knees, still clutching her son to her chest, and said a silent prayer of thanks.

One of Brad's neighbors had found him. Charlie had apparently wandered out of his father's house and down the street before crawling under a bougainvillea bush and falling into the sort of deep, trancelike sleep that only small children are capable of. He didn't wake up until the woman who found him had knelt down and shone her flashlight directly under the bush and into his face.

The thought of her two-year-old son outside and alone after dark, where he could have been hit by a car, or drowned in a neighbor's pool, or attacked by an alligator, or abducted, or hurt in an endless number of ways, made Anna's insides shift queasily whenever she thought about it. She let Brad take over the job of thanking the police and his neighbors who had helped with the search. Anna just sat there, with Charlie—now sleepy again—cuddled in her arms, while hot tears of relief leaked from her eyes. Even when Margo came out, sobbing with happiness and relief and wanting to give Charlie a hug of her own, Anna wouldn't let go of him.

But when Charlie saw his grandmother, he reached out to her.

"Gigi," he said sleepily. Margo took the opening as an opportunity to bundle the little boy into her arms, while she burst into loud, weepy tears.

"Anna," Brad said, and Anna turned to look at her ex-husband.

"No. Not now," she said simply, shaking her head. "We'll talk about it tomorrow. Now I'm going to take Charlie home."

Brad nodded. "I'm so sorry," he said, lifting his hands up, palms facing out, as though waiting for his punishment.

Anna just looked at him. It was a heartfelt apology, she knew, and yet there wasn't any point. It wasn't like she'd ever be able to forgive him.

Or herself, for that matter.

"I'll drive you home," Noah said quietly from behind Anna. "Both of you."

Anna turned to look at Noah. She'd forgotten that he was here. His face looked taut and strained, so unlike he had earlier that evening when they'd laughed and talked and made love in his car.

God, that was only five hours ago, Anna realized, and suddenly felt a wave of exhaustion hit her. One moment she was running on nerves and adrenaline, and the next she felt like she was about to keel over.

"No," she said. "Thanks, but my mom's here. She'll drive us home."

"Are you sure?" Noah asked. He stepped closer and rested a

hand on her arm. "If you don't want to be alone, I can stay with you. On the couch, of course," he hastened to add.

"My mom already has a seat for Charlie in her car," Anna said. She wondered if she was making more sense than she thought. "It'll be easier if she takes us."

Noah pulled Anna toward him and kissed her on the forehead. "Try to get some sleep. I'll call you tomorrow."

"Okay." She turned away from him, back to where her mother was standing, covering Charlie in kisses while he giggled and squirmed in her arms. Anna made up her mind right then and there.

When Anna thought she could actually balance parenthood with a personal life, she'd made a terrible mistake. And with that mistake she'd put her son's life at risk. Anna had come too close to losing Charlie.

It wouldn't happen again.

She turned suddenly, running back after Noah, who had already reached his car.

"Noah, wait," she said, her breath coming in little puffs when she reached him.

"Change your mind about the ride?" Noah asked. In the dim light of the streetlamp she could see that he looked exhausted, but he managed a crooked grin.

"No. I just wanted to say... thank you for tonight. For staying and helping," Anna said.

"Of course I stayed," Noah said. He reached out and brushed the back side of his hand against her cheek.

This deliciously intimate touch caused goose bumps to spring up on her shoulders and the back of her neck. Anna shivered but stepped back.

Despite the darkness, Noah read something in her face. His frown was quizzical, questioning. Anna nodded slightly, as though he'd already asked the question.

"Tonight was great, but... it was just tonight," Anna said softly.

Noah shook his head slowly. "You had a bad scare tonight. I understand. But there's no need to make any big decisions about where you and I stand. We can talk about it later, tomorrow, or in a few days."

But Anna shook her head in reply. "No. I know this seems harsh, and I'm truly sorry for that, because…well." Anna swallowed. "I care about you. More than I thought I would. More than I wanted to."

Noah's expression softened. "Anna—" he said.

"But I can't do this," Anna continued, as though he hadn't spoken. "I just can't. Not now. Not while Charlie is so young. I know it's not what you want, but he has to be my first priority. My only priority. I'm just not one of those women who can juggle ten things at once and be amazing at all of them."

"You don't have to be. I don't need you to be amazing. I just want to spend time with you. Get to know you better," Noah said softly.

"The thing is," Anna began. She stopped and swallowed before continuing. "You'll be better off without me. You will. You'll meet some nice woman, one who doesn't already have a child and an ex-husband. And when you get married and start a family, you'll both be doing it for the first time."

Noah looked away, his face unreadable, and Anna was sure then, sure with a sickening certainty, that she was right. That Noah knew he really would be better off with a woman who came with less baggage.

But then Noah looked back, right at Anna, his dark eyes holding hers. And although his voice was quiet and hoarse with fatigue, she felt the force of his words as surely as if he'd been shouting them at her. "I've been engaged four times. Each time, I was as wrong as I could be. Maybe you have a history that's messier than some; maybe you come with a few extra strings attached. But I'd rather have the mess, and the strings, and at the end of the day know I'm with the right person."

Anna just stared back at him, her mouth sagging open. It was perhaps the most romantic, most amazing thing any man had ever said to her.

It took all of her effort to shake her head.

"I'm so sorry," she said, her voice no louder than a whisper.

"Anna! We should get Charlie home," Margo called to her across the lawn.

Anna looked back to where her mother stood holding Charlie and saw that the search party had broken up. The neighbors were melting away, heading back to their homes to salvage what sleep could still be had. The police cruiser was backing out of the drive-way. Brad was standing a good distance away from Margo, as though it was as close as he dared get to his son, and Bridget stood even farther away, her arms wrapped around her body.

"I have to go," Anna said without turning back, keeping her eyes on her son, who looked like he was sleeping again, his head lolling against his grandmother's shoulder. It took all of her self-control not to look back to see if Noah was watching her go.

sixteen

Chloe

Chloe shifted William from her right arm to her left in order to dial Anna's cell-phone number.

"Hello." Anna sounded exhausted.

"It's me, Chloe. Are you okay?" Chloe asked, immediately concerned. "Did something happen on your date last night?"

Anna sighed. "Yes, but that's a long, long story. I'll tell you about it when I see you," she said.

"Actually, that's why I was calling. I wanted to see if you were up for a walk. I thought maybe we could head down to Manatee Park. I read in the paper this morning that there have been some manatee sightings. I thought Charlie would get a kick out of seeing them," Chloe said.

"I'm sure he'd love that, but we can't. Not today. I'm actually at the hospital."

"*What?* What's wrong? Is it Charlie?"

"No, not Charlie. It's Grace. She fell yesterday."

"She fell?" Chloe repeated. She thought of her great-aunt Marge, now deceased, who had once taken a nasty spill down some stairs and broken a hip. But Marge was an old lady at the time, with frail, brittle bones. Grace was a young, vivacious woman.

"They think it was that diet tea she's been drinking. Remember how she got dizzy yesterday? Well, they think it happened again, only this time she fell, and she"—Anna paused and took in a deep, sighing breath—"hit her head first on the corner of the kitchen table and then on the tile floor."

"*What?*" Chloe shook her head in disbelief. She hated to ask her next question. "But she's going to be okay, right?"

Anna hesitated. "I don't know. The fall caused her brain to swell, and until the swelling goes down...they're not going to know," Anna said. "Louis is in talking to the doctors now."

"What about Grace's kids?" Chloe asked. "Where are they?"

"Her dad and stepmom are staying with them," Anna said.

"That's good. Okay. What can I do?"

"Unfortunately, there's nothing to do but wait," Anna said. She sounded as though she were near tears, which just made Chloe feel even more helpless. She had to do something.

"Then I'll come down there and wait with you," Chloe said.

"Can you? That would be great. It's been a bit unnerving sitting here alone," Anna said. "I talked to Juliet a little while ago, and she said she'd come too."

"I'll be there in a half hour," Chloe promised.

She hung up, just as James came into the kitchen. He had his hands in his pockets and was whistling off-key.

"Hello, my family," he said. He leaned over to kiss first William, then Chloe, before stepping back and gesturing at his red golf shirt. "What do you think? It's my Tiger Woods look. I thought a touch of the Tiger might help my game."

"Game? What game?"

"I have a one o'clock tee time. I'm meeting Jack and Fritz. Didn't I tell you? No? I thought I did." James gave her a fond pat on the rump, and then turned to rummage through the kitchen cupboard. "Is there anything to eat?"

"No," Chloe said.

"I'll just make a sandwich," James said, pulling down a jar of peanut butter.

"I meant no, you can't go golfing today. I just found out that Grace is in the hospital. She's unconscious. I said I'd go down, so you'll have to stay and watch Wills."

James stared at her. "But I have a tee time," he said.

"*James.*" Chloe shook her head, not quite believing that he was arguing about this with her. "My friend is in the hospital. That's more important than your golf game."

"But you said she's unconscious, right? So she won't know whether you're there or not," James said. His boyishly handsome face looked petulant, and Chloe was suddenly overcome with the urge to slap him. Wills, watching his parents solemnly, blew a spit bubble.

"James, I'm going."

He decided to try another tack. "Can't you take Wills with you?"

"To a *hospital*? No, of course not." Chloe thrust the baby toward James, who fumbled for a moment as he juggled Wills in his arms. He finally shifted his son, holding him under the armpits and looking down at William uncertainly. The baby responded with a gummy grin.

"Chloe," James said, but she cut him off before he could lodge any additional protests.

"I have to get dressed and go," Chloe said. She turned and walked out of the kitchen.

The ICU was on the ground floor of the hospital, in the same wing as the third-floor L&D unit where Chloe had delivered William. Chloe arrived brandishing a huge bouquet of sunflowers and stopped at the nurses' station.

"Excuse me, I'm looking for Grace Weaver. She's a patient here in the ICU," Chloe said.

The nurse glanced up. "You'll have to stay in the waiting room for now, until the doctor clears Mrs. Weaver for visitors. Oh, and you can't bring flowers back into the ICU."

"Oh . . . right. Sorry," Chloe said. She turned toward the waiting area the nurse had gestured to. Four rows of gray hard-shell chairs, bolted into the industrial tile floor, were separated from the ICU by a heavy set of automatic doors.

"Chloe! Over here!" Anna was sitting in the first row of chairs, Juliet by her side. They both looked tired, their faces pale and drawn. Chloe hurried toward them.

"Hey," she said. "Have you heard anything?"

Anna shook her head. "Not yet. Louis hasn't been out in a while."

"Oh." Chloe bit her lip and glanced at Juliet, who suddenly looked, oddly enough, angry. Her blue eyes had narrowed, and her lips were pressed tightly together. Two spots of color had appeared on her thin cheeks.

"I, um, brought flowers," Chloe said. "I thought Grace would like to have something pretty in her room when she wakes up. But the nurse back there said ICU patients can't have flowers."

"Well, aren't you just wonderful," Juliet said coldly. "A regular Martha fucking Stewart."

Chloe felt the words like a slap. She stared at Juliet, trying to fathom the naked hostility on her friend's face.

"Juliet!" Anna said severely. "That's not funny."

"Neither is writing an attack piece about someone you're supposed to be friends with," Juliet snapped.

"An attack piece? Oh...oh." Realization hit Chloe, and she felt her knees go wobbly. "Are you talking about the *Mothering* article?"

"The *Mothering* article," Juliet agreed, her voice scornful. "Forgot about that, did you?"

"Actually, I did. Oh, Juliet, I'm so sorry. I...I wrote that months ago...before I got to know you. Before we became friends," Chloe said in a small voice.

"What are you two talking about?" Anna asked.

"You know, Anna, the article. The one about working mothers. Haven't you read it? You're quoted in it too, although not quite the way I was," Juliet said. "You see, I made a joke to Chloe about Patrick being my housewife—you know, Chloe, a *joke*, as in *ha-ha*—and Chloe quoted me as though I seriously meant it. And, on a related note, Patrick's taken the kids and left me. So thanks for that."

"Wait—Patrick *left*?" Anna repeated, looking stunned.

"Yesterday afternoon. He took the girls to his parents' house."

Anna reached out to touch Juliet's arm, but Juliet stood, and Anna's hand fell limply back to her side.

"Juliet, I'm sorry. I'm so, so sorry. I feel…*awful*," Chloe said. She looked like she was about to be sick.

"I don't give a damn how you feel," Juliet said. She looked at Anna. "I have to go. I have to get out of here."

"Juliet—" Anna began.

"Call me if Grace's condition changes," Juliet said. And she turned and strode away.

Chloe sat down shakily and buried her face in her hands. Anna patted Chloe on the back.

"Shit," Chloe said. "Shit, shit, shit. I forgot all about that stupid article."

"Was it bad?"

Chloe lowered her hands, but kept her head bowed. "I didn't misquote her. I swear I didn't. I always record all of my interviews for just that reason. Juliet really did refer to Patrick as her 'housewife,'" Chloe said. "And honestly, I didn't know she was joking at the time. Now that I've gotten to know her better and I know what her sense of humor is like…but then…and when I wrote the article…" Chloe's voice trailed off. "Oh, God, I really screwed up. Juliet's never going to speak to me again."

"I'm sure she'll calm down eventually," Anna said, although she sounded uncertain. "She can't stay mad forever."

"You don't think?" Chloe asked hopefully.

"Well…" Anna hesitated. "No one can stay mad forever, right?"

Chloe groaned, and again covered her face with her hands.

Chloe spent the afternoon at the hospital with Anna, getting infrequent updates from Louis and feeling completely helpless. Louis, who was pale with fear, kept running his hands through his thinning copper hair, vacillating between tearful desperation and manic optimism.

"I'm going to get some coffee," Louis said, when he came out into the waiting room at quarter to three.

"I'll get it for you," Anna immediately volunteered.

"No, that's okay. The walk will do me good," Louis said. "Would you mind going back and staying with Grace, though? In case...in case..." He took in a deep, ragged breath. "I don't want her to be alone if she wakes up." He pressed his lips together.

"Of course," Anna said.

"Will they let us go back?" Chloe asked. She looked questioningly at the nurses' station.

Louis nodded. "The doctor said it would be okay for a few minutes. And I won't be long."

Chloe had expected that she and Anna would be forced to stand out in the ICU hallway and look in at their friend through a glass window, like they did in the movies. So she was surprised when they were allowed to walk right in to Grace's room. The hospital room was surprisingly small—much smaller than the suites on the Labor and Delivery floor—and it was filled with glowing, flickering machines grouped around the bed.

I'd never be able to sleep with all of those lights blinking, Chloe thought, before remembering—and then she felt foolish and glad that she hadn't spoken the words out loud.

Because Grace wasn't just asleep as she lay in the hospital bed, her eyes shut and her skin so pale it was almost waxy. But she did look peaceful. That was the only word for it. Her face was smooth and untroubled, and Chloe was suddenly—and absurdly—reminded of Princess Aurora in the old Disney classic cartoon *Sleeping Beauty*.

She looks too peaceful, Chloe thought. In fact, Grace looked almost corpselike.

Chloe heard Anna's sharp intake of breath and then what sounded like a sob being swallowed back down. When she turned to look at Anna, Chloe wasn't surprised to see tears slicking her friend's cheeks.

"This can't be happening," Anna said faintly, and Chloe reached out and silently took her hand. They stood there, hand in hand, and looked down at Grace until Louis returned with his coffee. Chloe was ashamed at how relieved she was to retreat back to the waiting room.

"I have to get home," Anna said sometime later, after glancing at her watch. "Charlie's with my mom, but after last night I don't want to be away from him for too long."

Over the course of the afternoon, Anna had filled Chloe in on the events of the previous night, and now Chloe nodded, understanding.

"I should go too," Chloe said, rising to her feet. James got flustered when she left him alone with William. He acted as though William were a very complicated piece of machinery that needed to be constantly monitored and recalibrated. Chloe had tried explaining to him that babies weren't as fragile as they looked, and as long as James kept William fed, changed his diapers, and cuddled him when he cried, the baby would be fine.

"I can't wait until he's older and more interactive," James had said one night, when they were standing side by side in William's nursery, gazing down at their sleeping baby. "And then we can go out and throw a ball around, and I'll teach him to ride a bike and play golf."

"You don't have to wait until he's older to do things with him," Chloe had said.

"I don't think I can find a golf club small enough for him to hold," James teased.

"Well, no, he can't play golf yet," Chloe conceded. "But you could just hang out with him. You know—talk or read to him, hold up toys for him to look at. That's important too."

But James had just put his arm around her and planted a kiss on the top of her head before heading downstairs to watch SportsCenter. Chloe didn't think he'd taken in a word she'd said. Or maybe he just didn't want to hear her. He seemed to think that all newborn activities, like diaper changing and burping and rocking William to sleep, were not part of the daddy job description.

Which reminded her of something Juliet had once said: "Just because I'm the one with a uterus doesn't automatically make me the shitty-diaper changer."

Chloe smiled, until the memory jarred her back to the unpleasant reality that Juliet was monumentally pissed at her. And just when they'd started to become friends—good friends even, Chloe thought. Chloe, with William in tow, had met with Juliet for lunch a few times, and Chloe had even gone jogging with Juliet one morning. Well, sort of. Chloe had started jogging with Juliet but lasted only a half mile or so, at which point Chloe felt like her lungs were about to explode and she got such a sharp stitch in her side, she actually had to sit down on the curb for twenty minutes while Juliet ran on ahead. But still, Juliet had asked her, which meant a lot to Chloe.

And now Chloe had gone and screwed it all up.

I'll just have to find a way to fix it, Chloe thought, as she swung her Jetta into her driveway. *Maybe James will help me. He's always good at people problems.*

"Hello?" Chloe called out as she walked in through her front door. She dropped her keys in the tray on the hall table and glanced at the pile of mail.

"Hello, dear," a voice said, from the direction of the kitchen. It was a gravelly woman's voice, one that sounded as though its owner had smoked a pack a day for forty years. Chloe was so surprised that she started, wheeled around, and poked her head in the kitchen. There, sitting at the table, was a woman Chloe had never seen before. She was older, probably in her late sixties, and had a pleasant face, square-jawed and heavily lined. Her blue eyes were kind, and her plump face was framed by a short crop of steel-gray curls. She was wearing a coral T-shirt with shells screen-printed on the front and matching cotton shorts that stretched over her comfortably plump frame. William was next to her, sitting in his vibrating bouncy seat. He kicked his fat little feet up and chortled happily when he saw his mother.

"Hi," Chloe said. She smiled uncertainly down at the stranger who seemed to have made herself at home in Chloe's kitchen.

"Hello, dear. I'm Mavis Willert. I live two doors down from you. In the town house with the blue door and the rainbow wind sock."

"Oh! Right! Hi," Chloe said, smiling at her. "We haven't met many of our neighbors yet. It's funny how things change. When I was growing up, I knew every square inch of my street and all of my neighbors by name." Chloe bent over and kissed William on the top of his fuzzy head. "So, um, I see James got you some coffee?"

Which was rather shocking. She didn't know James could work the coffeepot. Or where Chloe kept the coffee, for that matter.

"No, I made the coffee. I hope you don't mind."

Okay. This is . . . well, bizarre, Chloe thought. *There's a stranger in my house, with my baby, making herself a cup of coffee. Where is James, anyway?*

"Oh . . . of course not. Um, where is my husband?" Chloe asked, looking around.

"I think he said he was going golfing," Mavis said. She stood creakily, with a groan. "But now that you're back, I suppose I'll be getting home."

"Wait—you mean, James left you here? Alone?"

Mavis smiled vaguely, unperturbed. "Not entirely alone. I had William here for company." She glanced up at the kitchen clock. "So that will be twenty-four dollars."

"Twenty-four dollars?" Chloe repeated, confused. She was still trying to get her mind around the part where James had left a complete stranger alone in their house to take care of William, while he went off to play golf.

"That's what your husband and I agreed on. Eight dollars an hour, and I was here for three hours," Mavis said conversationally.

Three hours? Chloe thought. *James has been gone for that long?*

"Oh. Right." Moving woodenly, Chloe reached into her purse and pulled out thirty dollars. She handed the money to Mavis. "Go ahead and keep the change," Chloe said.

"Thank you, dear," Mavis said brightly. She beamed down at

William. "He's a good boy. If you ever need a sitter again, don't hesitate to call me. It was nice to be around a little one again."

"Thanks," Chloe said faintly.

She walked Mavis out, said good-bye, and then returned to the kitchen. She sat down heavily at the table, and, as she looked down at William cooing happily in his bouncy seat, her rage began to swell. It burned in her chest and throat, moving outward until her entire body felt as though it were electrified with anger. She looked down at her hands; they were shaking. Chloe breathed in deeply, gulping in the air, and when she felt she'd calmed enough that she could speak without screaming, she stood and retrieved the telephone. She punched in James's cell phone number.

"Hey, babe," James said, sounding obscenely cheerful.

"Where are you?" Chloe asked, struggling to keep her voice calm.

James hesitated. "I'm at the golf course. Is everything okay?"

"So you didn't have some sort of an emergency that required you to go to the ER to get stitched up? A bagel-slicing incident, perhaps? Or a freak Jet Ski accident? You weren't attacked by a pack of wild rabid dogs?"

"What? We don't even have a Jet Ski. Are you okay, sweetie? You sound a little...weird. And you're not making a whole lot of sense."

"I'm just trying to get this straight: You left William with a total stranger so you could go *golfing*?"

"Oh! You mean Mavis. I thought she seemed real nice," James said. His Texas drawl was more pronounced, which always happened when he'd had a few beers.

Chloe gritted her teeth. "How did you find her?"

"I went and knocked on a few doors."

"You...*knocked*...on *doors*? You mean, you just went from house to house, asking someone to take care of our baby?" Despite her best efforts to stay calm, Chloe's voice rose shrilly.

"Why are you yelling?"

"I'm not yelling. I'm very calmly asking you if you really left our infant son with a stranger so that you could play golf. Because I'm finding it hard to believe that you would really do that."

"Chloe, calm down—"

"Oh, I'm calm. I'm perfectly calm," Chloe said. "In fact, I'm now going to very calmly hang the phone up on you."

And then she clicked the phone off, which felt good. It felt even better when James called back ten seconds later, and Chloe picked up the phone and hung it back up without a word. She thought for a few minutes, and then an idea came to her.

Do I dare? she wondered, with a thrill of recklessness. But then she thought about how James was willing to risk the safety of their son by leaving him with a complete stranger while he went golfing—*golfing*, for Christ's sake—and she thought, *Screw it. He has this coming.*

Chloe pulled the heavy yellow pages out from under the kitchen counter, flipped open to the locksmith section, and called the first company listed there.

James didn't come right home. He wasn't back by dinnertime, so Chloe ate alone, heating a can of soup in the microwave, before changing to go out for her evening walk.

He's probably waiting for me to cool off before he shows his face, Chloe thought resentfully. It hadn't worked. If anything, his absence just made her angrier.

When Chloe got back from power-walking around the neighborhood an hour later, pushing William in his carriage, James's blue Honda Accord was parked in the driveway. Chloe took a deep breath and steeled herself for the inevitable scene.

"I am not backing down," she told herself, as she pushed the stroller up the driveway. "He left our baby with a stranger. I am not going to let him pretend that it's no big deal."

But James wasn't sitting on the tiny front porch, in the Adirondack chair they kept there, as she'd expected him to be. In fact, she didn't see him anywhere.

Did he break into the house? she wondered, with a thrill of anger.

Chloe glanced into his sedan as she walked by, and she stopped. James was sitting in the car, in the driver's seat, his head lolled back and his eyes closed. Chloe stared at him for a moment while it registered. He was *sleeping*. They were having a fight, and not just any fight, but the biggest fight of their marriage, and he was *asleep?*

Then she spotted the bouquet of yellow roses, wrapped in plastic, on the passenger-side seat of his car. They looked a little shopworn, as though they'd spent a few too many days in the grocery store's florist case. The edges of the petals were starting to brown and curl, and the baby's breath looked limp.

Roses, she fumed silently. *He leaves our baby with a stranger while he takes off to play golf, and he thinks he can make it all right with a bouquet of cheap grocery store roses?*

Chloe's resolve hardened. She turned abruptly away and marched up to the house. She unlocked the door with her shiny new key, let herself in, and locked the door behind her, fastening the security chain for extra measure.

seventeen

Grace

When her eyelids fluttered open, it took Grace a long, groggy minute to figure out what was going on.

Where am I? And what am I doing here? And why does my head feel like someone clocked me with a baseball bat? she wondered woozily.

But then it clicked, and she knew exactly where she was. Orange Cove Memorial Hospital. She'd given birth to three babies here, and the room—with its painted concrete brick walls, orange upholstered visitors' chairs, and awful bleachy smell—was all too familiar.

Oh, Christ. I didn't have another baby, did I? Grace wondered, with a jolt of panic.

But no, that wasn't it. She wasn't pregnant. At least, not that she could remember...no, no. Definitely not pregnant. Thank *God.* So why was she here?

Louis was dozing in one of the visitors' chairs, his head leaning back against the wall. Grace frowned as she gazed at her husband. He looked awful, as though he hadn't showered or shaved in days. Usually, he was freakishly neat about his clothes, carefully ironing every last crease out of his shirt each morning before work. But now his clothes were wrinkled, and there was what looked like a coffee stain splattered on the right knee of his khakis.

"Louis," Grace said, or tried to say. All she could produce was a froglike croak. But the noise was enough to wake Louis, who suddenly sat bolt upright and looked wildly around the room, blinking.

His eyes focused on her—and widened with shock. She tried to smile at him, but her lips felt out of practice too.

"Grace." Louis jumped to his feet, and crossed the distance between them in two steps. He picked up her hand and peered down at her. "Gracie, you're awake. Can you hear me?"

"Water," Grace said creakily. This time the word actually came out, although she sounded like the Tin Man from *The Wizard of Oz* before Dorothy oiled him.

Louis beamed down at her, his eyes filling with tears. "Water? Did you say water? Oh, my God—that's the most beautiful thing I've ever heard in my life," he said, and he picked up her hand and pressed it to his lips. She could feel the warmth of his tears on her skin.

"The doctor! I have to get the doctor," Louis said. He picked up the call button strapped to the side of her hospital bed and began pushing it on and off, on and off, on and off.

"You're only supposed to push it once," Grace croaked. "And please get me some water."

A nurse—young, freckled, and wearing mint green scrubs—came flying into the room at a full sprint, her plain oval face looking grim, as though she was expecting the worst. But then she stopped suddenly when she saw Louis smiling down at Grace.

"She's awake," the nurse said unnecessarily, and her face broke out in a broad smile.

"She's awake," Louis confirmed. "And already bossing me around."

"Excellent! I'll go get Dr. Patil."

Dr. Patil turned out to be a middle-aged man with kind brown eyes and soft hands, and he stayed for a long time, asking Grace questions and checking her reflexes, while Louis stood nervously on the other side of the hospital bed, clutching Grace's hand. Dr. Patil finally pronounced Grace's prognosis to be "promising" and cautioned that they would need to run more tests before she could leave.

"Fine by me," Grace said. She'd had some water and was getting her voice back, although she still sounded husky. "Lying in a bed, with everyone waiting on me hand and foot, and no diapers to change—throw in a few margaritas, and I'll think I'm at Club Med."

Dr. Patil laughed as he left the room, but when Louis turned back to Grace, he wasn't smiling. Instead, his eyes were narrowed and his lips were thinned into a tight line.

"What's wrong?" she asked.

"How can you joke about this?" he asked, his voice strained.

Louis looked thin, Grace thought, as though he hadn't been eating well. She felt an odd mix of guilt and jealousy. She decided to try to coax him out of his anger.

"I'm serious. After five years of sleep deprivation, I could use a little vacation. In fact, are you sure I was even in a coma? Maybe I was just sleeping really, really hard," Grace joked.

But Louis didn't laugh. Instead, he crossed his arms and glared at her through bloodshot eyes. "Grace, it isn't funny. You almost *died*. Do you not understand that? That tea you were drinking almost killed you," Louis said.

Grace blanched. "God, don't even say it," she said, shivering a little.

"I'm going to say it, and you're going to listen." Grace had never heard Louis sound so stern. He crossed his arms and glowered down at her, just as he did at the girls when they were misbehaving. "You have to promise me, right here and now, that you won't ever drink that poison again. And you have to promise me, no more crash diets."

Grace, remembering her eleven-pound weight loss, hesitated.

No, she thought rebelliously. *No. I'm not giving up being thin. No way.*

"I asked my paralegal to do some research on that tea. Did you know that ten women in the U.S. alone have died while taking it?"

"Really? Why? Did they get dizzy and fall like I did?"

"No. The research indicates that the laxative effects of the tea caused an electrolyte imbalance, eventually causing heart failure," Louis said.

Grace gave another shiver. *Heart failure.* "No, I didn't know that," she said in a small voice.

"Grace, listen to me." Louis sat down on the edge of her bed and folded her hand into his. "I can't do this without you. Any of it. I need you, the girls need you. They can't grow up without a mother. For my sake, for *their* sake, you have to promise to stop," Louis said. His voice cracked, and his eyes were welling with tears again as he looked at her. "I couldn't stand to lose you," he said simply.

Tears were now stinging at Grace's eyes too. The thought of her family going on without her broke Grace's heart. "Okay," she finally said, nodding. "I promise I'll stop."

"Maybe you should talk to someone," he said.

"Talk to someone? You mean a shrink?"

"Or a therapist. Someone you can talk to about why you feel so bad about yourself. Why you have such a negative self-image that you would risk your health like this just to lose a few pounds."

The tears began to spill out of Grace's eyes and run hotly down her cheeks.

"But I needed to lose the weight," she said. "I looked awful before. I was bloated, and pudgy, and ... and—"

"Beautiful." Louis's voice was firm. "You had just given birth to our daughter, and you were beautiful."

Louis leaned forward and wrapped his arms around her. Grace winced when his arm hit the IV needle taped to her arm, but she didn't let go. Instead, she held him to her, gently stroking his hair, just the way she always did when one of their daughters was upset.

"Fill me in on all of the gossip," Grace demanded. It was Tuesday, the first day the doctor had cleared her to have nonfamily visitors, and Grace had been crazed with boredom. She'd never felt so disconnected from her life.

Anna laughed. She kicked off her flats, and tucked her feet up underneath her on one of the ugly visitors' chairs. "You've only been in here for three days," she said. "It's not like the Orange Cove social scene ever shifts that dramatically."

Grace shook her head. "Come on. You're going to have to do better than that. I want gossip."

"Well, I don't think this qualifies as gossip, considering she is one of our closest friends, but I assume you've heard that Juliet and Patrick are having trouble?" Anna said.

Grace's expression turned grim. She nodded. "Yes, and I can't believe it. Do you know what's going on? Juliet was in here earlier, but she didn't really tell me anything, other than that Patrick's taken the twins down to his parents' for a few days."

"That's all I know too. I've tried calling her, but she doesn't answer her phone and she hasn't called me back. How did she seem when you saw her earlier?"

"She was acting a little strangely."

"How so?"

"Well, for one thing, she looked awful. She was wearing sweatpants, and her hair was all sticking up, like she hadn't brushed it in days," Grace said.

Anna's brow wrinkled. "Sweatpants? So she wasn't coming from the office?"

Grace shook her head. "I don't think so. Louis told me that when he called in for his messages, his secretary said Juliet wasn't at the office today or yesterday."

"That's not like her."

"Tell me about it. And she was sort of manic, hyper even, like she'd been knocking back shots of espresso, and—get this—she was talking about doing some work around her house," Grace said.

"Housework?" Anna's eyebrows rose in surprise. "Juliet doesn't do housework."

"I know. That's why I thought it was weird. Apparently, she's painting. She brought in a stack of paint chips with her when she visited me, so that I could help her pick out colors. In fact," Grace paused and ducked her head, her cheeks flushing a rosy pink, "she said she wants to hire me to help her redecorate once I get back up to speed."

"That's a great idea!" Anna enthused.

Grace shrugged, as though it wasn't any big deal, but her smile gave her away. "I told her that it's the professional version of a pity fuck. But, hell, I'm not proud. I'll take it."

"Will you stop," Anna said, although she laughed.

"I think I'll get her to take some before-and-after pictures. It's about time I started getting a portfolio together," Grace mused. She stretched and looked disconsolately around her. "I know I've been joking about how I had to land myself in the hospital in order to get some sleep, but I have to say, I'm going to be glad when I can finally get out of this hellhole. I swear, there's a vampire in here taking blood samples every other hour." She lifted her arm to show Anna the needle pricks on it. "I look like a junkie covered in track marks."

Anna looked sympathetic. "Do you know when you're getting discharged?"

"No." Grace sighed and kicked back the hospital sheets. "Every time I ask Dr. Patil, he just says, 'We'll see.' But he's already run every possible test there is to run on me, and other than having a nasty bump on my head, he hasn't been able find anything wrong with me. Hopefully, they'll let me out soon. So, come on, give me some more news. I can't tell you how boring it's been in here."

"I really don't have any—Oh! Wait, I do! I saw Mandy Rider yesterday, and..." Anna paused dramatically. "She's pregnant again."

"Oh, yawn. I wanted juicy gossip," Grace complained. But then she reconsidered. "Still, you just know the Wonder Twins aren't going to cope well with a new sibling. They may even stop composing symphonies and start scribbling on the walls with crayons like normal kids. It'll be fun to watch."

"You're evil."

"I know. Have you seen Chloe? She came by this morning too."

Anna shook her head. "I haven't seen her since Sunday. Why, what's going on?"

"You didn't hear? Jesus, I've been in a coma, and I still have better gossip than you. Apparently, Chloe's locked James out of the house. Is it just me, or does it seem like everyone's marriages are suddenly imploding all over the place?"

"What, Chloe and James?" Anna asked, looking shocked. "But they seemed so sweet together."

"Except for the part where he spent her labor and delivery passed out in the bathroom," Grace said wryly.

"Except for that," Anna conceded. "What happened?"

"Something about how James left the baby with a stranger while he went golfing, although I think it's more than that. General assholery. Chloe had the locks changed on the house, and he's been living outside."

"What, in his car?"

"At first. But then one of their neighbors took pity on him and lent him their RV. So now he's living in that, parked in the driveway," Grace said. She grinned at the image.

"Is that why they have that camper in front of their town house? I noticed it on my way in to work this morning," Anna exclaimed.

"That would be it. The Trailer of Shame."

"Well, you have to give James credit. At least he's not going away."

"I didn't know Chloe had it in her to stick to her guns. I'm actually proud of her," Grace said.

"Like you'd ever lock Louis out of the house," Anna scoffed.

"If he left our baby with a stranger, I damned well would," Grace said. She rattled the ice cubes in her plastic water mug and then sipped at the straw while she eyed Anna thoughtfully. "Are you ever going to tell me what happened between you and the wine-store guy, or am I going to have to beat it out of you?"

"Tough talk from a woman who's hooked up to an IV."

"Oh, come on—please?"

"There's nothing to tell," Anna said, and promptly belied her words by flushing bright pink.

"Uh-huh. So you slept with him, hmmm?" Grace grinned.

But Anna didn't return her smile. She just bit her lip and looked down at her hands. "Yes, but I wish I hadn't."

"Oh, no. It was that bad? Like, bad-breath-and-no-foreplay bad?"

"No, no. Nothing like that. It was just bad timing for us."

"What are you talking about?"

"The whole dating-with-kids thing—it's too complicated. More complicated than you'd think." Anna shrugged. "I just can't do it right now."

"Oh, no. You're not really going back to that whole I'm-not-going-to-date-while-Charlie-is-young thing, are you?"

"Well...yes. Pretty much."

"Anna—" Grace shook her head, but Anna jumped in before Grace could start her lecture.

"This isn't just paranoia. Really. I don't know if Juliet or Chloe told you, but while I was with Noah, while we were...well, *together*, Charlie was over at Brad's house, and Brad wasn't watching him closely enough. Charlie ended up wandering out of the house. Alone. In the dark. Right near the beach. We're lucky as hell that he didn't go toward the water and—" But Anna couldn't bring this thought to its terrible conclusion. She just shuddered and wrapped her arms around herself.

"Juliet mentioned something about it, but I didn't realize that Charlie was out alone at night. I thought he just went out the door for a minute."

"Try four hours. The police came. It was awful."

Grace gasped. "Oh, my God! Did you kill Brad?"

"I wish it were that easy," Anna said grimly. "I think a nicely planned murder would be easier to pull off than getting his visitation revoked."

"You're trying to keep Brad from seeing Charlie?" Grace asked, trying not to sound as shocked as she felt. She could understand Anna's anger, but surely this was going too far.

"I'm going to sue for full custody and to have Brad's visitation scaled back. And I want his visits supervised."

"Anna..."

"What?"

"I know Brad screwed up, and I know you're angry—Christ, I'd be furious if I were you—but maybe you should think this through before you do anything drastic. You know it's important for Charlie to have a relationship with his father."

"Not if his father is too busy screwing some bimbo to watch him," Anna said stubbornly. She crossed her arms in front of her. "Did Juliet tell you that part? That the reason Brad didn't notice our two-year-old son got out of bed and let himself out the front door—the *unlocked* front door—is that he was upstairs getting it on with his new girlfriend? One night. He couldn't even take one night off to spend some quality time with his son. I mean, who does that? Who lets his own child get away from him like that?"

Grace wondered if Anna would have been so angry if Brad had been distracted by a football game rather than a woman, but upon seeing the mutinous expression on her friend's face, she refrained from sharing this insight with her.

Instead, Grace said, "Well, I did."

"What? What are you talking about?"

"Molly got away from me."

"What? When?"

"It was just after Hannah was born. Hannah had colic and was up screaming all night, and both Louis and I were dragging around like zombies right out of *Night of the Living Dead*."

"I remember that. It went on for months."

"The longest three months of my life," Grace agreed. She plunked her water cup down on the over-the-bed table. "I've never been so tired. Anyway, one morning, after a particularly bad night where I hadn't slept at all, I'd finally just gotten Hannah to fall asleep in her swing and I collapsed on the sofa. Molly was a toddler, and she was sitting at the coffee table, coloring, so I let myself close my eyes. I remember thinking, *I'll just rest for one minute*—and the next thing I knew, the doorbell was ringing. It was Sandy Howard, who lives two houses down from me, bringing Molly home. While the baby and I slept, Molly had let herself out of the house and was halfway down the block when Sandy spotted her."

"Oh, no! Grace! You never told me that!"

"I was too embarrassed to tell anyone."

"You must have been beside yourself," Anna said sympathetically.

Grace nodded and shuddered. "I was a mess. I felt like a complete failure as a mother. For weeks after, I had nightmares about what might have happened to Molls if Sandy hadn't seen her. She could have been hit by a car, or grabbed by some creep, or fallen into someone's pool..."

Anna was quiet for a minute. "I know where you're going with this. But my situation is different. Brad didn't lose track of Charlie because he'd been up all night for months on end with a screaming baby."

"No. He screwed up, and I'm sure he feels awful about it. But sometimes that's what it takes. You have a close call like that and it wakes you up. That night Louis put security chains on every door in the house. And we haven't lost one of the kids since," Grace said, now smiling wanly. She rapped on the over-the-bed table. "Knock on wood. Or plastic. Whatever this is. Just promise me you'll think this through before you do anything drastic, okay?"

Anna didn't say anything for a minute, but finally she nodded and said, "Okay."

"And remember, if you do decide to date, Charlie will be *fine*. Kids are adaptable."

But Anna just shook her head and pressed her lips together in a tight line. Grace decided to change the subject.

"Back to Mandy Rider. Please tell me she looked bloated when you saw her," Grace said, settling back against her reclined hospital bed.

Grace was finally discharged on Thursday afternoon, and she was thrilled to get home.

"Mama's home," she called out, dramatically throwing the front door open. Louis was following behind her, her overnight bag slung over his shoulder, being overly solicitous. He kept trying to hold on to her elbow and guide her into the house, as though she were a doddering old woman, until she finally swatted him away and said with exasperation, "Louis, let go of me! I can walk on my own."

"Just tell me if you're feeling dizzy again, okay?" Louis said, his face knit with concern.

"Mommy! Mommy's home! She's here!" Hannah and Molly came rocketing down the stairs and hurled themselves at their mother, nearly knocking her off her feet.

"Girls! Be careful with your mommy, she's still not feeling well," Louis said sternly.

But Grace ignored him. She swooped down and pulled both of the girls to her, breathing in their deliciously familiar smells, a combination of strawberry shampoo, girly sweat, and lavender-scented talc. They hadn't been allowed to come see her at the hospital—which was probably just as well, Grace thought, since it might have scared them to see her so incapacitated—and she'd missed them to pieces. Five long days. It was the longest she'd ever gone without seeing her girls.

"Come here and cover me with kisses," she said, and the girls giggled and wrapped their arms around her neck.

"Honey, welcome home," Victor said, hurrying out from the kitchen and pulling her into another hug. Alice followed behind him, holding Natalie perched on one hip. Alice was smiling, but it looked forced.

"Hello, Grace," Alice said.

"Hi," Grace said breezily.

She and Alice hadn't ever resolved their spat over Alice's re-decorating project. It was a typical pattern for them. They'd argue, and rather than reconcile, they'd just keep their distance from each other for a while, and eventually they'd forget to be mad. Now Grace was in the uncomfortable position of being indebted to Alice for coming to watch the girls all week, while not yet ready to forgive her stepmother.

"Come here, Nat," Grace said, reaching out for her youngest daughter, but Alice stepped back, moving the baby out of Grace's reach.

"I really don't think you should hold the baby just yet," Alice said. "What if you have another one of your attacks and end up dropping her?"

Grace's cheeriness at being home instantly evaporated. "I'm fine, really," she said evenly, stepping forward and pulling Natalie from Alice's arms.

Alice's mouth thinned into a disapproving line, but she remained silent while Grace cooed down at Natalie, who was kicking her dimpled legs and grinning up at her mother.

"She's started sucking her toes," Victor announced proudly, as though Natalie had started solving quadratic equations.

"Always a useful skill to have," Grace said, laughing down at her baby girl.

After dinner, the men tag-teamed the kid's bed routines—Louis gave the baths and Victor read the stories—and Alice finished up the dishes. Grace had been firmly instructed by everyone that she was not to exert herself, so she decamped to the family room, where she curled up in her favorite armchair—a battered old leather club chair from the thirties that she scored at a thrift store—with the stack of interiors magazines that had arrived during her absence. She flipped through a few pages of one issue—green was the in color this year, she noticed, and wallpaper was still popular. As usual, her pleasure at seeing the pictures of beautiful rooms artfully arranged was dampened by a pang of regret that it wasn't her work on display, her design that the writer was gushing over.

And then suddenly she remembered.

Oh, shit! The stain!

Grace had forgotten all about the chocolate-milk stain that she hadn't been able to get out of the sofa. She'd meant to camouflage it before Alice's next visit—maybe with an artfully draped throw or a large pillow—not anticipating, of course, that she'd be unconscious in the hospital when her stepmother arrived.

But when she looked over at the spot where the stain had been on the right back cushion, it wasn't there. Grace peered at it, confused. She stood and walked over to the couch so that she could get a closer look. Maybe Louis had flipped the cushions around—but, no, the stain was completely gone. Scrubbed clean.

Grace knew instantly who was responsible: Alice. But rather than feeling pleased that the ugly stain on her newish sofa had come out, Grace just gritted her teeth. It wasn't just the stain. It was one more way for Alice to feel superior, one more failure for her to keep track of, Grace thought, feeling ruffled as she settled back down on her chair.

Just then, Alice breezed into the room. "Do you have everything you need?" she asked Grace. "I know the doctors said you're supposed to be taking it easy."

It was an innocuous-enough statement, yet the underlying tone was unmistakably critical. It was as though Alice was taking Grace's convalescence as a personal insult.

"Fine, thanks," Grace said. She lifted up her magazine and attempted to hide behind it.

But Alice was not to be put off so easily. She sat down on the now stain-free sofa, facing Grace. Alice was wearing a white sleeveless cotton sweater and perfectly ironed blue seersucker capris. Grace wondered, as she often had, how the woman managed to get through the day without a single wrinkle.

Freak, Grace thought. *The woman is a freak*.

"Actually, I'm glad to get you alone for a minute. I have a bone to pick with you," Alice said pointedly.

Gah. When Grace was a teenager, those words—*I have a bone to pick with you*—had always struck fear in her heart, as they were inevitably followed by a lecture about Grace's weight (too heavy), or clothes (too slutty), or attitude (bad), or school performance (merely average), or any other area in which Grace fell short of Alice's expectations. That was to say, pretty much everything Grace did, including breathing, which, Alice had informed her on occasion, she did too loudly.

Grace put down her magazine. "What does that mean, anyway? 'A bone to pick with you'? Where do you think that came from? Do you think it dates back to cavemen, beating one another with dinosaur bones?" Grace asked, in an attempt to distract Alice from her bone-picking.

It didn't work.

Alice sighed heavily and brushed some invisible lint off one of the pillow cushions.

"I know I'm not your mother," she began. "But I like to think that we've formed a special relationship over the years. And I think I've earned the right to offer you the sort of guidance your mother would have given you, had she lived."

Oh, Christ. I know I'm not going to want to hear whatever it is she's about to say, Grace thought. And yet, perversely, Grace couldn't bring herself to stop Alice. It was like worrying at a canker sore— as much as it might hurt, you can't leave it alone.

"I know no one wants to say anything that might upset you, but I think it's time you heard the truth," Alice continued.

"The truth," Grace repeated.

"Yes. The truth. And don't look at me like that." Alice held her hand up, palm facing out. It was an imperious gesture and had the effect of making Grace want to slap her.

"Because the *truth* is, if everyone wasn't so worried about you, what with the coma and all, they might actually tell you how furious they are at you for being so stupid," Alice continued. "Thank goodness you were alone when you fell! What if you'd been holding Natalie and you dropped her? Or what if you'd been driving with the girls in the car when you had one of your attacks? What then?"

Grace shuddered at this grim thought, and her guilt over the danger she'd posed to her daughters momentarily edged out her annoyance with Alice.

"Please don't," she said quietly. "I can't bear to think about that."

"Well, I think you should think about it. I think you should think long and hard about how much damage you could have caused. As it was, you were lucky. You only hurt yourself. What if something had happened to one of those girls? You would never have forgiven yourself."

"I know. I was very lucky," Grace said, struggling to keep calm.

"I don't think you do know. Have you thought about what this has done to Louis? What you've put him through? Or the girls? Or your father?"

"Alice. *Please*. I know how lucky I am that my girls weren't hurt. You don't think it makes me sick to my stomach that it could have been one of them lying in that hospital instead of me? That I could have been the reason they were in there? You don't think I know how stupid I was? I *know* I screwed up. I *know* that."

Alice crossed her arms and pursed her lips. "I should hope so," she said severely.

Grace's anger, contained until that moment, suddenly flowered. "You know, Alice, it's not exactly like you're blameless in this," Grace said slowly.

Alice's face puckered in surprise. "*Me?* I fail to see how any of this is *my* fault."

"Oh, you don't, do you? So the fact that you spent pretty much my entire childhood lecturing me about my weight, and putting me on one diet after another, and *weighing* me, and then making me feel worthless for not being stick-thin—that wasn't your doing?"

"What I've always told you is that staying thin requires discipline. You need to exercise and be careful about what you eat. I never suggested that you could lose weight just by drinking some tea," Alice said scornfully.

"Actually, yes, you did. You were the one who told me about that tea in the first place."

"I did not."

"Yes, you did. Christ, Alice, you never let it go. You have this way of always making me feel worthless just because I don't measure up to your standards. So if I have weight and body-image issues, well, I lay at least some of the blame at your feet."

Alice sighed dramatically. "Oh, Grace. You always have to paint me as the evil stepmother. I would have thought you'd have grown out of that by now."

"And I would have thought you'd have stopped being such an insufferable, hypercritical bitch by now!" Grace retorted.

"Grace!" Victor Fowler strode into the living room, his face pale with shock. "Don't talk to your mother like that."

Alice, predictably, burst into tears. It had been her favorite move back when Grace was a teenager and Victor caught the two feuding. Alice would cry, and Victor—always uncomfortable with conflict—would take his wife's side.

"She's *not* my mother," Grace said flatly.

"I'm not staying here. She's always hated me...never appreciated me...has always resented me...," Alice said between great heaving sobs. She stood and threw herself in Victor's arms, burying her head on his shoulder. "I want...to go home...not staying another minute in this house..."

"Shhh. Shhh." Victor patted Alice on the back. Grace swallowed hard and crossed her arms.

"Grace, I think you should apologize," Victor finally said.

Of everything her father could have said at that moment, this was the one thing that made Grace the angriest. Flashes of the injustices, large and small, that had scarred her childhood came rushing back to her. Alice counting out the number of baby carrots Grace was allowed for lunch every day. Alice refusing to buy Grace the bikini she wanted, insisting that with Grace's hips, she was better off in a one-piece. Alice turning away two of Grace's classmates who were selling Girl Scout cookies door to door, saying with a tinkly little laugh, "Grace doesn't need the extra calories."

No, Alice hadn't always been awful, not all of the time. There were some good memories too, wedged in among the painful ones: Alice taking her to the Breakers for tea when Grace was eleven, just the two of them, as a special treat. Alice in attendance at Grace's dance recitals, jumping to her feet to applaud Grace's solo. Alice on Grace's wedding day, doing up the satin buttons that ran down the back of the gown and then, when Grace spun around, announcing that she'd never seen a more beautiful bride. (Although this last memory was a bit marred by the fact that Alice had suddenly narrowed her eyes and said, "The dress is a bit tight in the bust, though. Have you put on weight since your last fitting?")

But the inconsistency was almost worse; it had just given Grace false hope that Alice would suddenly look on her with softer eyes and hand over the one thing Grace had always wanted from her stepmother: her approval.

"I'm not sorry. In fact, if anyone is owed an apology around here, it's me. She," Grace pointed at Alice's back, "owes me an apology for belittling me for years. And you," Grace turned her finger to her father, "owe me an apology for inflicting her on me."

At this, Alice sobbed even louder and then turned and rushed dramatically from the room. Victor stood and watched his wife go, before turning to face his daughter. Grace had expected his expression to be thunderous, but instead he just looked tired. Resigned. Defeated.

When Victor finally spoke again, his voice was quiet and controlled. "I know she can be inflexible. I know that, Gracie. I'm not blind. And I know . . . I know she didn't always make things easy for you when you were growing up."

These words jolted Grace. He *knew*? He *knew* what Alice had put her through, *knew* how unkind she'd been, *knew* that she'd spent years—*years*—picking at Grace, tearing her down, undermining her self-esteem? Yet he'd never once stuck up for Grace. Not once. He'd always taken Alice's side after every fight. Alice would cry, Victor would calm her, and then Grace would be forced to apologize. Time and time and time again.

"But she's my wife," Victor said simply, raising his hands and then dropping them to his side. "She's my wife."

That was his explanation. Brief, but complete. And Grace knew it was all she'd ever get out of him.

"Then I suppose you'd better go after her," Grace said quietly.

Later that night, after Victor and Alice had left—the latter making a dramatic, tearful exit—Grace lay in bed, trying to read a paperback novel. But the story wasn't holding her attention, and her mind kept drifting back to Alice and their conversation.

"Nat's down, the girls are asleep. My work here is done," Louis announced, as he walked into the bedroom.

"I should feel more upset," Grace said distractedly, flinging her book aside.

"Are you having one of those conversations in your head again?" Louis said. "Because it sounds like I'm coming in on the middle of it."

"I'm talking about Alice. Usually she makes me nuts. I mean, she makes me crazy even when she's not saying anything, when she's just sitting there, twitching silently. Fighting with her should make me insane, right? Especially since she pulled the whole drama-queen routine and my dad took her side, yet again. I should feel upset. But I don't. It's weird. I actually feel sort of... peaceful."

"It must be the drugs. Didn't they load you up on painkillers at the hospital?" Louis said, climbing into bed next to her. He stretched and then turned over on his side to face her.

"No, that's not it. I think I've just finally started to reach a place where she doesn't get to me anymore. Or at least not as much as she used to."

Louis didn't say anything, although his eyebrows arched in a way that made it clear he found this hard to believe.

"I'm serious," Grace insisted. "I spent my teens hating her, and my twenties mad and resentful that my father married her, but now I'm tired of feeling angry. I don't like her, and I probably never will, but not liking her doesn't have to control my life," Grace explained.

In reply, Louis leaned forward and kissed her gently. "Good," he said.

"Not that I'm giving up the right to complain about her from time to time," Grace added quickly. "Because she is still the most annoying woman to ever live."

Louis laughed and kissed her again, this time letting his lips linger against hers. Grace reached up and gently rested the palm of her hand against his cheek as she kissed him back. There was a knock at the door. Grace's lips, still pressed against her husband's, curved into a smile.

"Which one of the munchkins is that?" she whispered.

"Shhh. If we stay quiet, maybe they won't hear us," Louis said.

"Mama," a voice piped up, muffled through the door. "Daddy?"

It was Hannah. Their middle daughter had never been a good sleeper, from the time she was a colicky infant.

Does any of us ever really change? Grace wondered. *Or are we just born the way we're born and carry that personality with us through our lives?*

And then Grace wondered where she would have ended up had her mother lived and had been the one to raise her, instead of Alice. Would she be a happier person? More secure? Thinner? Would she have married Louis, had the girls? Maybe—but, then again, maybe not.

Mothers matter. This much I know, Grace thought. *For better or worse, we matter.*

"Come in, baby," Grace called back.

The door swung open, and their pink-pajama-clad daughter came running in, her mess of brown curls streaming behind her. She climbed up on the bed.

"Hi," Hannah said brightly. She looked alarmingly wide awake. "I couldn't sleep."

"So I see. Do you want to lie down with Mama?" Grace asked.

Hannah grinned in reply and then climbed over her mother, snuggling in between Louis and Grace.

Grace wrapped her arms around Hannah, closed her eyes, and breathed in her little-girl scent, luxuriating in the deliciously solid feel of her daughter pressed against her. Someday these nighttime visits would stop, and the girls wouldn't let her cuddle them. The realization caused Grace a sharp jab of pain. When she opened her eyes again, she saw that Louis was smiling in the direction of the door.

"We have another visitor," he said.

Grace looked over, and Molly—grumpy and half-asleep, her dark hair sticking up in every direction—was standing in the doorway.

"What's everyone doing in here?" Molly asked sleepily. And then, without waiting for an invitation, she clambered up over the end of the bed, settled down next to her sister, and closed her eyes. She seemed to fall asleep instantly.

"That's two of the Three Stooges," Louis said. As if on cue, Natalie started to fuss, her cries clearly audible over the baby monitor. They both waited to see if she'd settle back down, as she sometimes did, but the grizzling turned into a squall. Louis sighed and stood up.

"Might as well bring her in here," Grace said. She rolled her eyes upward in mock exasperation but was secretly enchanted with the idea of having all of her family around her, lying close.

Louis returned a few minutes later with the baby in his arms. Natalie grinned when she saw her mother. Grace reached out, and Louis gently laid Nat in her arms.

"Do you think she's hungry?" he asked, as he climbed back in bed with a groan. "I could go get her a bottle."

Grace felt a momentary pang of guilt. She hadn't been able to nurse while she was in the hospital, and Nat ended up having to wean much earlier than Grace had planned. She'd nursed the other two girls until their first birthdays.

"No, I think she was just lonely. She knew her sisters were here with us, and Nat didn't want to miss out on the fun," Grace said fondly. Nat gave her mother another gummy smile.

"I missed you, baby doll," Grace said softly, kissing her youngest daughter on her downy head. "I missed you like crazy." Her two older daughters were now both asleep, curled up side by side, their heads close together. "This is sort of nice. Usually when the two of them are together, all hell is breaking loose."

And when Grace looked up at her husband, a grin on her face, she saw that he was smiling down at her, at all of them curled up together in the bed. For a moment she could have sworn that there were tears glinting in his eyes. Maybe he, too, was realizing that the days when they'd be together like this, as a family, were finite, and that one day the girls would grow up and move away.

And what then? Grace wondered. *What will our lives be like without them?*

Louis leaned over and kissed Hannah and Molly lightly on the head.

"Are you okay?" Grace asked. She reached out and touched her husband's cheek.

"Better than okay," he said. He grabbed her hand and pressed it to his mouth. "I'm perfect. And really, really glad that you're home."

"Me too," Grace said, snuggling back against the pillows, Natalie nestled in her arms. "Me too."

eighteen

Juliet

Ding-dong!

Juliet ignored the doorbell. It was probably just the UPS man, and anyway, she was too busy painting the upstairs hallway a serene shade of celadon. Grace had recommended the color, insisting it would go nicely with the maple hardwood floor. Juliet hadn't been at all sure, concerned that the color might be too wishy-washy, but it turned out Grace was right; it was the perfect shade.

Ding-dong! Ding-dong!

"Oh, for Christ's sake," Juliet snapped. She rested the roller on its orange plastic pan, marched down the stairs, and yanked the front door open.

Anna and Chloe, with baby William strapped to Chloe's chest in a carrier, were standing there. Chloe had her head down, staring at her shoes like a schoolgirl about to be yelled at by the principal. Anna was smiling, although that faltered when she saw Juliet.

"Jesus," Anna said. "What happened to you?"

Chloe looked up at this, and her face registered surprise, her mouth forming an O.

"What are you talking about?" Juliet asked.

"You're a mess," Anna said bluntly.

"You've got paint on your…," Chloe began, touching her own cheek, but she trailed off when Juliet glared at her.

"Well, I was painting, so…" Juliet said impatiently. She glanced down at herself, and her voice trailed away. She was *covered* in paint. Patches of pink from the girls' bathroom mixed with the cerulean blue from the kitchen, topped with splotches of white from the downstairs bathroom, and, finally, the celadon.

"May we come in?" Anna asked gently. Then, without waiting for Juliet's reply—which was going to be a firm *no;* she still had lots more painting to do—Anna walked in. Chloe hesitated for a minute and then followed Anna.

"This actually isn't a great time for me," Juliet said.

"Well, I tried calling, but you haven't answered any of the eight billion messages I left for you. When was the last time you ate something?" Anna asked.

"Um…" Juliet tried to remember but couldn't. There had been some saltines, somewhere between the pink and cerulean blue.

"I'll make some tea," Chloe said, and hurried off toward the kitchen.

"Why did you bring her with you?" Juliet hissed at Anna.

"Because she was worried about you too," Anna said simply. "You haven't returned her messages either. She's been wanting to apologize to you."

"I don't want an apology," Juliet said, knowing that she sounded like a petulant five-year-old but not caring. Maybe it wasn't entirely Chloe's fault that Patrick had left, but that damned article certainly hadn't helped matters.

"Good. Then we can just move on and spend our time catching up instead," Anna said. She turned and followed Chloe's path to the kitchen. "Do you have anything to eat?"

"You know that's not what I meant," Juliet called after her.

When Juliet got to the kitchen, Chloe had already put on the kettle and was searching for tea bags, while Anna rummaged through the freezer, letting out a cry of triumph when she uncovered a bag of frozen muffins. Juliet watched them, her arms crossed indignantly. She didn't want company, not now, not when she still had so much painting to do, and she sure as hell didn't want to sit around and chat over tea. Why couldn't they just leave her alone?

"Sit down," Anna ordered, as she arranged the muffins on a plate and popped them in the microwave. "Do you have any milk for the tea? Wait, here it is." Anna sniffed it doubtfully, then checked the sell-by date. "Is it any good?"

"Anna," Juliet said, her voice steely. "Why are you in my kitchen sniffing my milk?"

Anna and Chloe exchanged a meaningful look.

"Why do you think we're here?" Anna asked. "We're worried about you. Louis said you haven't been at the office all week and that no one there has heard from you either."

"Oh," Juliet said dully. She'd meant to call in to work but somehow kept forgetting. She pulled back one of the kitchen chairs and sat down, belatedly wondering if she'd get paint on the chair, then deciding she didn't care if she did.

"And then we get here and find you covered in paint, looking like you haven't slept or eaten in a month," Anna continued, setting the plate of warmed muffins on the table in front of Juliet. "So you can imagine we're a bit worried."

"You don't have to worry about me," Juliet said defensively.

"Of course we do," Chloe said gently, setting a steaming mug of tea down next to the muffins. "You're our friend."

Juliet looked at her, raising her eyebrows skeptically. Chloe colored.

"Juliet, I am so, so sorry," Chloe said, sitting down across the table from Juliet. "I truly didn't mean to hurt you. And I never meant to cause trouble in your marriage. I just feel terrible about everything."

"Well, obviously our marriage was in serious trouble before that article came out, or else that on its own wouldn't have been enough to make Patrick leave," Juliet said grudgingly. In truth, her anger at Chloe had been receding. Maybe it was just that she was suddenly so tired, too exhausted to hold on to it. Or maybe it was that she knew, deep down, Chloe hadn't really meant any harm.

"Is there anything I can do to help? Anything to make it up to you?" Chloe asked hopefully.

"No," Juliet said dully. "There's nothing to do."

"So—" Chloe began, before stopping. "Are we...are we okay?"

Juliet sighed, and then nodded once. "We're okay."

"Good," Anna said. She settled down at the head of the table. "Now that that's settled, let's move on to the next matter of business."

"Which is?" Juliet asked.

"What's going on with you?" Anna asked. "What's with the painting? And why do you look like a drug addict who's hit rock bottom?"

"Oh, that's nice," Juliet said sarcastically. But then she drew in a deep breath and closed her eyes, which were so scratchy, it felt like sand had been rubbed into her corneas. Another wave of exhaustion swept over her. She hadn't slept in two days, not since she'd started painting on Tuesday afternoon.

When she opened her eyes, she saw that Chloe and Anna were watching her closely.

"I just wanted to get the painting finished," Juliet said, knowing this response sounded feeble.

"Why?" Chloe asked.

"Because...because..." And suddenly, Juliet felt tears, hot and salty, stinging at her eyes. When she finally did speak, her voice was a husky whisper. "I want the house to look nice for when Patrick and the twins come home."

"When are they coming back?" Anna asked gently.

Juliet was immensely grateful that she hadn't phrased the question as, *Are they coming home?* Which was, of course, exactly what was scaring the crap out of her.

"I don't know," Juliet said. Her shoulders sagged. "I don't even know if they will. If they want to."

Then Juliet, who had always prided herself on her ability to keep her own counsel, told them everything: How she and Patrick had been fighting for months. The long hours she'd been working in the hope of making partner. The crushing pressure she'd been feeling over money. Her fear that she was missing out on the twins' childhood. Her flirtation with Alex. And, finally, what had happened between her and Alex at the Sands.

Juliet had expected her friends to be horrified by her actions, especially Anna, since her marriage had ended over an infidelity. But they didn't look away, their faces etched with revulsion. They just listened and nodded, and gradually, as Juliet unburdened herself, she felt . . . well, not better, exactly. But lighter. Like she could draw in a deep breath for the first time in days. When she'd finally talked herself out, she was surprised to see that she'd drained the cup of tea and eaten an entire muffin.

"Does Patrick know about Alex?" Chloe asked.

"No. And I don't want him to find out, so don't go sticking that in one of your articles," Juliet said, although she tempered the sharpness of her words with a wan smile.

Chloe blushed. "I wouldn't do that," she said.

"I know," Juliet said.

"And the painting?" Anna asked.

"And the painting . . . well, maybe the painting was me hitting rock bottom," Juliet admitted. "I was just itching for something to do, and I thought—I know this sounds stupid, considering all that's happened—maybe it would make a difference with Patrick. That he'd see this new domesticated me"—she looked down at her paint-splattered clothes and smiled ruefully—"and want me back."

"*Juliet*. I'm sure Patrick doesn't want a new you. I think he wants the old you—the you who was, yes, a self-reliant career woman. But the you who was also reachable," Anna said softly. She leaned forward and rested her hand on Juliet's. "I don't think he's angry that you've been working too hard—more that you've been working to the exclusion of everything else in your life."

"Except when I'm checking in to hotels with my boss," Juliet said bitterly.

"Well, okay, that wasn't the best idea you've ever had," Anna said.

But Chloe cut in. "I think you're being too hard on yourself. I can see how something like that could happen. Sometimes when you're under a lot of stress and you bottle it all up inside, the pressure just grows and grows until it has to burst out somewhere. I think that's what Alex was, maybe. A pressure valve. Not," she hurried to add, "that it was a good decision to go to the hotel with him. Obviously, that was self-destructive. But it was understandable, considering the pressure you've been under."

But Juliet was not quite so ready to forgive herself. She stared down at her tea mug and said, "I have to quit my job."

"Quit?" Anna exclaimed. "But what about partnership? Everything you've worked toward?"

"I can't work for Alex. Not now. Not after what happened— what almost happened—between us. No." Juliet shook her head. "My marriage is more important than my job. Besides, I won't have a problem finding another position." She smiled wryly. "Alex wouldn't dare give me a bad reference now."

Once Anna and Chloe left—which they did only after Juliet swore up and down that she wouldn't go back to painting—Juliet stripped off her grimy, paint-splattered clothes and got into the shower. She turned the water on as hot as she could stand and stood with her face turned up, letting the water stream down over her. She washed and conditioned her hair and soaped her body over and over and over again, scrubbing the paint off her skin.

Finally, when the water started to turn cold, she got out and toweled herself off with a clean, fluffy white towel. And then, with the towel wrapped around her, she climbed into bed and almost instantly fell into a deep, dreamless sleep.

It was a long-standing tradition at the law firm of Little & Frost to begin the weekend as soon as the bosses cleared out of the office on Friday afternoons. Paul Little, who was semiretired, rarely even came in on Fridays. Alex usually cut out at around four, as did the other partners—Orson Smith, Gerald Pitt, Steven Spitzer, Farley Robard—and the associates began emptying out of their offices about ten minutes later. (Any earlier and they'd risk running into one of their bosses in the parking garage.) Even Richard, the most dedicated of ass kissers, was out the door by six. Neil usually stayed late but he rarely left his office, so Juliet was reasonably sure that she wouldn't run into anyone when she showed up at seven o'clock on Friday night to clean out her desk.

She brought two empty document boxes in with her, and as soon as she got to her office she set about packing up her personal files, calendar, the potted cactus garden Patrick had given her for Valentine's Day, remembering how he'd joked it was the only plant she couldn't kill. She took her framed diplomas and license down off the wall and gathered up the detritus of her professional life—the spare black suit jacket she kept at the office, a travel umbrella, allergy medicine—and piled it into a box. She worked quickly but methodically until everything was packed, with the exception of the larger framed items, which would have to be carried down separately.

It wasn't until she got to the snapshots of her family in spare silver frames that she felt the first tug of emotion. Juliet looked down at the smiling faces of her husband and two daughters as they mugged for the camera on Christmas morning. A second photo showed the twins frolicking on the beach. In the third, taken on the day Emma and Izzy were born, Patrick was sitting in a chair in the hospital nursery, a tightly swaddled twin in each arm and grinning so broadly it looked like his face would split in two.

My family, she thought. Suddenly she was missing them so much, it hurt to breathe.

Then she heard Alex's voice, and froze.

"Neil, I want to talk Monday about the Steele Insurance case," he was saying from out in the hallway. She could tell he was coming this way and, from his jovial tone, seemed to be in a very good mood.

And then he was there, about to pass by her office, his hands thrust casually into his pants pockets, his face bright, when he saw Juliet and stopped.

"You're here," he said. He looked back over his shoulder—probably checking to make sure that Neil hadn't ventured out—and then stepped into Juliet's office. "Where have you been?"

"I've been at home," Juliet said.

Alex's eyes flickered toward the boxes on her desk. "You're leaving?"

"Don't tell me you're surprised."

"Of course I'm surprised. Why would you leave?"

Juliet tucked her hair behind her ears. "Because I can't continue working with you, Alex. Not after—well. You know. Here." She handed him the letter of resignation she'd typed out. Alex stared down at it.

"I told you that wouldn't affect our working relationship," he said.

Juliet raised her eyebrows. "How could it not?" she said simply.

"Look. It was . . . well, I'm not going to say it was a mistake, because I don't regret it." Alex smiled then, looking rather wolfish for a moment. "But if you don't want to get personally involved with me, I'll respect your decision. Besides, I have good news."

"What's that?"

"We won the motion for summary judgment in the dead-baby case. Or I should say *you* won, since it was your motion. The decision came down yesterday, and the defense has already responded by making a sizable settlement offer today," Alex said.

Despite everything, Juliet felt a thrill of pleasure at this news. It *had* been a good motion. She'd worked damned hard on it.

"That's great," she said. "Really, really great. Our client will be relieved."

"Wait, there's more." Alex's voice dropped even lower. "You're making partner. It's official. We decided this afternoon. The announcement will be made next week."

"Partner?" Juliet echoed. Suddenly, her legs felt shaky, and she sat down in one of the visitors' chairs that faced her desk.

Partner . . . I've made partner.

Alex grinned at her and ripped her resignation letter in two. "So unpack your stuff. As far as I'm concerned, this past week has been a well-deserved, long-overdue vacation."

"Alex, that's just...," Juliet began, but the words left her, and for a long moment she stared down at her hands. Finally, she looked back up at him, at his pale eyes and sexy smile, and there it was, the familiar desire, plucking at her. Less intense than before, but it was still there. Maybe her feelings for him would go away in time.

Then again, maybe they wouldn't.

"Thank you," Juliet said. "But no."

Alex's smile faded. "Are you sure this is what you want?" he asked softly.

Juliet looked down then, at the photos of her family. At Emma and Izzy, joyful, as if they were lit up from inside. At Patrick's sweet smile. She touched the photo of him gently, her finger smudging the glass, and decided.

"Yes," she said. "I'm sure."

Juliet did not sleep well that night. First the room was too hot, so she got up and turned up the air conditioner, and then five minutes later she was freezing. Then, just when she was getting comfortable temperature-wise, she had to get up to pee. Once back in bed, she tossed from one side to the other, the sheets tangling uncomfortably around her legs. And, worst of all, every time she turned to face Patrick's empty side of the bed, she felt a fresh stab of pain at his absence.

When Juliet woke, much later than usual, the sun was already fragmented through the blinds. She showered, dressed, and poured a bowl of cereal, although she was so nervous, she didn't have much of an appetite.

She had decided: She was going to get her family back.

Patrick had asked her for some space, and she'd given it to him. A whole week in which to decide whether they had a future together. Now it was up to her to change his mind and talk him into coming home.

On the drive down to Boca, Juliet rehearsed what she was going to say to Patrick when she saw him. But thinking about it, and how he might respond, made her too nervous—Christ, she could hardly believe she was nervous about seeing her family—so Juliet tried to think about work instead. And then she remembered she didn't have a job anymore to think about. She finally just switched on the radio and tried not to think about anything at all. Which, oddly enough, worked—or, at least it did until Bill Withers's "Ain't No Sunshine (When She's Gone)" came on, with its sappy breakup lyrics, and Juliet abruptly turned the radio off.

It was eleven by the time Juliet pulled up in front of the security gate that spanned the entrance to her in-laws' subdivision. She gave her name to the security guard, who called to the house. There was a tense moment during which the guard hesitated over whether he should allow her in, and Juliet wondered if her in-laws had instructed him to keep her out. But he finally waved her through.

Just as Juliet pulled into the driveway of her in-laws' peach stucco home, the front door opened and Emma and Izzy spilled out of it. Juliet was out of her car in a flash, and she opened her arms to her daughters. A second later she was hugging them, pulling them close to her.

"Hi," Juliet said, kissing them each on the top of the head. They were wearing matching floral tank bathing suits—Patrick's mother, Trish, always insisted on dressing them alike—and their hair smelled like sunshine and chlorine. The girls stumbled over each other to talk.

"We just got out of the pool, but we can go back in if you want to swim with us," Izzy offered.

"Ooh, yes, come swim with us!" Emma said.

"Pops was playing Polo Marco with us," Izzy said.

"Marco Polo," Emma corrected her.

"Oh, yeah, right," Izzy giggled.

"Look, Mama, I got earrings!" Emma announced.

"We both did! I have emeralds, and Emma has rubies."

"What?" Juliet asked. She pulled back to look at her daughters— and at the earrings glinting in their newly pierced ears. "Who took you to get your ears pierced? Daddy?"

"I had nothing to do with it," Patrick said. Juliet looked up, startled. She'd been so caught up in her reunion with the twins, she hadn't heard him approach. Now, seeing him there, squinting into the sun, his dark hair a little too long on his neck, his skin glowing with a tan he hadn't had a week earlier, Juliet was overcome with the urge to stand up and wrap her arms around him. But she didn't. She continued to kneel next to the twins, who were turning their heads from side to side, gleefully preening as they showed off their new earrings.

"Gran said she needed a way to tell us apart," Izzy announced.

"For what it's worth, I've already given my mom hell about it," Patrick said.

"Daddy told Gran that she crossed a line," Emma informed Juliet.

"He said that we were too young to wear earrings," Izzy continued.

"And Gran told Daddy that we were becoming young ladies, and that he can't keep us babies forever," Emma said.

"Then she said that it was a good thing she was there to do these things for us, because God knows you won't," Izzy finished.

"Izzy!" Patrick said sharply. "That's enough."

"I was just saying what Gran said," Izzy grumbled.

But the words hit Juliet like a sucker punch to the gut. She stood slowly while she tried to regain her composure and not give in to the impulse to storm into the house and shake Trish until her teeth rattled out of her silly, vapid head.

Instead, Juliet smiled down at her daughters and then grabbed on to each girl's hand. "How would you two like to go out to lunch with Mommy? Just the three of us?"

"Well..." Izzy hesitated. "Gran was going to take us to get manicures today."

"Manicures?" Juliet asked. She looked up at Patrick, who had the grace to flush.

"I swear I didn't know anything about it," he said. "Come on, girls. Go in and get dressed. You can go get manicures with Gran another time."

"Oh," Emma said, disappointed. "But she said that I could have my nails painted red."

"How about if I take you to get your nails painted after lunch," Juliet suggested, and the twins immediately brightened. "Go on in, get dressed, and we'll go when you're ready."

The twins scurried back in the house, jabbering happily. Juliet watched them go.

"I've missed them," she said simply. She glanced back at Patrick, who was now staring at her with his eyebrows raised. "What?"

"You? In a nail salon? I'm having a hard time picturing that," he said.

"I've had my nails done before," Juliet said defensively.

"When?"

Juliet tried to remember, and when she finally did, she smiled. "In Vegas. The day we got married. I had a manicure in the casino beauty parlor. Remember? It was part of the package that we bought. It included a 'day of beauty,' which roughly translated to a twenty-minute manicure."

Patrick grinned too, and Juliet knew he was also remembering that day, which had seemed so magical and glamorous despite the hot, tacky surroundings of downtown Las Vegas and the crowds of glum senior citizens milling about in track suits and visors.

"That's right. I remember," he said. The corners of his eyes crinkled when he smiled.

Juliet had always loved his eyes, which were a clear, steady blue, loved the contrast they made with his pink cheeks and dark hair. Now, looking at him, she felt a swelling in her throat and had to swallow several times.

"Patrick . . . ," Juliet began.

"I know. We need to talk," he said. The smile left his face, and he folded his arms over his chest. But before he could say anything else, the twins were running back out of the house, wearing cotton sundresses over their swimsuits. Izzy had a little denim purse slung over one wrist, and a naked Barbie doll with teased-up hair was sticking out of it.

"Ready!" they shrieked.

Despite the cold fear clutching at her from Patrick's *we need to talk*—words that had never, ever, in the course of human existence preceded good news—Juliet couldn't help but smile down at her daughters. How had she, of all people, managed to produce such girly girls? Barbies and manicures? And yet she loved it, adored the sweet silliness of her daughters. When she was with them, they made her laugh and got her out of her own head. They were good for her, Juliet knew. Probably better for her than she had been for them.

But from now on, she thought, *that's all going to change.*

"We'll talk later?" Patrick asked quietly.

"Later," Juliet agreed. "Come on, girls. Let's go get our nails painted red."

"I don't want red. I want pink," Izzy said, as they turned away from Patrick and walked to Juliet's car.

"Then pink it is," Juliet promised.

"What color are you going to have your nails painted, Mommy?" Emma asked.

"I don't know. Why don't you two pick out a color for me? You can surprise me."

The twins squealed with excitement at this idea. And although Juliet didn't glance back, she had the distinct feeling that Patrick was smiling again as he watched them leave.

When Juliet and the twins returned from their outing, Juliet was sporting purple nail polish, the color of a grape lollipop.

"Don't laugh," Juliet said warningly to Patrick, who had greeted them at the front door of his parents' house. She held up her hands, fanning them out to show off her manicure.

"I think it suits you," he said, as he stepped aside so that Juliet and the twins could enter. "Purple is clearly your color. It reminds me of..." He stopped, trying to remember.

"Disco Barbie," Juliet said. "They picked it because it's the exact same color that Disco Barbie wears on her nails."

"Disco Barbie," Patrick repeated, grinning.

"Hi, Gran," Emma sang out.

"We got our nails done!" Izzy said.

Juliet turned and saw Trish lurking by the kitchen door.

Probably trying to eavesdrop, Juliet thought resentfully. She still hadn't forgiven Trish for the newly pierced ears or the bitchy comment to go along with them.

"Hello, Juliet," Trish said, smiling but looking a little ill at ease, as though she thought Juliet was at any minute going to make a scene.

Trish darted forward to kiss Juliet on the cheek, which Juliet did her best to endure without flinching. She even bent down to receive the kiss. Her mother-in-law was a surprisingly petite woman—especially considering how tall Patrick was—and although she'd been beautiful when she was younger, she hadn't aged well. Trish compensated for her pouching eyes and puckering lips with a vast battalion of cosmetics. If the cosmetician at the Chanel counter in Neiman Marcus worked on commission, Trish was probably single-handedly supporting the woman.

In fact, Juliet had never seen her mother-in-law without makeup on and had long suspected that Trish even slept fully done up. Today, Trish had dusted her face with bronzer, giving her a weird, seventies-television-star glow. And then there was the tattooed-on eyeliner, three shades of blue eye shadow, navy mascara, brown lip liner, and matte brown lipstick. She wore her hair short and dark, with heavy blond highlights on the crown.

Oh, my God, Juliet thought, as she suddenly realized who Trish reminded her of. *She looks like David Bowie in his* Ziggy Stardust *phase!*

Juliet had to swallow several times to keep from laughing out loud.

"Will you be joining us for dinner?" Trish asked solicitously. "I made a roast chicken."

"What she means is that she bought an already roasted chicken," Sean Cole said, following her out of the kitchen. He was as tall as his wife was short, making them a strikingly mismatched couple. When he slung his arm around her shoulder, the top of her head didn't even reach his armpit. "Hi, Juliet."

"Hello, Sean."

"I made the side dishes," Trish protested.

Sean grinned down at her. He always delighted in teasing his wife. "Rice and salad?" he asked.

"Oh, stop," Trish said, flapping a hand at him.

"Yuck. I hate salad," Izzy said darkly.

"Iz," Juliet said warningly.

"That's why I made you fruit salad, princess," Trish said.

"Me too?" Emma asked, her forehead creasing with worry.

"You too," Trish assured her with a smile. She looked back at Juliet. "So you'll stay?"

"Thanks, Mom, but I think Juliet and I are going to go out for a little while. I'm not sure if we'll be back in time for dinner," Patrick said.

Juliet glanced up at him, wondering where they were going. But Patrick's expression was inscrutable. For all she could tell, he could be taking her to a divorce attorney.

"Do you mind watching the twins?" Patrick asked his parents.

"Of course not," Trish said. "Come on, girls, let's go swimming."

At this, the twins whooped with delight and raced off toward the pool.

"Wait for me," Trish called after them. She looked beseechingly up at her husband. "Sean, go watch them. Those little monkeys will be in the water before you know it."

"I'm on the job," Sean said, hurrying off after his granddaughters.

"We'll be back in a bit," Patrick said, jingling his car keys in his hand. He was standing close to Juliet, just behind her, but she could feel him holding himself away from her. He didn't lay his hand on her back, as he would have once done. Juliet desperately missed that hand.

"Okay. Oh, and Juliet?" Trish stepped forward, looking worried. "About the twins' earrings—I'm sorry about that. I shouldn't have had their ears pierced without asking you first."

Juliet was stunned. She could not remember her mother-in-law ever apologizing to her about anything. And that included the time that Trish took it upon herself to throw Juliet and Patrick a surprise wedding reception after their elopement, even when they had specifically forbidden her to do so. They showed up for dinner one night and were greeted by seventy-five guests. Even worse, Trish had invited a priest, insisting that since Juliet and Patrick had a civil ceremony in Vegas, they weren't officially married according to Catholic law. She'd then attempted to force them into repeating their vows. Juliet, who was not Catholic, had firmly refused, not backing down even when Trish cried.

So an apology—this was no small thing. Trish was actually waving a white flag.

"Thanks, Trish. I appreciate that," Juliet said.

Trish smiled and self-consciously smoothed her hair.

"And thank you for all you've done with Izzy and Em this week. They were telling me all about it at lunch today. They've had a wonderful time," Juliet said.

"Oh, well, it's a grandmother's prerogative to spoil her grandbabies," Trish said.

Juliet smiled briefly and wondered what kind of grandmother her own mother would have made. Lillian had been a disappointment as a mother, but maybe she would have tried to make up for that once she was a grandmother.

Who knows? Juliet thought. *Stranger things have happened.*

She felt Patrick's eyes resting on her, and when she looked up at him, he had a quizzical expression on his face.

"Shall we go?" Patrick asked her quietly. Juliet nodded and exchanged a brief smile with Trish before following Patrick out the door.

They left their shoes by the wooden stairs that led down to the beach and strolled barefoot down toward the water. As they walked, Patrick kept his hands in his pockets and Juliet crossed her arms in front of her. The tide was coming in, rolling toward them in large, white-capped waves. A few high-school-age boys were surfing, or trying to, doing their best to show off in front of the teenage girls lounging about in skimpy bikinis. Juliet could see a few boats off in the distance, looking small against the horizon. Gulls swooped down before them, bickering over the remains of picnic lunches.

"I quit my job," Juliet said.

Patrick came to an abrupt stop, and Juliet had to turn to look at him.

"What?" he asked.

"I quit my job."

"But...*why?* When?"

Juliet looked down at her toes—painted the same garish purple as her fingers—sinking into the wet sand.

Should I tell him about Alex? she wondered, clenching her hands so tight, her nails dug into her palms.

She wanted them to have a fresh start, to not have any secrets from each other, but she also didn't want to hurt her husband. Or inexorably damage their already fragile relationship. Even though she hadn't had sex with Alex, that would be a small consolation to Patrick upon learning that his wife had made out with another man in a hotel room. He wasn't the sort of guy—if such a guy existed—to laugh off some friendly heavy petting and say, "Oh, well, as long as his penis didn't enter your body, no harm done."

And then Juliet had a revelation: If she confessed, she'd be doing it for herself, to alleviate her own guilt. It wouldn't help Patrick move on; it would devastate him. The kindest thing, the most loving thing she could do, would be to carry her own burden of guilt and not pass it off to Patrick.

"I thought you'd be happy I quit," she said instead.

"I just...What about making partner?"

"They offered me a partnership. I turned it down."

"You turned it down?" Patrick's voice was incredulous.

"You said that something had to change. So I changed it," Juliet said simply. She stepped forward and reached out for his hand. There was a long moment where he didn't reach back to her, a moment where Juliet couldn't breathe, but then...then he did. He entwined his fingers with hers, and they held their hands between them like a bridge.

"And now what?" he asked.

"Come home. I miss you. I miss the twins. I miss my family," Juliet said, her voice soft but steady. She tried to ignore the nervous *thump-thump-thump* of her heart and the breath that seemed trapped in her chest.

"I've missed you too," Patrick said quietly.

"And if you want to go back to work, we'll find a way to make it work," Juliet said.

"What about the twins?" Patrick asked.

"Well, their school has an after-hours program. They'd probably really like going to that. And I'm going to find a job that will let me have more flexibility. Maybe one where I could work at home a few afternoons a week," Juliet said. She hesitated. "I'll almost certainly have to take a pay cut, though."

Patrick didn't say, *There are more important things than money.* Nor did he puff out his chest and say, *Don't worry, I can support us.*

Instead, he said, "Would you be okay with that?"

And the fact that he understood her so well, that he actually *got* her, caused Juliet to feel a warm whoosh of love for him.

"Yes," she said. "I'm okay with that."

Patrick swung their hands gently back and forth between them.

"It hasn't just been your job," he said seriously. "You've been distant—even when you're around."

"I know," Juliet said, remembering how many hours she'd wasted fantasizing about having a relationship with Alex. "That's going to change too."

Patrick let go of her hand and squinted into the sun. Juliet got the feeling that the jury was now deliberating, weighing the persuasiveness of her promises against the cold reality of her past behavior. But Patrick surprised her.

"It wasn't just you," he said suddenly, thrusting his hands back in his pants pocket. "I get some of the blame for this too."

Juliet thought of Alex again and shook her head. "No. This was all me."

"No, it wasn't," Patrick said firmly. "I knew why you were working so hard. I knew you were doing it for us, for the girls. And I didn't exactly make it easy for you, always nagging you to come home early and putting you on guilt trips."

"I deserved the guilt trips."

But Patrick shook his head. "We're supposed to be partners, not adversaries. We're supposed to support each other."

'That's what I want. More than anything," Juliet said.

"Me too."

Patrick smiled at her then, and relief coursed through Juliet. She knew then that it was going to be okay. Patrick pulled her close, wrapping his long arms around her waist, until her body molded against his. She felt his chest rise and fall, and she matched her breath to his.

"We'll figure it out," Patrick said, kissing the top of her head.

"We'll figure it out," Juliet repeated. And she held Patrick close, not wanting to let go.

nineteen

Chloe

As she fumbled with her keys, Chloe nearly tripped over the bouquet of tulips lying by her front door. Just the sight of the flowers enraged her, and for a moment she considered punting them off the porch. Or maybe getting out her kitchen shears and leaving a pile of mutilated stems and petals by the front door of the ridiculous trailer James had insisted on parking in their driveway.

"When is he going to get a clue?" Chloe muttered to herself, pushing the flowers off to one side with her foot.

Every evening since she'd kicked James out of the house, there'd been a bouquet waiting for her by the front door. And every evening, Chloe had ignored the flowers, stepping over them as though they weren't there. The next morning, the bouquet would still be languishing there, pathetic and wilted in its raffia-tied cellophane. And each evening, the old flowers would be whisked away and new ones would appear in their place.

And every time Chloe saw the flowers, it pissed her off even more.

"Hello," Chloe said, as she walked into the kitchen and set her purse down on the table. Mavis—her neighbor and Wills's new babysitter—was sitting in her usual seat at the table, a cup of coffee in front of her. "How'd he do?"

"He was perfect," Mavis said. "I gave him a bottle an hour ago, and then he went right to sleep. Sweet as a lamb."

"Oh, good. Thank you so much for watching him," Chloe said warmly.

"Always happy to," Mavis replied. "Did you have a nice dinner?"

"I did, thank you. I met a few of my girlfriends out. One of my friends is the restaurant reviewer for the newspaper—"

"Oh! I've read her column. 'Silver Spoons,' right?"

"Yes, that's right. We were trying out that new Italian restaurant over on Olive Street," Chloe said. "And, I'm happy to report, the food was excellent. Although Anna thinks they knew who she was, since the waiter brought us over a complimentary bottle of wine." Chloe looked closer at Mavis. The older woman's face had clouded over, and she was twisting her hands nervously in front of her. "Mavis, is everything okay?"

"Well…" Mavis paused, and when she began to speak again, the words came out in a breathy rush. "He asked me not to tell you, but I thought you should know—your husband stopped in while you were out. He wanted to see the baby," Mavis said worriedly. "I hope that's okay. I wasn't sure if I should let him in, but I also didn't feel like I could tell him he couldn't come into his own house."

"It's fine, don't worry," Chloe said soothingly.

"Are you sure?"

"Yes, really, it's fine if James wants to see Wills. I'm sure he misses the baby."

Mavis's face cleared. "Oh, good, I was so worried. And, just between you and me, I think he's a little lonely," Mavis said, as she stood and picked up her cardigan sweater and novel off the kitchen table.

"Really? Why?"

"He stayed for a while, even after I put William to sleep. We had a cup of coffee and talked. He seemed so sad," Mavis said.

"He did?" Chloe asked, and the thought of James being so lonely and despondent that he'd pour out his heart to this nice old lady caused her anger to defrost a bit.

"He said he doesn't even understand why you got so angry at him, especially since you hired me to babysit again." Mavis's expression became reproachful. "I hate to think that I'm the one who came between you two."

And back came the deep freeze.

Unbelievable, Chloe thought. *He actually manipulated Mavis into acting as his go-between. Not that I should be surprised. It's so typical of him, always trying to charm the world into doing his bidding.*

"Don't worry," Chloe said, as she walked Mavis to the front door. "This isn't your fault, believe me. By the way, how would you like some flowers to take home with you?"

There was a knock on the door the next morning. Chloe had just finished nursing William and was still in her bathrobe with her hair pulled back in a headband when she answered it. James was standing on the front porch, smiling nervously at her. He was dressed for work in the navy-blue suit she'd helped him pick out and a blue-and-white-striped shirt. There was a small square of toilet paper stuck to his jaw, covering a shaving cut.

Chloe folded her arms and looked coolly out at him. Or, at least, she hoped she looked cool and composed. The sight of her husband had actually stirred up a steaming cauldron of feelings within her: anger, sadness, regret, pain. And, yes, she missed him. She wished she didn't, but she did. The house had been so quiet without James's larger-than-life personality filling it.

"I saw you took the flowers in last night," he said. "I thought it was a sign that you were ready to talk."

"I didn't take them. I gave them to Mavis," Chloe said.

James's face fell, and his hands played nervously with his blue-and-green-striped tie. "Did Mavis tell you I stopped by to see Wills last night?" he asked hopefully.

"Yes, she did."

"Did she tell you about our conversation?"

"Do you mean how you tried to manipulate her into talking me into taking you back? She might have mentioned something about that."

"Manipulate...no! That's not what I was—honey, you're not being reasonable. You're completely overreacting."

The flames of Chloe's temper began to flicker.

"You don't get to tell me how to feel," she said.

"I'm not! I'm just...didn't you like the flowers?" James asked, his voice small and pathetic.

"No."

"Oh." He looked so disappointed that Chloe felt mean. But she was also tired of lying about her feelings to make him feel better.

"I thought you'd think they were romantic," James said sadly.

"Well, I don't. They remind me of every other time you've screwed up and tried to buy your way out of it by giving me flowers," Chloe said. She started to close the door, but James reached out an arm to stop her.

"Wait. I'm sorry. I'm sorry for the flowers, and for leaving William, and for everything," he said. He looked beseechingly at Chloe. "Just tell me what I have to do, and I'll do it. I'll change."

Chloe hesitated for a minute. He looked so miserable and so remorseful, she could hardly bear it.

What if I'm making a mistake? she wondered. *What if we really can work through this? What if this is just the normal growing pains of a couple adjusting to the pressure of caring for a new baby?*

And yet...Chloe was just too damned tired of being disappointed.

"I wish I could believe that. But, frankly, I just don't," Chloe said. She took in a deep breath. "I'm angry at you."

"Yeah, I sort of got that," James said. "But I thought it was time we made up."

Then James smiled at her. She'd seen that smile before. Charming, engaging, effortlessly charismatic. It was the sort of smile that got him the best seats in restaurants and upgraded when he flew and that caused people to trip over themselves to apologize to him for cutting ahead in line. But now it had the effect of propelling Chloe into a stratospheric rage.

He isn't listening to a word I say, she thought. *He never listens to me. Never. Not even now, when our marriage is at stake.*

Suddenly Chloe was so furious it felt like her head was going to split into two. She opened her mouth and the words that she'd been suppressing for so long finally began to flow.

"You know, I don't think you *have* gotten it. I don't think you've gotten it at all. I'm not just angry—I'm furious, and fed up, and sick to death of the way you've been acting! This isn't how it was supposed to be! I thought that when William came along, we'd be a real family, that we'd spend time together. But instead, I've been doing it all alone. All you do is work, or golf, or hang out with your buddies. Meanwhile, I'm up to my elbows in baby poo, and I hardly get any sleep, and I'm exhausted! You never get up with William, you never change his diaper. And the one time I asked you to stay with him, so I could visit my friend in the hospital, you dumped him on a complete stranger and WENT OUT GOLFING! DO YOU HAVE ANY IDEA HOW PHENOMENALLY IRRESPONSIBLE THAT WAS? DO YOU? YOU'RE A FATHER NOW! DON'T YOU GET IT? A FATHER! YOU DON'T GET TO ACT LIKE YOU'RE IN COLLEGE ANYMORE!"

Chloe's voice had been steadily rising as she spoke, until she was screaming. It wasn't until she realized just how loud she was, and just how out of control she sounded, that she stopped suddenly. She stood trembling, her breath coming in quick puffs. Chloe hadn't followed any of Juliet's tips for staying calm during a conflict—she hadn't squared her shoulders, or lifted her chin, or kept her voice controlled, or coolly laid out her argument.

James's smile had faded from his face.

"I don't know what to say," he said, fidgeting with his tie again. He seemed a bit shell-shocked from the force of her anger. "I'm sorry—really sorry. I want to fix this. Tell me what I can do to fix it. Anything, just name it."

William started to cry then, with a high-pitched urgency.

"I need to change his diaper," Chloe said, recognizing the indignant note that had crept into William's wail. She was distantly aware that she was trembling.

"Chloe, wait," James said, stepping forward. His face was pale, and his blue eyes were highlighted by smudgy dark circles. "Please. Tell me we can fix this."

But Chloe just swallowed, and after a moment she shook her head.

"I don't think we can," she said. And then she gently closed the door on her husband.

"You're all over the news," Grace said, when Chloe answered the phone.

"What are you talking about?" Chloe asked. She was sitting at the desk in her tiny home office, working on a story about diet frozen desserts for *Scale* magazine while William napped. Actually, she was trying to write the article but had mostly spent the afternoon chewing on the end of a pencil and failing to come up with a way to make Fudgsicles sound sexy.

"I was just online, and I saw your story about Fiona Watson on Google's home page. Listen: *Actress Fiona Watson Disgusted by Breastfeeding. Fiona Watson has made her fame and fortune playing the girl next door. With her all-American good looks and famous smile, she's graced the covers of dozens of magazines and been compared to the legendary actress Grace Kelly. Her famous blonde locks have been copied so often in beauty salons across the country, the hairstyle has been nicknamed 'The Fiona.' And even though Watson failed to win the Oscar for her role as Fanny Price in last year's screen adaptation of* Mansfield Park, *there's no doubt: Fiona Watson is white-hot.*

"When I met with Watson recently, she was relaxing in her Palm Beach hotel room and preparing to attend a fund-raiser at Donald Trump's famous Mar-A-Lago resort. My first impression of the actress was that she is smaller and more fragile in person than she appears on screen. But despite her diminutive size, Watson exudes a powerful magnetism. This effervescent charm, which practically guarantees box office bank, was very much in evidence as we chatted about her new movie, Lamp Light—*or it was right up until the moment when my infant son began to cry in the next room. Despite being a mother herself—although one armed with a battalion of nannies and personal assistants—Watson appeared enraged at the interruption. And*

*things only got worse when my breast milk began to leak through my
shirt, a common predicament for nursing moms. Watson was so re-
pulsed at even being in the same room as a lactating woman, she ordered me out of her presence.*

"Sound familiar? The entertainment news has picked up the
story, and the bloggers are all over it. Apparently, some breast-
feeding activists—oh, my God, they call themselves *lactivists*, if you
can believe that?—are going to stage a nurse-in at the *Lamp Light*
premiere. In this story here, one of the protest organizers is
quoted as saying, 'If Watson was grossed out by the presence of
one lactating mother, imagine how she'll feel when she faces two
hundred of us breast-feeding when she walks down the red carpet.' Wow, a nurse-in. That's hard core. But you have to admire
their spunk," Grace concluded cheerfully.

Chloe dropped the pencil she had been holding.

"The story's on the Internet? With my name on it?" she asked.
Chloe was shocked. At Juliet's encouragement, she'd typed up the
Watson story when she was still upset over being ejected uncere-
moniously from the Breakers, but she never thought for a moment that *Pop Art*—known for its sycophantic celeb pieces—would
ever publish it. Maia Bleu had practically told her as much when
Chloe handed it in.

"It's great, but I doubt the brass will clear it," Maia said. She
laughed. "I've heard rumors that Fiona can be an imperious bitch,
but I think this takes the cake."

But *Pop Art had* published it. *Wow*, Chloe thought, stunned at
this development.

"Yes! All of the news Web sites are running with it—Google,
the Drudge Report, E! Online—and they're all mentioning you
and your article in *Pop Art* by name," Grace said. "You're famous.
I'm going to e-mail this article to everyone I know."

"Oh, my God," Chloe said. She clicked open the Internet and
saw that Grace was right. It had been a slow news day—no one
had blown anything up or invaded another country—so the news
that Fiona Watson was *anti-boob*, as one Page Six columnist caus-
tically called her, was huge.

"Hey, do you want to come over for dinner on Sunday? I think we're going to cook out. Louis said he's in the mood for ribs," Grace said. "Juliet and Patrick are going to come too. And maybe Anna, if I can ever get hold of her."

"Sure, that sounds great," Chloe said distractedly. She was still clicking on the various stories, all of which pointed back to her original story, which was now on the front page of the *Pop Art* Web site. And her byline was there, in prominent fuchsia letters: CHLOE TRUMAN.

Grace said something, but Chloe was so immersed in surfing through the Fiona Watson stories, she didn't hear her.

"Sorry, what did you say?" she asked.

"I said, have you let James back in the house yet?"

"Oh...no. Not yet," Chloe said.

"Is he still leaving you flowers?"

"No. He finally seemed to figure out how much it was annoying me."

"You're the only woman I know who would be irritated by flowers," Grace said. "If Louis brought me flowers every day, I'd keel over in shock. Wait, can I say that? Or is it considered bad taste, considering I did keel over?"

"Ha-ha. And don't even try to pretend that Louis is anything less than the perfect man."

"Louis? Perfect? Are you serious?"

"Yes, I'm serious. He's amazing," Chloe said. Ever since she'd seen how he'd hovered over Grace while she was in the hospital, Chloe had become Louis's biggest fan. Especially since she couldn't help but compare his behavior with James's pitiful performance at William's birth.

"Okay, let me disabuse you of that idea right now. Louis is far from perfect. He's a bear until he's had his morning coffee. He untucks the sheets on the bed—which drives me crazy; I like them tucked in—and he leaves his wadded-up, used towels on the bathroom counter instead of hanging them up. I don't think he's ever actually put a single dirty sock in the laundry hamper. Oh! And when he has allergies, he does this disgusting, phlegmy, throat-clearing thing. It sounds like he has a mucus-covered hair-ball." Grace imitated the sound.

"Okay, that is pretty gross," Chloe conceded. "But not as bad as leaving your baby with a total stranger."

"I thought you'd decided to hire your neighbor as a regular babysitter?"

"That's besides the point. I only asked her to sit for Wills *after* I ran a background check on her," Chloe retorted.

"So what are you going to do about James?"

"I don't know," Chloe said, feeling a twist of anxiety in her stomach. "I haven't seen much of him lately. Although he has been doing stuff around the house."

"Like what?"

"Yesterday he washed my car. The day before that, he planted a border of hibiscus trees by that big front window. And he finally fixed the section of our back fence that was damaged in the hurricane last summer before we even bought the place, which I've been asking him to do for months."

"Ohhhhh," Grace sighed. "That's so romantic. As I always tell Louis when he's sniffing around for sex, there's nothing more attractive than a man who vacuums."

Chloe snorted, but the truth was, she didn't know what to think about James's sudden spate of DIY projects. It wasn't like him. And she was starting to wonder if her husband had really meant it when he'd promised to change.

The Fiona Watson story got bigger over the next few days. It came out that Fiona didn't just dislike babies and breast-feeding mothers—she seemed to hate all children, possibly even her own. Stories came flooding in. There was the maître d' at an upscale Manhattan eatery who claimed Fiona made him evict a young family because she didn't want to have to look at children while she ate. A flight attendant came forward with a tale of how Fiona had screamed abusively at her on a Miami-to-L.A. flight because there was a baby twenty rows back in coach class who wouldn't stop crying.

"If it won't shut up, try throwing it off the plane," Fiona had purportedly snapped.

And then there was the young woman who had once worked for Fiona as a nanny who was now a hot property on the talk-show circuit, enthralling viewers with a portrait of Fiona as an absentee mother who spent all of her time working or indulging in bizarre beauty treatments (including allegedly getting her bottom bleached, although Chloe wasn't sure what that could possibly involve) and rarely saw her children. Fiona was threatening to sue the nanny for violating their confidentiality agreement.

After years of having to hunt down every story assignment she got, magazine editors were finally coming to Chloe with assignments. Practically overnight, she had more work than she could handle. First she was asked to write a follow-up article about the backlash against mothers who nurse in public for *Pop Art*. Then *Mothering* magazine called to ask her to do a piece on the pros and cons of early potty training. And then a maternity magazine hired her to write a story on the drastic steps some celebrities take to lose weight after having a baby.

Chloe hired Mavis to sit with William in the afternoons while she worked, and she often stayed up late into the night, tapping away at her laptop. And, slowly, her days took on a sort of routine that helped distract her from the almost unbearable sadness she felt over James's absence.

Chloe hadn't even wanted the bracelet. It was a faux-bamboo bangle made out of clear brown Lucite, and not at all her taste. Yet she couldn't help herself. She picked up the bracelet and slid it on. It felt cold and hard on her wrist. And Chloe felt that familiar rush of exhilaration, a tantalizing cocktail of intoxication and fear. Her pulse picked up; her heart drummed in her chest.

William let out a squawk from his stroller and kicked his feet impatiently. He liked to be in constant motion when they were out and about and resented the stop.

Chloe glanced around to see if anyone was watching her or had been alerted to her presence by William's grousing. But Saks was deserted. There were a few women back behind the cosmetics counter, wearing white lab coats and chattering to one another, but Chloe doubted if they could see her from their vantage point across the floor. A zoned-out middle-aged woman clutching shopping bags and dressed in head-to-toe taupe passed by, looking absentmindedly at a rack of earrings. But she didn't seem to notice Chloe, and a moment later she moved on.

Now, Chloe thought. *Now!*

She removed the bracelet from her wrist and pretended to set it back on the display case, but then she palmed it and slipped it into her diaper bag hanging off the back of William's stroller. She felt the familiar rush of exhilaration and had to force herself to continue to browse calmly through the accessories. She feigned interest in a display of Isabella Fiore purses and then in a rack of metallic-hued belts before turning and resolutely pushing William toward the back entrance of the store.

She was just reaching out to open the door, feeling her victory swell up euphorically in her chest, when a hand clamped on to her arm. Chloe spun around to see who had grabbed her, trying unsuccessfully to pull her arm back as she did so.

It was the taupe woman—only now she didn't look so glassy-eyed. The woman reached into one of the paper shopping bags and pulled out a small walkie-talkie.

"I've apprehended the subject," the taupe woman said into the unit while Chloe stared at her uncomprehendingly. "I'll bring her up now." The woman dropped the walkie-talkie back in the bag and pulled on Chloe's arm. "Come with me."

"No, wait," Chloe protested. She clutched the handle of William's baby stroller. "Obviously there's been a mistake."

The woman reached forward into Chloe's black nylon diaper bag and pulled out the ugly Lucite faux-bamboo bangle. Chloe went cold. Fear seized at her, and her throat closed.

"Please," Chloe whispered. "Please. I'm with my baby."

"You should have thought of that before you shoplifted," the taupe woman said. And then, still holding on to Chloe's arm, she propelled Chloe—and, by extension, William in his baby stroller—with her.

Chloe felt numb as she sat holding William in the back room of Saks. The baby was awake and looking around with interest. It wasn't what Chloe had expected a detention room to look like—the sort of grim interrogation room you see on *Law & Order*, with bars on the window and a single steel folding table in the center of the room. This looked more like a small break room. There were several tables, a water cooler, and a cork message board with flyers and announcements tacked to it: an advertisement for a personal defense course, someone looking for a good home for a golden-retriever mix, a reminder for employees to put in their vacation requests six weeks in advance.

The taupe woman who'd apprehended Chloe was standing by the door, deep in conversation with a short, squarish woman wearing a white security uniform. Chloe couldn't hear what they were saying other than occasional snippets, such as "file charges," "official complaint," and—worst of all—"call child-protective services."

At this last one, Chloe felt like her heart had been dipped in ice.

Did they mean . . . are they going to take William away from me? Just for stealing a bracelet? Oh, please, no, she thought desperately. Chloe had never been particularly religious, but she began to bargain with God. *Please don't let them take William. Please. I promise I'll never steal anything ever again, if you'd just please grant me that one request. And I'll start going to church and volunteering at a homeless shelter and whatever else you want—just don't let them take William.*

"Ms. Truman." In her panic, Chloe hadn't noticed that the short, square woman in the uniform had crossed the room to speak to her, and she was startled by the security guard's sudden appearance in front of her.

"Yes?" Chloe asked, her voice high and strained.

The security guard held out a portable phone to her. "It's store policy to allow you a phone call. Is there someone you could call to come pick up your son?"

"Yes," Chloe said gratefully, so relieved that they wouldn't just take William from her and put him God-knew-where that she didn't even care what they were planning to do with her afterward. "Thank you so much."

The guard nodded brusquely and handed her the phone, then walked back to continue her argument with the taupe woman. Chloe sat, cradling William in one arm and holding the phone in her free hand, while she tried to figure out who to call. Juliet was the obvious choice—she was a lawyer—but Chloe didn't want Juliet, or any of her friends for that matter, to find out that she was a thief. Her parents were too far away to help. The only other person she knew in town was Mavis, but Chloe had already learned that the older woman loved to gossip, and she didn't relish the entire neighborhood hearing about this.

Which left only one person: James. Chloe didn't have a choice, she *had* to call him. She shifted the phone awkwardly to her other hand and dialed his cell phone number. He answered after one ring.

"Hello," he said. His voice sounded tinny and distant.

"Hi, it's me," Chloe said.

"Hey," he said, his voice softening. "Where are you calling from? I didn't recognize the number."

"I'm in West Palm at the mall, and...well, I'm in trouble. I need you to come get William," Chloe said. "Now. It's an emergency."

When James arrived, his boyishly handsome face was taut and pale. The female uniformed security guard led him in, and Chloe's first thought was how out of place he looked in the dingy room, dressed for the office in a crisp white shirt, pale-purple silk tie, and navy-blue wool pants.

"Mrs. Truman, your husband is here," the guard said unnecessarily.

"Chloe, Jesus, what's going on?" James asked, crossing the room quickly. Chloe stood and wordlessly stepped into his arms, which he wrapped around her. "Where's William?" he asked softly.

"Right here, in his stroller," Chloe said, turning to look at William, who'd been lulled into a milk-sated sleep. "Will you take him home? I don't know how long they're going to keep me here or what they're going to do to me...." Her voice, quavering with fear, trailed off.

"What happened?" James asked. "They said they were holding you for shoplifting a bracelet. I told them they must have made a mistake, that you must have gotten distracted by the baby and forgotten that you were holding it. Right?"

Chloe buried her head on his shoulder and closed her eyes, feeling her forehead press against the soft cotton of his shirt. She knew she could lie, say that it was a mistake, and that James would believe her. But she couldn't. Not only was she a terrible liar—a liability for any thief—but she didn't *want* to lie. Not now, not anymore. She shook her head slightly.

"No," she whispered. "I took it."

"But why?" James asked. He was being careful to speak quietly, so that the guard wouldn't overhear him.

Chloe shrugged, shaking her head more vehemently. "I don't know. I just...did," she said faintly.

"Did you think we couldn't afford it?"

"No, that's not it. It wasn't even that expensive. I just felt this...urge, I guess. It's happened before," she said.

"Oh, Chloe," James said with a sigh, and Chloe felt an almost unbearable sadness wash over her. She'd disappointed him. It was an awful feeling.

"Don't admit anything to them," James said. "In fact, don't say anything to anyone. I'll call your friend, the lawyer, and ask her to come represent you."

"No!" Chloe said, louder than she meant to. She took a step back and peered up anxiously at James. "Please don't tell her. I don't want anyone to know. *Please.*"

"Okay, shh, okay," James said soothingly. He took her back into his arms, and Chloe relaxed against him. Having him there made her feel like everything might be okay after all.

"Mrs. Truman?"

Chloe turned. It was the short, squat security guard, frowning at her. The guard was homely, with coarse features and brushlike hair, and she had a name tag pinned to her white polyester uniform blouse that read MONA STANWICK. But despite the stern expression on Mona's face, there was a kind light in her brown eyes. Chloe knew Mona was just doing her job, which, in this case, was catching thieves.

Well, she's caught one, Chloe thought. And feeling bolstered by James's steady presence beside her, one arm wrapped around her shoulder, she decided it was time she took responsibility for her actions. The term *scared straight* was making a hell of a lot of sense to her right now.

"Are you going to press charges against my wife?" James asked.

"No, we're not," Mona Stanwick said. "The value of the item you took was rather insubstantial, under fifty dollars, so we're going to let you go with a warning, Mrs. Truman. This time. I can promise you that if it happens again, we won't be so forgiving," the security guard said, arching her eyebrows for emphasis.

"Thank you," Chloe breathed, so overcome with gratitude, she was surprised she was able to speak at all. "Thank you so much."

"All right," Mona Stanwick said. She nodded at the door. "You're free to go."

Chloe staggered out of the door with James following behind her, pushing William's stroller. Chloe felt woodenly self-conscious as she walked through the store toward the exit. *Are the salesclerks looking at me? Does everyone know?* For a moment Chloe faltered and had to reach out and grab on to a rounder of women's sale jackets to steady herself.

But then James caught up with her and took her hand in his, which gave Chloe the courage to start moving forward again, putting one foot in front of the other.

It wasn't until they were outside, in the warm stillness of the afternoon, that Chloe was finally able to speak.

"Thank you," she said, turning to face him.

"For what?"

"For coming down here."

"Of course I came. You know I would." James frowned suddenly. "Don't you?"

"Yes—well..." Chloe hesitated. "I wasn't sure you'd want to, after...after everything that's happened between us."

"Chloe." James touched her arm lightly. "You're my wife. You're my *family*."

"But it's all been so...so *awful* lately."

James nodded. "You were angry. And rightfully so."

"But we never fight. We never have before," Chloe said.

"Maybe we should. Maybe if we actually did, we could work out some of our problems and we wouldn't get to this point—me living in a trailer in the driveway, you stealing bracelets at Saks. And you were right about everything you said that day. About how I need to step up and be a better dad. Maybe it took you shouting it at me for me to finally hear it. I'm so sorry."

The relief that rushed through her took Chloe's breath away. So he had heard her. For once he'd really listened to her.

And yet Chloe hesitated. "But how do I know that things won't go back to the way they were before? With you off golfing every weekend and me never getting a break from taking care of Wills?"

"They won't. I won't." James smiled wryly. "I've learned my lesson. Learned what it's like to live without my family. I don't want to ever go through that again."

"I don't either," Chloe said. "And I'm sorry too."

"You don't have anything to be sorry for. I'm the jackass here."

"Well, I'm the one who just got caught shoplifting," Chloe said, shrugging. She stared down at her feet. "It isn't exactly something I'm proud of."

"Why did you do it?" James asked.

"I'm not sure, really."

James fell silent, and Chloe didn't have the nerve to look back up at him. Instead, she stared down at William's sweet round face, still slack with sleep.

How could I have done this when William was with me? she wondered, and a fresh wave of horror washed over her. What if she'd been arrested? What if they'd taken him away from her? And what if she hadn't been able to get hold of James? Where would they have put William? It was too awful to consider.

Whatever I have to do to get control of this, I'll do, Chloe thought. *I have too much to lose to ever take a chance like this again.*

"It's over. I won't ever do it again," Chloe promised. She'd made the promise to herself in the past, but this time she meant it. Saying it out loud, saying it to someone else, made it more than a promise. It was now an oath. "But I think I'll need help. Maybe I should try talking to someone, like a therapist."

"I think that might be a good idea. Maybe we should go together and talk about some of the problems we've been having."

"You'd do that for me?"

"Chloe." When James looked down at her, his eyes were soft. "I'd do anything for you. You and William are my family. I love you."

"Oh," Chloe said. "I didn't know."

"You didn't know I loved you?"

"No, I knew you loved me, it's just…" But Chloe stopped. It was just that she always thought she was the one who loved more. There was always one person in a relationship who did. But maybe she'd been wrong about that. Maybe both people could love equally. Or maybe they could take turns being the one to love more. She looked at James, suddenly feeling shy with him.

"What are you doing now?" Chloe asked.

He shook his head. "Nothing. I thought I was going to take Wills home, so I took the rest of the afternoon off."

"Do you want to go home and talk?"

James looked at her for a long moment and then reached up to brush a stray curl back from her forehead.

"More than anything," he finally said.

"Good," she said. "Let's go home."

twenty

Anna

Anna hadn't wanted to fight with her mother. But sometimes the fight just found you. Or at least that's how Anna con-
soled herself when she was in a philosophic frame of mind.

The argument had come about when her mom began to
question Anna about her relationship—or lack thereof—with
Noah.

"When are you going to see Noah with the sexy smile again?"
Margo asked.

"First of all, it completely weirds me out when you refer to a
man I've dated as sexy. Second, you do remember the part about
him having four ex-fiancées, right? And third, I'm not going to see
him again," Anna retorted, trying to ignore the way her stomach
felt like it was falling out of her body whenever she thought about
Noah.

"Four fiancées." Margo waved her hand dismissively. "It's not
like he's had four *wives,* for goodness sake."

"It's not much better," Anna muttered.

"Why aren't you going to see him again? Has he called you?"

"No, but that was my choice. I told him not to."

"Why the hell would you do something stupid like that?"
Margo had asked, her voice sharp.

"Mom, shhh," Anna said, giving her a pointed look and then
nodding in Charlie's direction.

They'd taken Charlie out to the Orange Cove Grill for dinner
and ordered cheeseburgers, fries, and chocolate shakes all around.

Anna didn't want to get into her nonrelationship with Noah in front of Charlie, even if he (a) was only two, (b) hadn't yet mastered the English language, and (c) was too busy pushing packets of sugar around the table, pretending they were trains, to pay any attention to what Anna and Margo were talking about.

"Choo choo," Charlie said happily.

Just before her mother had started in, Anna was mulling over an idea for an article: *The Best Cheeseburger in Orange Cove.* The Orange Cove Grill—an overly grand name for what amounted to little more than a burger shack—would top the list. Despite the humble surroundings, the cheeseburgers there were excellent, dressed in dill relish and homemade mayonnaise and served with thick steak fries made from scratch. Delicious. Anna had been savoring her burger, right up to the moment that Margo—who was incapable of letting anything go—had to go and ruin dinner by bringing up Noah.

"Men like Noah don't come around every day. You know, you won't always be this young and pretty," Margo continued mulishly.

"So what are you saying? That I should run out and find a man before my looks fade?" Anna asked incredulously.

"That's exactly what I'm saying."

Anna rolled her eyes. *Give me strength,* she thought. "*Mother.* Stop it. My love life is none of your business."

"What a ridiculous thing to say. Of course it's my business."

"No, it's not," Anna hissed. "And I've already told you, I don't want to discuss this in public. Charlie, aren't you hungry? Here, eat some french fries."

But Charlie, who didn't share his mother and Gigi's taste for greasy junk food, just poked disdainfully at his cheeseburger. "Grapes?" he asked hopefully.

"Grapes? I give you french fries, and you ask for grapes?" Anna asked, with a laugh. "Clearly you are not my son."

"You're my daughter, and the mother of my grandson. Whom you date is certainly my business," Margo continued.

Anna sighed, trying—and failing—to swallow her irritation. "Well, then, you have nothing to worry about. Because I have no intention of dating anyone right now or in the foreseeable future. In fact, well past the point when my looks start to go," she said stubbornly.

Margo looked scandalized. "I didn't raise you to be a quitter."

"Quitter? I'm not quitting anything." Anna set her half-eaten cheeseburger down, her appetite gone. "I'm simply choosing to content myself with my life as a single mother rather than risk exposing Charlie to the sort of men who—" Anna stopped, realizing a moment too late what she'd been about to say.

"Go ahead. You don't want to expose Charlie to the sort of men I exposed you to," Margo said, her voice suddenly cold.

Well, I'm in it now, Anna thought. She sighed.

"Mom, for all that we joke about how off the wall some of those guys were, let's face it: It's dangerous to expose your child to strange men. You were taking an enormous risk bringing men that you barely even knew around me," Anna said.

"I can't believe you'd say that to me. I would never—*never*— have risked your safety," Margo said, her voice now quavering.

"But you *did*." Anna shrugged. "And luckily, nothing ever happened. But that's just what it was: dumb luck."

"It was *not* dumb luck. I would never have dated the sort of man who would have hurt you! I can't believe you'd suggest that I would!"

"How would you know? Do you think pedophiles have a giant P tattooed on their foreheads?"

"Do not patronize me, Anna Catherine."

"Mom—" Anna began.

"No parent is perfect, but I can tell you this: I did my best, my absolute level best, to keep you safe and happy when you were a child. God knows, your father wasn't any help, and I had to do it all on my own, but nevertheless, you were always my top priority. And so for you to begrudge me a life of my own—"

"I don't begrudge you anything," Anna interrupted her. "All I said was that I wasn't going to do the same. Aren't I allowed to make my own choices, to live my life the way I think best?"

"No," Margo said, suddenly strangely calm. "Not if you're going to be so stupid about it."

Anger pulsed in Anna. She struggled to keep her voice calm and level, so as not to upset Charlie. "I see. So you can question my judgment, but I'm not allowed to question yours?"

"That's right," Margo said. She buttered a slice of bread for Charlie, who grabbed it from her and jammed it into his mouth.

"Bread and butter," Charlie chortled, as though he were a Dickensian orphan who'd been subsisting on little more than watered-down gruel.

"And it's about time you stopped being so rigid," Margo continued.

"What? How am I being rigid?" Anna yelped.

"Like with Brad. He made one little mistake, and *poof,* you divorced him, just like that," Margo said, waving an airy hand.

"What do you mean, *poof*? He cheated on me! Besides, you hate Brad!"

"I don't hate him. Well, okay, yes, I do. But that's not the point," her mother said. "The point is you never give anyone a second chance."

Anna stood. "Mom, I'm sorry, but you're out of line on this one," she said wearily. "Come on, Charlie. You can eat your bread and butter in the car."

Margo didn't talk to Anna for two weeks, other than to exchange the necessary information about Charlie when Anna dropped him off or picked him up. Anna got so tired of the cold-shoulder treatment, she contemplated avoiding her mother altogether, but she didn't have the heart to keep Charlie and his beloved Gigi apart.

The price of motherhood, Anna thought, with a sigh. *I can't even avoid the people I want to avoid.*

Case in point: Brad. Once her temper had cooled, Anna decided to take Grace's advice and didn't file for a change in the custody arrangement. But Brad had been annoyingly eager to please ever since Charlie's big escape. He'd even hired a company that specialized in childproofing to come over and make his house completely Charlie-proof, and he was so excited with the new child safety locks, door alarm, and oven lock that he'd insisted Anna come over to give her approval.

"And look over here!" Brad said, gesturing toward the living room with a flourish. It looked... empty. The leather couches were still there, but not much else.

"What did you do? Where did all of the furniture go?" Anna asked, frowning, as she tried to remember what Brad had kept in his living room. All she could remember was lots of glass and chrome.

"The woman from the childproofing company had me put all of it away. She said that Charlie could easily pull something down on himself or fall on it and cut himself," Brad explained.

"Oh, right. You know," Anna said, not able to resist, "I did mention that to you a while ago."

"Did you? Really? I don't remember."

"Yes, I did. Really. Look, this is great, but you probably spent way too much money. You could have gotten most of this stuff from the Home Depot and installed it yourself."

"I know. But I wanted to make sure it was done right and that I didn't miss anything. Anyway, now you don't have to worry about leaving Charlie here again. This place is like a fortress," Brad said. Anna recognized his tone and the swagger that accompanied it: Brad was just selling again. But instead of selling pharmaceuticals, he was selling himself as a responsible father.

And the most irritating part of it was that it was working.

Anna looked over at Charlie. He was playing with the train table Brad had bought and set up for him in the corner of his living room, giving the whole space a different atmosphere— suddenly it was more Nickelodeon, less Playboy Mansion. She had to admit: Charlie looked happy here. He was confident and re- laxed, basking in the glow of his father's attention.

"All aboard!" Charlie called out happily, waving one of the trains in the air.

Anna turned back to Brad. "Okay. You've convinced me."

"So does that mean...will you actually let me have Charlie over again?" Brad asked tentatively.

And as much as her reaction irritated her, Anna couldn't help but feel touched that Brad was being so deferential. It was just so thoughtful and considerate—and so completely unlike him.

"Yes," she finally said. "But I swear, Brad, if anything like that ever happens again..." Her voice trailed off, the implied threats unspoken.

Brad nodded solemnly. "I know you hate it when I promise something, but on this I really and truly do give you my word. I'll keep him safe, Anna. He's my son too. I love him more than anything in the world."

Anna nodded in return, slowly, reluctantly. "Okay. But I'm going to hold you to that," she said.

When Brad smiled, the corners of his eyes crinkled up. "I wouldn't expect anything less."

Despite herself, Anna couldn't help smiling back at him.

"Come give Mama a kiss good-bye, Charlie," she said. "Daddy's going to take you swimming in the ocean! Won't that be fun?"

Anna did what she always did when she was stressed out: She cooked. A lot. Since the argument with her mom, Anna had made a frittata, two peach pies, carrot cake, a big pot of gumbo, moussaka, lasagna, and a sour-cream chocolate chip cake. She felt like the very hungry caterpillar from Charlie's picture book, only instead of eating her way through the week, she was cooking her way through it.

Finally, in despair, Anna turned to her fail-safe stress-buster: bread. She spent an entire Saturday morning mixing up two huge bowls full of dough, letting it rise, and then pummeling it, while Charlie and Potato romped underfoot.

Is Mom right? Am I too rigid? she wondered, as she oiled her big stainless-steel mixing bowl, prepping it for another batch of bread dough. *Was I too quick to end things with Noah?*

Noah. Her heart squeezed. She missed him more than she'd thought possible. It had been so amazing to have something in her life other than Charlie, work, and her friends. She hadn't even realized there was something missing until Noah came along. And now that he was gone, the hole was back. A Noah-shaped hole.

Yes, it was true he had a worrying history, what with his four ex-fiancées. But that was just it—Anna had believed Noah when he'd explained the scary-high number to her. She had. So if it wasn't that . . . well, it wasn't that. It was her. Her—and Charlie.

Anna looked down at her son, who was now lying on his stomach in the middle of the kitchen floor, happily scribbling in a coloring book with a thick orange crayon. Potato lay next to Charlie, in a nearly identical position, chewing on a blue crayon she gripped with her front paws.

What was it Grace said? Anna wondered as she leaned over to take the crayon away from Potato. *Charlie will be fine. Kids are adaptable.* Was that true? Was she avoiding Noah not for Charlie's sake but because she was frightened of being hurt?

This thought startled her with how true she immediately knew it to be. She *was* afraid. Afraid of being hurt, afraid of being left. Afraid of another Brad. Afraid of taking a chance and being let down again.

The doorbell rang, interrupting her thoughts.

Noah! Anna thought, her heart lurching. Could it possibly be him? Had he somehow sensed that she was thinking about him?

Anna wiped her hands on a dish towel, stepped over Charlie, and hurried to the door, anticipation swelling inside her. She yanked the door open, and—

"Hi, honey," her mom said.

Of course it wasn't Noah, Anna thought. She didn't know why she felt so disappointed. She'd told him to stay away, and he was respecting her decision.

"Gigi!" Charlie crowed happily, rushing forward and flinging his arms around his grandmother's legs. Potato cavorted after him, yipping happily.

"Hi, Mom," Anna said.

"I don't want to fight anymore," Margo announced. She was holding a plant with a big white bow wrapped around the pot, which she thrust at Anna. "It's a peace lily. Peace?"

Anna laughed. She shifted the plant to her left arm and hugged her mom with her right, breathing in the familiar scent of her Joy perfume. Margo had worn it for as long as Anna could remember, and the fragrance clung to all of Anna's childhood memories.

"Peace," Anna agreed. "Come on in."

"What smells so delicious?" Margo asked, shutting the front door behind her.

"I'm baking bread," Anna said, leading Margo—who had picked Charlie up and perched him on one hip—back to the kitchen. "Would you like some coffee?"

"Yes. Black, please." Margo sat down at one of Anna's cane-back kitchen chairs and fixed her daughter with a penetrating look. "So what's wrong?"

"Wrong? What do you mean? Nothing's wrong," Anna said. She poured a cup of coffee from the drip pot and put it on the table next to Margo. "Do you mind if I work while we talk? I have to knead this dough."

"You only bake bread when you're upset about something," Margo said. She blew on her coffee and took a careful sip. Charlie brought over his coloring book to show his Gigi and beamed happily when she said, "That's a gorgeous picture! What a talented boy!"

"No, I don't," Anna said.

"Yes, you do. You don't think I know my own daughter?" Margo asked.

"It's nothing." Anna shrugged. "It's just been hectic at work. And you and I haven't been speaking."

"Mmm-hmmm," Margo said, clearly not believing this was the whole story.

Anna sighed and tucked her hair behind her ears. "And...
well. I've been wondering..." This was hard to admit. "Maybe you
were right. About Noah, I mean. And about my being too rigid."

Margo's face lit up with a huge, self-satisfied smile. *"Really,"*
she said, drawing the word out.

Grrr, thought Anna.

"Look, never mind," she said grumpily, and went back to
pounding her dough.

"Anna." This time Margo's voice was gentle, and when Anna
looked up, she saw the concern on her mother's face. "Just don't
make the same mistake I did."

"What mistake?"

Margo sighed and wrapped her hands around her coffee mug.
"After your father left, I swore I'd never let another man do that to
me. Desert me, leaving me alone and wounded."

Anna stared at her mother, not comprehending. "What are
you talking about? You dated all the time," she said.

Margo nodded. "That's right. I *dated.* I went out and had fun,
and as soon as I sensed the man was getting too attached—
or, even worse, if I was getting too attached—I stopped seeing
him."

Anna struggled to make sense of this new perspective. Her
mother—her vain, flirtatious mother—was a commitmentphobe?
Even more disturbing, her mother's confession that her fear had
kept her from getting too close to another man mirrored Anna's
own revelation about herself.

"I never knew you felt like that," Anna said.

"Oh, yes. Then you grew up and moved out, and now I'm all
alone," Margo said sadly.

"You're not alone. You still have me. And Charlie."

Margo smiled fondly down at Charlie, who had dragged his
toy xylophone out from his room and was now banging away at it.
She had to raise her voice to be heard above the cacophony.

"Yes, of course I do. And I have my work." Margo was a nurse
and worked part-time for an orthopedist. "But still. It would

have been nice to have someone to come home to. Someone to travel with."

"I can see that," Anna said, thinking, *Oh, my God, is this how I'm going to end up? Lonely and miserable because Charlie's grown and I don't have anyone to go on a Caribbean cruise with? And I'll just get older and older, and Charlie will probably marry some awful woman who won't want me to move into their in-law suite, and they'll stick me in some horrible retirement home and only visit me once a year on Mother's Day?*

It was such a depressing vision of her future that Anna felt wobbly for a minute, and she had to draw in a deep, steadying breath and grip the counter.

"Are you okay?" Margo asked, her brow knitting in concern.

"Fine. I'm fine." Anna took in one more deep breath and then decided what she had to do. She'd made a mistake—a terrible mistake—and now she had to see if she could make it right.

"Mom, would you mind watching Charlie for a bit? I have an errand I have to run."

"Of course," Margo said, with a knowing smile.

"Thanks." Anna pulled off her apron and smoothed down her pink oxford shirt. *Should I change? Slap on some makeup? And, oh, God, what's going on with my hair?* Anna raised a self-conscious hand to her chopped locks, which were still in the growing-out stage.

"You look beautiful," Margo said. She stood and wiped some flour off the tip of Anna's nose. Then she placed a cool hand on Anna's cheek. "You've never looked lovelier."

"Thanks, Mom," Anna said. She took in another shaky breath and wondered why she suddenly felt like she was going to cry.

"Now go get him," Margo said. She picked up the peace lily and handed it to Anna. "Give him this."

"Really?" Anna asked, looking at her lily doubtfully.

"Yes, really."

"Okay, I'm going. Wait—what about Charlie?"

"Charlie will be fine. I'll take him over to the playground."

"I know he'll be fine *now*. But what about later?" Anna asked.

"He'll be *fine*, Anna. He'll be fine because he's your son."

And suddenly Anna's eyes were blurring, and her nose got the tingly feeling it always did when she cried.

"Okay. Wish me luck," Anna said. And then, the peace lily tucked under one arm, she walked out into the glittering Florida sunshine.

The bell tinkled as Anna walked into Bacchus, clutching the plant to her chest like a safety blanket.

"Hi, can I, like, help you?" a young woman behind the counter asked. She was pretty, with lots of dark eye makeup and hair dyed the color of maraschino cherries. She was also thin, with—Anna couldn't help but notice—very large, very perky breasts.

Oh, God, Anna thought. *What if Noah's started dating his store clerk?* Suddenly her imagination began to spin out of control: *Noah noticing the nubile young woman, admiring her as she stocked the shelves... The two of them kissing and clutching at each other in the back room... Noah's newly found appreciation for young, pert breasts not made saggy by breast-feeding. Oh, no, no, no*, Anna thought, as an even worse possibility occurred to her. *What if he's proposed to her? He does have a track record of doing that.*

She was just about to back slowly out of the store and bolt to her car when Noah came out of the back room, holding a heavy crate in his arms. He stopped when he saw Anna, his eyes looking very dark and guarded behind his metal-framed glasses.

"Hi," Anna said.

"Hi," Noah said. He turned to the shopgirl. "Leah, why don't you go take your break."

"Sure thing," Leah said, grabbing a canvas tote bag from behind the counter and bouncing off happily. The doorbell tinkled again as she left.

Hmmm, Anna thought. *Okay, so they're probably not dating, or she wouldn't have been so thrilled with being asked to leave. Well,*

*Unless she's so self-confident in her perfect body that she doesn't view
me as competition, that is.... No, no, no. Of course Noah isn't sleeping with his shop assistant. He's too ethical for that.*

And then there was the not-so-small matter of the way Noah
was looking at her, as though he wasn't exactly unhappy to see
her, but a bit warily, as though not sure why she was there.

"I just stopped by to give you something," Anna said. She
thrust the lily at him.

"Thanks. What is it, exactly?" Noah asked.

"It's a peace lily," Anna explained.

"A peace lily?"

"Yes. You know—it's a plant."

Noah finally laughed, although his chuckle seemed reluctant.
"Yeah, well, I sort of figured that part out on my own," he said.

"The peace lily," Anna gestured toward the plant, "is meant to
be a symbol of peace and reconciliation."

"Isn't this the plant people give to mourners after they've lost
someone?" Noah asked, frowning down at the lily.

"Yes, that too. But that's not how I meant it."

"So you're not giving me a plant of death?"

"No! I'm trying to—oh, crap. This isn't coming out right at all.
When my mom gave it to me this morning, she—"

"Wait: Your mom gave this to you?" Noah asked, his forehead
wrinkling with confusion.

"Well, yes," Anna said. "But she told me to give it to you."

"Your mother told you to give me your plant?" Noah repeated.
"And why exactly did she want you to do that?"

"Because..." Anna stopped and took a deep breath. *Here goes
nothing,* she thought, hoping that he really, truly wasn't involved
with his shop assistant. Or anyone else, for that matter. Or that
he'd decided that neurotic single mothers were too high mainte-
nance for him. Or that that he wanted to take a break from dating
altogether.

Gah, stop it, Anna told herself sternly. *Just tell him how you
feel. The worst thing that can happen is that he says no, he doesn't feel*

the same way. That would be mortifying beyond all sense, true, but you'll survive.

"Okay, what I wanted to tell you is…" She drew in another steadying breath. "I made a mistake when I said I didn't want to see you anymore. A big mistake. And I've missed you. So that's why I came over with the stupid plant, to tell you that. And to say I'm sorry. For everything," she finished awkwardly.

Noah was quiet for a minute, and Anna found herself holding her breath as she waited for his response. Then, not able to stand the silence anymore, she blurted out, "But if you don't want to give me a second chance, I totally understand. All you have to say is no, and I'll go away and never bother you again. Or bring you plants."

Anna couldn't bear looking at him, so she stared down at the dark-stained floorboards of the shop.

"A second chance?" Noah finally said.

"Yes," Anna said. "I know I don't deserve it, but—"

"Don't deserve it?" Noah said. This time his voice was incredulous. "You just need a second chance. That's nothing. I'm the guy with four ex-fiancées looking for a fifth chance."

Only then did Anna let herself look at him and really see him for the first time since she'd arrived, peace lily in hand. She saw the angular planes of his face—the slightly crooked nose, the strong jaw, the just-too-thick eyebrows. She saw his eyes, which looked more hazel than brown today. She looked at the soft curve of his mouth as it smiled down at her. Anna's heart sped up a bit, and a magically warm feeling flooded through her.

I love him, she thought. *I really do love him. When the hell did that happen?*

"A fifth chance. I think I can manage that," Anna said softly, and a smile spread across her face. And she kept smiling, even after Noah pulled her close and kissed her.

Then suddenly she pulled back and looked up at him. "Why didn't you ever call me?" she demanded.

"What?" Noah asked.

"You never called me. Not once. You just stopped by to drop off my purse that day after...well, you know," Anna said, blushing a bit. "After our last date. But you never called."

"You told me not to call. I was trying to respect your wishes," Noah said. He looked perplexed.

"Yes, but how did you know I really didn't want you to call? How did you know that I wasn't just playing hard-to-get? That I was *saying* don't call but that it was really a test to see if you *would* call?" Anna asked.

"Because we're not sixteen years old?" Noah said, now looking amused.

"Hmmm," Anna said suspiciously. "You're not seeing anyone, are you? You haven't gotten engaged to anyone since we last spoke?"

Noah snorted. "No."

"How about Leah?"

"Leah? You mean Leah that was just in here? With the bright red hair? And the ten tattoos?"

"Yes, that Leah. Wait—how do you know she has ten tattoos?"

"You're jealous." Noah smiled down at Anna, and wrapped his arms around her waist and pulled her close against him. "Mmmm, I like it when you're jealous. And when you go into reporter mode and start interrogating me." He bent forward and nuzzled her neck.

"You haven't answered my question," Anna said.

"No, I'm not seeing Leah. And I know she has ten tattoos because she spends an inordinate amount of time wondering out loud where she should place her eleventh tattoo."

"Oh. Well. Okay, then."

Noah kissed her again, this time more intently. Leah came back in, holding a pink fruit smoothie in one hand. When she saw Noah and Anna embracing in the middle of the store, she stopped, and her mouth formed an O.

"Should I, like, come back later?" Leah asked.

"No," Noah said firmly. "We have to"—he gave Anna a sly glance—"go take care of something. So you're in charge, Leah."

" 'Kay," Leah said, her combat boots clomping on the wooden floor as she made her way back to the counter.

"Where are we going?" Anna whispered, as Noah put a hand on her arm and started to guide her out of the store.

"My place," Noah said decisively. He shot her a sideways smile. "As fast as my car will drive us there."

epilogue

Three Months Later

"Hey, sweetie, it's me," Grace said when Anna answered the phone.

"Hey, you! How are you feeling?" Anna asked.

"I wish everyone would stop asking me that," Grace grumbled.

Anna laughed. "So, what's up? I can't talk now. I'm right in the middle of my column."

"I was just calling to see if you and Charlie wanted to come over on Saturday night for a farewell party."

"Absolutely," Anna said. "Can I bring anything?"

"You could bring Noah."

"Or a peach cobbler," Anna said.

Grace sighed with exasperation. "You're going to have to do it sooner or later."

"Okay, then I choose later," Anna said. She'd been as yet unwilling to let Noah meet Charlie. Or, more accurately, unwilling to let Charlie meet Noah, until she was sure where her relationship with Noah was going.

"You've been dating for months," Grace said.

Anna shrugged, before remembering that they were talking on the phone, and Grace couldn't see her. "I just want to be sure first," Anna said. "Really, *really* sure."

"At least think about bringing him," Grace said.

"You're starting to sound like my mom. And I don't mean that as a compliment," Anna said.

Grace laughed. "How is your mother? Is she still dating that guy she met through the online personals?"

"Yeah, actually, she is. I think it's getting serious. They're taking a trip to Savannah next week."

"Good for her," Grace said warmly. "Oh, crap!"

"What?"

"Literally: crap. I have to change Nat."

"I'll see you Saturday."

"See you then."

It was a typical south Florida summer night—hot and unbearably humid. Anna was running late, as usual, so by the time she and Charlie got to Grace's house, everyone else was already there. The kids were splashing around in the pool and shrieking wildly. Chloe was paddling in the water too, pushing William and Natalie along in a little inflatable boat. Grace and Juliet, dressed in tank tops and shorts, were sitting by the edge of the pool, their feet dipped in the water. The three husbands sat in the shade of the covered patio, drinking bottles of sweating beer and talking golf.

"We're here!" Anna said. Charlie, spotting the pool, stopped dead in his tracks and began stripping off his clothes.

"Charlie, wait," Anna said, trying to hold him back. "I have to go in with you."

"It's okay, Anna, I'll watch him," Chloe said.

Anna held on to a squirming Charlie just long enough to fasten on his water wings. As soon as she let go, he catapulted into the pool, giggling manically.

"Stay with Mrs. Truman," Anna called after him.

"Come sit down with us, Anna," Grace said. "Louis, will you get Anna a glass of wine?"

"Coming right up," Louis said. "Does anyone else want one? Chloe? How're you doing?"

"I'm fine," Chloe called back. "Still nursing my iced tea."

"There's something I have to tell you first," Anna said. She took in a deep breath, but before she could continue, Grace interrupted her.

"You're engaged!" Grace announced.

Anna stopped and blinked. "What?"

"Is that your big announcement? You're engaged?" Grace asked hopefully.

"No! And shhh," Anna said. She gave a meaningful look in Charlie's direction, although he was too busy paddling around under Chloe's careful supervision to hear anything his mother was saying.

"Sorry," Grace said, rolling her eyes at Juliet. "I wasn't thinking. Clearly, I must edit myself in front of the two-year-old."

"*Anyway*, I was just going to say that—" But before Anna could finish her thought, Noah walked in through the back gate, carrying a Pyrex baking dish.

"I come bearing bread pudding," Noah announced.

"Noah!" Grace said excitedly, twisting around to beam up at Anna. "You brought him!"

Anna held up her hands and widened her eyes at Grace. "Yes," she hissed. "And we're trying to keep it low key." She bobbed her head toward Charlie again.

"Ohhhh," Grace said, realization dawning. She paused. "But wait. Didn't you just come together? Or did you drive separately?"

"No, we came together. We're just not making a big deal over it," Anna said, as Noah joined her, still holding the bread pudding.

"Hi, Noah," Grace said.

"We're glad you talked Anna into bringing you," Juliet said.

"It didn't take much convincing. I just had to promise not to hold her hand or pretty much make any physical contact with her in front of Charlie," Noah said, grinning at Anna and bumping her arm gently with his.

"Hello? That was physical contact," Anna said, stepping away from Noah and looking nervously over at Charlie.

"Maybe I should go over and join the guys," Noah said. He held up the Pyrex dish to Grace. "Where should I put the bread pudding?"

"Chocolate bread pudding with bourbon-pecan caramel sauce," Anna corrected him.

"Just something you whipped up in your spare time?" Juliet teased.

"It sounds *yum*," Grace said.

"I'll take it," Louis said, bringing over a glass of chilled white wine for Anna. "In fact, why don't the rest of you leave me and the bread pudding alone."

"Ha-ha," Anna said. She accepted the wine, then kicked off her sandals and sat down next to Grace at the edge of the pool, dipping her feet in the water.

"Come on, Noah. I think the women want to talk about you behind your back," Louis said.

"We don't mind talking about him in front of him," Grace said.

"Thanks, but I think I'll pass on that kind offer," Noah said, as he followed Louis back toward the covered patio, where he was greeted by Patrick and James.

"Suit yourself," Grace said.

"James," Chloe called out. "Will you come and take over with the kids? I'm missing out on all the gossip. Here, come get in the boat, Charlie."

Chloe scooped up Charlie and settled him in the boat next to William and Natalie. James set his beer down, pulled off his shirt, and—with a wide grin—cannonballed into the deep end of the pool. Emma squealed as she got drenched with water.

"Ham," Chloe said affectionately. James kissed her lightly on the mouth.

"Come on, guys. Let's go *brrrrm* like a motorboat," James said, buzzing his lips and pushing Charlie, William, and Natalie in front of him as he kicked his way down the pool. Chloe climbed out of the pool, water streaming off her body, and grabbed a towel from the back of a deck chair before heading over to her friends.

"Hey," Chloe said happily, settling down next to Juliet as she toweled off her hair.

"Ack! You're dripping all over me," Juliet complained.

In response, Chloe shook her head like a dog drying off, spraying Juliet.

Juliet leaned away, grimacing as the water splattered her. "Oh, that's very mature," she said.

"You're going to miss me when you're gone," Chloe said. She pouted. "I can't believe you're moving away."

"I know. It's going to be so weird not having you around," Grace said.

"So you're really leaving Monday?" Anna asked.

Juliet nodded. "The moving company is coming first thing Monday morning. Patrick's going to stay and supervise the movers, and I'm going to drive the kids down."

Juliet had accepted a job as in-house counsel for an insurance company. The pay was good, and the hours would be more flexible than what she'd had at her old job. The only downside was that the job was in Boca. Which, as Juliet and Patrick had decided, wasn't such a bad thing. And Patrick had also already secured a new job, this one at the Boca Raton Fire–Rescue Services Department. Patrick's mother, Trish, had offered to help out with the girls, picking them up from school on the days when neither Juliet nor Patrick would be able to.

"Well, we'll just have to meet up a lot," Juliet said firmly. "You're not getting rid of me that easily. And I'll come back up for the baby."

"You will?" Grace asked, breaking into a smile.

"I promise," Juliet said.

Anna reached over and patted Grace's stomach. "You're already showing," Anna said.

"I know. I started showing about five minutes after the conception," Grace said. She shook her head in disbelief. "Do you know what the odds are of getting pregnant after a vasectomy? Do you?"

Actually, they all did know this nugget of information, as Grace had told them about two hundred times since she'd learned that she was pregnant.

"Less than one percent!" Grace continued.

"Did you ever figure out how it happened?" Juliet asked.

"Well, as it turns out, *Louis*"—Grace stopped to shoot her husband a venomous look—"was supposed to go back in and give his urologist a semen sample after the vasectomy. They check to see if there are any live sperm present before they give you the all-clear. And he claims he got so busy with work, he forgot to go in." She rolled her eyes.

"I thought you said you were happy about the pregnancy," Anna said.

"I am. It's just taking some time for the shock to wear off and the reality that I'm going to have four—four!—small children under the age of seven to set in," Grace said. She patted her tummy. "I'm hoping this one will be a girl too. The news that he'll have to pay for four weddings is the worst possible punishment I could think up for Louis."

The others laughed, and Grace turned to Anna.

"Your turn. What prompted the change of heart about bringing Noah?" she asked.

Anna shrugged and kicked at the water. "I thought about what you said. And I knew you were right. It was time to bring the two men in my life together," she said.

"It looks like it's going well," Chloe said, nodding toward Charlie, who was waving at Noah.

"Noah! Come swim!" Charlie chirped as he slid off the boat and dog-paddled to the edge of the pool. He'd recently learned how to swim with water wings on and loved to show off whenever possible.

"You've got it," Noah said. He pulled off his shirt and dove into the pool. Charlie cheered and paddled after him, arms churning wildly.

Anna watched them, while a knot grew in her throat. She gripped her hands into fists.

"Noah's great with Charlie," Grace said.

"Did you see that?" Anna asked, her voice barely audible. "Did you see Charlie asking Noah to come play? That's a good sign, right? Don't you think that's a good sign?"

Grace slung an arm around Anna's shoulders and gave her a quick hug.

"A very good sign," Grace said. "You see? I told you, it's all going to turn out just fine."

The women fell silent, their eyes fixed on their offspring. The twins and Molly were doing handstands in the shallow end. Hannah was trying to imitate the older girls, but she kept forgetting to hold her breath underwater and would pop up like a cork, spluttering, each time she tried. Noah was pretending to be a shark and was swimming underwater and grabbing on to Charlie's ankle, making the little boy scream with laughter. William and Natalie were happily taking in the sights from their inflatable boat.

"I can't believe William's already six months old; it doesn't seem possible. It feels like I just brought him home from the hospital," Chloe said, shaking her head in wonderment. "The time is going by way too fast. The next thing I know, he'll be heading off to college."

"My mom's always said that's the hardest part of being a parent," Anna said. "That if you're raising your kids right, you spend the whole time preparing them to leave you."

"But we have them now," Juliet said, so uncharacteristically sentimental that the others turned to look at her. Juliet's eyes were hidden behind her sunglasses, but a faint smile played at her lips.

"We have them now," Chloe repeated quietly.

"Oh, Christ, you're going to make me cry," Grace said, sniffing. "It's these damned hormones."

"That's your excuse anyway," Juliet teased her. She tipped back her glass and drained the last of her wine.

"Louis, Juliet needs a refill," Grace called.

"Coming," Louis said, walking over with the bottle of chardonnay in hand. Juliet held her glass up, and he filled it. "Anyone else?"

"I'm good," Anna said.

"I'll take a splash," Chloe said. "No, you don't have to get me a fresh glass. Just dump some in here."

She held up her empty iced tea glass, and Louis poured some wine into it.

"I'll take some," Grace said hopefully.

"Not a chance," Louis said.

"Being pregnant seriously sucks," Grace said, but she grinned as Louis leaned over and kissed the top of her head as he passed by.

When Louis had returned to the cluster of guys, who were now all admiring his new grill, Anna said, "I think we should make a toast."

"Good idea. What to?" Grace asked.

"How about Juliet? This is her farewell party," Chloe suggested.

"No, that's too depressing," Juliet said. "Besides, you're not really getting rid of me. I'm not going that far away."

"So what should we toast to, then?" Anna asked. "Our health? The future? The kids?"

"Why don't we just toast to being mothers?" Grace suggested.

"I like it," Chloe said. "After all, that's how we all ended up as friends, isn't it? Through Mothers Coming Together. At least, that's how I met all of you."

"This is true," Grace said. "Juliet?"

"Fine by me," Juliet said.

"So let's drink to us," Grace said. She lifted her glass of lemonade up in the air. "To motherhood."

"To motherhood," the others chimed in. And then they clinked their glasses together.

Whitney Gaskell briefly—and reluctantly—practiced law, before publishing her first novel, *Pushing 30*. She lives in Stuart, Florida, with her husband and son, and is at work on her next novel. You can visit her website and read her blog at www.whitneygaskell.com.

DON'T MISS
WHITNEY GASKELL'S

Testing Kate

Available from Delta Trade Paperbacks

Testing Kate

WHITNEY
GASKELL

Author of
She, Myself & I

One

When I was twelve years old, I froze right in the middle of the three-meter springboard diving competition.

I'd been taking diving classes at the local YMCA. When I'd stand at the edge of the rough board, my toes curled over the end, and stare down at the sprinklers spraying over the surface of the water, the whole world would go quiet. And then I'd take three steps back, turn, balance my shoulders over my hips and my hips over my feet, lift my arms out, and then it was three steps back again to the end of the board. With one final bounce, I'd leap straight up and then out, stretching my body into an arrow and slicing into the cold water, feeling like a mermaid.

At the end of the summer, the Y hosted a fun meet called Splash Day. The swimmers raced like a pack of sleek dolphins, and the synchronized swimmers spun around and fluttered their hands in time to a Christopher Cross song, and the divers sprang fearlessly from the board.

But when it was my turn to dive—a forward half-twist dive I'd been practicing for months—I stood at the edge of the springboard, staring out at the crowd, at my parents sitting side by side on the wooden bleachers, and smelling the chlorine in the air, and I just … froze. I don't mean that I had a moment of anxiety, or even that I decided not to dive and retreated back down the ladder. Oh, no. I was incapable of movement. I just stood there in my navy blue Speedo suit, shivering a little, my arms wrapped around myself in a hug, and I listened to the crowd first grow quiet and then, becoming restless at the holdup, start to call out either encouragements or barbed jokes, their voices echoing over the water.

"You can do it, honey!" (My mother.)

"Just jump already!" (Mr. Hunt, father of Bobby, who for some inexplicable reason wore sweatbands on his wrists when he swam the hundred-meter freestyle.)

"Damn, that water must be *really* cold!" (Mindy's dad, Mr. Camp, who thought—incorrectly—that he was hilarious.)

The voices just made it worse. I don't know why. I don't even know what it was that stopped me from making the same dive I'd completed hundreds of times in practice, the dive I'd been so sure would secure the blue ribbon. But even as I told my legs to *jump now*, they refused to obey.

In the end, Ms. Hadley, my coach—one of those sturdy, capable women with a square jaw and bushy brown hair cut in a severe bob—had to climb up onto the board, take my limp hand in hers, and lead me down and away. As soon as my bare feet hit the wet tiled pool deck, I dashed for the locker room—disobeying the sign that forbade poolside running—where I sat huddled on the wooden bench while hot tears of shame dripped down my cheeks. It was the most humiliating moment of my life.

Until now.

As I sat in my very first class on my very first day of law school, only one terrified thought had crystallized in my mind:

Which one of us will he call on first?

Actually two thoughts, the other being: Please, please, please, God, please don't let it be me.

Law schools are infamous for their use of the Socratic Method, where the professor singles out a student and questions him or her on the finer points of case law. And despite my performance anxiety, which had been lingering since the diving incident seventeen years earlier, I hadn't worried about the Socratic Method when I first applied to law schools.

Getting called on in class? Big deal, I'd thought as I paged through the glossy admissions catalog.

But as I sat in the too-cold lecture hall for the first time, a queasy, oily fear slid through me. And I wasn't the only one. Everyone around me was sitting a little too straight and rigid; heads were bowed over casebooks, eyes flickering around nervously.

Professor Richard Hoffman had finished his curt introduction to Criminal Law and stood leaning forward against the wood lectern, his flat gray eyes scanning row after row of students, all of whom did their best not to make eye contact with him.

Please don't let it be me, I thought again. My hands tensed into two fists, the nails pressing into the tender skin of my palms. Please, please, please don't let it be me. Not today, not when I hadn't done the reading assignment, or even bought my case-book, for that matter. Not the one day of my academic career when I was completely and totally unprepared.

"The sixth row to the right. The young woman who didn't seem to think it necessary to bring her textbook to class," Professor Hoffman said.

Which row was I in? One, two, three, four . . . shit, shit, shit. He couldn't possibly be . . . was he really? . . . oh, God . . . he *was*. . . .

I looked up and saw that all of my new classmates had swiveled around to face me, a sea of strangers, their faces stamped with relief that they hadn't been singled out as the first member of our class to be called on.

Dumb fucking luck, I thought.

You know those people who fill out a sweepstakes entry form on a lark and end up winning a new flat-panel television, or who always manage to make it to the gate just in time when they're running late for a flight, or who find priceless antiques for next-to-nothing in the back room of a dusty thrift store?

I'm not one of them.

I step in wads of gum the first time I wear a new pair of shoes, and get stuck in traffic when I have an appointment I can't be late for, and my first and only new car was dinged by a hit-and-run driver less than half an hour after I drove it off the car lot.

So it really shouldn't have surprised me that I was the very first person to get called on by the professor on the very first day of class. It was just more of the freaky bad luck that had been hanging over me since the day I was born (which just happened to be right in the middle of one of the worst blizzards to hit central New York in forty years).

"Your name?" Hoffman asked.

My skin felt very hot and very tight stretched over the bones of my face, and my throat closed up. "Kate. Kate Bennett," I croaked.

"Ms. Bennett, please stand."

"Ex-excuse me?"

Hoffman sighed dramatically. "If you are not capable of speaking loudly enough for the rest of the class to hear you, you must stand. Up. Now," he said. He raised his hand, with the palm facing up.

But all I could do was gape back at the professor, while the eyes of my classmates burned into me. And just like that, I was twelve years old again, frozen at the end of the diving board.

Twenty minutes earlier, I'd been standing on the Freret Street sidewalk and staring up at the imposing three-story brick facade of John Giffen Weinmann Hall. The morning sun cut down at a sharp angle, and I had to hold my hand up for shade to get a good look at the building that housed the Tulane School of Law, where I was now officially enrolled as a first-year law student.

I was sweating. Heavily.

Perspiration beaded up on my forehead, rinsing away the tinted moisturizer I'd so carefully applied that morning, and my white cotton T-shirt dampened under my armpits in two wet crescents.

Great, I thought, shifting my black leather knapsack on my shoulder and plucking the thin cotton of the shirt away from my skin. Nothing like making an elegant first impression.

It was only nine in the morning, but it must have already been ninety degrees in New Orleans. The late August humidity made the temperature even more oppressive, blanketing the city with a heavy wet heat that was causing my blonde wavy hair to rise up from my head in a halo of frizz. And I thought we'd had heat waves back home in Ithaca, those brief summer spells that baked the spring mud until it was dry and cracked. Graham and I would sit in front of an oscillating fan set on high, wet towels wrapped around our necks, and bemoan our lack of air-conditioning for those nine days a year when we actually needed it.

Back home... Only Ithaca wasn't home anymore, and I no longer shared an old Victorian house, with a wraparound porch, poky kitchen, and hideous blue floral wallpaper in its one dated bathroom, with Graham.

Now I lived in New Orleans, in a shabby shotgun-style apartment on the corner of Magazine and Fourth, on the second floor of a converted Greek Revival house. The house had probably been grand in its glory days but had long since faded into a state of genteel decay. My apartment had no closets, the toilet ran nonstop, and when I walked barefoot across the narrow-planked wooden floors that ran from the living room to the bedroom, the bottoms of my feet turned black from decades of worn-in grime.

My new roommate was a cockroach the size of a rat, which had leapt out at me the night before when I went into the kitchen for a glass of water. I'd shrieked and dropped my glass, only remembering at the precise moment that it shattered on the black-and-white linoleum tiled floor that I still hadn't gotten around to buying a broom and dustpan. Afterward, I huddled in my bed, giving myself the heebie-jeebies by wondering if the ticklish feeling on my arm was the roach climbing into bed with me.

"You said you wanted to get out of Ithaca," I now muttered to myself. "And this is out. Hell, they even have palm trees here." Palm trees were exotic, the stuff of vacation resorts and *Miami Vice* reruns.

Students streamed past me, most walking in small chatty clusters, on their way into the law school. I still had a few minutes before class started, so I held back and tried to figure out what the hell I was smelling. It wasn't the sweetly Southern aroma of magnolias and mint juleps I'd expected, but instead an odd odor of burned toast that hung in the air.

Just then, a tall, thin woman strolled by. She had a sleek dark bob that reminded me of Uma Thurman's in *Pulp Fiction,* and she looked effortlessly elegant in slinky jeans, a slim-fitting charcoal-gray T-shirt, and black leather thong sandals. An equally tall skinny guy with spiky brown hair and a nose ring loped along next to her. He was gesticulating wildly as he talked, and the brunette threw back her head in appreciative laughter at what-ever it was he was saying. I watched them turn into the law school, disappearing behind the heavy glass doors.

Was I the only person at this goddamned school who didn't know anyone?

"Excuse me," a voice said. I pivoted around to see who it be-longed to.

The man standing there was roughly my age—late twenties, or possibly early thirties—and he was gazing at me expectantly. He had short dark curly hair that rose in peaks over his high fore-head. His nose, peeling from a sunburn, was a little too big for his face and his chin was a little too long, but he had the brightest blue eyes I'd ever seen. "Are you talking to me?" I asked.

"Yeah, actually, I've been trying to catch up with you since we got off the streetcar," he said.

I had heard someone calling out after me as I'd trekked across campus. But since I didn't know anyone in New Orleans, much less anyone at Tulane, I'd assumed that whoever it was wasn't talking to me.

"I'm sorry…have we met?" I said. I looked at him a little closer. "Actually, you do look sort of familiar."

"If I had a dime for every time a woman said that to me. I used to think it was because I was starring in everyone's sexual fantasies," the guy said. "Let me guess, I look just like the brother of one of your friends. Or the friend of one of your brothers."

I laughed. "No, I don't think so. I don't have a brother."

"No? Really? That's usually it. Well, then maybe it's because we live in the same building."

"We do?" I asked. I hadn't met any of the other three tenants in my new apartment building. I hoped he wasn't the person who lived in the other second-floor apartment. Every time I stood on the narrow landing at the top of our shared staircase, fumbling with my key and sticky dead bolt, I could smell cat urine wafting out from under his door. And then, last night, while I was trying to fall asleep after my run-in with the gargantuan cockroach, I'd heard what sounded like someone over there tap dancing, their steps reverberating through the cheap hardwood.

He nodded. "Yep. I live in the bottom right apartment. I saw you leaving today, and we were on the same streetcar. I was right behind you. We both had to run to catch it...."

I nodded. "Oh, right. That must be it."

Now that he mentioned it, I did have a vague memory of someone getting on the streetcar right behind me, joking with the driver as he boarded. I'd taken the rattling green streetcar from my stop at Fourth Street all the way up St. Charles Avenue to the Tulane campus, gawking out the open window at the Greek Revival mansions we passed along the way, sitting like dowager queens on their carefully manicured lawns.

"But that's not why I was trying to stop you. You have a ..." His voice trailed off, and he looked uncomfortable.

"I have a what?"

"A ... thingy. Um. Something. Stuck to ..." He made a vague gesture toward my hips. "On the back of your skirt," he said. He blushed and averted his eyes.

I reached back, brushing at my skirt, trying to figure out what he was talking about, what was causing him such obvious embarrassment. And then I felt it.

Oh. *Shit.*

There was a maxipad stuck to my ass.

I could feel the blood flooding to the surface of my skin as I peeled the pad off my skirt and stuffed it into my knapsack. It wasn't used—thank *God*—but still. *Still.* I'd just walked across the entire campus with a sanitary napkin stuck to my skirt.

"Ah. Um. Thank you," I said stiffly, trying to regain some

smidgen of dignity. I glanced nervously at the law school, wondering how many of my new classmates had seen me. Would I spend the next three years known as the Maxi Girl? "Well. Um. I'd better get to class."

"Are you a law student too?" the guy asked.

Too? Oh, no.

"Please tell me you're not a first-year law student," I said, briefly closing my eyes in the hopes that he would disappear. When I opened them, he was still standing there, looking a little confused.

"Yeah, I am."

"Of course you are," I said dryly. "Because this wouldn't have been sufficiently mortifying otherwise."

At this, he laughed. It was a nice laugh, full and deep.

"Don't worry, I won't tell anyone. So you're a One-L too? I don't remember seeing you at orientation," he said.

"I wasn't there. My U-Haul truck broke down in Pennsylvania. I spent three days outside Pittsburgh waiting for a replacement," I said.

"You didn't miss much," he said. "They made us wear name tags."

"Yeah, but now everyone knows everyone else," I said. "Except for me."

"You know me."

"No, I don't, actually."

"That we can remedy immediately. I'm Nick Crosby," he said.

"Hi, Nick. I'm Kate. Kate Bennett," I said. I sniffed again as the burned-toast aroma became even stronger. "What is that smell?"

"What smell?"

"You don't smell that? It smells like burned toast."

"Maybe someone burned some toast," Nick suggested.

"I don't think so. I smelled it earlier, when I was leaving my apartment. Unless people are burning toast all over the city, all at once," I said.

"Did you know that carob trees smell like semen?" Nick said.

I blinked. "What?"

"I thought we were having a conversation about things that smell weird."

"No. Just the one smell," I said.

"Right, sorry. So what classes do you have today?"

I consulted the slip of paper the school had sent me over the summer. "This morning I have Criminal Law with Hoffman. And then Torts with Professor Gupta," I said.

"Excellent. We must be in the same section," Nick said. When I looked at him questioningly, he explained. "They break the One-Ls into four sections. Each section has all of their classes together."

"Just like at Hogwarts in the Harry Potter books," I said.

Nick laughed. "Minus the magic and all of the other cool stuff. Come on, we'd better get in there."

We walked up the steps, and then Nick held a glass door open for me, and I stepped inside. The ground-floor corridor of the law school was bustling with students standing around in groups or winding their way through the crowd en route to class. Up ahead, to the left, there was a student lounge furnished with green upholstered chairs and couches and lined with glowing vending machines that spat out soda cans with a loud clatter.

"We have mailboxes in there," Nick told me, pointing to the lounge. "Only they're not really boxes, they're hanging folders; but, whatever, they call them mailboxes. The Powers That Be have ordered us to check them once a day."

"You see, you did learn something at orientation. Did I miss anything else?" I asked.

"No, not really. They gave us a tour of the building, told us what to expect at lectures, stuff like that. Mostly it was just a chance for people to meet and settle into cliques at the earliest possible point," Nick said.

"Oh good. That makes me feel better," I said, rolling my eyes.

We turned left and walked to the end of a locker-lined hall, where even more students were milling around, some of them shoving heavy legal books into the lockers before slamming them shut. The hollow metallic clang reminded me of high school. The law school smelled like a high school too, that unmistakable bouquet of tuna fish sandwiches, new sneakers, and freshly shampooed hair.

"Do we have lockers assigned to us?" I asked.

"Yeah, but to get one you have to fill out paperwork at the reception desk we just passed back there," Nick said. "Give the Powers That Be your student ID, take a blood oath that you won't deal drugs out of it, promise them your firstborn, and they'll give you your combination."

When I laughed, the tangle of nerves in my stomach loosened.

Directly ahead of us was a set of heavy wooden doors. Just through it was a large, sunken lecture hall, so that when we stood at the doors, we were at the highest point in the room, looking down. At the front of the hall, a wooden lectern sat on a slightly raised platform. Long tables were bolted into the floor across the center of the room, set up in a stadium style, so that each was on a lower level than the one behind it. There were two sets of staircase corridors—the one where I was standing, and another to the right of the long tables. The room was already half filled with our new classmates sitting in green upholstered task chairs lined up behind the tables. Their voices, buzzing with excitement and anxiety, echoed around us. The chic dark-haired girl I'd seen earlier was there, I noticed, along with her skinny companion with the nose ring.

"Do you want to sit here?" Nick asked, gesturing to one of the shorter tables just to our left, which was still empty.

"Sure," I said. We sat down, and I got out a yellow lined legal pad and a pen. Nick unzipped his black messenger bag and pulled out a thick brown textbook with gold lettering on its face: CRIMINAL LAW, 8TH EDITION, ALAN M. HOFSTEADER.

"You already got your textbook?" I asked him.

Nick's eyebrows arched. "You didn't?"

"No, I just got into town on Saturday, and since then I've been unpacking and getting groceries and things. I figured I'd just go to the bookstore today after class," I said, trying to keep the shrill edge of panic out of my voice.

Nick nodded. "That must have been your U-Haul parked in front of the house on Saturday. I saw it when I came back from the library."

"The library...you mean you've already started studying?"

"Yeah, we had a reading assignment for class today."

"*What?*"

"That's right—you weren't at orientation. They posted the first class assignments over by the student lounge. This class was the worst. We had two chapters to read, and the cases were unbelievably boring. I thought Crim Law would have been the most interesting assignment, but apparently not," Nick said.

"Oh, no," I said, slumping forward. "I'm already behind. Stupid U-Haul..."

"Don't worry, I'm sure you won't get called on. What are the odds? There must be over a hundred students in here," Nick said.

"Called on? He's going to start *calling* on people today?" I asked, and when Nick nodded, my stomach did that dropping thing where it feels like you're falling off a tall building. I *never* thought the professors would be calling on us on the first day of classes.

"Hoffman is supposed to be the worst of the worst when it comes to humiliating students in class. The upperclassmen call him Professor Satan. Actually, I think that's him there," Nick said, nodding at the back of a man cutting through the students.

I turned and saw a middle-aged man making his way down the stairs. He led with his crotch as he walked, and the fluorescent lights shone on his pate. He reached the front of the room, stepped up on the platform, and turned to face us. From where I sat, he didn't look outwardly satanic. Just your average academic type. He wore the hair he had left a bit too long, and his blue oxford shirt was rumpled. His pants were low on his hips to accommodate his stomach paunch. The professor crossed his arms and leaned forward against his lectern, looking blandly disinterested as he waited for the noise level to drop to a nervous buzz before finally tapering off. When silence stretched across the room, he continued to stare back at us for a few uncomfortable moments.

"This is Introductory Criminal Law. I am Professor Hoffman.

If you are in the wrong place, please leave. for those of you who are in the right place, I'm going to go over the ground rules. First, do not be late to my class. We will begin promptly at nine a.m. on Monday, Wednesday, and Friday.

"I will be passing around a seating chart. The seat you are now sitting in will be your seat for the remainder of the semester. Locate your seat on the chart and fill in your name in large block letters.

"My system for calling on students is as follows: Everyone will be called on at least once over the course of the semester. If you volunteer to answer a question during class, you will inoculate yourself from being called on for the rest of that week.

"Office hours are Wednesdays from two to four p.m. Do not bother me at any other time, including before and after lectures. And do not waste my time during office hours by asking questions that were addressed during the lecture. If you attempt to do so, I will not be pleased. And I assure you, ladies and gentlemen, you do not want to displease me. Any questions? Good. Open your casebooks to chapter one," Hoffman said. His biting voice had just the faintest trace of a Northeastern accent. Connecticut? I wondered. Rhode Island, maybe.

Nick opened his book and moved it between us on the table so that I could share it with him. I shot him a grateful look and began speed-reading through the introductory paragraphs of the chapter, praying that I wouldn't be called on.

"Ms. Bennett, I don't like to be kept waiting," Hoffman snapped. "Stand up now."

Finally my legs obeyed me, and as I stood shakily, my chair rolled backward, turning as it went, so that the hard, curved plastic of the armrest was pressing into my right thigh. My hands shook slightly as I clasped and then unclasped them, and I tried to resist the urge to wipe my slick palms on the front of my skirt. Nick gave me a tight-lipped smile of encouragement and pushed his book even closer to me.

"Define *mens rea*," Professor Hoffman said. He continued to stare at me blandly, with eyes that were light and flat, like a shark's.

"I don't know," I admitted. "My moving van broke down, and so I missed orientation and I didn't know there was a reading assignment due today. I'm sorry. I'll be prepared next time."

I started to sit down.

"I didn't tell you to sit. I asked you to define the term *mens rea* for the class," Hoffman said.

My mouth went dry and my throat was so scratchy, it felt like I'd swallowed a handful of sand. He wasn't going to let me off the hook, I realized. He was going to make an example out of me in front of everyone. I slowly stood back up, my legs shaky.

"Um...I don't know. I'll have to pass," I said lamely. I crossed my arms in front of me, pressing my elbows down so that no one would be able to see my sweaty armpits.

"I don't allow passing in my class," Hoffman said.

Mens rea, mens rea, I thought wildly. I'd watched every episode of *Law & Order* at least three times. Hadn't Assistant District Attorney Jack McCoy used that term during that episode with the teenager who'd killed his friend? It had something to do with...

"Is that...does that mean...the mental state of a...um, criminal...person?" I asked, stumbling over the words.

"Are you asking me or telling me?" Hoffman asked.

Asshole, I thought, biting down so hard, the muscles in my jaw twinged.

"*Mens rea* refers to the, um, mental state of a criminal," I said loudly.

"And why is that important?"

"Because a person's intent when they commit a crime is important for...um...determining...um...what kind of a crime... it is," I said, hoping that that made sense. I had a feeling that Jack McCoy had been more eloquent when he was explaining it to the police detectives.

"And what are the four levels of criminal intent under the Model Penal Code?" Hoffman asked.

Four levels? I didn't have the slightest fucking clue. *Law &
Order* wasn't going to save me now.

"Ms. Bennett?" Hoffman said.

I shook my head. "I don't know," I mumbled.

Hoffman strode to the whiteboard behind his lectern, picked
up a black Magic Marker, and began writing: PURPOSELY,
KNOWINGLY, RECKLESSLY, NEGLIGENTLY. Then he drew a line
under the four words, and below the line wrote: STRICT LIABILITY.

"This is a basic concept of criminal law," Hoffman said, pointing to the board with the uncapped marker. "Your inability to answer does not bode well for how you'll do in my class. I gather it
would be a waste of everyone's time to ask you for a summary of
Staples v. U.S.?"

Somehow his bland, sneering tone was worse than if he'd
yelled at me.

"Yes," I said in a small voice.

"You can sit down now. And don't come to my class unprepared ever again," Hoffman said.

I reached behind me for my chair, sat down shakily, and edged
it back toward the table. Resting my hands on my forehead, I
stared at Nick's casebook, but the words on the pages didn't make
any sense. They just floated around, an impenetrable sea of tiny
type.

"That wasn't so bad. Could have been a lot worse. At least you
were able to answer a few of his questions," Nick whispered. His
breath was warm on my ear and smelled like mint toothpaste.

I just shook my head at him and tried to focus on the case-
book. If that was how Hoffman treated a student who was unprepared, I could only imagine how he'd deal with our whispering in
the middle of a lecture. I certainly wasn't about to find out.